With her arms pressed against her sides for warmth, Rachel made her way to the dance house. The drumbeat didn't alter in rhythm. Stepping close to the building, Rachel peeked in through a wide break in the boards.

Jason was the drummer. He stood, his feet apart and his back straight. His hair, usually tied back neatly, hung to his shoulders in heavy waves. His snug, dark trousers and white shirt with the billowing sleeves gave him the air of a pirate on the bow of a ship. He was watching her. Their eyes met and Rachel's heart leaped in fear and surprise. Momentarily panicked, she stepped backwards, then turned and ran blindly toward the cabin. A hand grabbed her from behind, and she was stopped, finding herself pulled against a firm, hard chest. She tensed.

"Don't run from me, Rachel." Jason's voice was husky and close to her ear.

His touch melted her. She bit her lip to keep from crying out. He'd awakened all the sensual nerve endings in her body with a single embrace and the whisper of her name. She wanted to fight him, to pull away and run far and fast to escape the f-- nited inside her.

"Rachel." H_____her hair.

Suddenly he_____slumped against him. .

HEAT OF A SAVAGE MOON

JANE BONANDER

SMP

ST. MARTIN'S PAPERBACKS

HEAT OF A SAVAGE MOON

Copyright © 1993 by Jane Bonander.
Excerpt from *Forbidden Moon* copyright © 1993 by Jane Bonander.

Cover illustration by John Ennis.

ISBN: 0-312-92859-9

Printed in the United States of America

St. Martin's Paperbacks edition/June 1993

10 9 8 7 6 5 4 3 2 1

Dedicated to my husband, Alan,
for his love, patience, and belief that I
could do it

Special acknowledgment to Professor
Dorothea Theodoratus,
Sacramento State University,
who invited me along to experience the
timeless, haunting beauty of
the Big Head

To be ignorant of what happened before you were born is to be forever a child.

—Cicero, 108–43 B.C.

Some of the agents, and nearly all of the employees, we are informed, of one of these reservations at least, are daily and nightly engaged in kidnapping the younger portion of the females for the vilest of purposes. The wives and daughters of the defenseless Diggers are prostituted before the very eyes of their husbands and fathers, they dare not resent the insult, or even complain of the hideous outrage.

—from a San Francisco newspaper, 1856

Author's note

During the course of my research, I learned of the atrocities heaped upon the Indians of Northern California, many so hideous and revolting, it's almost impossible to believe one people could do such things to another. And to presume one man has a right to take what has belonged to another for thousands of years is, at the very least, arrogant. In Anthony Jennings Bledsoe's *Indian Wars of the Northwest* (San Francisco: Bacon and Co., 1885) p. 7, he says, "The Indians of Northern California have been here for at least five thousand years." "Recent evidence," adds Jack Norton in *Genocide in Northwestern California* (San Francisco: Indian Historian Press, 1979), "has indicated that Indians occupied areas of Lake County for ten thousand years. This means that before Abraham was visited by Yahweh, before the Great Pyramid was conceived, thousands of years before Solomon or Caesar existed, or any other specific identifiable event occurred in Western history, the natives of Northern California lived within their beautiful lands."

These people, who were treated by many pioneers as subhuman, began and ended each day with prayers. They were urged to "keep a good heart," "do not think badly of people," "be kind and respectful of the old" (Norton, p. 27). Cicero was right. If we don't know what happened before we were born, we'll always be ignorant.

Jane Bonander
P.O. Box 3134
San Ramon, CA 94583-6834

🎀 Prologue 🎀

Dakota Territory—1868

*I*t was Aunt Billie's voice that woke her. She sounded funny, whispering like that. Snuggling deeper into her bedding, Rachel Hammond ignored the hand that shook her shoulder and pretended to sleep. It was a game. They played it every morning.

"Don't tickle, Auntie," she murmured around a grin.

Cold air rushed over her as her covers were yanked off. She drew up her legs.

"Rachel, honey," Auntie whispered again. "Up. You must get up!"

Rachel squinted up at the lamp in her aunt's hand, then at her face. Auntie looked scared. Immediately Rachel's stomach felt strange, kind of hollow and sick.

"We have to hurry, Rachel. Your mama and papa are waiting by the door with George and the baby. Come quickly," she ordered, no longer whispering and certainly not smiling. "No time to lollygag."

As Rachel slid to the edge of her bed, Auntie grabbed her hand and pulled her upright. She wanted to ask what was wrong, but she knew better. Staying quiet was better. Stay quiet, watch and listen. She'd learned that early on.

Auntie nearly dragged her down the hallway. Rachel stumbled, stubbing her bare toe on the wood floor. It hurt a lot, and she winced, but didn't cry out. She'd just turned eight; she was getting too old to cry.

Mama and Papa stood by the door. Mama clutched Rachel's six-month-old brother, Lucas, close to her chest. Papa looked worried. His face was white beneath his whiskers and his eyes were bright and unnatural looking. That made Rachel's stomach hurt ever more. `

"C'mon, Rachel," her cousin George shouted as he slid his arms into his jacket. "Gotta get outa here before the Injuns come."

"George, hush." Papa's voice was harsh and cold. "No need to scare the girl."

She saw the rifle in her father's hand, then tossed her mother a fearful glance. Mama gave her a wide smile. It didn't help the feeling in Rachel's stomach, for Mama's face was wet and her eyes shiny. When she turned away, Rachel realized her mother was crying. "Mama?"

Suddenly, their Indian friend, Elbee, was at the door. He had a rifle, too. "We have to hurry. They're coming. Now."

"Who's coming, Elbee? Who's coming?" Rachel's voice rose with fear, for Elbee wasn't smiling. Elbee *always* smiled, especially when he saw her. He picked her up, holding her easily with one arm.

"I'll take her, Elbee," Papa said, reaching for her.

The Indian shook his head. "I can carry her easier. You take care of the missus and be ready to shoot. I'll protect the girl."

Rachel saw a brief flash of uncertainty in her father's eyes. Then, because there was no time to argue, Papa stepped forward and kissed Rachel's cheek. "Be a good girl, Rachel, mind Elbee. Your mama and I love you."

Rachel lunged for her father, but Elbee held her tight. She felt like crying, but she wouldn't. She wasn't a baby anymore. But she wanted to be with Papa!

Once outside, everyone fled into the cornfield. The corn was dry and pale, snapping and cracking beneath Elbee's feet as he ran. An occasional leaf slapped Rachel in the face, but she pushed it away, mindless of its dry, cutting edges. The corn was so high that if Elbee hadn't carried her, she would have gotten lost among the tall, spiky stalks.

Lucas started to cry, and Mama tried to keep him quiet, "shushing" him jerkily as she ran.

Rachel bounced against Elbee's shoulder, her eyes glued behind her, on her home. Suddenly, flames erupted on the roof of the cabin, shooting high into the night sky. "Papa, the cabin's burning," she shrieked.

Mama, who ran beside Elbee, faltered and looked back. "Oh, Lyle!" she cried. "My things. My beautiful things!"

Papa turned, grabbed Mama's free arm and pulled her along. *"Things*, Faye," he said sternly. "They're not important. I'll buy you new things."

Aunt Billie and George ran ahead of them.

"Them dirty Injuns," George shouted, his high-pitched voice wobbling as he ran. "I'll kill 'em. I'll cut their stupid guts out!"

Rachel continued to stare at the burning cabin. Her lower lip quivered and she sucked it into her mouth, biting down hard. Indians were back there.

She stole a glance at Elbee's face and wondered what he was thinking. Those were his people burning down her house. She looked away, back toward the cabin again. She didn't see anyone, only the orange and yellow flames that ate up her home.

Shots rang out. Elbee didn't even duck. Rachel put her face down, against his shoulder. After a moment, she looked at her parents and her aunt. No one had stopped; they continued to run on through the corn.

More shots. Aunt Billie groaned, arched her back, then stumbled to the ground.

"Ma!" George fell to the ground beside her.

"Auntie? George?" Fear pressed into Rachel's throat and her stomach felt like someone had punched it. "I wanna see George!" She tried to wiggle out of Elbee's grip. He held her tight.

Elbee slowed down some. "Your ma all right?" he asked when George poked his head up through the corn.

George was crying. "She ain't movin', Elbee. She ain't movin'."

"Come on, boy. They'll just get you if you stay."

"No! I'm gonna kill 'em. They shot Ma! They shot Ma!"

George stood, then turned and ran the other way, stumbling back toward the burning cabin with his fist in the air.

"George! George!" Rachel screamed so hard, she thought her eyes might pop out. "Stop it, George! Stop it!" She was crying so hard now she nearly choked. "Wh . . . why is he going back, Elbee?"

Elbee glanced back but didn't answer her.

Another burst of shots, and George yelped with pain. He struggled on for a few steps, then another volley of shots hit him and he fell into the tall corn.

Rachel wiggled against Elbee and hit his shoulder with her fist. "George," she cried. "I want to see George."

"Shut up, girl. You wanna die, too? Shut up or they'll know where you are."

She no longer felt safe with Elbee. Something about him had changed. "Elbee, I want to get down. Please, Elbee."

"Shut up." He squeezed her hard and she bit back a whimper of pain.

Her eyes stung; tears ran down her cheeks. She tried to catch her breath and made wet, hiccoughing noises in her throat. Looking ahead of them, she saw Mama and Papa. They had stopped and were waiting for her and Elbee to catch up.

Suddenly, Elbee raised his gun and fired. Rachel's mother screamed; her father swore. Lucas continued to cry.

"Rachel!" Mama's voice split the night air, and Rachel wiggled wildly in Elbee's grip.

"Rachel, run!"

Elbee shot again, and her mother was quiet.

"Mama! Mama!" Terrified, Rachel squirmed to get out of Elbee's grip. She pushed at his face, his nose, scratching and clawing to get free. Instinctively, she grabbed a hank of his long black hair and tugged for all she was worth.

The Indian grunted, briefly losing his grip on her. She slid to the ground and staggered away through the corn, the dry stalks cutting into the tender skin on her legs as she ran. She had to get to Mama. Mama was hurt! Elbee . . . why had Elbee hurt her? Elbee had always been their friend.

Frightened and confused, Rachel raced toward her mother, intuitively knowing that she couldn't call out to her.

Mama! she screamed in silence. She couldn't let Elbee hear. If she found Mama, she would have to stay quiet, or Elbee would find her and hurt her, too. Suddenly she hated Elbee. She *hated* him! But, she thought, hurt and confused, how could she hate him when she'd loved him for so long?

Papa shouted something at Elbee. Swearing . . . saying those words he'd told her and George never to say. Rachel slowed down and listened. Elbee screamed, the sound sending icicles up her back. There was another shot, and her father's angry voice stopped, almost in the middle of a word . . . So did her baby brother's wailing.

Oh, Papa! Lucas! She wanted to go to them, too. But now she knew she had to hide. She'd find them later. Everything would be all right. They were just being quiet so Elbee wouldn't hurt them anymore. They'd want Rachel to be quiet, too. And Lucas was probably asleep. Crying always made him tired.

And Auntie and George were just hurt. They'd all be fine, once the Indians went away. They were only pretending— everyone knew to stay quiet and play dead.

But why would Elbee hurt them? He'd worked alongside Papa in this very cornfield. He'd eaten at their table. He'd given Rachel presents that he'd made himself . . .

She continued to run through the corn until she saw the riverbank. Realizing where she was, she felt a little twinge of hope. She was close to the little cave where she and George had often hid from Mama and Auntie when it was time for chores.

Watching for the familiar outcropping of rocks, she crept along the edge of the field, keeping the river in sight.

There it is. Rocks pointing into the air like church steeples. She felt safe. A little safe, anyway. Her chest hurt so much she could hardly breathe, and her bare feet burned from running through the corn. Finally slipping into the dank opening of the cave, she collapsed on the ground.

Drawing her legs up under her, she listened. And waited. Maybe Elbee and the others would go away.

Then a new realization wormed its way into her head. *Maybe they wouldn't.* Maybe they'd come looking for her.

Spontaneous sobs choked her. Oh, how she hated that awful Elbee! Mama'd always told her that hate was bad. But she couldn't help it. She *hated* him!

She swiped her sleeve across her eyes and stared at the opening to the cave. She was so scared . . .

As she sat alone in the dark, she remembered what Mama had taught her whenever they read stories about Jesus. Jesus promised that when people die, they go to heaven and meet all the people they've loved who have died before them. Rachel had been scared, telling Mama that she was afraid to die.

Mama had put her arm around her. *Don't be afraid, Rachel. I'll be there waiting for you.*

Mama's devotion should have been enough for her, but it wasn't. Finally, after stewing and hurting inside, she finally asked, *But Mama, what if I get there and can't find you?*

She remembered Mama's face crumpling into tears as she pulled Rachel against her chest. *Don't worry, darling. I'll find you . . .*

Sucking in a shaky, tear-filled breath, Rachel glanced again at the opening of the cave. Oh, she hoped everyone was just pretending to be dead. But if they weren't . . .

Mama always told Rachel that when she was scared, she should pray. And she was so scared . . .

> . . . *If I should die before I wake,*
> *I pray the Lord my soul to take* . . .

❧ Chapter One ❧

Northern California—late January, 1880

The air was still and deathlike in the murky glimmer of dawn. A mourning dove perched on the crumbling chimney atop a cottage at the edge of the Pine River Indian Reservation. Its funereal *oooh-oo-oo-oo* floated on the invisible currents of the morning air.

From her hiding place inside the fireplace wall, Rachel Weber strained to hear the haunting cry of the dove. It kept her from slipping into a mad place from which she might never return. She closed her eyes, squeezing them tight, desperately wanting to block out what she'd seen.

It didn't help. Visions of the bloodbath filled the empty space behind her eyes and she forced them open, staring, instead, at the tiny ray of gray light that filtered in through the small hole in the stone fireplace wall.

Eventually she'd have to face what had happened. Eventually, but not yet. Not yet. She shivered, both from the cold and from the fear that crippled her mind.

She wondered again why she'd come to this place, but deep down, she knew why. She'd decided that she belonged with Jeremy, her husband, wherever he was. It didn't matter that he'd told her not to come. He'd reminded her that she hated Indians with good reason, but she'd wanted him to understand that she loved him more. It was an uncivilized land, he'd said. Not safe. She'd argued that if they were together, everything would be all right. But she wouldn't be happy living among the vicious savages, he'd said. I'll be living with you, not them, she'd answered.

His warning was fresh in her mind, but he'd been gone so long. Two years. Two long, unhappy years . . .

A cramp gripped her calf, knotting the muscles. Gritting her teeth, she pressed her thumb against the spasm and rubbed, welcoming the pain. She took a deep, quiet breath and buried her face against her knees, circling them with her arms. She didn't want to think. She wanted to wake up and heave a shaky sigh into her pillow, but she knew that what she'd seen hadn't been a dream. Dreams weren't that vivid, that terrifying—or that loud.

Now it was quiet. No birds chirped in the trees, and no wind whistled down the chimney. It was so still; the sounds from the massacre still rang in her ears.

How she'd wished there had been someone to help them. But no one had come. Frustration and anger welled up inside her. They were alone in this godforsaken hole at the brink of the world. The only human beings around were the savages who lived back under the trees, less than a quarter of a mile away. And they certainly wouldn't help. Indians stuck together.

And for all she knew, the murderers could live right behind them, on the reservation. Trembling, she realized that she knew better than anyone never to trust an Indian, even if he professed to be your friend.

A tremor shook her. Her hiding place inside the cold wall didn't allow her to move and she was getting numb. But she preferred it that way. She didn't want to move. She didn't want to feel. She didn't want to leave her protective nook, and she wasn't even sure she wanted to live.

Suddenly there was a noise beyond the wall. Swallowing hard, she slowly pulled herself forward and peered out into the room. She gasped, covering her mouth with her hand. Someone was there.

She looked out the hole again and her heart vaulted upward, into her throat. A man stood before the two dead bodies, one of which was her husband's. The room was lighter, but morning shadows still played upon the walls, preventing her from seeing the man's face. Hardly daring to breathe, she watched him hunker down beside the other body, that of the schoolmaster. He stood abruptly, removed his shirt and appeared to consider laying it over the bodies. But he shook his head, muttering something under his breath as he moved away and faced her.

Rachel's gaze was drawn to a glimmer of white on his chest as the morning sun glanced off his solid frame. Her breath caught in her throat as she stared at the scars that zigzagged across his torso from his nipples to his navel. They looked old, for they blazed white against his brown skin, but the age of the scars made them no less menacing.

Suddenly aware that he hadn't moved, she pinched her eyes shut and slumped back, her heart thundering as she awaited discovery.

Minutes passed. Rachel cried—silent, inward sobs that choked her throat and strained her lungs. *Oh, God, let it be over.* She wasn't sure why she feared him. He was not dressed like a savage, nor did he further desecrate the bodies by rifling through the clothing and robbing them of their coins or their watches. Yet fear was the only emotion she felt. She expected him to rip away at the wall to get to her, and finding her, ravage or murder her. Some small part of her told her she wasn't being reasonable. A louder, stronger voice urged self-preservation.

She hugged her knees again, clutching them so tightly her arms ached. She gasped, sucking in great gulps of air to fill her starving lungs. The noise of her breathing shattered the silence and she was suddenly drenched in an icy sweat. Surely he'd find her now. She leaned her head back against the wall, tears coursing down her face and neck as she waited. But nothing happened. Holding her breath again, she listened. There was no sound but the rumbling of her own heartbeat.

She looked out and saw that he'd gone. But still she waited—uncomfortable, cold, and afraid to move. She endured the taut stinging of her cramped muscles.

The sun rose, hovering over the oak trees and spilling in through the window across from the fireplace. It seemed like hours since she'd looked out and seen the man with the scars. She'd begun to feel the walls of the small space crowding in around her, and knew she had to get out. Pushing on the door, she suddenly remembered that Jeremy had thrown the latch when he'd shoved her into the crawl space.

Swallowing her panic, she groped along the floor around her, searching for something long and narrow to use to flip the lock. Her fingers touched a long, thin shard of wood, and she expelled a sigh of relief. Before shoving it between the door and the wall, she sat quietly and listened for footfalls. Hearing none, she slid the wood up and flipped the latch, then slowly forced open the small door. Grimacing as she moved muscles that had been frozen with fear, she inched her way out into the cold, sunny room.

She stood, her hands gripping the rough stone fireplace as she leaned against it for support. Glancing at the floor beside her, she spotted Jeremy's long, trouser-covered legs. Slowly she allowed her gaze to move up his body until she saw the blood pooled in the folds of his shirt. His right arm was flung across his chest, and it took Rachel a moment to realize that his hand was gone, cut off at the wrist. Choking back a sob, she quickly looked away. *Why?* Why would they do that to him?

Finding it difficult to breathe, she slowly moved her gaze to Jeremy's face, carefully avoiding his mangled arms. Death had interrupted a scream, for her husband's features were frozen into an ugly sneer.

She stumbled to the sofa and retched into the spittoon that sat on the floor nearby, although there was nothing in her stomach to throw up. Running her shaky fingers through her tangled hair, she slumped to the floor. She tried to swallow, but spasms clutched her throat, causing strangled gasping sounds to echo in the quiet room.

The bodies lay lifeless and cold on the floor in front of her. Jeremy, her handsome, muscular husband, was dead. And poor Harry Ritter, the shy, young reservation schoolmaster . . . She attempted to drag air into her lungs, and the sound was punctuated with grating sobs.

What was she going to do? They were both dead. *Dead*. Ritter's shock of blond hair was dark, matted with his own blood, and the side of his handsome young face was gone. A splotch of red drew her gaze to his groin and she sucked in another ragged, wrenching breath. *Oh, God . . .*

His trousers were ripped open and his genitals were gone —hacked off, the blood still oozing brightly in the morning sun. She swallowed convulsively, pushing back the bile that slithered up her throat. Screaming voices in her head silently questioned why someone would do such a thing. She had no answers. She just knew that savages didn't need a reason to kill.

Fearing she might vomit again, she turned away, shivering as she attempted to focus on something else. She nervously wiped her hands on her dressing gown, suddenly noticing the streaks of blood that smeared over the sooty dirt covering the light blue fabric. Opening her fists, she looked down at her hands. Her nails had dug into her palms with such force, she was bleeding.

She wished she felt some pain. She needed to feel something, for she'd done nothing to prevent what had happened. She'd been useless, eager to hide and avoid the confrontation and conflict, just as she always had. Common sense told her there was nothing she could have done. Guilt whispered that she should have tried.

She wondered why she'd been spared again. Painfully, hating the haunting memories, she thought back to the day twelve years before when she'd lost her parents, her brother, Lucas, Aunt Billie and George. The sounds and smells of that dark morning invaded her senses, and she closed her eyes, pressing her hands over her ears. What had she done to earn such wrath from a gentle God?

The smell of blood reached her nostrils. She sucked in great gulps of air to clear her head. Scanning the outer perimeter of the room, she pulled herself up, trying to avoid the bloody scene before her. The thick, cloying scent of death permeated the stuffy room, and she knew she had to get out. Later she would do something, but not now. Not now . . .

She staggered outside, gulping in the fresh air as though it were an opiate that could numb her soul. With her hand shielding her eyes from the morning sun, she lurched forward.

Mindless of the frosty air that scraped her lungs, she tottered down the pebble-strewn road toward town. A chill wind had picked up with sunrise, flattening her nightgown and her robe against her body. Stones gouged the delicate soles of her slippers, digging into the fleshy pads of her heels. She tripped over a half-buried root in the road and fell, scoring her already bloody hands with dirt when she put them out to break her fall.

She pulled herself up and stumbled on, leaving thick tracks of mud on her tear-streaked face as she pushed her long, heavy hair out of her eyes. Suddenly, she stopped. Someone was coming up behind her. She could hear the creaking of the wagon and the clip-clopping of the horses. She turned and stumbled toward the noise, trying to run, until her head became light and black spots danced before her eyes.

"Please," she choked out, waving her arms weakly over her head. "Please . . . help me . . ."

Jason Gaspard's Karok blood steamed through his veins, blinding him to the familiar surroundings. He forced himself to dig his heels gently into his stallion's ribs, mindful that the animal should not have to suffer the effects of his anger. They flew across the vineyard acreage, eating up the ground beneath them. Row upon row of dormant grapevines slid by, blurring together as horse and rider rushed on.

Seldom did Jason allow his anger to fester as it did now. Years of education and self-discipline had honed him into a civilized, law-abiding citizen. He had little use for anyone who couldn't control his emotions. But what he'd just seen was inexcusable. Unjustified. Totally outside any realm of reasonable human behavior. And he had a sick feeling in the pit of his stomach that he knew who might be responsible.

Spying the large, newly painted cabin that sat in the field on the boundary of the vineyard, he nudged his mount toward it. The cold winter sun glimmered off the clean porch windows, slowly melting the frosty film that edged the steps beneath them. Jason leaped from his horse and stormed to the cabin door. It opened before he had a chance to beat on it with his angry fists.

Sky, the overseer for the Gaspards' vineyard, stood in the doorway holding a cup of coffee. His square face was still strong and handsome, although he was over fifty and had lived a spartan, though not entirely unhappy, life. "Good morning, Two Leaf."

Jason nodded, responding as easily to his Indian name as he did to his white one. He immediately checked his anger, giving his father's friend an appropriate greeting. "I hope you and your family are well."

"We are, despite the cold sting of the Wolf Moon." Sky's eyes were warm with fond remembrance.

Jason was forced to smile. "You haven't forgotten." He stepped into the house, the aroma of fresh, hot fry bread washing over him.

"How could I? You had such enthusiasm when you learned there were others like ourselves living in the east." He studied Jason a minute. "What tribe spoke of the Wolf Moon?"

"The Algonquin," Jason answered.

"Ah, yes. The tribes that live on the shores of the other ocean."

"And elsewhere," he added, clapping Sky on the shoulder.

Sky pressed Jason's hand. "Your mount tore up the ground as you rode up. You come in haste, or you are angry."

"Both," he answered, his anger returning. "I've come to see Buck. Is he here?"

At the mention of his stepson's name, Sky nodded. "In there," he answered.

Glancing into the kitchen, Jason saw his young friend

Buck Randall, tough, rangy, and lean, sitting at the table, his gaunt face more haggard than usual. Though seven years Jason's junior, Buck had not grown into adulthood easily, and appeared almost as old as Jason's thirty years. The chubby little "Cub" who had followed him around like a shadow hadn't existed for almost two decades.

"Weber and Ritter have been murdered," Jason said without preamble. He watched Buck's face for some sort of response. There was none.

Buck pushed his chair back, wincing as he stood, and crossed slowly to the window. "Well, there *is* a divine spirit. You know I hated that bastard's soul."

Jason's eyes narrowed; he knew which man Buck referred to. "Enough to kill him yourself?"

Buck's weak, mirthless laughter became a cough, and he hunched over, presenting Jason his back. "Seems someone beat me to it. How do I know it wasn't you?"

"I don't kill my enemies."

Buck snorted, his shoulders still hunched forward. "Don't tell me you've never thought about it."

"I didn't come here to open old wounds." Frowning, he stared at Buck's unusual stance. "What's wrong with you?"

Buck tossed him a quick glance over his shoulder. "Not a damned thing. Thanks for bringing me such pleasant news. Now, get the hell out of here and leave me alone."

Jason and Buck had butted horns constantly over the past few years, their long friendship tested time after time as they took different sides on every issue facing their people. But that wasn't what bothered Jason now. Buck held his torso stiff and straight, altogether different from his usual "don't-screw-with-me" posture.

He joined Buck at the window and touched his shoulder. Buck reeled away, staggering into the wall.

Surprised, Jason stepped back, too. "What happened?"

Glaring at him, Buck pressed his palm against the upper right-hand corner of his chest. "I was in a fight last night, outside a bar in Redland." He slumped back into the chair. "I got knifed. That's all."

Jason pushed Buck's hands away and unbuttoned the younger man's shirt. He peeled off the blood-soaked bandage. "Why were you trying to hide it from me?"

Buck scowled. "Because I hate like hell to listen to your priggish preaching, that's why."

Buck's mother, Shy Fawn, limped into the room with fresh bandages. The years had been kinder to her than they had been to her eldest son. Her skin was still smooth and her hair barely held a hint of gray. Her limp, the result of a beating she'd received when she was pregnant with Buck, had fortunately not gotten worse over the years, for Sky, with the aid of Jason's father, Nicolas, had found a bright, young doctor to help her. That doctor had been Jason's own reason for going into medicine.

"I wanted him to see you right away, Two Leaf, but he refused," Shy Fawn said. "You know I can't do anything with him."

After scrubbing his hands at the sink, Jason examined the wound. It was jagged and deep, and appeared to have been made with a knife with hooked teeth—definitely a wicked weapon. "It could have killed you. You're lucky it didn't pierce your stubborn, mutinous heart."

Buck continued to glower. "Free medical advice, or just your personal opinion?"

"Take off your shirt."

Buck carefully shrugged out of his shirt, exposing a smooth, tightly muscled chest and firm, well-defined arms. "What were you doing at the reservation?"

"Mary Deerflower went into labor. After I delivered the baby, I passed Weber's cottage. The front door was wide open."

Buck didn't flinch as Jason probed the wound. "How did the bastards die?"

Jason glanced up, nodding a thank-you toward Shy Fawn, who brought him a basin of warm water and some homemade salve. He waited for her to leave the room.

"Weber was stabbed in the chest, probably through the heart. And his hands were cut off." The significance of that made the list of suspects endless. It was also puzzling. It was often easier simply to use poison. The method of mutilation was used frequently by the plains Indians. To Jason's knowledge, though he knew his people could mutilate as well as any others, leaving a message by specifically removing body parts wasn't a common occurrence. But it was clear that by cutting off Weber's hands, everyone would know that he'd been considered a thief.

"They used a club on Ritter. The side of his head was bashed in." Jason waited a second, then added, "And they cut off his balls."

A lopsided smirk cut into Buck's angular face. "Ah, the punishment of choice for the bastard's crimes."

Jason eyed him closely, looking for some sign of guilt. There was nothing in Buck's flat black eyes that gave him away. But then Jason hadn't really expected to find any remorse. There had been too much hatred.

"They were dead when I arrived."

"You don't know who did it then, do you?"

Jason merely shook his head, ignoring the smug tone in Buck's voice. He remembered that not a single person from the reservation claimed to have heard any noise. Hell, he hadn't heard anything either, and from the warmth of the bodies, the murders had to have happened while he was delivering Mary's baby. Unfortunately, the Deerflower cabin was built deeper into the woods than the others, and trees muffled most of the day-to-day clamor.

"This isn't the way to handle things," he reminded Buck.

Buck's head jerked up, and he glared at Jason. "Dammit, I told you I was in Redland last night, and I've been here since midnight. Don't try to hang this one on me."

Jason tied the flapping ends of the bandage together beneath Buck's wound. "It's a very tidy convenience that Ritter was mutilated that way."

Buck shoved Jason's hand away. "Do you think my wife is the only squaw he coaxed into a barn with his sweet talk, then raped? Was she the only woman on the reservation, or anywhere else for that matter, who died because of that little weasel? Hell, Jason, I can name a dozen men who wanted that son of a bitch dead as much as I did."

This was true. Relief nudged Jason's suspicions aside. "I had to be sure."

Pinning Jason with an angry gaze, Buck grabbed his shirt off the table and carefully slipped into it. "You sound like you're sorry they're dead."

A flash of hot rage seared Jason's chest. "Of *course* I'm sorry they're dead. Do you realize how much this sets our cause back? You can't get rid of the weed by hacking away at the plant. You have to dig out the root."

Buck snorted. "That means killing every politician and army officer from here to Washington, D.C."

"It doesn't mean *killing* anyone," Jason answered. "You know damned well what I mean." Jason's frustration with the Bureau of Indian Affairs had begun when his uncle, Jake Gaspard, had retired from the post some years before. Weber, an army lieutenant, had taken over the post two years ago. He'd done nothing but line his pockets with Bureau money ever since.

Buck stood up, sighing dramatically. "Yeah, I know what you mean. And I think you're wrong. We can't fight the Whites on their level. We have no *rights*, dammit!"

"And we'll never have any rights or anything else if we keep killing their leaders," Jason reasoned strongly.

Swearing again, Buck went to the stove and poured himself a cup of coffee. His hands shook visibly. "We'll never have any if we don't, either. Hell, we don't have anything anyway. You know as well as I do that if shit were worth something, Indians wouldn't have assholes." He reached into the cupboard and pulled out a bottle of whiskey.

Jason grimaced, both at Buck's comment and at the picture of him spilling the liquor into his coffee. "You've already got the shakes. That stuff will kill you."

"So what?" Buck turned and glared at him. "Maybe it's what I want. What do you care if I drink so much that I have to open my shirt collar to piss?" He took a long drink, then sucked air in through his teeth. "Tell me what in the hell I have to live for?"

"You have your son," Jason reminded him, curbing his anger at Buck's flagrant carelessness with his life in spite of his responsibilities.

Buck glanced at the closed bedroom door. "Dusty's better off here with Ma and Sky."

Jason clenched his fist, wanting to smash it into Buck's face. "It sounds like you've already decided to abandon Dusty and drink yourself to death." Frustration whipped up his anger. "You're not that stupid, are you?"

He gave Jason a familiar smirk. "Maybe I am. Or maybe I just don't give a goddamn."

Jason washed his hands again, then turned to leave. Reasoning with Buck was like trying to argue with a stone. "Say goodbye to your folks. I have to tell Tully about the murders and arrange for their burial."

"If you need someone to friggin' dance at the funeral, let me know."

Jason gave him a look of disgust.

"Ah, c'mon, Jason." Buck's teasing had a sharp edge to it. "Get that ramrod out of your ass. Don't you ever have any fun anymore? When was the last time you had your dick out of your pants for anything besides taking a leak?"

Jason gave him a grim look. "Life's one big drunken brawl to you, isn't it?"

Buck shrugged, tossing him a dismal half-smile. "If I can get away with it."

Jason left, but all the way to town he worried about Buck's impulsive behavior and his excessive drinking. Some of his attitude could be excused. He was, after all, still in mourning. It hadn't been quite a month since Ritter had forced himself on Buck's young wife, Honey, beating her into submission before raping her. It wouldn't have mattered if Ritter had known that Honey bled and bruised easily. But it *would* have mattered if she'd been found before she bled to death.

Jason dismounted outside the smithy, flipped a coin at the

young boy who took his mount, then headed for Marshal Tully's office. •

Jason left the jail, feeling the winter chill in the air for the first time all morning. Maybe it was because of Tully's ominous premonition regarding the deaths. *Damned right there'll be hell to pay. How d'ya think it's gonna look for two government officials to be slaughtered that way, right under our noses? We're in for some serious inspection, Jason, and I mean serious.*

He jogged the last few hundred yards to his office and stepped inside. Ivy Masterson, the owner of the cafe, sat on his cot, cradling a young girl in her arms.

"Ivy?"

"Lord, Jason," she answered, pulling the child closer. "Where have you been? I found this here gal stumbling along the road from the reservation. She's got cuts and bruises everywhere. I tried to clean her up," she added, "but you know I ain't much good in a sickroom."

Jason crossed to the washstand and washed his hands. As he poured clean water over them from the pitcher, he studied the girl. It didn't surprise him that Ivy, the bleeding heart of Pine Valley, had found another child in need. But they were usually abandoned or orphaned half-bloods, children whose parents had been killed by the Whites. This one didn't look much like an Indian. A tangle of wild light brown hair hung over her face, wreathing her tiny head. She moved, just enough so that the sunlight caught a fat curl, touching it with fire.

Her dress, or robe, or whatever the hell it was, was dirty and smeared with blood and dirt and her hands were folded, prayerlike, in her lap. He noticed that her nails were grimy. The soft slippers on her tiny feet were dirty and dusty, and her bare ankles looked as though they hadn't seen soap and water in a month.

"I don't believe I've seen her around here before." The girl kept her head down, her unruly curls hiding her face. From the sound of her sniffles, Jason imagined she'd been crying off and on for hours.

"I came here just . . . just last week," she said in a meek, teary voice.

"Her name's Rachel. Rachel *Weber*," Ivy offered.

The towel he was using hung suspended for a brief second. *Weber?* He crossed the room, crouched down and stared at her. She still wouldn't look at him, her gaze seemingly frozen on her dirty hands, which were still folded in her lap. "I didn't know Weber had any children." He tried to keep the surprise from his voice.

The girl raised her head and looked at Jason through her spiral of brownish curls. There was a vacant look in her light gray-blue eyes, a look he'd seen many times before. He had no doubt that it masked something she didn't want to think about, or remember. *God, if she saw what happened* . . .

"She's not Weber's *daughter*, Jason," Ivy admonished. "She says she's his *wife*."

Shock flooded him. He lifted her chin to get a better look at her. "Good God," he whispered, his voice laced with disbelief. "You're just a child."

Shaking her head, she pushed his hand away. "I'm . . . I'm not. We've . . . been married over two years." She appeared to run out of breath. Then, after a few seconds, she added, "He . . . he just didn't want me to come out here. . . . too uncivilized." Her voice rattled with tears. "Oh, God . . ." The words caught in her throat as she dissolved into tears.

"There, there," Ivy soothed. "Lord have mercy, Jason. Ain't you got something you can give her? She's shakin' like fish jelly. And get something on her hands. Just look at them," she added, turning the girl's palms up and presenting them to him.

Jason saw the deep gouges and knew they'd been made by her fingernails. He went to the tall cupboard with the glass doors and took out a jar of salve. Returning to the cot, he pulled up a chair and straddled it, then he reached for the girl's hands.

She was listless, allowing him to smear the salve on her

palms even though he knew it must sting. Suddenly her small shoulders shook and she started to cry again.

"I . . . I'm s-sorry," she whispered, swiping at her eyes with the sleeve of her robe. "I . . . I can't seem to stop . . ."

A number of emotions surged through Jason. But pity, though she was obviously in a pitiful state, was not one of them. Whether she knew of her husband's dirty dealings or not made little difference. Jason knew it wasn't fair, but to him, she was guilty by association.

"Is she staying with you?" he asked Ivy as he wrapped the girl's hands with a light bandage.

"Well, of course she's stayin' with me. Where else would the poor dear go?"

He shook his head. "I had to know before I gave her a sedative. What happened to her, anyway?"

"Someone came in and killed her man, that's what happened to her."

The memory of the massacre, fresh and harsh, swelled before him. "Was she . . . *hurt* in any way?"

"Oh," Ivy muttered. "Oh," she repeated, giving Jason an understanding nod. "I don't think so. 'Course, I ain't sure, but she says her man shoved her into the storage hole beside the fireplace before the ruckus started." She turned to the girl sitting beside her. "Isn't that right, honey?"

The frail-looking thing on the cot bobbed her head but said nothing.

Jason swore. He'd had the strangest feeling when he'd stepped into that cottage that he wasn't alone. He even remembered staring at the fireplace, sensing something, but he'd shrugged it off.

He swung himself off the chair and crossed to the glass cupboard again. Rummaging through the clutter of bottles and jars, he found the small white packet he was looking for. He handed it to Ivy.

"Take her home and put her to bed. Mix half of this in water and give it to her now, and the rest tonight, before she goes to sleep. That is," he added, not attempting to hide his disdain, "if she really needs it."

"Your bedside manner is lackin'," Ivy said, her black eyebrows arched at him.

He swung away from her. "Ask me if I care."

"Now, Jason, I—"

"Bring her back in a couple of days and I'll change the bandages," he interrupted. He tossed the stethoscope back over the chair and waited for them to leave. When he heard the door close, he realized that he felt some shame, but he couldn't dredge up any sympathy for the pathetic creature who claimed to be Weber's wife.

He walked to the window and watched them cross the street, his eyes following the small, mousy woman as she leaned on Ivy's arm.

His *wife*? He swore under his breath, imagining how hard it must have been for Weber to see this creature arrive on his doorstep. They didn't appear much of a match, but then, looks could be deceiving. She could just be a consummate actress. He refused to get suckered in by her helplessness like Ivy had. Hell, no doubt she'd have the whole town feeling sorry for her in no time at all.

He wondered if she'd seen her husband's killer. Had she seen *him*? If she were really as troubled as she seemed, she probably hadn't seen much at all. Or at least, nothing that registered. He shuddered as he pictured her stumbling from her hiding place into the bloody, body-strewn room.

Shaking his head, he left the window and crossed to his desk where he made out a chart with Rachel Weber's name on it. After jotting down a few notes, he slipped the chart on top of the others and thought about Weber's activities. It occurred to him that his little wife might know nothing about them. She appeared naïve and a little simple. He wondered if she'd even noticed that her husband's hands were missing, or that the little bastard Ritter's genitals, balls and all, were gone.

He cleared his throat, feeling a little foolish at where his thoughts were going. If he wasn't careful, she'd have him in her pocket just like she had Ivy. And no doubt the marshal would be treating her like a long-lost daughter.

He'd check on her in a day or two and hope she'd be fit to travel. He wanted her out of town. Any trace of Ritter and Weber was going to leave a bitter taste in everyone's mouth. Hopefully, now that Weber was dead, his frightened little rabbit of a wife would hightail it back to where she came from.

🮡 Chapter Two 🮡

A light drizzle descended on the gravesite. The lonely sprig of winter flowers from Ivy's window garden clung to the wet brown casket cover. Rachel tossed a furtive glance at the lone woman who stood beneath the wide branches of an oak tree as she adjusted the hood of her borrowed woolen cape. She pulled it closer around her face, careful not to crush the flower she would throw on Jeremy's coffin before it was lowered into the ground.

She glanced at the minister. His lips were moving, but she didn't know what he was saying. She couldn't concentrate. None of this seemed real.

Jeremy had been so vital, so handsome and strong. It just didn't seem possible that he was . . . gone. Swallowing a sob, she tried to make sense of it all, but she couldn't. She'd lost the one person who could have made her life happy. He'd been ripped from her side by the army and called to duty so quickly after their wedding, they hadn't been allowed to even plan their life together. And now she was expected to live on without him.

Forcing her thoughts onto another path, she scanned the tiny group of mourners. Only a handful of people had shown up. The weather was bad, but that shouldn't have mattered. It had been weather like this, maybe worse, when her parents, Aunt Billie, and her cousin George had been buried, and the circle of mourners around the gravesite had been wide, warm . . . loving. Where were all the Indians Jeremy had come to help?

Unappreciative savages. This was the gratitude he got for trying to civilize them and make them decent human beings. He and his father had been right. Indians were inferior. They didn't appreciate the help they got, so didn't deserve it. Why, then, had Jeremy put his life on the line trying to help them?

Oh, darling, look what your good intentions got you. The bite of anger and hatred she felt toward all Indians returned and churned in her chest.

She glanced at the few people scattered beside the grave, particularly noting the tall, dark man who stood with his coat collar turned up against the rain. The faces of the other mourners were covered, either by umbrellas, veils, or hats pulled low over their eyes. Ivy and Marshal Tully stood on either side of her, framing her, protecting her, holding her up. She was so obliged for their support these past few days, she didn't know how she'd ever repay them.

Briefly, a blustery gust of wind coaxed out a ray or two of sunshine, whipping off Rachel's hood. Pulling it back in place, she stood before her husband's casket and closed her eyes, trying to forget what lay before her. The unknown frightened her; it always had. Fear of the future was what had kept her from attempting to change it, despite her unhappy, unfulfilled life. And she was well acquainted with grief. Long before she'd grieved for Jeremy, she'd ached with despair at the loss of her family.

But Jeremy was the reason she'd come to California—against his wishes, of course. She'd hoped to awaken something that hadn't been allowed to bloom, to rescue something that might have taken a miracle to save. Hero that he was in her heart, Jeremy just didn't understand what his absence did to her.

Ivy's hand squeezed hers and she felt a wealth of love for this woman who'd been the mother she hadn't known in twelve years. She and the marshal were the only friends Rachel had left in the world, and she hadn't known them a week. It was a sad commentary on her life.

Once again, she sneaked a glance at the woman standing

away from them, under the oak tree. Dressed all in black, including the veil that hung over her face, she shook visibly. Rachel thought she must be very, very cold. A blond curl had escaped from beneath her hat and now lay damp and limp on the woman's shoulder. Rachel felt sorry for her, standing there all alone.

Suddenly she realized that the minister had stopped speaking.

"Rachel, the flower."

Ivy's whisper shook Rachel from her reverie. She stepped forward and tossed the flower on the casket. The minister said a final prayer, and it was over.

She stared down at the box that held her husband's body. *Oh, Jeremy. We could have been happy. We would have been happy.* A brief picture of the stunned look on his face when he saw her on his doorstep flickered before her. She shook it away. He'd been surprised that she'd come and unprepared for her. That was all. She couldn't blame him for that.

"C'mon, honey."

She looked up, her eyes meeting Ivy's. Ivy had a friendly face, one that appeared comfortable with the way the years had whittled away at the once-beautiful contours, leaving gentle lines around the mouth and fine crinkles at the corners of her warm, brown eyes.

"How are we doing?" Ivy put her arm around Rachel as they walked away.

"I'm fine, really," Rachel answered, her voice quavering as she leaned into Ivy's embrace. "I'm . . . I'm just so tired—" She pressed her lips together, hoping to stem the flow of tears.

They walked toward the buggy where the marshal stood, ready to help them in. "Well, of course you are. You ain't slept good one night since you been stayin' with me."

Rachel smiled slightly. "Now, how do you know that?"

"These old ears still hear better'n most," Ivy answered.

Rachel turned to respond and saw the woman in black walking slowly behind them. "Ivy?"

"Yes, love?"

Rachel nodded toward the woman. "Who's that?"

Ivy looked in the woman's direction, cleared her throat and lifted her head in the air. "I ain't really sure," she answered, pulling Rachel toward the buggy.

Again, Rachel thought about the few mourners. "It must have been the rain," she said to herself.

"What, dear?"

She got to the buggy and the marshal helped her inside, giving her a fatherly kiss on the cheek. She gave him a grateful smile. "The service was so small. It must have been because of the weather."

Ivy adjusted herself beside her. "Yes, might be that."

Marshal Tully stood at the buggy door. "Ivy, maybe it's time we—"

"Hush your mouth, Earl Tully. Just get up there and drive."

Rachel smiled wanly at the bickering twosome. It seemed they did quite a lot of that, in spite of the fact that she could tell they really cared for one another.

The buggy lurched forward, gently swaying its passengers. Rachel looked out at the wet, gray day and shivered as they passed the harsh, flat slabs that stood sentry over the dead.

She wasn't sure what she was going to do. There was really no reason to stay here, but she had no place to go, either.

Jason watched the buggy leave the cemetery. What a shock it had been to see the mousy widow standing bravely between Ivy and Tully. For some reason, he'd envisioned her falling apart, throwing herself over the wet, brown casket and mewling like a whipped dog. But she hadn't. And when the sun had caught shimmering strands of gold in her cognac-hued hair, and the wind had pressed her dress against her bosom, he'd suddenly been struck with the realization that she was neither a rabbit nor a mouse. She was flesh-and-blood woman, and he began to see what Jeremy Weber might have found desirable about her.

* * *

Rachel warmed her hands around the hot cup of coffee and brought her arms in close to her sides. The cafe was nearly empty; it was too early for the lunch rush. She'd confided her plight to Ivy, and the woman had been such a dear, assuring Rachel she could use the spare room for as long as she liked. She'd even told Rachel she really didn't want to see her go, and if she could have seen any way to hire Rachel herself, she would have. But that wouldn't have been fair to the two employees, both Indian women, on whom Ivy counted to help her run the cafe.

"Mrs. Weber?"

The masculine voice had a soft, Southern quality to it, for her name had come out sounding like "Miz Webbah." She looked up at the tall, lean man who stood in front of her. His hair was a mass of barely tamed black curls, shot with gray, and his eyes were so dark they reminded her of unlit coals.

She suddenly realized he wasn't as young as she'd first thought. He didn't seem to be a threatening sort of man, but she felt threatened anyway. Men had always threatened her one way or another, ever since she'd had to move in with her mother's brother, Uncle Gabe, and his family in Bismarck. It was Uncle Gabe's callous treatment of her that had made her realize that all men weren't as sweet and kind as her father.

"Yes?"

"Name's Bram Justice." He drew up the end of his name, making it sound like a question. Giving her a brief bow, he added, "I own the Western King Saloon. May I sit down?"

Puzzled, Rachel nodded as he took the seat across from her.

He shook his head sympathetically, then reached across the table and pulled her hand into his. His hands were soft —a rather unpleasant sensation from a man, she discovered. She also decided it was an inappropriate gesture from a stranger, but she didn't pull her hand away.

"First of all," he began in that slow, deliberate drawl, his brow knitting genially, "I am so sorry to hear of your loss, ma'am."

"Thank you." His touch was warm and firm, no doubt meant to put her at ease. It didn't. There was something ingratiating about his behavior.

"The lieutenant—your husband—was a good friend of mine. A good friend." He patted her hand, then released it at the same time she'd decided to extricate her fingers herself. "I want you to know that." Watching her carefully, he added, "I feel sort of responsible for what happened."

"Oh? Why is that?" She couldn't imagine why he should feel it was his fault that Jeremy was . . . murdered.

Putting his elbows on the table, he steepled his long, lean fingers and looked at her over the top of them. "We were savin' him a chair at the poker table that night. It had been planned for weeks." He gave her a small, knowing smile. "I guess he sort of forgot about his old cronies when you swept into town, lightin' up his life again."

Oh, dear heaven. If only Jeremy had done what he'd planned, he might not be dead in the ground right now. If only . . . Dreams were built and shattered on those words.

He reached into his pocket and pulled out a piece of paper. "I don't know any way of doing this that won't be a shock, so I won't pussyfoot around it." He shoved the folded paper toward her.

Rachel reached for it. "This is for me?"

He straightened his immaculately tailored waistcoat. "In a manner of speakin'."

She unfolded it and looked down at the familiar script. "This . . . this is Jeremy's writing," she said.

"Yes, ma'am."

She glanced across the table at Mr. Justice, then down at the paper, and read: *I owe Bram Justice and the Western King Saloon $3,000. Jeremy A. Weber, Lieutenant, U.S. Army.*

Rachel's stomach dropped. "Jeremy owed you money? Why?"

Mr. Justice took a deep breath. "Well, you know he was a mighty heavy poker player—"

"Did Jeremy play poker a lot?" she interrupted. Her stomach continued to twist into knots.

"Uh, yes, ma'am, he did. And he owed me a bundle of money because of it."

Frustrated and confused, she continued to stare at the note, then at Mr. Justice. "I don't understand. Why would you let him play cards if he didn't have the money?"

The saloon owner gave her a condescending smile. "It's part of the deal, ma'am. It doesn't do me any good to have my friends stop patronizing my place just because they're out of money."

Rachel stared at him. His words made absolutely no sense. It wasn't logical to give people money just so they could lose it. She turned back to Jeremy's signature. Her husband had made a reasonably good salary, she knew that for a fact. Not that she'd seen much of it, but she'd always figured he was salting the bulk of it away for their future. At least, that's what he'd told her . . .

She kept her head lowered, but peered at the man sitting across from her through the thick veil of her lashes. She was usually uncomfortable around all men. This one was no exception, but the situation gave her a certain amount of strength to overcome it.

"I . . . I'll see what I can do, Mr. Justice. Perhaps when I get Jeremy's final pay voucher, I can pay you part of this. But," she added, feeling her chest tighten and tears well in her eyes, "I don't think there will be enough to cover such a huge debt." Tears clogged her throat, and she wanted to scream. When was she going to stop this infernal blubbering?

Bram Justice muttered something under his breath. "I'm real sorry to have to hand you this problem, ma'am. But you have to see this from my side. If I were to forget about every IOU that crossed my desk, I'd be out of business."

Rachel swallowed hard, trying to get control of herself as she waved away his concern. "I understand, Mr. Justice. I really do. I . . . I'll do the best I can, but please," she said, giving him a pleading look, "give me some time."

Justice stood. "Of course. And, again, I'm real sorry for your loss."

Rachel nodded and watched him leave. When he was gone, she took out her handkerchief, blew her nose and wiped her eyes. Gambling? Jeremy had been *gambling* with their money?

She took a sip of her now lukewarm coffee, trying to make some sense of what she'd learned. The acidic brew burned as it rolled around in her stomach. Where was she going to get that kind of money? Suddenly, she knew. The bank. *Of course.* Jeremy certainly had a bank account.

A bud of hope flowered in her chest. Maybe there *was* money, after all. Maybe there would be enough to pacify Mr. Justice, at least until she could get settled somewhere and find a job. Oh, Lord . . . this was all so new to her.

Fighting a sudden feeling of panic, she shrugged into Ivy's cape and left the cafe, heading toward the bank. That would be a logical place to look, wouldn't it? Surely the bank would know about Jeremy's finances.

Rachel was ushered into the bank president's office. The thin, bespectacled man with the receding hairline looked up at her from behind his pedestal desk, the center panel adjusted at a special height for reading.

"Morning, Mrs. Weber. So sorry to hear of your loss." He was unconvincing.

"Th-Thank you, Mr. Bailey," she answered, gingerly sitting down on the edge of the chair in front of the desk.

He continued to work on some papers. "I'll be with you in a moment."

Rachel nodded and clasped her hands in her lap. That was the best way to keep them from shaking. Glancing around the room, she noticed that the furnishings were expensive and highly polished. She stared at the walnut Eastlake bookcase and cabinet, noting the shiny brass hinges and pulls. The books behind the glass doors stood in an orderly fashion, as if they hadn't been disturbed in years.

Glancing at the side wall, she found her reflection in a

large, rectangular mirror that hung over a shiny walnut single-door commode. She quickly looked away and sat up straight, hating the image of herself cowering in the chair like a beggar.

"Now," the banker said, setting his papers aside. "How can I help you, Mrs. Weber?"

Rachel looked into his cold blue eyes. He didn't like her. And he didn't even know her. "I . . . I've come to see about my husband's account." Her voice actually sounded confident. Maybe there was hope for her after all.

"His *account?*" Abner Bailey smirked.

Her confidence crumbled. "I assume he has an account with you. You're the only bank in town," she added with more assurance than she felt.

The banker pushed his chair back, rose and adjusted his brown morning coat. He walked around to the front of his desk, and leaned casually against it. "Mrs. Weber, your husband's account exists only on paper. There's no money in it."

Rachel's hand automatically went to her throat. "I . . . I don't understand."

Mr. Bailey cocked his head and sighed. "I don't know what else to tell you. Your husband spent money faster than he could earn it."

Rachel slumped back against the chair. "All of his army pay?"

He nodded. "I can show you the paperwork." He shoved back from the desk. "I'm afraid he also had an outstanding loan with me."

"A *loan?*" Rachel couldn't believe it. Not another debt.

He nodded again. "And, because he had no other collateral to put up, he gave me this." He crossed to the floor safe, returning with a small black box which he handed to Rachel.

Rachel held the box, almost afraid to open it. Willing her hands not to shake, she lifted off the cover and looked inside. Her heart dropped to the tops of her shoes.

"My mother's cameo!"

She threw the banker a look of confusion and despair. "I . . . I thought I'd lost this." She picked up the brooch and lovingly touched the pearl-encrusted border.

Abner Bailey shook his head. "I'd like to give it back to you, Mrs. Weber, but you must understand," he said, retrieving it from her shaking fingers, "that until the loan is paid off, it belongs to me."

Rachel was aghast. Jeremy had purposely taken the only thing that had meant anything to her, the only thing that she had left of her mother's, and exchanged it for money. Money for—what? More gambling?

"I . . . I guess I understand," she said, refusing to let him see her cry. "If . . . if I can pay you the money, it's . . . mine again?"

He nodded, then slipped the cameo back into the box.

She swallowed hard, dreading the answer to her next question. "How . . . how much did he owe you?"

"One thousand dollars, plus interest."

Rachel gasped. "A thou—" She couldn't even get the words out. She hadn't the foggiest notion where she was going to get the money to cover *this* debt, much less three times the amount to cover the debt to Mr. Justice. Suddenly, she realized that Jeremy was a man she hadn't known at all.

She stood, nervously straightening the folds in Ivy's cape. "I see. Well, then I guess I'll have to make some arrangements. Would it . . ." she added when she reached the door, "would it be possible to pay you in installments, Mr. Bailey?"

"Any way you like. But I'm afraid the brooch is mine until the full sum is paid off."

Rachel bit her lip and nodded, then left his office. Once outside the bank, she sank onto a wooden bench beside the building, so weak she was afraid she'd topple to the ground.

She dared not concentrate on the amount of money she had to come up with. All she knew was that she couldn't leave Pine Valley without setting things right. Her marriage hadn't been perfect. But still, the words had been spoken before the minister, and she knew full well that marriage, good or bad, meant sharing everything. Including Jeremy's debts.

Jason stood at the window and watched Rachel Weber sit down on the bench in front of the bank. She pressed her hand over her mouth and leaned back against the building. Somewhat concerned, he watched her carefully, wondering if he should go to her and ask if she needed help. Obviously, something she'd learned from Abner Bailey had shocked her.

His gaze roamed over her figure, partially hidden beneath the voluminous cape, and he remembered the gentle swell of her breasts as the wind had caressed them at the funeral. No, she was no longer the dirty, bedraggled urchin he'd imagined after first meeting her. Now, there was a frightening, haunting familiarity about her. He hadn't wanted to dwell on it then, and he didn't want to now.

As she got up slowly from the bench and made her way down the street, he wondered what she'd learned at the bank. The longer she stayed in town, the more puzzled Jason became. Each bit of bad news she learned about her husband —if, in fact, she hadn't known it before—should have sent her scurrying off, leaving her husband's creditors in her dust. He really felt it was just a matter of time. At least that was his fervent hope. Unwittingly, this innocent-appearing child-woman was playing havoc with his senses.

"Oh, Marshal, you're going to spoil me." Rachel sniffed the sweet aroma of the hot chocolate that Marshal Tully had put in front of her, along with a piece of Ivy's apple pie. "You keep this up and I'm going to get fat as a toad."

Tully pulled up a chair and sat across from her. "That'd take some doin', Rachel. A healthy gust of wind'd blow you clean off your feet."

Rachel gave him a wan smile. "I'm hardly that small."

"You're about swimmin' in Ivy's dresses. Sure you don't want me to go out and get your things from the cottage?"

"No," she answered quickly. "I . . . I have to do that myself. I *have* to. I'm . . . I'm just not ready. Not yet."

The thought of stepping into the room where Jeremy had been murdered frightened her more than anything. She'd ruminated about it for hours on end. She even woke up in a cold sweat many nights, dreaming she was still inside the crawl space. But, more often than not, during those dreams savages usually found her and hauled her out, dragging her by the hair.

No, she was positive she couldn't set foot in that place ever again. She also knew that meant that she had to. She had to start facing her fears.

She took a sip of the chocolate, closed her eyes and sighed. "Oh, I know it's silly. But if I don't . . . don't try to get over this awful fear I have, it will haunt me forever." She opened her eyes and gave him a warm smile. "Do you understand that? Foolish as it may sound?"

He took her hand and squeezed it between his two big, rough paws. " 'Course I do. An' you're about the bravest little gal I ever met."

Rachel shook her head. "I'm not brave. I'm frightened, Marshal." Her newfound anger enabled her to fight back her tears, although she'd discovered that she cried just as easily when she was angry as when she was upset. It was ironic that she didn't feel confident enough to do much of anything well, but one thing she could do better than anyone was bawl. "I'm so very, very frightened."

Marshal Tully's gray eyes softened even more. "Here," he said, taking her cup. "Let me warm that up."

"Oh," she answered, finally getting control of herself. "Thank you, but really, I have to check with Mrs. Weaver at the general store to see if that job is still open."

Tully put her cup on the table and clucked his tongue. "Shore wish I could come up with somethin' for you. There was a nursin' job outside of town, but I'm afraid Nellie Bluehorse took it just a couple of days ago."

A nursing job. That sounded so perfect. At least it was something she could do without any instruction. Working for her board and room in North Dakota as her uncle's nurse had prepared her, and she had proven competent, once she'd gotten used to the blood.

"Well, something will show up, I'm sure of it." No, she wasn't sure at all. Mrs. Weaver was her last chance. She'd checked every single shop in town; no one needed help.

The cafe door opened, and a tall, well-dressed man in a dark gray morning coat and light gray trousers stepped into the room. He looked vaguely familiar to Rachel.

Marshal Tully looked up and smiled. "Mornin', Doc."

Rachel studied the man. Of course. He was the doctor Ivy had taken her to the day of the massacre. She'd also seen him at the funeral. She continued to watch him, an odd feeling in her chest. It had to be fear, for he was a forbidding sort of man.

He walked toward them, his gait easy and fluid. He was as tall as the marshal, but wider through the shoulders. And his clothes appeared to be just a facade—something to hide the fact that beneath them he had the instincts, though possibly calloused, of someone well acquainted with the wild. That's what made him frightening. Her assessment surprised her. She didn't usually look at a man long enough to make one.

"Earl," the doctor answered, giving Rachel a slow, lazy glance.

"You remember Miz Weber, don't ya?"

Rachel's neck was warm, and probably red—a familiar peculiarity of hers when she met strangers, especially if they were men.

"Of course. How are you doing, Mrs. Weber?" he asked politely.

Rachel had the sensation that he wasn't sincere, although he wasn't as obvious as the banker. "I'm . . . I'm fine, thank you," she said.

"I had told Ivy to bring you back. How are you healing?" He sat down across from her, obviously expecting her to show him her hands.

For some inexplicable reason, her hands shook. Still, she turned them over on the table and showed him her palms.

He made her feel like a child being scrutinized for dirty fingernails.

His touch was firm and warm. He ran his thumb gently over the flat expanse of her palm, sending exciting little shocks up her arm. Immediately she felt guilty that his touch didn't repulse her. Her hands began to sweat, and she felt further embarrassment creep up her neck into her cheeks.

"Has Ivy been medicating them for you?"

A bristle of annoyance germinated in her chest, *almost* overriding her embarrassment. "I'm . . . sorry, but I'm quite capable of doing it myself."

He glanced up at her, one cynical black eyebrow raised. Staring at him, she realized she'd never seen eyes like his before. They were deep brown, almost black, and it was as if his lashes were so heavy, they pulled on his sloping lids. It gave him a look of superiority, as if he were looking down his nose at her. But that hadn't been her first thought, the one that accompanied the odd fluttering in her chest. *That* had been that she'd never seen such slumberous, stirring eyes. It was as if he'd just tumbled out from between warm, rumpled sheets.

Shame! Those kinds of thoughts were inexcusable. Her guilty flush deepened, and she was grateful he couldn't read her mind.

He still hadn't let go of her hand.

"Rachel's lookin' for work, Doc. Seen anything around?"

The doctor finally released her hand, sat back in his chair and stared at her. She couldn't tell what he was thinking. It was most disconcerting.

"So you're going to stay around here a while?" He spoke with an indolent drawl. He didn't seem to like her, either.

"Well," the marshal started to say, "she's had a bad—"

"I need some traveling money, that's all," she interrupted, giving the marshal a stern glance. She was surprised that she could get the words out, but she had no intentions of airing her dirty laundry in front of the arrogant doctor.

"And," she added, hoping to keep the marshal from saying more, "I have to wait until my . . . my husband's final pay voucher arrives."

The doctor quirked that wicked black eyebrow at her again. "It could be mailed to you."

She squelched the urge to squirm. He sounded anxious to be rid of her. Again, she briefly wished she could say something flirty such as, *Wouldn't you miss me if I were gone?* But that in itself would be hilarious. She was quite possibly the only woman on God's earth who didn't know how to tease a man. And, if the truth were known, quite possibly the marshal's presence was the only thing that kept her from scurrying away like a frightened rabbit.

The doctor was, indeed, menacing, although Rachel had the feeling it was an automatic reflex with him, not necessarily done to frighten her.

"I . . . I suppose it could," she answered, hating the insipid sound of her voice, "but I—" *I have no place to go.* "I feel that . . . that it will be here soon. Otherwise, if . . . if I change my address now, it could take months for the army to get it to me."

Marshal Tully looked at her strangely. She caught his gaze, hoping to signal him to stay quiet. He gave her a look of disapproval, but said nothing.

Tully pulled out his pocket watch. "Well, time for me to get back." He shoved himself away from the table and stood.

There was no way Rachel was going to be stuck in the cafe with the imperious doctor. "I'll go with you, Marshal. I want to see Mrs. Weaver, remember?"

She hurriedly grabbed Ivy's cape off the coatrack near the back of the cafe and rushed past the table. When she got to the door, she turned and looked at the marshal, who was staring after her.

"Are you coming, Marshal?" The question was a plea; she hoped he got the message. She didn't want him telling the doctor her private business behind her back.

Earl Tully scratched his chin and shook his head. "Right behind ya, Rachel."

* * *

Jason watched them leave. A slow, disparaging smile spread across his face. Damned if the widow hadn't already wrapped Tully around her little finger. He'd followed her out of the cafe like a lag-tongued pup.

There was that familiar tug again. But it sure as hell wasn't her voice. For some reason, her Yankee twang had surprised him—and disappointed him. But the tug was there, just the same, and it was stronger, now that he'd seen her up close and without something covering her head. The fire in her hair had drawn him. It was a more powerful lure than he could have imagined.

Nancy Brown, one of Ivy's helpers, ambled into the cafe from the kitchen. "Mornin', Doc. Coffee?"

Jason nodded. "Do you see much of the Weber woman?"

Nancy came out from behind the counter and placed a steaming cup of coffee on the table in front of him. "Oh," she said with a shrug as she removed Rachel's cup and the plate that held the uneaten piece of pie, "now and then. I don't pay much attention to her. She's quiet as a mouse."

Jason laughed softly. "Seems the Widow Weber leaves everyone with that impression." He still wondered if it was real or contrived.

Nancy shrugged again. "Maybe she's just scared. She's real good at avoiding Jessie and me."

Or maybe, Jason thought, taking a drink of coffee, she didn't like Indians any more than her husband had. The woman was a damned puzzle. But why? She didn't appear to have any more depth than a sheet of paper. He didn't know why he couldn't figure her out. But if she was going to stay around Pine Valley much longer, she bore watching. She couldn't possibly be as innocent as she appeared. No one married to Jeremy Weber could be. And besides, Jason admitted with a wry smile, he was curious.

🎵 Chapter Three 🎵

*R*achel stiffened on the wagon seat as she and Ivy approached the cabin. An odd sense of detachment spread through her as she looked at the small, square building; she prayed the sensation would continue when she was forced to step inside.

It was strange that she hadn't noticed just how badly the place needed repair. The adobe, chipped away around the windows, was cracked along the length of the wall that held the fireplace. Huge chunks of the hardened clay had fallen away where the outside surface met the beetling eaves of the roof.

She glanced at the dried-up hollyhocks and sunflowers. Someone had planted them long before she had come, and now they seemed to grieve, their heads drooping like graveside mourners. And the weeds . . . she'd meant to get out there and pull them so they wouldn't choke the roses . . .

A sad smile played on her lips. This run-down adobe cabin wasn't what she'd had in mind for her dream house. A whitewashed cottage with upstairs bedrooms, a paneled parlor, and big kitchen had always been her dream. And flower beds. At least six, scattered here and there over the landscape . . . And a swing hanging from an oak tree, for the children . . .

She sucked in a ragged breath and quickly looked away as the wagon stopped in front of the building where Jeremy had been killed. She sat, unmoving, for a long, silent minute, no longer feeling detached. She wouldn't have thought she'd feel any affection for this place. But deep down, she knew she did, and she knew why. It had been her last chance to make her marriage work. And this tiny, sorry-looking cottage would have been a place of her own—something she'd never had, not with her uncle and his family who had raised her, and not with Jeremy, who had insisted she live with his parents these past two years. No, it wasn't her dream cottage, but it still would have been a place of her own.

She'd come West wanting to start all over again, hoping to bring about that special something her parents had had in their marriage. That something she'd never known in hers, because she and Jeremy hadn't had a chance to make it work.

Ivy shifted beside her. "You sure you really wanna do this? I can get your things for you, honey."

Rachel sniffed and cleared her throat. "That's all right, Ivy. I can't pretend this didn't happen. If I don't face the place sooner or later, it will haunt me forever."

"Want me to go in with you?"

Grateful, Rachel nodded.

Ivy stepped down and started toward the building, stopping when Rachel didn't follow.

"There's nothin' inside that can hurt you," she said softly.

Oh, but there is, Rachel thought, the collection of noises and smells rushing back at her like swill water.

Don't be a coward. The voice in her head was so loud, it startled her. Pulling her shawl tighter around her, she walked to the door, stopping as it loomed in front of her. Closing her eyes, she briefly pictured the room as it had been the last time she'd seen it.

"I'm sorry . . . I can't," she whispered, tossing Ivy a plaintive look.

"Take your time." Ivy gripped the heavy metal handle, pressed on the latch and pushed the door open. Dust that had settled on the mantel and the tabletops suddenly came to life, moving in whorls as the room filled with sunlight and air.

Rachel stood rooted to the entry, and stared inside. The

room hadn't been cleaned very well. Swallowing convulsively, she stared at the cedar floorboards, which still bore the stains of blood, dark and dry. Though someone had tried to wash it off, the blood had soaked permanently into the wood, just as the memory of the massacre was carved into her heart. A brief, violent picture of that morning flashed into her mind, but she shook it away.

She looked around the rest of the room. Everything else was as it had been then. Shuddering, she glanced again at the spot where Jeremy had fallen. His handsome face floated before her, the ugly death grimace that haunted her sleep now obsessing her conscious mind.

Choking back a small cry, she ran into the back room, pulling in great gulps of air. Fighting back tears, she pulled open the small country wardrobe and yanked out her clothes, tossing them onto the bed.

Ivy came in behind her. "Where are your bags?"

Not trusting her voice, Rachel pointed to the shelf on the wall next to the window.

Ivy lifted off her valise, put it on the bed and opened it. "I just wish I could afford to hire you at the cafe, honey."

Rachel tried to control her emotions. None of this was Ivy's fault. She didn't want her to feel guilty.

Fingering the scalloped trim at the edge of her heavy white cotton slip, she answered, "Oh, that's all right. I'll find something, I'm sure of it."

But she wasn't sure at all. Mrs. Weaver at the general store had been her last chance, and she'd told Rachel she had just hired her niece. Every merchant in Pine Valley was sympathetic, but no one needed any help.

She pushed down her panic. The enormity of Jeremy's debts still staggered her; she didn't know if she'd ever get over the shock. And she had no idea how she was going to pay them. But discovering that he'd stolen her brooch had been the deepest blow of all.

"I'm so sorry you have to go through this, dear." Ivy's motherly voice broke into her reverie. "Must be just awful to have to keep thinkin' about that awful mornin'."

"I just want to get it over with," she answered with shaky determination. Her figured batiste garden dress with the soutache braid and open oversewn lace lay crumpled on the bed. A brief, happy memory of her wedding day—the last time she'd worn it—danced on the fringes of her mind. She quickly rolled up the garment, shoving it into her bag.

Ivy gasped. "What did you just do to that beautiful gown?"

"Oh, what does it matter?" Rachel stuffed her blue cotton skirt with puffing, tucking, and eyelets into the bag on top of the dress.

Ivy pulled out the dress and the skirt, folding them carefully before putting them back in the valise. "Your life isn't over, honey."

Tears clogged Rachel's throat again. *Darn*. When was she going to stop this abysmal sniveling?

The raucous cry of a hawk exploded outside, and Rachel jumped, bringing her hand over her heart. She shook herself and began packing again. "You don't know how much I wish someone had come along to help us," she said, swallowing her hurt. "Why couldn't someone have . . . have been driving by?"

"Those are the kinds of questions that just can't be answered, dear." Ivy sighed, then asked, "You hadn't been here very long before this happened, had you?"

"No. It's been less than two weeks since I stepped off the train, and I hadn't been here a week when . . ." Rachel wondered how twelve days could seem like such a lifetime.

"Did you know your man real well?"

"What a silly question. Of course I knew him," Rachel answered, a little too quickly. "We were married for over two years." Again, the memory of her shock at discovering Jeremy's gambling debt sifted through her mind. It was hard to admit that she really hadn't known him at all. She'd loved him desperately, but she hadn't known him. The realization that you can't truly love someone you don't know spread through her, but she pushed it away.

Ivy cleared her throat. "We haven't talked much about Harry Ritter."

Rachel briefly stopped her frenzied packing and gave Ivy a sad smile. "Poor Harry. He was so sweet and shy." Rachel remembered how timid he'd been around her. Barely said a word to her, always ducking his head to avoid looking at her when he came inside to talk to Jeremy.

Ivy cleared her throat again. "Well, to be perfectly honest, dear—"

"Afternoon, ladies."

Rachel turned toward the door just as Marshal Tully entered the room. He was so tall, he had to stoop to get through the door or he would have hit his head.

"Lord in heaven, Earl." Ivy's voice was tinged with impatience. "I tried to find you when we left. What the devil are you doin' out here?"

"Had to check on some reservation business. Saw your wagon, and thought you might need some help."

" 'Course we could use the help. You don't expect we can haul that trunk out of here ourselves, do you?"

"Now, Ivy, I'm here, no need to nag me." Tully actually appeared to blush.

"Somebody has to," she retorted.

Rachel felt a tug of envy as she listened to them. Over the past week she'd discovered that the bristly way Ivy talked to the marshal was only for the benefit of others. She'd often caught the warmth in Ivy's eyes when Earl Tully entered or left the room. It was sweet, this quiet love they seemed to have. Rachel's envy deepened.

"I got a few more questions, Rachel, honey. Somethin's come up. Now, I know you've told me everything you can remember, but," he said, running his forefinger along his steel-gray mustache, "I thought that mebbe you'd remember somethin' else now that you're in the house again."

Rachel fiddled nervously with the bodice of her borrowed green and brown calico print housedress, remembering the picture that had flashed through her head shortly before. Not wanting to think about it further, she folded another skirt and pushed it into her bag. "I . . . I'm really sorry, Marshal. I've told you everything."

"Earl, don't badger her," Ivy scolded. "She's been relivin' the nightmare from hell to breakfast every day since it happened. Can't we just let it lie?"

Tully stepped to the window and looked outside. "I'd like to, you know I don't enjoy browbeatin' women, Ivy."

Rachel's heart bumped her ribs. "I . . . is it that important?"

He turned, giving her a sympathetic look. " 'Fraid so. We don't have a notion as to who killed your husband, Rachel. Any little thing you can remember will help. For instance," he added, "d'ya know whether or not he had any valuables stashed in that safe of his? It's standin' empty in the other room, if you noticed."

She hadn't. "You think the savages stole what was in it?"

Tully ran his big, calloused fingers through his silver hair. "Well, now that's puzzlin'. It's empty, there's no doubt about that, but it ain't been broken into. It was opened clean."

Rachel fiddled with a loop of her hair. "Maybe . . . maybe Jeremy had opened it himself."

He nodded, digesting her comment. "Mebbe. But I just got word that he'd had some—" He shot Ivy a quick glance before continuing. "I heard he'd gotten a lump of money from . . . from some business deal. Now, we know the bank don't have it on record. I have a strong hunch that money was in the safe that mornin', and now it ain't."

"Then . . . then the savages stole it. What else could have happened to it?" Oh, Lord, what she could do with that money, no matter how much or how little it was.

Tully clucked his tongue. "I don't know too many Injuns who can open a safe without blastin' it to kingdom come. 'Course," he pondered, "there are a few."

"What . . . are you trying to say?"

"Oh, it's nothin'," he assured her with a wave of his hand. "Just a thought. Anyway, can you think of anything else that might have happened that mornin' that might help us?"

"Now, Earl," Ivy chided softly. "Can't you see how upset all these questions are makin' her?"

Rachel drew in a deep breath, letting it out slowly. "No, it's all right, Ivy. There *is* something else. Until I stepped back into this place, it had completely slipped my mind. I . . . I know I forced myself not to think about it. It was so . . . so awful . . ."

"Of course it was, dear," Ivy crooned.

"Dangit, Ivy, quit treatin' her like she was just whelped."

Ivy clucked her maternal tongue and turned her back on him.

"Now, Rachel, what do you remember?"

"The Indian who murdered my husband." The savage's face blurred in her vision, but his eyes, so filled with hate, were sharp and clear in her memory.

"What about him?"

"Jeremy stabbed him." She looked at the marshal, then pulled her gaze away. There was something terribly disconcerting in his expression.

"Your husband stabbed his killer?"

Nodding, Rachel swallowed hard. She brought her hand up to her right shoulder. "Here."

Tully's eyes were narrow slits. "On the right side?"

She nodded again. "Jeremy was left-handed." She sat down slowly on the edge of the bed and stared at the wall. "I'm sorry I didn't think of it sooner. I don't know how I could have forgotten that. I don't . . . I didn't think I'd ever forget that savage's face." She shuddered, remembering the wild look in his eyes as the light from the kerosene lamp undulated across his features.

"I see," Tully answered, turning back to the window. "Can you remember somethin' about that face?"

Rachel closed her eyes, trying to picture it. Only the eyes remained. She shook her head. "I'm sorry, it's hard to describe. I know I said I'd never forget it, but you have to understand that I didn't think about memorizing it at the time." Shrugging her small shoulders, she added, "He was an Indian." She gave him a doleful glance. "I . . . I haven't told you, but one of the reasons I didn't follow Jeremy out here sooner was because . . . because I didn't want to be surrounded by . . . by savages.

"When I was just a little girl," she said quickly, her face pinched with pain, "my family . . . was killed by Indians. Right . . . right before my eyes. Mama, Papa, Lucas, my aunt Billie and my cousin George. One of the Indians . . . was a man we all trusted. He was almost like family. At . . . at least, that's the way we treated him." Elbee's face as she'd last seen it loomed before her.

She choked back a sad little laugh. "Now, my husband's been killed by Indians. Just thinking about them scares me to death. I can hardly look at one without remembering that terrible, dark morning when . . . when they burned our cabin and chased us through the corn."

Pressing her fingers against her lips, she turned away toward the window. Her fear and hatred of Indians had been fed first by Uncle Gabe, then by Jeremy and his father. She'd honestly tried to come to terms with her own feelings, and she'd made progress just by coming out here, where she knew she'd have to face many Indians. And now, they had killed Jeremy, and her bitterness toward every savage who walked the earth was compounded.

She turned back to the marshal. "They all look alike to me. Don't you see? Every time I see one, I only see someone I've learned to hate and fear. Someone who might hurt me. All they've ever done in my life is hurt me." Sobbing again, she put her face in her hands, loathing her weakness.

"Oh, Earl," Ivy quipped, "you're about as sensitive as a sack of hog turds." She scurried to the bed, sat down and pulled Rachel into her arms. "I hope you feel right good about makin' her cry." She hugged Rachel, rocking her back and forth. Rachel sagged against the older woman's shoulder.

Tully ignored the comment, crossed to the bed and hunkered down in front of them. He reached out and touched Rachel's arm. "I'm sorry, Rachel. Thanks for tellin' me about the stabbing. It might help." He chucked her under the chin. "I hope we still have a date for church tomorrow night."

Rachel gave him a watery smile. "Yes, thank you. And I'm sorry I'm blubbering so. I just can't seem to stop."

He gave her a wicked grin, one intended to cheer her up. "Don't you give it another thought, sweetheart. Wouldn't miss a chance to walk you home." He nodded in Ivy's direction. "Lucky fer us she has to work, ain't it?"

"You behave yourself, Earl Tully," Ivy chimed in, giving his hair a tug. "You're old enough to be her pa, and then some."

Tully picked up Rachel's trunk. "I'll toss this in the back of the wagon," he said as he left the room, his husky laughter floating in his wake.

After he'd gone, Rachel quickly packed up the rest of her things, anxious to leave the cottage behind her. But foremost in her thoughts was the look on Marshal Tully's face when she'd mentioned the savage with the knife wound. Because she was a quiet, introspective person, she'd made it a point to study the faces of those around her. And Earl Tully's face told her he knew something he wasn't willing to share.

Rachel nodded to the minister as she left the church to catch up with the marshal, who had gone out earlier for a smoke. "That was a very nice service, Reverend Toland."

"Thank you, Mrs. Weber." His voice was fine, generous and sincere. Rachel liked him.

"Do you have someone to walk you back to the cafe?"

"Yes," she answered, pointing toward the big, bushy oleanders. "The marshal. He's right over there."

The reverend smiled and nodded, then went back inside the small white frame building, leaving her alone on the steps. She heard him lock the door, and moments later, saw the lights extinguished inside. She knew he would go out the back door and make his way to the parsonage, a short block away.

Turning from the church, she could see the round red fire

from the marshal's cigarette as he inhaled. He was standing by the fence. Carefully making her way down the steps, she crossed the grass and was almost in front of him when he suddenly pushed her to the ground. Simultaneously she heard a small explosion and a deep, low groan from Tully.

She lay there, confused, unable to understand what had happened. Tully groaned again.

"Marshal?" Part of his upper body was still on top of her, although she could tell he was trying to move away. Scooting out from beneath him, she grabbed his arm as he tumbled to the grass. "What is it? What happened?"

"Shot," he said, his voice gritty and hoarse.

Her hand flew to her chest. "What!" She knelt down beside him, looking around wildly for some light in the black sky.

Tully sucked in a deep breath. "Holy hell," he swore, struggling to sit up. "I've been shot."

Rachel couldn't see anything. It was too dark. "Where?"

"Leg . . ." he croaked.

Automatically she ran her hand along his leg. Her fingers touched the warm, sticky liquid that oozed from his wound and her first response was to recoil. It was always worse to touch something you couldn't see.

She frantically looked around her. They were alone. "I have to get some help," she finally said. "I'll . . . I'll get the reverend."

Tully grabbed her arm. "No, don't bother him."

"But why not? He's not that far—"

"No," he interrupted, his voice raspy. "His wife's pretty sick. He's gotta get home to her and his kids."

Rachel felt panic push at the heavy weight in her chest. "The doctor. I'll get the doctor."

"Ain't no use. He's out at the reservation," Tully answered, his breathing labored.

"Then . . . then I'll get Ivy—"

"Dadburnit, not Ivy. I don't want her to—"

"Earl Tully," Rachel interrupted impatiently, "just stay put. I'm going to get Ivy whether you want me to or not.

Have you a handkerchief or something to hold over the wound?"

"Here," he answered, untying the one around his neck and handing it to her.

She folded it into a small square and pressed it over the wound. "Hold it there until I get back. Press hard."

"Now, Rachel—"

"Sit still and be quiet." Lifting her skirts, she turned and ran down the darkened street toward the cafe.

She raced up the steps, the hood on her woolen cape flapping out behind her. Her lungs burned and her heart drummed painfully.

"Ivy! Please, help!" She gasped for breath, panting as she leaned against the door frame.

Ivy hurried out from behind the counter. "What in the devil is wrong? You hurt, honey? What is it?"

Rachel waved away her concern. "No," she said, trying to catch her breath. "It's the marshal. He's been shot."

Ivy's hands flew to her cheeks. "Oh, *Lord*. Earl? What happened? Where is he?" she asked, grabbing her cape off the peg as she followed Rachel out the door.

They raced down the street. "We were just outside the church. Everyone else had gone. Then . . . then suddenly," Rachel said, her voice bouncing as she ran, "he pushed me down. He must have seen something. I didn't know what had happened until he told me."

They turned on El Suyo Street and raced on, the grinding of the gravel under their shoes and their labored breathing the only sounds in the cold night air. Reaching the corner, they found the marshal sitting up, his back against the fence in front of the church and his hand still pressed against his calf.

"Earl! Earl!" Ivy cried, rushing to his side.

"Oh, now hang on to your bustle, Ivy girl. It ain't as bad as all that."

Rachel hovered over them. "We'd better get him to the doctor's office," she suggested briskly. "Even if he isn't there, we can clean up the wound."

Ivy agreed, and with the marshal draped between them, they stumbled down the dark street.

Jason was bone-tired. Two full days at the vineyard and another at the reservation weren't usually enough to tire him out, but two cases of croup, three deliveries, and a false labor had kept him up two nights in a row. Grinning wryly, he wondered what had happened nine months ago that had led to the rash of births this past week.

Leaving the smithy, he dragged himself across the quiet street to his office. The sun was just staining the eastern sky, throwing soft shadows against the sides of the buildings. Opening his office door, he stepped silently into the room. *What the hell—*

His practiced gaze took in the transformation in seconds. No clutter. No mess. The windows sparkled and the floor had been scrubbed. He should have been pleased; instead he was annoyed. The place looked as though the Ladies' Aid Society from the Methodist church had come in and raised holy hell.

Breathing deeply so he wouldn't lose his temper, he moved slowly about the room. His medical books, always open and strewn around so he could use them when he needed them, were where they "belonged." They stood stiff and closed in a neat row on the top shelf of the battered, pockmarked bookcase he'd dragged home from college years before. He peered closer—and swore. They were alphabetized. *Diseases of the Chest*, by William Stokes, stood sentry at the end of the shelf, shoved tightly against the heavy bookend. On the other two shelves, the rest of his books were arranged according to height and color. His annoyance grew.

His gaze went to the wall beside the washstand where his stethoscopes hung neatly from hooks instead of from the backs of the chairs—where he'd purposely put them so he could grab them faster. He grunted again.

Glowering, he shoved his hands into his pockets and scrutinized the rest of the room. The sun glinted off the glass-covered doors of his cupboard. No dust, no fingerprints. Hell, the glass was so clean, it looked as if it weren't there. He felt a bubble of anger churn in his stomach. Not wanting to lose his temper, he dragged in another slow, deep breath.

He stood, glaring at the bottles inside the cupboard, their labels facing out. Winslow's Baby Syrup and Kopp's Baby Friend beamed at him like damned shiny smiles. He didn't need to see the labels to know what things were; hell, he knew every bottle by heart.

If he'd wanted his office to look like his mother's parlor, he'd have done it himself. He wondered who'd had the *nerve* to do this to him. The only people he could think of were Ivy, or maybe Nell—and they'd already nearly come to blows over the state of his office. He hated fighting with women, but it seemed he'd been doing it most of his life.

Heaving a sigh, he walked slowly to his desk, hardly recognizing the clean surface. It had been years since he'd actually seen it. He flipped through the charts and papers that were stacked on top, noting that they too were alphabetized. Scanning the far side of the desk, his gaze caught a flash of color. Pinning it with a glare that could melt rock, he scowled at the vase of yellow and white daisies that sat perched at the corner on top of a frilly white doily.

He spun around and stormed into the back room where he kept his extra cot and stopped short, his heart meeting his throat. Earl Tully was asleep on the bed, his left leg outside the bedding, resting on a pillow. Stepping closer, he saw the bandage around the marshal's calf. Spots of blood colored the surface, seeping into wide reddish-pink circles against the white cloth.

Jason's heart all but stopped when he glanced at the big easy chair by the stove. Curled up, sound asleep with her feet tucked under her and her head resting on the arm of the chair, was Rachel Weber.

He stepped closer and stared down at her. The familiar memory, old yet still painful, finally lunged to the surface of his mind.

Regina.

The kerosene lamp flickered on the table beside Rachel, flinging its quivering light over her as she slept. Her hair, the rich, thick color of cognac, shimmered with red, brown, and gold streams of light. *Regina.*

He couldn't believe the emotions that battered his insides. Years ago he'd purged himself of all feelings for the pretty, shallow woman for whom he'd almost changed his life. Now, suddenly, all of those feelings came back to him.

He studied Rachel. She still looked young. Too young to be involved with an unprincipled man like Weber. And damn, she was a pretty creature, in a delicate, porcelain kind of way—if you liked the type. He'd decided long ago, after Regina broke their engagement, that he didn't.

Rachel's long, dusky lashes lay on her cheeks, the curved ends feathering lightly along the rims of her eyelids, so thick, they bunched up in the outer corners of her eyes. Her face had a child's roundness to it, and suddenly she swallowed, pulling her mouth tight, causing dimples to delve deeply into the sweet pinkness of her cheeks.

His gaze roamed over the rest of her. Full, round breasts pressed against a white batiste blouse that had some sort of frilly design and a high, hand-embroidered neck.

Bringing his gaze back to her face, he was momentarily startled to discover she'd awakened and was looking at him. Big, blue-gray eyes held his.

"What happened to Tully?"

She cringed visibly at the sound of his voice. He hadn't meant for it to come out quite so harsh.

"Oh, I'm . . . so . . . so sorry," she stuttered, struggling to sit up in the chair. "He . . . he was shot, and I'm afraid it's my—"

"Shot?" He couldn't ignore the husky, sleepy tone of her voice. "How did it happen?"

She slipped her feet out from under her blue skirt, pushed back her hair and rose from the chair. She was taller than he remembered. Her chest was high and full against her blouse, and her waist was tiny, her skirt flaring gently out over her hips. And her hair . . . the brandied mass smoldered like kindling in the light. He shook his head, emptying it of poetry.

"We were standing outside the church," she began, nervously smoothing down her skirt. "Everyone else had . . . had gone, and he was going to walk me back to Ivy's." She brought her small hand to her chest, unconsciously displaying the finger that held her thin gold wedding band. "He . . . he shoved me to the ground and we heard a gunshot. He was hit in the leg."

Her no-nonsense recitation surprised him. The flat, Yankee twang annoyed him. Even though he'd spoken to her before, he'd somehow expected to hear the sweet confection of a Georgia drawl—like Regina's. He'd also expected her to start to cry, as she had the first time he'd seen her. He had a ridiculous urge to jump at her and shout "Boo!"

"Did you see anyone?"

She looked at him and frowned, then averted her eyes when she found him watching her. "No, I'm sorry, no."

"Was there much bleeding?"

"Um . . . no. Not too much. I'm afraid the bullet is still in there." She blinked nervously, then swallowed, unconsciously revealing dimples.

He glanced at the marshal, then turned to leave. "How long has he been asleep?"

"Not long," she answered, looking at the pendulum clock that hung on the wall. "Maybe a few hours. I'm sorry, but it took a little time to make him comfortable," she added, timidly following Jason into the larger room.

He crossed to the cabinet and pulled out a bottle of salve. "The dressing was wrapped quite capably. Where did you learn to do that?"

"My uncle. He was a physician in North Dakota. I . . . I used to help him."

The clipped, clean cadence of her speech was becoming more familiar. He still preferred a softer, more vulnerable sound.

"Why did you feel the need to clean up my office?" He tried to keep the irritation from his voice.

She cleared her throat, an anxious sound that seemed forced. "I'm sorry if I did something wrong. I . . . I thought I was doing you a favor."

"I happen to like it the way it was," he snapped.

Nervously twisting a long, loopy curl through her fingers, she said timorously, "I'm sorry, I was just trying to help—"

"Dammit, can't you say anything without apologizing for it?"

"Excuse me?" Her voice quavered.

"You're always apologizing for something. Why?" He slammed the glass door on the cabinet so hard, he was surprised it didn't crack.

She jumped, then stared at him, her big light eyes filled with confusion. "I . . . I'm sorry, I don't know what you mean."

"Just what part of the sentence didn't you understand?" he grilled, immediately regretting the words. Dammit, *now* she looked as though she were going to cry.

"Never mind," he muttered, picking up a wad of bandages. God, but she really was a mousy thing. He still couldn't imagine how she and Weber had ever gotten together. She had all the earmarks of a frightened virgin. He couldn't figure her out.

"May . . . may I go now?"

He turned and stared at her. She looked as if she didn't have a friend in the world. Her small shoulders sagged and her head was tilted to the side as she looked up at him, those big, light eyes seeming to beg for—something. He softened ever so slightly. "Are you leaving Pine Valley soon?"

She looked at her toes. "I . . . I can't leave just yet. I'm still waiting for . . . for the voucher."

Oh, yes. He remembered. That possibly nonexistent pay voucher from the government. He hadn't known Weber any better than he'd had to, but he knew the man had probably died without a cent to his name. He wondered what the widow was living on in the meantime.

"Do you still need a job?" He could have bitten his

tongue. He wanted her tiptoeing around his office about as much as he wanted a broken nose.

Her head jerked up, her glance taking in the room she'd just cleaned. Then she stared at him, innocently batting those big, vulnerable eyes. "Here?"

He nodded, swallowing his exasperation. "Here." He could see a mixture of excitement and fear flutter over her features.

"I . . . yes, I could use the job."

"Fine. But I'll warn you right now," he added, watching her carefully, "I treat whores, drunks, and Indians."

Her eyes closed, and she swayed to one side. He frankly thought he was going to have to catch her.

She shuddered, pressing her fingers against her mouth and turning away.

"Forget it," he said, dismissing her with a wave of his hand. "I need someone I can depend on. Not someone who's going to run crying into the street when she comes face to face with someone who doesn't meet her standards."

"Oh, please. I'm sorry, I—"

"Good-bye," he said, turning away from her and going into the back room to remove the bullet from Tully's leg. In a funny way, he was disappointed, and that was the rub. She brought out a dog-in-the-manger attitude in him that confounded him. He sure as hell didn't want her around, but if she was going to be around, he wanted to watch her. He was curious, *that's all.*

After a long silence, he decided she'd gone. So much for trying to help her. He wasn't sure which—whore, drunk, or Indian—had offended her the most. No doubt all three. Yet Regina's final words came back to haunt him. *Lawd, Jason. Ya don't expect me to live with savages, now, do ya?*

Turning back to the sleeping Tully, he heaved a deep, resigned sigh. He'd have to give the Weber woman a job if she showed up on his doorstep tomorrow. He needed the help, and she had the experience, or so she said. And, he reminded himself, he could keep his eye on her. Never before had he met a married woman who acted so innocent and uncomfortable around him. She had an inherent shyness that didn't fit with her status.

He hadn't wanted to elaborate on that thought, but a brief picture of her naked body sprang into his head. At the apex of her thighs, instead of the regular female equipment, he imagined there was a sprig of daisies. He snorted a laugh. No doubt the daisies on his desk had come from there.

Visualizing her breasts, he was sure they would be pale and full. Her nipples—probably pink, sweet, and tasty. All-day suckers . . . Strawberry. He'd always had a preference for strawberry-flavored suckers . . .

He swore. There was a stirring in his groin. He muttered a stronger curse as the picture filtered through his mind again. He'd better get a grip on things before tomorrow, because if he didn't, and she showed up, he was going to have one hell of a time explaining why he laughed every time he looked at her below the waist, and his mouth watered when he looked at her chest.

❧ Chapter Four ❧

The Queen Anne fret-carved mirror reflected Rachel's image. Worrying her lower lip between her teeth, she glanced at her gown. The red and white floral design against the deep blue background seemed to wash her out today. She pinched her cheeks, then stood back, studying her reflection. It would have to do. She couldn't deny that she was nervous about going back to the doctor's office. Maybe he really meant for her to forget about the job, and would tell her to disappear. But that was a risk she'd have to take. She needed the job, and she needed it badly.

He'd picked up on her flaw immediately, asking her why she apologized for everything. And he'd been so sarcastic. *Just what part of the sentence didn't you understand?* she mouthed sassily into the mirror. Oh, for the courage to tell him then and there that she could dissect the sentence as deftly as she wanted to dissect him! But that was always her problem—finding the clever thing to say hours, or even days, too late.

She shook her head, remembering that he'd been upset because she'd cleaned his office. And here she thought she'd done him a favor. She'd been cleaning up after someone ever since she moved in with her aunt and uncle. It was a hard habit to break. And all the other men in her life, her uncle, her father-in-law, and Jeremy, had *expected* it of her. How odd to run across a man who didn't. Yes, she thought, worrying her lip some more, how very odd. She sighed, concentrating on pinning up her hair so she wouldn't have to remember the old hurts.

As she straightened her room, she thought about what the doctor had said to her the morning before. *I treat whores, drunks, and Indians . . .* She shuddered, suddenly uncertain that she could go through with it. Although she desperately needed the job, she wasn't sure she could actually *touch* an Indian if she had to. And no doubt, if she was going to assist him, she'd have to.

A funny tingling passed over her skin. Something else bothered her. It had caused her to lie awake much of the night. The doctor frightened her. And it wasn't just because she was a timid person, although that was something she was certainly going to have to work on, for she knew that it annoyed him.

He simply made her uneasy. He was so tall and, yes, handsome in a dark, mysterious way. And those eyes . . . His gaze left her breathless.

She shivered, remembering how she'd felt he could see through her clothes to her bare skin. Though why she thought that, she didn't know. There was no reason to believe that he found her the least bit attractive or interesting. After all, she wasn't a "looker," as her uncle had constantly pointed out. And that was fine. The only thing she had to prove was that she was a capable assistant. As she twirled away from the mirror and crossed to the dressing table, she realized she'd have enough trouble convincing him of that.

It wouldn't be like working with her uncle; at least she hoped it wouldn't. She just had to try not to preface everything she said with "I'm sorry." Sucking in a deep breath, she realized that wouldn't be easy; she'd always been that way, as if she were responsible for every plague and pestilence since the beginning of time.

Her silver-framed wedding picture on the bedside table caught her eye. She picked it up, wiped off the thin layer of dust, and frowned as she looked at the two of them. She vividly remembered wanting to smile for the picture that day.

The idea of marrying Jeremy Weber had been a dream come true, although she'd even admitted to herself back then that she was surprised when he'd asked her. She'd loved him from afar, like half the other girls in town, but she hadn't thought he knew she existed. She'd been so eager to leave her uncle's house, she hadn't cared that she and Jeremy had moved directly in with his parents. As she stared down at Jeremy's boyishly handsome face, some of the sadness she'd experienced since his death returned.

Clutching the picture to her breast, she sank down on the bed. There just wasn't time to mourn. At least not the kind of mourning that took so much from her that she had nothing left with which to fight for her own survival. And, she thought, a little peeved as she recalled Jeremy's debts and his theft of her brooch, even in death he'd found a way to make her life miserable.

Stop it. She felt a deep twinge of shame at her selfish thoughts. Jeremy couldn't help the way he was. She'd known when she married him that he'd been a pampered child, just by the way his mother had treated him as an adult. But he'd still been the most handsome man she'd ever known . . .

Heaving a long, sad sigh, she put the picture back on the table and rose from the bed. Maybe things would have been different if they'd had a child. Maybe . . .

Don't think about it.

She shook off her maudlin thoughts, taking the advice of the little voice in her head as she pulled on her heavy black cape. As she left her room, she squared her shoulders and crossed her fingers, hoping that the doctor wouldn't toss her out on her behind.

"Don't touch them, Dusty, not yet."

Rachel tentatively stepped over the threshold and peered into the room. Dr. Gaspard and a young boy of about five stood with their backs to her, the young boy on tiptoe, his head bobbing excitedly as he watched something in a box on the table.

"Look!" he exclaimed. "She's lickin' on 'em."

Stepping closer, Rachel could hear the familiar faint squeals of newborn kittens. A floorboard squeaked under her feet, and Dr. Gaspard turned, studying her with his brooding, cavalier gaze. It affected her strangely. She tried to hold his stare, but she finally blinked and looked away.

"So," he said, "you've changed your mind."

"I'm s—" Catching herself, she replied, "I didn't turn down your offer, Doctor." She was going to add that he'd withdrawn it, but thought it best not to remind him.

His gaze drifted over her, stopping briefly just below her waist. Thinking that perhaps she'd spilled something in her lap during her hasty breakfast, she looked down, but saw nothing. When her gaze met his again, he was watching her. He quickly looked away.

"After I mentioned who most of my patients are, I thought I was going to have to pick you up off the floor."

"I was . . . I was merely exhausted," she lied. "And it had been a while since I was in a sickroom. How's the marshal?" She slid her cape off her shoulders and hung it on one of the oak hall trees that stood by the door.

"He's resting," he answered, giving her a good once-over before turning back to the kittens. "Go back and check on him if you'd like."

The little Indian boy continued to stare at her with big near-black eyes. Scolding herself, she swallowed a shudder. Even the gaze of an Indian child sent fear and a stab of hatred up her spine. She fled to the back room.

Tully grinned at her from the cot, and she smiled back. "No ill effects from my nursing?"

"Naw," he scoffed, his grin widening. "Doc Gaspard might be one hell of a doctor, but sometimes he has the bedside manner of a polecat. I missed yer gentle touch, Rachel."

Rachel laughed softly. "Of course you did," she answered, humoring him. The dressing had been changed. She pretended to check it for blood.

"Does he have a large practice?"

Tully shrugged. "Fair. A lot of the townsfolk head over to Redland when they need major doctorin'."

Rachel looked up, puzzled. "Why is that?"

"Oh, I guess they're used to old Doc Hillman." When Rachel met his gaze, he just grinned again. " 'Never trust a doc who's young enough to be yer grandson,' and all that, y'know."

No, she didn't know. She'd have given anything to see some young competition for her uncle. In the months before he died, he'd gotten lazier and lazier in his treatment of his patients.

The doctor stepped into the room. "Could you give me a hand, please?"

Rachel caught a reassuring look from the marshal before she followed the doctor into the other room. Her steps faltered and her pulse raced when she saw the two unsmiling, stone-faced Indians sitting on the cot, their arms crossed over their chests.

One, the younger of the two, had deep-set black eyes that drilled into her the minute their gazes met. The other, considerably older, had a bulbous nose, bobbed gray hair, and wrinkled, squinty eyes. Rachel knew that had they been wild coyotes, her response couldn't have been any stronger. Her heart boomed in her chest and she was breathless. She was as close to fainting as she could be without actually falling to the floor.

"John Hart needs his dressing changed. Do you think you can manage that?"

His heavy-handed sarcasm wasn't lost on her. She swallowed and cleared her throat, gripping the edge of his desk for support. "What—" She cleared her throat again. "Where is his wound?"

"John," the doctor said to the younger man, "drop 'em."

John Hart closed his eyes and gave his head a violent shake. "Not in front of her."

Rachel felt the blush roll up her neck into her face.

"For godssake, John, she's a nurse."

John shook his head again. "Not in front of *her*."

My sentiments exactly. Rachel's heart was in her throat as she pretended to tidy up the doctor's desk. She kept stealing furtive glances at the two Indians. Oh, Lord—what had made her think she could actually do this?

Suddenly, the older man grinned at Rachel, showing wide pink gums. "I'll drop mine," he said, his voice crackling with age. With that, he hopped off the cot, untied the cord he used as a belt, and let his trousers drop to the floor.

Rachel gaped and gasped. The blush that had already stained her cheeks flared into her head, and she felt it to the very roots of her hair. The man wasn't wearing any underwear.

"Joseph!" The doctor swore, rushed to the old man and whisked his trousers up over his skinny legs and his shriveled privates.

Rachel couldn't speak. Her voice had fled. She repressed an urge to follow it.

"Father, shame on you," John Hart scolded softly. He looked at the doctor and tapped his finger against the side of his head. "This has been happening more and more."

Turning back to his father, he said, "How many times do I tell you to wear that other thing?"

The old man pushed the doctor's hands away and tied his rope around his pants. "I do not like it. It smothers my skin. My skin is old, it must breathe. I lived seventy winters in the mountains with little to wear but a blanket. I won't wear the white man's underwear. It strangles me everywhere." He looked at Rachel regally. "That is all I have to say."

John Hart's eyes were warm as he looked from his father to the doctor. "Next month he is doing the Ghost Dance at the Big Head. Will Two Leaf be there?"

A strained look passed over the doctor's face. "I'm not sure. Do you expect trouble?"

John Hart tossed Rachel a hard glance. "I think we're safe this time."

The doctor looked at Rachel too, as if what they were talking about had something to do with her. Heavens, she didn't even understand what they were saying. *Two leaf? Big head? Ghost dance?* They might as well be talking voodoo.

"John," the doctor said, "if we don't look at your wound, you might not live long enough to enjoy the next ceremony."

The man glowered. "I do not want a *White* looking at my wound."

Rachel was startled by the acrimony in the man's voice.

"She's my nurse, John. You might as well get used to seeing her around. She might save your life one day. Her name is—"

"I know who she is," John interrupted, giving her a hard look of contempt. "She will probably 'save' me like 'Oily Fingers' saved the reservation." He shook his head again. "She will not touch me."

Rachel turned away again, intensely embarrassed and confused. The Indian blatantly disliked her, and made no attempt to hide it. But why? She'd never seen the man before.

She heard the doctor heave a sigh behind her, obviously giving in to the man's whim.

"Rachel?"

Pulling her face into a bland expression, she turned around. "Yes?"

He gave her an apologetic look. "Maybe Earl needs something," he answered, glancing toward the back room.

She nodded and scurried away, knowing full well that her eyes were brimming with gratitude.

An hour later, Jason was at his desk, writing in John's chart when Rachel tiptoed in from the back room.

She began straightening the equipment. "He didn't like me. Why?"

Jason looked up. "John Hart?"

She nodded. "It can't just be me. I . . . I've never seen the man before."

Jason stifled a sigh. She evidently didn't understand who "Oily Fingers" was. "John had an unhappy experience with your husband."

Rachel frowned as she plumped up the pillow on the cot. "Really? What happened?"

He leaned back in his chair and looked at her. In between the high neck and the snug waist of her dress was her full bosom, and below it, the rest of her. He mentally peeled away her clothes and pictured the lollipop nipples and the flowered delta at the apex of her thighs. His mouth watered and stinging need burst in his crotch.

Swearing to himself, he slammed the chart on the desk and pushed back his chair. Imagining daisies between her legs had been funny yesterday, but today it was something else. Soon after she'd walked into the office, he'd tried to see the humor in it, but what he conjured up wasn't a bit funny. Somehow he knew that under all of her clothing her thighs would be smooth and white, and the tuft of hair crowning her sweet sex would be a dark, rusty red.

"Is . . . is it really that bad?"

He looked at her, momentarily confused. "What?"

"What happened between Jeremy and that . . . that man?"

He shook off his erotic musings and straightened the stack of files in front of him. It wasn't his duty to tell her what her husband had been up to. If she stuck around, she'd find out soon enough. But he sure as hell wasn't going to whitewash the bastard, either. "Your husband had some problems communicating with the Indians." He almost choked on the understatement.

"But," she answered, running nervous fingers over the sheet on the cot, "that has nothing to do with me."

"Are you afraid of Indians?" His question was blunt.

Her eyes widened and her hand went to her throat. "I think . . . I think you know I am."

He studied her. Yes, he knew she was. She was afraid of him, at any rate. He wondered just how much to tell her. Finally, because she was such a frightened little mouse, he said only, "Maybe John Hart is afraid of Whites."

She turned away then, confusion pinching her features. He continued to watch her while she straightened up the office, wondering if she would ever believe the things her husband had gotten involved in. Suddenly, he realized that he was beginning to believe in her just as Ivy and Earl did. He doubled his fingers into his palm and counted to ten, restraining himself from smashing his fist against the wall.

The Reverend Toland ushered Rachel and Jason into the small, tidy parlor. "Thank you so much for coming. Birgit didn't want you to go out of your way for her, Doctor, but I knew you wouldn't mind."

"How is she today?" Jason dug through his bag, searching for something.

A little girl of perhaps three peeked around the corner, then ran and hid her face in her father's lap.

"She's feeling a little stronger." Reverend Toland lifted his daughter onto his lap. "Is Mama ready for the doctor?"

The child nodded, then glanced at Rachel, and smiled. But her eyes went immediately to Jason, who was still rummaging in his bag.

"Are you waiting for your medicine, Gwennie?" Jason asked.

Little Gwennie's big blue eyes clung to Jason. "Yes, Dr. Gaspard."

Jason's face was stern. "Well, it should be here."

Gwennie looked at Rachel and pointed. "Maybe *she* took it."

"Hmmm." Jason frowned. "Nope," he said, discovering something at the bottom of his bag. "It's right here."

Gwennie jumped off her father's lap and ran to Jason with her hand outstretched.

"What do you say, Gwen?"

The child dug her bare toe into the worn rug and swung shyly from side to side. "Please, Dr. Gaspard?"

Jason grinned and held his hands behind his back. "Which hand?"

"That one," she answered, pointing to his left. Jason handed her a cherry lollipop.

"Thank you," she chirped. "Now I'll take you to Mama," she said, taking his hand and skipping from the room.

Rachel watched, fascinated.

"It's a ritual," Reverend Toland explained with a warm smile. "Each time Dr. Gaspard comes to visit Birgit, he and Gwen go through the same little scene."

Rachel didn't know what to say. Jason was absolutely charming when he wanted to be. "I . . . I hope your wife is better."

"If anyone can help her, the doctor can." He seemed to notice her surprise. "I have more faith in him than in any doctor I've ever met."

"He . . . he doesn't seem to have many patients," Rachel commented.

Reverend Toland sighed. "They'll come, slowly. Most of them will have to see proof that he's as good as I say he is." A small, wry smile lifted one corner of his mouth. "Before I went into the ministry, I thought about medicine. I learned enough to know a good doctor when I see one."

Rachel's hopes lifted. "Then you think that one day he'll have a good practice here?"

"Yes," he answered. "But it will take time. People don't want to trust someone different. And that's the shame of it."

Rachel didn't really understand what he meant by "someone different," but she didn't pursue the comment. She was just happy to know that even if other townspeople didn't have good judgment when it came to doctors, the reverend, whom she liked very much, obviously did.

"Bram made us bring her sorry ass over here, Jason. She's been loonier than a duck since this morning." The hard-looking woman with the low-cut dress took a nervous puff of her thin cigar, then blew the pungent smoke into the air. She pushed a brightly dyed lock of brassy red hair out of her eyes. "Is she gonna be all right? We gotta get back to the saloon."

"I'll let you know, Tess." He turned to the burly young

man who had carried the woman into the office. "Thanks, Harvey, for bringing her over here."

Much to Rachel's relief, the muscle-bound brute pulled his gaze from her, his toothpick still gripped between his teeth, and gave Jason a terse nod. The man hadn't taken his eyes off her all the while Jason and the woman called Tess had talked. No one had ever looked at her that way before. His arrogant, cocky stare probed her skin, making her want to hurry to the washbasin and scrub until she bled. She shuddered discreetly and moved as far away from him as she could get.

The woman called Tess strode by her on her way to the door. She smiled at Rachel, revealing a broken front tooth.

"Things workin' out for you, Miz Weber?"

Rachel tentatively returned the smile, a little surprised that the woman knew who she was. "Yes, fine. Th-Thank you for asking." She watched the woman disappear, noting that the bustle beneath her garish red gown swayed provocatively from side to side as she walked. She stopped, glaring back at the muscle man.

"Harv? Get your eyes back in that stupid head of yours. Miz Weber ain't your type."

The bartender gave Rachel a licentious grin, then swaggered out of the room behind the prostitute.

When both of them were out of sight, Rachel expelled a sigh of relief and went into the back room to the cot where Jason had laid the unconscious woman.

In the two weeks since she'd begun working for him, they'd treated more drunks and Indians than she'd thought could possibly live in one town. And strangely, none of the Indians she'd helped Jason treat had made her skin crawl like the burly white bartender. And, although Tess was the picture of every prostitute and saloon girl Rachel had ever read about, the one on the cot wasn't. She was young and vulnerable looking. Rachel almost felt sorry for her.

"Rachel, get me some water. We're going to have to cool her down. Her fever is pretty high."

Rachel hurried into the other room, lifted the full pitcher

of water into the basin, grabbed some towels, and dashed back to the cot. Jason was attempting to undress the girl.

"Do . . . do you want me to do that?"

He gave her a mocking smile. "I've undoubtedly had more experience undressing other women than you have."

Oh, no doubt you have, she thought. Of course, she could never say such a thing out loud. Never, never. She still wasn't used to his sarcasm. It stung her, even when it wasn't actually aimed at her. But he was fumbling with the bodice of the gown, so she put the pitcher and the towels on the table by the bed.

"Here," she said, pushing his hands away. "The hooks are probably in the back." Rachel rolled the young woman toward her, careful to keep her face from pressing into the pillow. "Can you do it now?"

Jason quirked his eyebrow at her, as if expressing that he had no doubts about the task, then settled himself on the cot and began unfastening the hooks.

She felt a blush work its way up her neck and wished she could stop it. Every time he looked at her, she blushed. If he smiled at her, which was rare, she blushed. If he became impatient, which wasn't at all rare, she blushed. If their hands accidentally touched as they worked on a patient, she blushed. If he knew what he did to her, he'd probably die laughing.

She watched him concentrate on the buttons. She could imagine his strong brown hands moving over the woman's dress, probably inadvertently touching her skin. Suddenly Rachel found herself wondering how those hands would feel on *her* skin. The image bloomed in her mind. She could almost feel him snaking his fingers beneath her clothes, touching her in places that hadn't been touched in—

Warmth spread into her stomach, heating up that place beneath it, that place that she'd long since believed was dead.

Sucking in a ragged breath, she scolded herself. A newly widowed woman should *never* think such thoughts. They were as bad as committing adultery itself. She tossed Jason a contemptuous look, one he didn't even see, before glancing down at the unconscious girl.

Why, she wasn't more than eighteen, Rachel thought, gazing at the girl's pixielike features. She brushed back a blond curl, feeling an odd sense of companionship with the stranger. She was someone's daughter. Did they know what she'd chosen to do with her life, or had she been left alone in the world, just as Rachel had?

"Let's roll her back." Jason's voice interrupted her musings.

They both heard the front door open, and Jason stood. "Can you manage it from here?"

"Of course," she answered. "Oh, by the way. What's her name?"

"Karleen."

She watched him go, then finished undressing the girl, leaving her in her camisole and drawers. As she sponged the girl down, she spoke to her softly.

Suddenly the girl moaned again, moving about restlessly on the cot.

"Shh, shh, Karleen," Rachel soothed, softly stroking the girl's forehead. "It's all right."

"Jeremy!"

Rachel froze. Her chest filled with a nausea that sank into her stomach. Mechanically she continued stroking the girl's face, waiting to hear more.

Karleen's eyes popped open. "Have you seen him?" She appeared lucid; Rachel was sure she wasn't.

"Wh-Who?" Her heart was pounding.

"Lieutenant Weber." Karleen gave Rachel a weak smile, her dry lips pulled tightly over her teeth. "He's promised to come for me," she said, her voice filling with tears. "I know he'll come. He loves me, don't you see?"

Rachel's throat worked as she tried to breathe and swallow at the same time. She felt as though someone had just pushed her off a cliff and the only thing to catch her fall was a pile of rocks.

"Oh, Jeremy," the girl said, her voice soft and sad. "Oh,

Jeremy, please . . . don't be dead. Oh," Karleen sobbed, tears running down into her hair, "don't be dead. I love you. I love you . . ."

The words were punctuated with sobs and slurred because of the fever, but there was no mistake as to the name she'd called out. Rachel gripped the cloth tightly to keep her hands from shaking. Jeremy and this . . . this whore? *Her* Jeremy?

A deep, welling sadness washed over her and she felt her own tears running down her cheeks. If only she'd come to him sooner he wouldn't have had to find his pleasures somewhere else . . .

The girl moaned again, and Rachel quickly resumed sponging her down, although now it was purely a mechanical motion. She realized that it had been Karleen she'd seen at the funeral. Yes, she was pretty, but what had Karleen been able to give Jeremy that his own wife hadn't been willing to give?

Rachel pulled out a handkerchief, pressed it against her eyes, then blew her nose. She just didn't understand. It hurt so very much to think . . . that Jeremy had thought so little of her that he'd openly slept with someone else. The thought that there had been others wormed its way into her head, and she took a deep, shaky breath.

They'd been apart so long. Perhaps other women tolerated infidelity, she didn't know. Would it have made a difference if she'd accompanied him when he first came out here? She hadn't wanted to stay behind—not really.

Liar. Her shoulders drooped and she sobbed quietly into her handkerchief. She hadn't wanted to come out here, either. Isn't that why she'd forced herself to live with her in-laws, even though she knew they didn't like her? The reality of what she'd pushed Jeremy into hit her hard. His unfaithfulness was *her* fault.

She touched Karleen's face, cringing as she did so. A tiny, spiteful part of her wondered why she had to care for the whore who'd stolen her husband. She looked at the girl again, imagining her and Jeremy together, naked, writhing in ecstasy.

"Oh, *God*," she whispered, tipping over the chair in her haste to get away. She ran toward the other room. Jason stood in the doorway.

Turning swiftly around, she rushed to the corner, sank down on the sofa, and buried her face in her hands. She cried, trying to swallow the sound. If she kept quiet, maybe he wouldn't discover her tears.

He sat down beside her and clumsily stroked her hair.

She refused to look at him until he touched her chin and raised her face to his. The look of pity she saw on his handsome features brought on a fresh urge to bawl. "Oh, *don't*—" That was all she could get out.

"Ah, Rachel," he said on a husky sigh.

"You heard, didn't you?" she accused, feeling violated because what had happened made her look so in need of pity.

He nodded. "I heard."

She sniffed and breathed in a shaky, hiccoughing sigh. "Did you know?"

He briefly looked away. When he looked back at her, he nodded again.

"Oh, Lord, I must appear such a fool." She blew her nose and wiped her face—a useless gesture, for her eyes filled immediately and tears spilled down her cheeks.

"Believe me, Rachel, we didn't know about you."

Her mouth fell open and she let out a hysterical little laugh. "Oh . . . oh *fine*," she blubbered. "He . . . he didn't even tell anyone he was married?" She was learning too many things, too fast . . .

He swore. "I don't know if he told anyone or not. He didn't tell me, but then," he added, his voice caustic, "we weren't exactly friends."

Suddenly, the knowledge that the entire population of Pine Valley knew about Jeremy's adultery was almost more than she could handle. But the fact that everyone was probably laughing at her still didn't hurt nearly as much as Jeremy's deceit. She collapsed into sobs.

She felt Jason's hands on her shoulders, tentatively at first, then he gently squeezed them, as if adding his emotional support. But she needed more, so much more, and her state of mind was far past rational thought.

She flung herself at him, burrowing against his chest, needing to be held. He was big and strong, and she wanted him to comfort her. Pressing her nose against his neck, she pulled his clean, spicy scent into her nostrils. His arms came around her and he pulled her closer, patting her on the back as one would a crying child.

"There, there," he crooned softly.

The patronizing sound of his voice made her angry. She pushed at his chest and glared up at him. "I'm not a child," she retorted, unable to keep her voice from wobbling.

"Of course you're not." He smiled down at her, hypnotizing her with his dark, drowsy eyes. She stared at them. The thick, dark lashes lined his lids perfectly. Her gaze slid down his smooth brown nose and cheekbones, across the faint shadow of his beard to his mouth. She swallowed nervously, her heart fluttering in her chest. His smile was gone.

He's going to kiss me, she thought.

She watched his face come closer and she trembled. Closing her eyes, she felt his lips touch hers. His mouth was warm and tender, his lips gently tugging at hers, pulling them ever so slightly between his. She gasped, the sensation was so sweet she could hardly bear it.

The moment her lips parted, he pressed for more. Gentle tugging became experimental probing, and she felt his tongue gliding suggestively over the rim of her lips. She moved her tongue to meet his, shyly at first, unable to understand why his kiss should cause her so much more pleasure than any other kiss she'd ever had.

Suddenly his lips clamped over hers, and his tongue thrust into her mouth, rubbing over, under, and around her own. Her nipples hardened, and the secret, numb bud between her legs burst with a sensation so hot and exciting, she thought she might faint.

As quickly as it had begun, it was over. He grasped her

shoulders and set her away from him. Confusion over-whelmed her. She stared at her lap, her hands pressed against her feverish cheeks. She had no idea what to say.

"I'm . . . I'm sorry." Her voice was so shaky and soft, she could barely hear it herself.

"Dammit—" He took her hands away from her face and squeezed them in his own.

She dared look up at him then. His eyes were hot and black. His mouth was open just a little; she could see the edges of his teeth. His lower lip was full and sensual. Surprise washed over her desire. Although she desperately wanted him to kiss her again, she was afraid. All of the feelings he'd unleashed in her excited her.

As if reading her mind, he pulled her against his chest and kissed her again. Her lips clung to his, and when his mouth opened this time, she needed no instruction—or invitation. Pushing back her fear, she moved her hands up over his shoulders to his thick black hair and ran her fingers through it, pulling it, gripping it.

"Ahem!"

She forced him away, shoving at his chest like a guilty child. Glancing at the door, she saw Earl Tully. He stood with his hands on his hips and his feet wide apart, grinning at them from beneath his big gray mustache.

"Sorry to interrupt," he drawled.

Jason rose to greet him, his manner so staid and dignified, Rachel was sure what they'd done hadn't affected him at all. "What is it, Earl?"

"Somethin's happened on the reservation, Jason. I think you'd better get over there, quick."

❧ Chapter Five ❧

*J*ason briefly eyed Rachel's flushed face. She looked as if she were going to fall apart. Why it mattered to him, he didn't know, but if what Earl had to say had anything to do with the reservation and Jeremy Weber's involvement, now wasn't the time for her to learn the cold, hard facts. "Let's go into the other room."

"What's happenin' ain't no secret, Jason."

He stopped at the door, tossing Rachel another quick glance. She didn't even seem to be paying attention. "What is it, then?"

Tully limped toward him, still favoring his injured leg. "There's been a fire."

Dread coated Jason's stomach. "What happened?"

"Nellie Bluehorse stopped by to see her sister. Seems her two nephews are runnin' fevers. Anyway," he continued, shifting uncomfortably off his bad leg, "sometime during the night she went outside to get some air, and saw that the boarding school was burnin'. It's gone, Jason. Burned clean to the ground."

"They were warned," Jason muttered under his breath.

"What?"

Jason shook his head. "Never mind. Incendiaries?"

"Looks like it to me."

"Anyone hurt?"

Tully nodded. "Some smoke inhalation when they tried to put it out. And the fire spread to John Hart's place." He shook his shaggy gray head. "Joseph tried to beat the fire out with a blanket. He's got bad burns on his arms."

Jason's fear escalated. He turned and looked at Rachel again, this time not caring what she was stewing about. After all, dammit, she was his nurse. "I'm going to need your help out there eventually. For now, see to Karleen."

Rachel stood slowly, her face pinched with worry as she gripped the arm of the sofa. "You . . . you want me to go back out there? To the reservation?"

"I hired you as my nurse, didn't I?" She cringed at the hard tone in his voice, and he watched myriad emotions play over her face.

She crossed to the cot like a sleepwalker and touched Karleen's forehead. "I'm . . . I'm sorry, but I . . . I don't think I—"

"I should have gone with my instincts," he interrupted, his impatience mounting. "Just stay here and stay out of my way."

"Aw, now, Doc," Tully interjected. "Go easy on her."

Jason strode into the other room, Tully at his heels. "Dammit, Earl, I don't have time to mollycoddle her. She knew full well that I treated Indians. It was the first thing I told her." He jerked his leather bag off the desk, yanked it open, and shoved supplies into it.

"Now, Jason—"

"No," he interrupted again, his anger spreading. "I've had my fill of these damned soldiers' wives who arrive with their noses in the air, ready to condemn everything they don't understand."

Tully pulled out a cigarette, put it in the corner of his mouth, and let it dangle there, unlit. "That don't sound like a description of Rachel to me."

Jason pinned him with an insulting look. "It didn't take long for her to get you on her side, did it?"

Tully laughed quietly. "Nope, it didn't take long at all." He continued to grin at Jason. "Seems to me she's kinda gotten to you, too. Or," he added, feigning ignorance, "was she kissin' you against your will?"

Jason gave him a black look but didn't answer.

"Christ, Jason," Tully went on, "what d'ya think she is, anyways? Some kind of spy?"

Crossing his arms over his chest, Jason leaned against his desk and stared at Tully. "How do you know she isn't?"

An incredulous look spread over Tully's rugged, weather-worn features. "What in hell is she spyin' on? Your imagination's takin' you for a real fast ride, Doc."

Jason continued to stare, refusing to back down, and ignoring Tully's remark about the kiss. "Maybe. But," he added, lowering his voice, "have you ever wondered how such a sweet, innocent young thing, as you seem to think she is, could have married a bastard like Weber in the first place?"

Tully glanced at the door to the back room, then threw up his hands dramatically. "So maybe she fell in love. What the hell difference does it make?" He studied Jason carefully. "Seems to me you're lettin' old hurts get to ya."

Jason refused to allow old memories to interfere. "I just don't believe she's everything you think she is." He opened another leather bag and dropped a handful of lollipops on top of some clean white flannel squares and a large jar of salve.

"Well," Tully added sarcastically, "she sure as hell ain't everything *you* seem to think she is."

It was unusual for the two of them to lock horns like this. "And how do you know that?"

Tully lowered his voice again. "Did you know her ma and pa was murdered by Injuns when she was just a little thing? And that the Injun what killed 'em worked at their spread and was almost considered family?"

Jason froze, then forced himself to continue packing. He didn't want to hear this. "No. I didn't know."

"Don't ya think it might make a gal a tad wary, havin' her folks *and* her husband done in by savages?"

Although Jason bristled at the use of that word, he felt himself soften a little toward Rachel, too. There were times when he could have ridden the fence on the subject of who suffered more from the Indian-White conflict. But there was no doubt in his mind that the Indian was always the underdog, and though most of his sympathy went to them, he'd seen a few white women and children who hadn't deserved the punishment they were given. Both sides mourned their dead.

So Rachel Weber was afraid of Indians. That wasn't news, but now at least he knew *why* she skittered about like a scared mouse. Now that he'd learned this news about her parents, he was surprised she'd taken him up on his offer at all. "Is that what she told you?"

He nodded. "Me 'n' Ivy."

"That's all well and good, Earl," he said as he swung the bags off his desk and headed for the front door, "but I need someone I can count on. Not someone who's going to hide in a corner when I need her the most. Tell her to start looking for another job."

Tully was behind him in a shot, bad leg and all. He grabbed Jason's forearm, his beefy fingers biting into the muscle. "Gawdammit, Jason, if you're gonna get rid of her, you'll have to do it yerself. I ain't doin' any dirty work for you, especially if it means hurtin' Rachel."

He was right of course, and Jason knew it. "All right," he answered reluctantly. "Tell her to stay here and watch the office. I'll get Nellie or someone else to help me at the reservation." But he still knew Rachel Weber was going to be as useless to him in the long run as, to put it in one of Ivy's unique phrases, "Tits on a bull."

Rachel stepped into the room after Jason had left. There had been no way to avoid Jason and the marshal's conversation, save covering her ears. Not only did she feel worthless, but she felt like a fool as well.

Tully crossed the room and attempted to console her.

"No," she said softly, pushing him away. "Everything he said was true."

He gave her a gentle grin. "That maybe you're a spy?"

She tried to smile, but failed. "No, but—"

"That you come to town with your nose in the air?"

"No, of course not. But I *am* afraid of Indians, and I've hated them for so long, I don't know if I can ever change. I thought I could. I really wanted to try . . ."

"So, what's stoppin' ya?"

She swallowed hard. "I couldn't go out there," she answered, forcing down her panic. "Not now. Not ever again." Twisting in her fists the damp cloth she'd used to bring down Karleen's fever, she added, "After I picked up my clothes at the cottage, I told myself I'd never have to go near that place again."

Tully finally lit his cigarette. "I don't blame ya." He blew out a cloud of smoke and dropped the match into the spittoon.

Rachel frowned. She'd thought he would try to convince her otherwise. "You don't?"

He shook his head expansively. "Doc can get someone else to help. It ain't no place for a white gal, anyways."

Wondering why the marshal's words hadn't made her feel better, she walked to the window. "You're right, of course. And," she added, looking back at him, ". . . and I'd just be in the way, wouldn't I?"

Tully pulled smoke in through his nostrils, then blew out a sequence of rings. "Nellie's worked with him before. And these are her people. White folks ain't much welcome out there, anyhow. Nellie's one of a kind. A gem. A real trooper, if ya know what I mean."

And I'm not. She felt a tiny prick of envy. "I'd like to meet her sometime. She sounds like quite a treasure. Why doesn't she work here?"

"Never could get along with the doc more'n a few days at a time."

"Why not?" For some foolish reason, it made her feel good to know Dr. Gaspard couldn't keep decent help. She knew all too well how hard he was to work with—and for.

"Nellie still likes to use a lot of tribal medicine. Doc Gaspard wouldn't mind, but she bullies her way into his practice whenever she can." He clucked his tongue. "Stubborn Injun is what she is."

Rachel envisioned a tiny, old Indian woman bullying Jason and she almost laughed. "But she *will* help him at the reservation?"

"Oh, yeah." He took another long drag on his cigarette. " 'Course, it won't be easy for the two of them, seein' as how there'll be so many children to care for, all coughin' and cryin' because of the smoke, achin' for someone to just hold 'em. But," he added quickly, "that don't make no difference."

Rachel's heart dropped. "Children?"

He nodded, knitting his bushy gray eyebrows nobly. "Yeah, poor little critters. But don't you worry none about it. You stay right here and take care of Karleen. And, when Karleen's ready to go back to the saloon, you jes' stick around and keep things tidy. Doc'll appreciate that."

She made a face. *Sure, stick around and tidy up, Rachel.* That was what she'd always been good for. "No."

Tully gave her an innocent look of surprise. "What say?"

"No. I can't possibly just sit around here, knowing there are children out there who might need me."

He gave her a stern glance. "Naw. You don't wanna go out there, Rachel. It'll be too tough on ya."

She couldn't believe he'd continue to discourage her this way. "Marshal, I *have* to."

Tully shook his head again. "I don't advise it, Rachel, honey. You're too delicate. You wouldn't last a day."

Feeling a bite of anger, she answered, "I'm a lot stronger than I look." That bite was sinking its teeth into her lethargic manner more and more often lately.

He appeared to consider what she'd said, looking her up and down, scrutinizing her small frame. He sighed. "Nope, I don't think you'll be able to handle it."

"But . . . but I can, really. I'm strong." Suddenly her anger burst forth. "And don't you dare pigeonhole me, Earl Tully, it's not fair." She felt her color rising and tears of frustration welling, but suddenly she didn't care.

Tully rubbed his hand across his mouth. "You know the reservation's gonna be a hard place to stay. Ain't no fancy meals or sleepin' arrangements," he warned.

Rachel was already prepared, reminding her inner voice that she had to do this for the children—and herself. And, oddly enough, she refused to be bested by this Nellie Bluehorse person, whoever she was. "I don't care about that. I'll survive."

"You're sure, now?"

"I'm positive." She turned on him sharply. "Is there someone else who could watch Karleen for the night? She should be able to go back to the . . . the saloon tomorrow."

Tully appeared to suck in a smile. "Don't get your knickers in a twist, gal. Tomorrow will be soon enough to get to the reservation." He snubbed out his cigarette. "I'll take you there myself. Be ready at dawn. Bring warm clothes."

Rachel nodded, feeling a burst of excitement as she walked the marshal to the door. "I'll see you in the morning, then."

"Right," he answered, slipping into his fleece-lined jacket. "And I'll stop by and tell Bram to pick up Karleen either tonight, or at first light tomorrow. And Rachel."

"Yes?"

He gave her a broad grin. "I'm proud of ya, gal."

She matched his grin and knew that her eyes were shining with nervous excitement. Catching a glimpse of his face as he limped away, she saw that it was wreathed in a broad, amused smile.

"Why, that old—" Her own smile turned lopsided and she shook her head. She'd been cleverly, but royally, flim-flammed.

Jason closed his eyes and rubbed the back of his neck. He and Nellie had worked straight through the night. More people had suffered because of the fire than Tully had imagined. One of Nell's nephews, the older one, already had a problem breathing. For some reason, he'd awakened during the fire and wandered toward it before anyone noticed he was there. Poor little tyke was still wheezing.

And he wasn't alone. The normally hushed winter night air had been punctuated with deep, bronchial coughs and the wailing cries of children.

He left Nell's sister's house and stepped outside. Bracing himself against the cold morning air, he dragged it into his lungs, watching it congeal into white vapor as he exhaled. The smell of smoke still drifted heavily on the light breeze. They'd been lucky the winds hadn't picked up until toward morning when all traces of the fire were out.

Glancing at the snow-fringed skyline, he watched the wind unravel the cloud cover. He loved it out here—always had. Many nights during his youth, after an argument with his father, he'd come here and stayed for days. The reservation had been new then, fresh, clean and well run. It hadn't been until years later that he learned why the old ones were so unhappy to be here. For him it had been an escape from a stern, hard parent.

The rolling mounds of the Cascade foothills folded and dipped, then swelled and parted, revealing more of the same, until one finally saw the thickly shadowed pines near the top of the peaks and the brilliant snow beneath them. It had been a wet winter so far, but not cold. More rain had fallen than snow, the massy gray clouds having dropped enough to turn the grass and the trees on the slopes a thousand variations of green, black, and even purple.

Wailing, from inside the house, brought him back to reality. He and Nellie could handle it alone, but it would be nice to have more help. He knew his mother would have come if she'd been home. He didn't expect his parents back from Washington, D.C., until next month. *It would be nice if Rachel were here.* His mouth curled into a snarl even as his mind welcomed the thought.

But Rachel wouldn't come. No, dammit, not Rachel. He wasn't surprised. What surprised him was that he even cared. His whole reason for hiring her in the first place had been curiosity. And he knew she needed traveling money. The least she could have done was fulfill her part of the bargain. He'd warned her about his clientele and he'd seen the distaste and the fear in her eyes. He should have based his decision on that observation, not his restless, curious need to have her around.

Nellie ambled up to him, appearing as weary as he. Herbal doctor for the reservation Indians, and any others who cared to use her, she was slightly older than Jason. They'd known each other most of their lives—and butted heads ever since Jason had returned from medical school. "Breakfast is cookin', boss."

He draped his arm across her sturdy shoulders. "Sounds good to me, Nell. I could eat an elephant, hide and all."

She leaned against him and put her arm around his waist as they crossed the dewy grass to the warm cooking-pit fire. A number of people huddled around the blaze, more for comfort and companionship than because they'd lost their homes, because most of them hadn't.

"Settle for tortillas, beans, and fry bread?"

He drew in a breath, the scent of the spicy bean mixture reaching his nostrils. "Even better."

She punched his chest lightly with her fist. "We work good together."

He laughed. "For a day or two."

"You just have to be reminded that Indian medicine is as good as white man's medicine."

Jason sighed. "Sometimes it's better, Nell, I don't argue that."

"Then why do we fight?"

Because you can argue the hind leg off a jackass. "Because we both feel we're right, I guess."

A buckboard rattled up the road toward them.

Nellie shaded her eyes with her hand. "Who's that?"

Jason shrugged, then recognized Earl Tully's gray mustache. "It's the marshal."

"Who's with him, then? Must be Ivy."

He squinted at the tiny form sitting beside Earl, enveloped in the dark wool cape. A funny jolt licked at his loins, bringing about an instant tightening and desire. "No," he answered, an odd mixture of feelings washing over him, "it's not Ivy."

Rachel huddled inside the warmth of her cape, her teeth clenched and her hands pinched together. Ever since they'd passed the cottage with the drooping sunflowers and hollyhocks, she'd had to force herself not to leap from the wagon and run back to town. She'd never been this far into the reservation before; Jeremy had told her it wasn't safe.

Yesterday's bravado with the marshal came back to haunt her. When she realized she'd been hoodwinked into this, she hadn't cared. She'd been going to prove to everyone, especially to herself, that she could overcome her hatred and her fears. Suddenly, as they pushed closer and closer to the reservation itself, she knew it wasn't possible. *I don't want to do this. I can't do this.*

"How ya doin', Rachel?" The marshal's voice was comforting. She hoped he'd stay for a while.

"Fine . . . just . . . just fine," she lied, taking a deep, shaky breath. The hood of her cape flopped low on her forehead, so she raised her head slightly and looked around. The remnants of a building lay charred and smoldering across the road and under the trees. She quickly pulled her gaze away, the sight of the ruin distressing her.

There was a large, communal fire burning in an open space ahead of them. Her stomach pitched when she recognized Jason, his arm around the shoulders of a tall Indian woman. A strange envy washed over her, and she quickly looked away.

"Mornin', Doc, Nellie," Tully called out, pulling the team to a stop beside them.

"Who's that you got there, Earl?"

The woman called Nellie disengaged herself from Jason's embrace and crossed to the wagon. She peered up at Rachel, her black eyes wide and curious in her round face.

Jealousy flared in Rachel's chest. So, she thought, this is *trooper* Nellie. The gem. Everyone's herbal sweetheart. Feeling instant remorse for her petty thoughts, Rachel glanced quickly away.

"This here's doc's nurse," he answered.

"His *what?*" Nellie's voice exploded as she turned to stare at Jason.

Rachel felt herself flush, and there was a nervous quiver in her stomach. This Nellie person detested her without even knowing her.

"This here's Rachel Weber, Nell."

The woman turned to glare at Rachel, then spun around again, giving Jason a look of disbelief. "You hired *her?*"

Rachel pushed down her feelings of fear and discomfort. She hugged herself beneath her cape, dreading the time she'd have to spend at this place. This cold, backward place filled with sullen, surly savages.

"Now, Doc," the marshal scolded, "don't tell me you didn't tell Nell about your new nurse."

Jason's eyebrows slammed down over his eyes and he gave the marshal a lethal look. He shifted uncomfortably and raked his fingers through his hair. "Well, I—"

"Nell, you should be grateful the doc has some help."

Nellie made a distasteful face. "But . . . *her?*"

Oh, Lord, thought Rachel, why didn't the woman simply hit her with a shovel? It surely couldn't be any more terrible than sitting up on the buckboard, the target of her obvious, but inexplicable hostility.

The marshal ignored Nellie's comment. "We had to make sure Karleen got settled back at her place. It took a bit of doin', otherwise we'd have been here last night. Right, Rachel?"

Rachel's gaze didn't leave her lap. Marshal Tully was trying to save her hide, and she appreciated it, but Jason knew better. She refused to look at him, not wanting to see what would be in his eyes.

"Well, we got Karleen settled this mornin'. Bram came by early, and we got here as soon as we could." The marshal sounded so matter-of-fact, one would have thought it had all been planned before Jason even left the office yesterday.

Rachel was grateful, but embarrassed that he had to cover for her.

Jason stepped closer to the wagon. "Karleen's fever is down, then?"

He was talking to her. She guessed she'd have to look at him. When she did, she sincerely wished she hadn't. She couldn't read the message in his sensual, hooded eyes, but she got lost in them anyway.

With an effort, she forced her gaze back to her lap. "Yes, she was much better this morning. Bram . . . Mr. Justice said he'd make sure Tess kept an eye on her, just in case. And . . . and Ivy will look in on her, too." It wasn't necessary to tell him she and Karleen hadn't found it imperative to carry on much of a conversation. Although Rachel didn't think Karleen had been aware of what she'd said during her lapse into delirium, she was *acutely* aware of who Rachel was. And Rachel, coward that she was, couldn't bring herself to broach the subject of Jeremy, for it would have verbalized, once and for all, her fears about his infidelity.

"Nell," Jason said, finally turning away, "get Rachel settled in with Dixie, then show her what we're doing."

Rachel felt Nellie's eyes on her, burning into her skin. If she could only get up the courage to beg someone to talk to her, she might learn why everyone seemed to hate her.

❦ Chapter Six ❦

T he matron of the boarding school, an older woman who had temporarily replaced Harry Ritter, had fled the reservation the moment she heard news of the fire. Jason had watched her leave, her lack of concern for the welfare of the children evident in her hasty departure.

As he picked his way through the debris, he couldn't help but feel ill at the waste. And Tully was right. This fire hadn't started by itself. Incendiaries, as sure as he stood in the ruins, had been used. But by whom?

Tully limped toward him from across the road. He arrived at the building and stood in silence for a moment. "Well, what do ya think?"

"I think you're right. This was set on purpose."

Tully scratched his chin. "Any ideas?"

"They'd been warned, you know," Jason answered, massaging his neck.

"Who'd been warned?"

"The day the boarding school opened, Ty Holliday and his bunch living up in the hills refused to send their children. Don't you remember the squabble we had over that?"

"Yep, I do remember. You think Holliday did this? Set fire to the school?"

"He's an ornery cuss. I think he'd be tempted." Jason dug the toe of his boot into a blackened board, flipping the wood into the air. It landed on a soft bed of soot, sending up great plumes of gray powder.

"Ya think he and his renegades done in Weber and Ritter, too?"

The memory of the unusually violent message left on the dismembered bodies made him shudder. It still puzzled him. "Maybe. But you know that whole group that refuses to live here had threatened to burn down the building before it even opened. The hills are full of Indian traditionalists, Earl. Ty is the most militant of them. But murder . . ." He sighed and shook his head. "I don't know. All the people living in the hills firmly believe that the white schools are undermining and disintegrating native culture." He picked up a book, the pages blackened and burned like an ancient scroll. Only the spine remained intact.

"Hell, in a sense they're right."

Jason tossed the useless book aside. "I know. But they're going about this the wrong way."

Tully pulled out a cigarette, glanced around at the destruction, and put the cigarette back in his pocket. "Not accordin' to them they ain't."

Jason remembered his conversation with Buck. "Did you check out Buck's story for the night Weber was murdered?"

"I've tried, but no one's talkin'. Especially if it means clearin' an Injun."

"I don't want to believe he had anything to do with the murders, Earl. He's like a brother to me."

"But he's a mighty angry young man. Hell, he had cause. And," Tully added, "it's a mighty big coincidence that he got that stab wound in the same place Jeremy Weber stabbed his killer."

"I know, I know," Jason answered, unwilling to believe the evidence. "And he feels the only way to get even is sabotage—even if it means sabotaging the system itself." But even as he said the words, he still hoped Buck wasn't responsible. As angry as Buck was about everything, Jason couldn't imagine that Buck would take part in the destruction of life and property.

A beam fell from the rafters at the far end of the building and landed on a charred desk. This "incident" sickened Jason. It went against everything he'd been taught. Property was valuable. The loss of the school would set the reservation back thousands of dollars.

Jason swung away from the ruins and wondered if Buck would come by later, after he'd heard the news. He just didn't want to believe Buck was involved. Maybe he was too close to see how much Buck had really changed. But Buck had ties here. He might be angry as hell at the way the world was treating his people, but he wouldn't do something to threaten the lives of anyone near and dear to him. And Nell and Dixie were Honey's sisters. Matthew and Martin were Buck's nephews. No, Buck wouldn't do anything to hurt them.

"The folks in town run scared when they hear things like this. Most of 'em don't understand why the Injuns are fightin' a decent education. 'Course," Tully added, pulling out the cigarette again, "it don't help when Injuns learn that the Whites won't allow the small tykes to speak the language they was born to speak."

Jason stepped over a heap of incinerated rubbish and walked away from the burned-out shell. "No one's going to win, Earl. We're all going to lose."

He looked up as Nell raced toward him. "Nell? What's wrong?"

When she reached them, Nell was hardly out of breath, but her face was drawn with pain. "It's Matthew. He's not breathing."

Rachel stood beside Dixie, frantic because she had no idea how to help. Little Matthew, whose breathing had been labored since the fire, lay lifeless in his mother's arms. Dixie rocked back and forth, chanting something Rachel didn't understand.

The door whipped open and Jason, the marshal, and Nell hurried into the room. Jason held his arms out so the other two would stay behind him. Slowly he hunkered down beside Dixie and the boy.

"Dixie," he said softly, "give the boy to me."

Dixie clutched the small body to her breast and continued chanting, the poignant sound pulling at Rachel's heart.

Rachel tossed Jason a hard look. Why wasn't he doing something? Why didn't he just take the child from her?

"Dixie, maybe I can help him. Will you let me help him?" Jason's voice was tender and earnest, but Rachel could sense the panic behind the gentle facade. Still, she wondered why he didn't just take the child away from the mother.

Suddenly Dixie thrust the boy at Jason. He took Matthew and immediately began to blow air into his mouth. Dixie continued to chant, the sound becoming higher and more frantic as Jason worked on her son.

Rachel felt someone pull on her cape. Turning, she found herself looking into Nell's agitated, hate-filled face.

"You," she hissed under her breath. "You don't belong here. Get out."

Rachel was dumbfounded. She looked at Jason for support, but he was oblivious, working hard to save the child. She didn't want to cause trouble, but she wanted to stay.

Nell tugged her toward the door. "Get out," she repeated. "I don't want you here. This is a place for family." They stepped outside. "And *friends*," she added vehemently.

Rachel stumbled away from her, sick to her stomach at the hate she saw in Nell's face. "Please . . . I . . . I'd like to help."

If looks could kill, Nell's would have been a stake through Rachel's heart. With an angry wave of her hand, she went back into the cabin, leaving Rachel bemused outside in the cold.

As she'd reluctantly settled into Dixie's cabin, ignoring the stares from the curious Indians around her, Rachel hadn't had time to think about her fears. Before she'd even gotten a good look at the room, the little boy, Matthew, had begun to wheeze and choke. Instinctively, she'd wanted to help, despite her earlier feelings of fear and hatred. But as she moved toward Dixie and the boy, a woman she didn't know held her back.

She watched in horror as Nell ran for Jason, leaving the

boy lifeless in his mother's arms. She could have done what Jason did; she'd done it once or twice before. Shuddering, she wondered what would have happened to her if she'd wrestled Dixie for the child.

Numb with an odd hurt, Rachel walked down the path that led to the other buildings. Her own private pain slowly fell away as she moved through the village. Numerous small structures had been built to form a square. She recognized the sawmill and the gristmill; she wasn't sure what the other two were. Four young Indian children, dressed in shabby, yet warm clothes, played kickball over the lush, grassy hillside.

An old man sat stiffly by an outdoor fire, picking at something on his arms. Recognizing him as Joseph, John Hart's sometimes-forgetful father, and remembering their last meeting, she felt herself blush. She continued to dredge up her feelings of confusion, wondering why John Hart hated her. Now, she could add Nell to that list as well.

Remembering that Joseph's arms had been burned in the fire, she approached him cautiously. "You're Joseph, aren't you?"

He looked at her, but there was no evidence of recognition. "My skin must breathe," he said, stretching both bandaged arms in her direction.

Strangely, Rachel felt neither fear nor revulsion. Of course, from the beginning she'd felt he was just a sweet, harmless old man, in spite of the fact that she'd wanted to run away when she'd seen him the first time. She sat down beside him on the log bench and took his hands in hers.

"You've been burned quite badly. They say you tried to put the fire out by yourself. You're very brave."

He gripped her fingers. "My skin must breathe," he repeated.

"But," she answered, "you mustn't think about that. Leave the bandages on. Please be patient, Joseph."

"I am a patient man. If I were not, I would be dead."

Rachel didn't try to decipher the cryptic statement. Instead, she examined the bandages. The only thing seeming to seep through the cloth was the salve.

"Then, if you're a patient man, you'll leave the bandages alone. Nellie and the doctor didn't wrap your wounds so carefully just so you could unwrap them. If you do, you could get an infection."

A tiny smile flickered across his lips. "You are not a bad woman. You are just a bossy one."

She guessed that was a compliment, but the statement also alarmed her. "Someone thinks I am a bad person? Who, Joseph?" Maybe she'd finally learn something.

He shook his head. "You are not a bad person, like John and Nellie think. That is all I have to say."

Frowning at this news, she tucked his bandaged hands and cold fingers beneath the blanket that rested over his knees. "I don't understand it, Joseph," she said, as much to herself as to him. "I just don't understand what *I've* done." She still felt that if anyone had a reason to hate, it was she.

She got up to leave. "Don't sit out here too long. It's cold today."

"I will get some nourishment soon," he answered.

Glancing at his bandaged arms and hands, she asked, "But how will you eat it?"

"I will manage."

She left him, but worried about him as she wandered away. Suddenly the memory of Elbee's bout with influenza burst into her mind, and she felt the familiar burning hatred and distrust once again. They'd brought him into the house when he'd gotten so sick, and Rachel had even given up her bed for him so her mother and Aunt Billie could treat him properly. Then, not three months later he'd killed them all . . . Too trusting. They'd been naïve and trusting. It wouldn't happen to her.

Briefly glancing back at Joseph, she steeled herself against his apparent helplessness, then walked toward a freshly painted log building that sat beneath the pines.

She crossed the hard, needle-covered earth, pulled open the door, and peeked inside. Fresh baking smells invaded her nostrils. An Indian woman was on her knees, kneading

bread on a thick, wide board. She looked up as Rachel
stepped into the room, then quickly went back to her work.

Rachel stepped closer.

"Can I help you?"

Rachel turned, noticing an older white woman stirring
something in a large cooking vat.

"I . . . I'm sorry, I smelled the bread as I was walking by,
and I had to find out—"

"You had to find out if Indians ate the same kind of food
as white folks, right?" The woman tasted what she was cooking, then put the large spoon on a plate near the stove.

"No," Rachel answered with a tentative smile. "I . . . I
thought maybe I could get something for Joseph. He's hungry, and he—" She couldn't believe what she'd just said.
Not a minute ago, she'd vowed to ignore Joseph. Now, she
was asking some strange woman to prepare his lunch. She
was, without a doubt, the weakest-willed woman alive.

"And he wants lunch," the woman interrupted.

Rachel gave herself a shake. Forget it, she thought. I don't
have to do this. But as she turned to leave, she found herself
saying, "Do . . . do you mind fixing him something? He'll
have trouble eating it because of his burns, but I'll help him
if he'll let me."

The woman looked her up and down. "You Weber's
widow?"

Rachel nodded, feeling a foolish flush spread up her neck.

The woman stared at her a while longer, then looked
away, a rather snide half-grin on her face. "You're not what I
expected."

"I . . . I'm not?"

Shaking her head, she pulled down a tin filled with tortillas, spread one on the counter and ladled some spicy-smell-
ing beans over it. "Sort of thought the 'great' Jeremy
Weber'd have a looker," she said, her voice laced with sarcasm.

And no one would look at me twice. I know. She was used to
such comments. They no longer hurt. And she'd stopped
thinking that Jeremy had married her because he'd been

madly in love with her beauty. The trouble was, she was honestly beginning to wonder why he *had* married her.

Rather than continue talking with the woman, she simply said, "I'll take the lunch out to Joseph."

The Indian woman crossed in front of Rachel and gave her a shy smile. It was the first pleasant look she'd gotten from anyone all day—other than Joseph. In spite of herself, she smiled back, then looked around the clean, well-appointed room.

"Not what you expected, huh?"

Rachel glanced at the older woman. "I beg your pardon?"

"Thought maybe they'd all be living in shacks and eating with their fingers, I suppose."

"I . . . I didn't really know what to expect." That wasn't entirely true. Jeremy had frightened her into believing she wouldn't be safe walking through the reservation, and, because of her fears, she'd believed him. Maybe she'd wanted to believe him, for it gave her an excuse to avoid the place. Now she could see that he'd deliberately lied to her. But why? To keep her safe? She couldn't think of any other explanation.

"Did you know my husband very well?"

The woman scowled, but didn't look up. "Well enough."

"You didn't like him," Rachel said with a sudden flash of insight.

" 'Twasn't up to me to like him or hate him."

Rachel crossed to the stove and touched the woman's arm. She gave Rachel a hard look, but said nothing more. "What did he do?"

"What *didn't* he do—"

"There you are!"

Rachel turned. Jason stood in the doorway. He swung his gaze from her to the woman at the stove. "I need some help, Rachel."

Disappointed that she hadn't been able to learn more, Rachel nodded to the two women and followed Jason outside. They stopped in front of the door.

"How's little Matthew?" She was almost afraid to hear his answer.

"He's breathing, anyway. Listen," he said, grabbing her arm and glaring at her. "If you can't stand to stay near me when I'm working, then you might as well leave."

"But, I—" What could she say that wouldn't sound peevish and spiteful? Her dignity rumpled by his callous remark, she pulled herself from his grip. "Believe me," she answered, "it won't happen again. But that Bluenose woman all but dragged me out the door. I couldn't do anything but follow her."

"Horse," he said, appearing to swallow a grin.

"What?"

"Blue*horse*."

"Oh," she whispered, feeling quite foolish. "Yes, of course. Blue*horse*."

"Well," he said, continuing to glare down at her, "come with me now." He walked away.

She didn't follow him. "I promised Joseph I'd get him some lunch." Jason's arrogance was really beginning to annoy her.

"All right," he said, his voice strangely accommodating, "let's get Joseph some lunch." He steered her back inside.

After Joseph had eaten, they left him rolled in a bed roll under a pine tree.

"Why won't he go into the cabin?" Rachel was concerned that the old man would catch pneumonia, or at least a cold, sleeping outdoors.

"He refuses to sleep in a building. Many of the old ones feel as he does. They prefer their antiquated shelters."

They walked in silence. Rachel noticed how completely at home he appeared to be here. Everyone loved him. Even the dogs followed him wherever he went.

"Why did you wait so long to breathe into Matthew's mouth?"

He glanced down at her, his dark, sultry stare making her uncomfortable. "You mean, why didn't I rush in and grab the boy from his mother?"

She nodded, falling headlong into his magical, heated gaze. "I . . . I would have thought . . . you were wasting precious time."

"I suppose I was. But what if I'd grabbed the boy and hadn't been able to save him? Dixie would have blamed me for his death. She'd have felt that her chanting might have saved him, but that I'd interrupted it. As it was," he added, "she gave Matthew to me willingly. Whatever the outcome, it was her decision."

It made sense—on a basic, primitive level. "Will he be all right?"

"I hope so," he said on a sigh. "I'm going to check on him now."

Rachel's steps faltered. Another confrontation with Nell.

"What's wrong?" he asked harshly.

"Oh, it's . . . it's nothing, really." She bent over and pretended to remove something from her shoe. "I . . . I just stepped on something, that's all," she lied.

They stopped at Dixie's cabin. He let her go in ahead of him. She stepped into the room, relieved to find Nell nowhere in sight. Dixie was lying on the floor in front of the fire, Matthew in the crook of her arm.

Jason hunkered down in front of her and touched the boy's cheek. "He's sleeping, Dixie. Why don't you get some rest, too?"

"I'll sleep here, with him."

Dixie tossed Rachel a quick look—one not nearly as hate-filled as her sister's. "Nell took Martin with her."

"Good," Jason answered. "Then you can rest without worrying about him."

Rachel glanced around the cabin. It appeared that Matthew's crisis had erupted during Dixie's chores, for there were dirty dishes in the sink and a scrub bucket on the floor, the mop leaning against the wall. There was also a basket of clothes on the floor near the fire. She didn't know if they were clean or dirty, but she wanted to be useful. Dixie's chores needed finishing, and if there was anything Rachel was good at, it was chores.

"Rachel? Are you coming?" Jason stood by the door.

She looked at Dixie, who was now asleep beside her son, then at Jason. "Was there something special we needed to do?"

"I'm going to check on some other people."

Rachel glanced around the untidy cabin. "Do you really need me?"

He grabbed her arm and pulled her outside, his anger so evident that when he breathed out through his nose, he looked like a smoking dragon. "Dammit, either help me or leave!"

"Stop badgering me!" Her hand flew to her mouth and she gaped at him, stunned at the way she'd blurted out the words. This wasn't like her at all. Not at all.

"*Badgering* you? Hell, woman, someone ought to. What are you afraid of now?"

"I'm not afraid of anything, believe it or not. Not even you! You've intimidated me from the very beginning, and I've mewled and blushed at every turn. Well," she added angrily, "no more." Words spewed from her mouth like vomit, and she couldn't seem to stop them.

Taking a deep breath, she said in a softer tone, "It's . . . it's just that Dixie's chores were interrupted when Matthew got so sick. It won't take me long to clean up for her. That's all I wanted to do. Now," she chirped, sounding to herself like an angry magpie, "if you'll stop browbeating me, I'll get busy and be completely at your disposal when I'm finished here."

Embarrassed at her outburst, she ducked her head, glancing at him quickly before going back into the cabin. He had the oddest expression on his face. Well, she thought as she slipped out of her warm cape, it was about time she stood up for herself. Staring at the fire, she smiled. My, but it felt wonderful! She had no idea why she hadn't done this before. *Long* before, when her uncle first began belittling her. She folded her cape over the back of a kitchen chair. Maybe she wasn't too old to acquire some self-esteem after all.

Crossing to the stove, she checked the kettle and found it

full of hot water. As she poured it over the dishes in the dishpan, she felt his gaze on her. "Did you want to help?" she asked sweetly. "Scrub the floor, perhaps?"

Hearing him sigh deeply, she held her breath until she was sure he was gone, then she sagged, breathless, against the counter.

Jason had finally convinced Joseph to come in out of the cold. Sitting him down in front of the fireplace in his daughter's cabin, he unwrapped the bandages on Joseph's hands and arms. The skin was red and blisters had broken in a few places, but all in all, the pine pitch and the salve had done a good job.

He spread some special cream over the worst sores, then began rebinding Joseph's arms with fresh gauze bandages.

Joseph mumbled something and let out a snort of disgust.

"Be patient, Joseph."

He glared at Jason. "I *am* patient. I told the woman I was patient. Do I not appear to be a patient man?"

Jason bit back a smile. "No, you are not always a patient man, Joseph. Brave, yes. Patient, no."

Joseph stared at him for a long moment. "John is wrong. The woman is not a bad person."

Refusing to look up, Jason continued to bind Joseph's burns. "What woman is that?"

"Two Leaf knows about whom I speak." Slight derision laced his voice.

"Yes," he muttered under his breath. "I know of whom you speak," he mimicked.

"Do not make laughter of me." Joseph's voice was stern.

"I'm not humoring you, Joseph." He couldn't very well admit that "the woman" had suddenly discovered her voice and didn't seem to know how to shut herself up. He wasn't sure which way he preferred her—meek or feisty.

A slow smile spread across his face. Oh, feisty and peppery was infinitely more interesting . . .

"What makes Two Leaf smile like a tomcat with a mouse by the tail?"

Jason finished wrapping the burns and clapped Joseph on the shoulder. "You're right, Joseph. The woman is not a bad person."

"That is what makes you smile?"

Jason remembered her feeding Joseph his lunch earlier in the day. She'd been patient and caring. If she'd been afraid or repulsed, she'd hidden it well. Then, his thoughts turned to what she was doing now, bustling around Dixie's cabin, her cheeks red and her hair clinging to her warm temples. He allowed his thoughts to linger on the daisy-tufted apex of her thighs, and suddenly realized that daisies no longer seemed appropriate. Quite possibly they'd been replaced by velvety red roses—complete with a few well-hidden thorns.

"Yes, old man. That is what makes me smile," he answered, grinning foolishly.

After changing a dozen bandages, looking in on the newest babies, and doling out handfuls of lollipops, Jason was ready for a cup of coffee. Deep in thought, he rounded the corner of Dixie's cabin and bumped against something hard. Whatever it was, he'd knocked it to the ground. He looked down and saw Rachel, sprawled on the grass.

"My God! Did I hurt you?" He reached out to help her up.

Rachel appeared to catch her breath, and when she did so, she gave him a dimpled smile. It transformed her, made her almost beautiful. He couldn't believe he'd never seen her smile before, because if he had, he surely would have remembered.

She put her hand in his and allowed him to pull her up. "I'm fine, thank you. I'm . . . I'm sorry, I wasn't even paying attention when I came around that corner—"

"No," he interrupted, still dazed by his discovery. "It was my fault." He continued to hold her hand in his. "You finished up at Dixie's? Was there any problem with Matthew? I was just going to check up on him." God, but he was prattling like an old woman.

"They were both awake when I left." She stopped smiling, but continued to stare at him. Her light eyes with their sooty

lashes intrigued him. Her skin, he noticed, was almost trans-
lucent. Now, because of her chores, her cheeks were pink
and her lips full and inviting. Dammit, he had to taste her
again. The itch in his groin exploded into an all-out craving.

He lowered his head and touched her mouth with his,
hearing her sharp intake of breath and feeling it, soft and
warm, against his face. But she didn't pull away. Drawing
back briefly, he saw that her pupils had dilated, and her lids
were heavy over her eyes. Looking swiftly about him, he
pulled her into the dark nook behind the cabin where they
wouldn't be seen.

Still gripping her hand, he drew it against his waist and
around to his back, holding it there. She was small, but she
wasn't short. Still, he wanted her against him so their bodies
would meet neatly, at the lips, at the chest . . . at the
groin. Knowing there was a box behind her, he lifted her
onto it. He gazed into her face, his blood heating and thick-
ening as he watched the wary desire spread deeper into her
eyes. The hood of her cape had fallen back, and wisps of
rich, brandy hair framed her face.

Slowly, carefully, he touched his lips to hers once again.
Her mouth was soft and compliant beneath his. He held
back, wanting to bury himself against her, but sensing it
would frighten her. Suddenly he heard her erratic breathing
and knew what she was feeling wasn't fear. The soft, sexy
sound encouraged him and inflamed him. His mouth opened
over hers and his tongue touched her lips. She opened for
him, allowing him in, tentatively probing with her own
tongue. She tasted sweet, wet, and desirable.

His hands dove beneath her cape, sliding up the sides of
her blouse to the fullness of her breasts. She let out a small
gasp but still didn't push him away. The sensual groping was
made more erotic by the dimness of the nook. He envisioned
undressing her here, in this secret place out of doors, or just
taking her swiftly and hungrily, her dress up around her
waist and her thighs hugging his hips. His groin was full and
hard.

As his thumbs moved over her nipples, he could feel them

tighten beneath her clothes. She was making tiny, excitable sounds in her throat, and pressing her breasts against his hands. He ached with need. But when he finally pulled her hard against him and pressed himself against her abdomen, she stopped, suddenly stiff as a board.

Ah, dammit! He didn't want to let her go. He moved away, but still gripped her waist with his hands and touched her forehead with his. Their breath mingled, warm, moist, and intimate, between them. He wanted more from her. More and more and more . . .

Abruptly she pulled away, shoving at his chest. "No!" Her voice held no indignant horror at the liberties he'd taken. It was a different sound, a sound more frightening to him than anger. She stared at his chin, unwilling to look at him. His touch softened, and he let her go. Before she stumbled away, she looked at him, and he was certain that her eyes were filled with fear.

🌿 Chapter Seven 🌿

A long table had been set up in the recreation hall for the evening meal. Jason strode into the room with some other men, sending Rachel's heart bumping against her ribs. Quickly looking away, she busied herself by examining her hands, which were clasped in her lap.

His sudden presence forced a blush into her cheeks, reminding her that she hadn't been able to get away from him fast enough just a few hours before. She'd thought of little else all afternoon. As she'd stumbled off like a silly twit, every nerve in her body had vibrated with fear—and desire.

Spending the remaining afternoon hours helping to prepare for the evening meal hadn't been in her plans, but she'd done it with gusto. Anything was preferable to running into Jason again. Fortunately, she'd discovered he was busy with the other men, preparing for some kind of dance ceremony.

Now, with him sitting on the other side of the table, her heart pounded painfully in her chest. She didn't have to look at him to know he sent an occasional glance her way. His gaze might well have been a branding iron, for it left her skin hot and tingly, as though it had been marked. Her skin always felt like that when he looked at her, but after what happened earlier, the feeling was intensified.

These emotions, these sensations were all so new to her. Had she been told she could feel so strongly for any man, she wouldn't have believed it. *Nothing* had prepared her for this, not even her marriage. Just knowing Jason desired her caused her heart to want to burst free from her chest. It surprised her that no one could see what she was feeling.

Shuddering, she closed her eyes and took a deep breath. It mattered little whether she opened them or not. His beautiful face was there, imprinted on her mind. And he'd kissed her like he couldn't help himself. *Her*. Rachel Kathleen Weber . . . the plain brown wren. She opened her eyes, shook her head, and frowned. Rachel Kathleen Weber—the witless, hopeless fool.

An elbow nudged her, and the child next to her passed her a basket of tortillas. She absently took one, dropped it on her plate, and passed the basket on.

She spooned a meat and bean mixture onto the tortilla, watching to see how others folded and rolled it to keep the contents from falling through. Having very little appetite, yet not wanting to dishonor her hosts, she zestily bit into the spicy tortilla.

As she ate, she listened to the sounds around her. Someone said something to Jason, and he laughed, making her stomach jump. She hadn't heard him laugh until they came up here, away from Pine Valley. It was a deep, warm sound. A happy, contented sound. It made her wonder what he found so special about this primitive, poverty-stricken place.

"Hey, Joseph," the woman on the other side of her shouted. "You ready for tonight?"

Across the table next to Jason, Joseph Hart nodded sagely. "I am ready." He turned to Jason. "Two Leaf ready?"

Watching Rachel carefully, Jason nodded, and she wondered again at the use of that name. It was probably one the Indians had given him. She'd often heard that white men were given Indian names when they'd endeared themselves to a tribe. There was no doubt that Jason had endeared himself to this one, she thought, watching him laugh and joke with the others.

Before the meal, when she'd been told where to sit, she'd also been instructed that all of those not participating in the dance had to sit on one side of the table. The other side was saved for the men—the dancers, chorus, and all others taking part in the dance.

She had no idea what was going to happen; she'd been given no clue as to what this dance was about. That hadn't surprised her, but before the meal, she'd seen Joseph off by himself having a smoke. Slipping away from the kitchen, she'd joined him in the shadows and shyly asked him what was going to happen.

He'd nodded, seemingly pleased with her curiosity. "It's good that you ask, you know . . . But keep a mind that is open." He'd puffed on his pipe, the glowing bowl smoldering like the mouth of a tiny volcano.

"It's the Ghost Dance," he'd told her. "My people know the world will be destroyed soon. The Whites have come." He'd given her a slow grin. "I don't mean to offend you, but now the world is no longer pure. The earth lodge," he'd said, pointing to the circular semisubterranean building across the road, "is where we will take refuge when the world ends. It is also our dance house. My son, John, is our Dreamer. He dreams the rules we dance to. Tonight we dance to celebrate all of our people who have gone on into the spirit world before us."

She'd had a dozen questions for him, but decided she could wait. After all, she probably wouldn't even be allowed to observe.

Now, as she watched the camaraderie on both sides of the table and the way everyone ignored her, she was pretty certain she'd be spending the rest of the evening alone.

Fully clothed, using her cape as another blanket, Rachel tried to stay warm in Dixie's extra bed. Even with the fire blazing in the fireplace, she couldn't shake off the chill. And Dixie's cabin was quiet. The only sounds came from the crackling of the fire, her own breathing, and the purring of Matthew's kitten, which was curled against her beneath the covers.

Had it not been for the constant, unchanging drumbeat and the chanting male voices from the dance house, she'd have sworn she was alone in the woods. Even the children were included in the celebration. But, she thought, shivering under the bedding, not an outsider. It made her feel a little sad, and that surprised her. A week ago it wouldn't have occurred to her that she might wish to be included in an Indian ceremony. Heavens, a week ago she'd have been disgusted and sickened at the thought of it.

Wide awake, staring into the fire, she began to feel restless. Uttering an impatient sigh, she tossed back her bedding, slipped into her shoes, and pulled on her cape. Maybe if she went for a walk, she'd get tired enough to sleep.

With her arms pressed against her sides for warmth, she walked out into the frigid winter night. The cold air stung her nostrils, making her gasp when she attempted to pull in a deep breath. She made her way toward the dance house, noting that firelight flickered through the gaps in the vertical pine slabs that made up the walls. The drumbeat didn't alter in rhythm. Stepping close to the building, Rachel peeked in through a wide break in the boards.

Jason was the drummer. He stood, his feet apart and his back straight. His hair, usually tied back neatly, hung to his shoulders in heavy waves. Though he wore no costume, his snug, dark trousers and white shirt with the billowing sleeves gave him the air of a pirate on the bow of his ship.

He stared, his face expressionless as he pounded out the monotonous beat. He fit perfectly into the primitive, tribal setting. If she hadn't known better, she'd have thought he was as much an Indian as the rest of them. She watched, marveling at his strength. There hadn't been a break in the drumbeat or the chanting for at least half an hour, maybe more.

The drum was a long, heavy slab of log and Jason stood on it, pounding one end with a heavy, elongated piece of wood.

In front of Jason stood a group of men, one rhythmically slapping some sort of rattle against his palm. He intoned an eerie chant as the others interjected rich answering sounds. All of the men stamped their feet to the rhythm of the drum.

There were two dancers in the room. Among them she recognized Joseph, wearing an extravagant costume. The skirt appeared to be fashioned out of tule rushes, and the headgear was made up of a mass of long, feathered spines. In the light of the fire, she could tell they were brightly painted in red and black. The headdress was enormous. She wondered how he ever made it into the dance house through the narrow corridor that served as the entrance.

The other dancer, the one who faced Joseph from across the fire, was leanly muscled. From the waist down he wore long white leggings that looked like underwear, and he was naked from the waist up except for a wide necklace that covered his shoulders. As he danced, the muscles in his thighs beneath the leggings bunched and rippled, and his chest and arms were heavily corded with long, hard sinew. His movements were graceful and strong, causing the feather-tipped wires attached to his headpiece to vibrate and quiver.

Glancing back at Jason, she found him watching her. Their eyes met, and Rachel's heart leaped in fear and surprise. She stepped backward, wanting to get away before anyone else realized she'd been observing them. Abruptly, the music stopped. As she hurried away, she hoped it was an automatic break in the dance—not because they'd found her snooping.

Momentarily panicked, she ran blindly toward Dixie's cabin. A hand grabbed her from behind, and she was stopped, finding herself pulled against a firm, hard, chest. She tensed, waiting to be punished for her actions.

"Don't run from me, Rachel." Jason's voice was husky and close to her ear.

Relief cascaded through her and she slumped against him. "I'm sorry," she said, her voice catching as she spoke. "I know . . . I know I shouldn't have been watching."

"It's all right. Stop apologizing. I thought we'd cured you of that habit." He ran his hands up her arms, through the slits in her cape, then inside. "Anyway, I don't think anyone saw you but me."

His touch melted her. His scent, now heavy with wood-smoke, filled her. She wanted to cry, the poignancy of her need was so foreign to her. She tried to pull away.

"Rachel." His voice was a whisper against her hair as his hands gripped her waist.

Standing in the darkness beneath the trees, they were hidden from the rest of the world. She stood, shivering not from the cold but from the warmth that sneaked under her skin at his touch. She looked up at him, unable to see his face in the darkness. But she could feel his breath, warm and moist, on her cheek.

"Rachel," he repeated, drawing out the sound in a long, husky whisper. His hands slid up her sides again as they'd done earlier in the day. There was a yearning inside her that blossomed each time she was close to him, the feeling so intense she wondered how her chest could hold it. She wanted to run, but she was rooted to the ground, anticipation clinging to every pore.

His thumbs crept up and slowly encircled her nipples again and she bit her lip to keep from crying out. He'd reawakened all the sensual nerve endings in her body with a single embrace and the whisper of her name.

"I want to touch you." His voice was barely audible against her ear as he fondled her breasts. "I want to see you, naked before me, naked beneath me."

Rachel couldn't get enough air, yet she knew she was breathing rapidly. Her breasts felt heavy, swollen, and her nipples ached with longing. She wanted to tell him not to say such things to her. She wanted to fight him, to pull away and run far and fast to escape the feelings he'd ignited inside her. Suddenly her knees gave way, and she slumped against him.

He scooped her up easily and strode off into the darkness. She heard the battering of his heart against her ear but refused to think ahead as to what would happen once they arrived at his cabin. She clung to him because the world was topsy-turvy and her legs wouldn't hold her. She clung to him because what he'd said had scared her—and filled her with an urgent, untimely need. She clung to him because if she hadn't, she'd have fallen to the ground. She clung to him because what she felt for him was so dreadfully wonderful, she knew she'd fallen into the deepest pit of sin.

He kicked open the door.

"Well, well." The voice was deep and silky, the tone deadly. "What have we here?"

Jason stopped in his tracks. Rachel stopped breathing. All traces of desire faded. Slowly she was released, and she slid to the floor, her knees holding her once more.

"What are you doing here?" Jason sounded angry, although his question was asked with great restraint.

The man sat indolently in an easy chair in the corner, his leg thrown over the wide, cushioned arm, his face hidden in the shadows. "You're not happy to see me? I helped organize the dance, Jason. Surely you don't expect me to hide."

"I know what you're doing at the reservation, Buck. I asked what you're doing *here.*"

Rachel backed away, blindly groping for the door. Whatever the problem was between the two men, it wasn't any of her business. As she inched backward, guilt replacing desire, she felt a jolt of shame. Had nothing interfered, Jason would have seduced her here, in his cabin. And she would probably have let him.

Her fingers quietly gripped the doorknob, but as she opened the door, the hinges creaked.

"Rachel?"

Jason sounded surprised, as though he'd just remembered she was there. She didn't answer him, but slipped out the door and ran, careless of the cold, uneven ground, to Dixie's cabin.

Ignoring Buck, Jason crossed to the fireplace and fed the fire.

"*Rachel?*" The voice held intense sarcasm. "Weber's mousy widow? God," Buck said with a disparaging laugh. "I know I encouraged you to find something else to do with your dick, but—"

"Shut up," Jason ordered.

"Is she any good? Did you tell her that as long as you had a face, she'd have a place to sit?" Buck sneered.

Jason crossed to the chair and dragged him out, clutching his shirtfront in an iron fist. "Shut up," he ordered again, his voice angrier than it had been before. As he glared at Buck, it was all he could do not to smash his fist into the smug, hawklike face.

"Did you know," Jason said between clenched teeth, "that Weber stabbed his killer before he died?"

Buck didn't break eye contact. "What's that got to do with me?"

Jason released Buck's shirt, pulling it to the side to expose his scar. "He stabbed him exactly where you've been stabbed."

Buck's mouth curled and he twisted free of Jason's grip. "Dammit, I told you. I was in a bar fight."

"But no one will verify it, Buck. Next time, pick a better alibi—one you can prove."

Buck glared at him. "So. You think I'm guilty, too?"

Jason had been angry initially because Buck so crudely insulted Rachel. And he'd let it color his judgment. Now he was sorry his temper had gotten the better of him. The last thing he wanted was to believe Buck guilty of murder.

"No," he answered, his voice showing traces of regret. "I don't want to believe it, you know that."

"But you can't just take my word for it, can you?"

Jason stared into the fire, thinking of all the reasons why Buck was the perfect suspect. "No, I can't."

Buck paced behind him. "Got anything to drink?"

Jason nodded reluctantly toward the cupboard. Out of the corner of his eye he watched Buck pull out the bottle of whiskey and pour himself a healthy shot.

He took a long pull on the drink, then quickly poured himself another. "So, what's she doing here?"

Jason turned away, feeling the warmth dissipate as he left the fire. Joining Buck at the cupboard, he splashed a small amount of whiskey into a glass for himself. He took a swig, feeling the liquor burn a path all the way into his stomach. He welcomed it. "She's helping me with the burn victims."

Buck snorted a laugh. "I heard you'd hired her. Does she know why?"

"I needed a nurse," he answered blandly, refusing to be baited.

Buck laughed again. "Like hell."

Impatience ate at Jason. He gripped the tumbler hard, feeling the ridges of the glass press into his palm. "Why don't you tell me why, then?"

"God only knows." Buck laughed, a sharp, intense sound that had nothing to do with humor. "She's sure as hell nothing to look at. What is she—a good piece of ass? Widows can be—"

Jason's fist cracked into Buck's jaw. He used all of his self-control to keep from hitting him again.

Buck stumbled away, still clutching his drink. Regaining his stance, he grinned and gingerly touched his chin, moving his jaw around to check for damage. Finally he took a long drink of whiskey, sloshing it around in his mouth before swallowing it.

"Well, well, well." His voice was smoky, filled with sudden understanding. "So that's the way the wind blows."

Jason drained his own glass, slamming it on the table when he'd finished. "I don't know what you're talking about." He didn't like it when Buck got the upper hand. And that only happened when Jason felt vulnerable.

Buck poured himself another shot. He laughed, incorporating in it a harsh obscenity. "My old friend. If I thought for a minute that you were beginning to have feelings for the widow bitch whose family has been responsible for so much *shit* in your life and mine, I'd kill you."

Jason's own anger blistered to the surface. "Like you killed her husband?"

Buck turned and spat into the fire, sending a sizzle of smoke up the chimney. When he looked back at Jason, his face was grave, but his eyes were wary. "If you can believe I did that, then all the years we've been closer than brothers have meant nothing."

Jason knew Buck better than anyone. Yet now, his feelings for him tugged in two different directions. He desperately wanted to believe in his innocence. Yet, he knew there was a good chance he was guilty. Unlike Jason, Buck hadn't learned to deal with his feelings of revenge. He'd made it clear from the moment he found Honey's body that whoever was responsible for her death was going to pay for it.

"If I discover that you had anything to do with the bastard's death, I'll drag you to Tully so fast, you won't have time to think."

Buck smirked and raised his glass in an impudent toast. "Your death if you've been between her legs . . . or mine if I killed her husband." He took a long drink then gave Jason a smug smile. "Sounds like a fair exchange to me."

Rachel had had a sleepless night. She was relieved when the first shadows of morning winked outside the cabin window. After splashing water on her face and climbing back into the same clothes she'd worn the day before, she made a pot of coffee.

Matthew wiggled out of his mother's bed, his new kitten under his arm. "From Dusty," he lisped, dragging the feline to a box of sand in the corner where he unceremoniously dropped it.

"I'm surprised we didn't smother the thing," Dixie said around a yawn. Raising herself up on her elbow, she stared languidly at Rachel. "You're so efficient," she said. "It's like having my own maid."

The innocent-sounding remark caused Rachel to bite back a grin. "I do these things automatically."

Dixie got up and slipped into an old chenille robe. "Then I'm lucky you're staying with me."

Watching Matthew play with the kitten, Rachel remembered that first day she'd gone to work for Jason. He'd called that little boy with the box of newborn kittens Dusty. "Who's Dusty?"

"He's my nephew. My . . . my sister's boy," she answered, turning away.

"Nell's?"

Dixie gave her a brief, sad smile. "No. My youngest sister, Honey." Poking at the fire, she added, "She died a while back."

"Oh," Rachel said on a sigh. "I'm so sorry. I . . . I didn't know." As she watched Dixie gaze into the fire, she felt she'd opened a wound that was best left closed. Stepping quickly to the cupboard, she began preparing some cereal for Matthew. She felt comfortable with Dixie, who was so different from Nell. Perhaps it was time to learn something.

"Dixie . . . what can you tell me about Jason?"

Dixie stood at the window, her back to Rachel. "I've known him all my life. He and his sister, Summer, were adopted by a couple—she's white, he's a breed—about twenty years ago, I guess. Their mother, a Karok who lived way up near the Oregon border—"

"A *Karok*? What's that?"

"It's a tribe. I'm a Wintu." She turned, giving Rachel an odd glance. "Didn't you know he was a breed?"

Rachel stood frozen, unable to move. Her surprise hadn't come from the fact that Jason hadn't discussed his family. It had come from the knowledge, so casually given, that Jason was an Indian. "No. I didn't know . . ."

"Well, she was afraid the Whites were going to kill her, and she didn't want her kids to die. Nicolas Gaspard, Jason's adoptive father, took the kids when they were small. He hid them and a bunch of others up in the mountains somewhere to keep them safe from the Whites."

Dixie came back to the table. "That's when Nicolas met the woman who was to be his future wife." She grinned, shaking her head. "He needed a teacher for all these little Indian kids, so he kidnapped the one his father had hired to teach in Pine Valley."

"*Kidnapped?*" Rachel was stunned.

"Yeah. I guess it was really something."

"I see." Rachel turned back to the stove. *Jason is an In-*

dian. She allowed the sentence to move through her brain a number of times. Her heart beat rapidly, and there was an odd sensation in the pit of her stomach. *Jason is an Indian*.

While stirring Matthew's cereal, Rachel allowed her thoughts to go back to the day before, when she'd first realized she was falling in love with Jason. But how could she? How could she love the very kind of man who had killed her parents and her husband?

But he isn't that kind of man. No, she thought, he isn't that kind of man. Still, she wondered why he'd kept his Indian blood a secret from her. Maybe it was because he, more than anyone, knew how she felt about Indians.

Grabbing a bowl off the counter, she ladled a scoop of cereal into it. "Matthew," she called absently. "Your breakfast is ready." The boy ambled to the table, crawled up onto a chair, and attacked his cereal with enthusiasm.

"Rachel, I should apologize for Nell's behavior."

"Well," Rachel said slowly, "it isn't just her." She was a little reluctant to expose her feelings to someone she'd just met, but the need to talk about it was stronger. "I . . . I get the same feeling from a lot of people."

Dixie gave her a wide-eyed, innocent look. "Oh, really? Who, for instance?"

Rachel rolled her eyes. "Where should I begin? The banker, the saloon owner, Jason, people I've never met who see me on the street in Pine Valley," she added, ticking off the names on her fingers. It felt so good to sit and talk with someone—someone who didn't seem to hold a grudge against her.

"I know this is going to sound like a foolish question," Dixie began, "but . . . did you know what your husband was doing out here?" Her voice was noncommittal, but there was an intensity in her eyes that made Rachel uneasy.

She slowly took a seat at the table, watching Dixie carefully. "He was working as an Indian agent."

Dixie studied her fingernails, her thick, brushy lashes hiding her eyes. "Did you see the tall fence at the entry road when you came in from Pine Valley?"

Rachel frowned, trying to remember. "Yes, I think so. It's made of logs, isn't it?"

Dixie nodded. "Did you look behind it?"

"I had no reason to do that," she answered, a little perturbed. "Why?"

"Because behind it are all the broken-down farm implements your husband refused to replace or repair."

"Farm implements?"

Dixie nodded again, piercing Rachel with her strong gaze. "Plows, saws, wagons, gates—anything that needed fixing or replacing ended up behind that fence."

Rachel tried to keep her face impassive. She didn't like someone else loudly professing Jeremy's failures. Karleen's face flashed through her mind and she realized that it was dreadfully hard to face the fact that Jeremy hadn't been the Prince Charming she'd thought he was.

"The people here seem to be well cared for," she answered inanely, in her husband's defense.

"No thanks to Jeremy Weber," Dixie added, her voice clear, without animosity or blame.

Rachel stared at her. Dixie's lively black eyes had gone cold. "You're telling me my husband *deliberately* made life miserable for these people? I can't believe that. No," she added, shaking her head, trying to dispel the horror of the truth. "I can't believe he'd do that."

Dixie shrugged. "Ask anyone on this reservation what they thought of your husband, Rachel. I don't think you'll like the answer."

Rachel's stomach continued to burn. The feeling seemed to ooze up into her chest, for she felt sickened by the possibility that what Dixie had told her was true.

She looked up and found Dixie staring at her. "What about you, Dixie? Did you dislike my husband?"

Dixie gave her a cold, humorless smile. "There are a lot of reasons I didn't like Jeremy Weber. But ask me why I hated Harry Ritter more."

Rachel let out a short laugh. "Harry? How could anyone not like Harry?"

"Oh, *God!*" Dixie gasped. Before she turned away, her face was pinched with revulsion.

"What's wrong? What did I say?"

"Ma!" Matthew, who had been playing with his kitten in front of the fire, toddled to her, his arms outstretched. He grinned and threw himself at her lap. She ran her fingers through the boy's coarse black hair while contemplating Rachel.

"You didn't know Harry very well, did you?"

"No," Rachel answered cautiously. "I . . . I only met him a few times."

"And he seemed like such a *nice* young man, right?"

"Well . . . yes. He was always shy and polite around me." She had no idea what Dixie was getting at.

"Harry Ritter murdered my sister."

Rachel's jaw dropped . . . and so did her stomach. *"What?"*

"He was a nasty little fornicator who had a preference for Indian girls."

Rachel shook her head, unable to speak. This woman clearly didn't know what she was talking about. The idea that Harry could . . . could do *that* was ludicrous.

"He'd been after Honey for weeks, you see." She had a faraway look in her eyes. "Honey was beautiful. And not just her face, she was a beautiful person *inside*. She never liked to hurt anyone." She gave Rachel a sad smile. "She was always after Nell to be nicer to people, and Nell always warned her that her sweet, generous nature was going to get her into trouble one day." Dixie let out a long, sad sigh.

Rachel tried to picture the pink-cheeked Harry as perverted. She couldn't. The bloody memory of what he'd looked like when she'd last seen him forced itself into her head, but she shook it away.

"Every day," Dixie said, "when Honey would drop Dusty off at the school, Ritter would make some sort of pass at her. Oh," she added, "don't get me wrong. He was smooth as molasses on a summer afternoon. And that sweet, innocent act he put on for them . . ." She shook her head, snorting indelicately. "One day, for some reason, he must have broken through Honey's defenses. Probably bribed her with a cheap trinket. Honey had a weakness for jewelry—*white* man's jewelry."

Rachel clasped her hands in her lap. She didn't want to know anything more, but found herself asking anyway. "What . . . what happened to her?"

"Jason found her and told Buck—"

"Buck?"

"Buck Randall, her husband. Jason's closest friend." She studied Rachel further, as if trying to decide whether to go on. "He found her in the barn, behind a wall of hay bales. She'd been raped. She bled to death."

The picture made nausea heave up into Rachel's throat. She forced it back. "And . . . this boy, Dusty, is her son?" When Dixie nodded, Rachel thought back to the morning in Jason's office when the boy had studied her so intently. She remembered the watchful fear in his eyes. Had it mirrored her own?

Her thoughts immediately returned to Harry. A rapist? In spite of Dixie's convincing story, it still seemed preposterous. "I . . . I don't want to call you a liar, but there must be some mistake—"

"Why?" Dixie interrupted, her voice sharp. "Because you don't want it to be so? Because only *Indians* do such terrible things? I've heard what happened to you, Rachel, and I'm truly sorry. No one deserves to lose so many loved ones, no matter what the circumstances. But," she added, "what I've told you is the truth. Your husband was a cheat and a thief, and Harry Ritter was a murdering fornicator."

🌾 Chapter Eight 🌾

Rachel moved numbly through the rest of the morning as she made rounds. She forced herself to concentrate on the burn victims, but whether she believed Dixie's accusations or not, the words had upset her. If Dixie had tossed them at her angrily, as Nell would have done, she'd have thought it was merely to hurt her. To shock her. To drive her away. But Dixie hadn't even raised her voice.

She had to talk to someone. But not here. Not on the reservation. If any part of what Dixie had told her was true, whatever happened between Jeremy, Harry, and these people was something they certainly couldn't talk about rationally. She, as well as anyone, knew that.

After finishing rounds, she returned to Dixie's cabin. She poured herself a cup of coffee, taking it with her to the window. She stared out at the bright, clear day and watched the smoke meander torpidly into the air from the outdoor fire and the chimneys. No breeze disrupted its upward path.

Her thoughts went back to her first days in Pine Valley, when everywhere she turned, people gave her cold, hard looks. Now that she thought about it, most of them were Indians. The others, like Mrs. Weaver at the general store, had looked at her with more pity than anything else. And after Jeremy's funeral, she remembered that the marshal had wanted to say something to her. Ivy had hushed him up.

She'd noticed quick, secretive glances between them many times, usually after she'd said something about Jeremy, but she'd thought little of it. At least, she hadn't wanted to pursue it. And even that day at the cottage, when she and Ivy had come to pick up her things, Ivy had been ready to tell her something, but the marshal had walked in. Ivy had looked relieved at the interruption—and not only because she was always happy to see the marshal. It had been obvious to Rachel for weeks that Ivy's brusque manner covered the heart and soul of a woman in love.

She smiled softly. Not that Ivy would ever admit her feelings to anyone. A strange yearning cramped in Rachel's chest as she remembered the night she'd sneaked into the restaurant kitchen for a glass of milk. She hadn't bothered to bring a light, for the moon was full and had flooded the room with a white glow.

Ivy and the marshal had come out of Ivy's private little suite of rooms, hand in hand like young lovers. They hadn't noticed her, and she'd held her breath, hoping they wouldn't. It wasn't because she wanted to spy on them; she didn't want to embarrass them or interrupt them.

Ivy's black hair had flowed over her shoulders and down her back. As the marshal had bent to kiss her, he'd buried his fingers in the sable mass. At that point Rachel had turned away, feeling like a voyeur. Her own loneliness had only been compounded by watching the lovebirds. But she did wonder why they were so secretive about their affair. Ivy had been widowed years ago, and as far as she knew, Marshal Tully had never married.

She felt something rub against her foot. Looking down, she watched as Matthew's kitten attempted to climb her ankle. She scooped it up into her arms, listening to its tiny, asthmatic purr.

"So, little guy, did you have a nice nap?"

The kitten climbed onto her shoulder and nibbled at her earlobe as she continued to look outside. Absently stroking the pet, she watched as life went on beyond the confines of the cabin.

Suddenly feeling restless, she put down her coffee cup and gently dumped the kitten onto the bed. Grabbing her cape, she slipped into it and hurried outside. She approached the outdoor fire where a small group, including Jason, was engaged in animated conversation. He stood tall among the others, his bearing fierce and determined. She realized his height had been one of the things that had disguised his heritage, for the Indians she'd seen in Pine Valley and here, at the reservation, were considerably shorter and rounder.

As she neared, they stopped talking, turned and stared at her. She wanted to evaporate like smoke into the air, but Jason motioned her closer.

"It's all right, Ben. I think Rachel should hear this," he said.

Ben, a short yet well-muscled man with long black hair and shoulders that seemed too wide for the jacket he wore, scrutinized her carefully, then turned back toward the others. "As I said, I've changed my mind, you know . . . I don't want my boy to learn the White ways."

Rachel wondered if Ben and his son had been touched in any way by Jeremy's ineffectual leadership. A feeling of guilt overtook her sympathy when she realized that Jeremy may not have done everything in his power to help these people. Suddenly she was aware of the change in her feelings. Only a few days ago she'd been fearful of every Indian who breathed. Now, she was more concerned for their future than for her own.

"How long has he been staying with the Wilson family?" Jason's voice was subdued, restrained.

"Two weeks. And already," Ben added, scanning the faces of the others, "he learns that he can't speak the language of our fathers."

"Ben," an older man said, "we rarely speak it anymore."

"But we can if we wish to." Ben raised his voice in frustration.

"Have they mistreated him?" Jason asked.

Ben shook his head. "Of course not. In some ways—" He stopped, his face showing lines of weariness. "Please, you must understand that I would never want any harm to come to my son, but . . . in some ways, I almost wish they had mistreated him. Then my anger would be justified. Others

could see why I had to steal him back. But these Whites—
they are not unkind. They have given him more material
things than I ever could. He eats at their table. He wears
fine clothes. They teach him with a patience usually re-
served for their own. But it all comes with a high price." He
looked around at the group, his eyes coming to rest on Rachel. "*Too* high."

"How does the boy feel?" Jason asked quietly.

Ben looked at the ground. "He was happy to see me. But I
know that if I leave him there, I will lose him forever."

"In other words," Jason interpreted, "he enjoys the White
life."

Ben nodded. "Too much."

"Then what makes you think he won't return of his own
free will?"

Giving Jason a long, hard glance, he answered, "Maybe
one day he will, you know . . . But it won't be because I
agreed to it, and he will not go against my wishes. Not yet.
One day, I expect him to leave. But at least he will leave
knowing his heritage and why it is important not to let it die
or be wiped out by the Whites."

Jason clamped his hand on Ben's shoulder. "We'll talk
later."

The man nodded and, with the others, wandered off to do
something, leaving Jason and Rachel alone by the fire.

"I suppose you're curious to know what that was about."

Rachel looked at him and her heart ached. He was mag-
nificent, his coat collar pulled up against the cold and his
dark hair a harsh silhouette against the cold winter sky.
She'd discovered so many things about him since they'd
come to the reservation, his commitment to these people
because he was one of them, his ability to listen and dis-
pense his knowledge sparingly. Now, with Ben's problems,
Jason's face had taken on Ben's despair.

"How often does something like this happen?" She wondered if these people had tried to find other lives for themselves and their children while Jeremy had been in control.

Jason fed the fire, jabbing at the embers to enliven them.

"Many Indians have been persuaded to leave their children in the care of White families. They promise to educate them, to teach them their ways. It's no small temptation to do this, for the children are fed, clothed, and kept warm during the cold, angry winter." He stared out beyond the hills to the black trees that clung to the snowy mountain ridges. "It's a tremendous temptation. Unfortunately, the price is very high."

As Rachel listened to him talk, she realized he sounded more and more the Indian and less the educated doctor. She also began to see that if what Dixie had told her was true, Jason would have had no respect for her late husband—with very good reason. "It costs them?"

"Not in money." He faced her, a wariness in his eyes that hadn't been there before.

"Then . . . then how does it cost them?" She drew away from his hard look, somehow feeling responsible for Jeremy's alleged crimes.

"The white culture is very enticing. I should know," he added, piercing her with an arrogant stare. "I was raised to understand both. It puts me in an awkward, and sometimes unhappy, position."

The meaning of his bold look wasn't lost on her. Though she'd learned he was part Indian just recently, she felt his love for his people was so strong, she wondered why she hadn't noticed it before. Again, she realized that discovering his heritage hadn't been a horrible shock. It still didn't seem very important. Learning about Jeremy and Harry had been worse—far worse.

She let her gaze slide to the ground. "I don't understand why it would be bad to know both cultures."

"It wasn't for me. It isn't for my brothers and sisters. But we're the exception. We were raised with every benefit the white man has to offer, yet we were never allowed to forget the language we spoke as children, the spiritual life and stories of our people, or the harsh truths that have haunted us since our world was invaded by the Spanish."

"How are things different for Ben's son? Wouldn't he benefit more from having the knowledge of both environments?"

Jason stared off into the distance, a proud look of possession tensing his features. "This beautiful land," he said, spreading his arms expansively toward the mountains, "is only a small part of the total lands we still own. There are millions of acres across the country still held by the tribes. The Whites want them."

"And you won't sell them?"

He shook his head. "But the Whites are clever. Very, very clever. They want to keep the tribes from congregating and gathering strength. They take the children into their homes, treat them well, educate them. The only thing they require is that the Indian child never speak his native language or practice his own religion. All the old ways have to be erased from the child's mind. Acculturation is necessary."

"Acculturation?"

"Retraining. Cleanse his mind of what he's been taught by his own people. If that's done, one day he'll be as white on the inside as the white man is on the outside. Then," he added, his voice growing sad, "he will happily sell the land to the Whites, for it will seem like the only sensible thing to do."

"And what if Ben's boy chooses to go back?"

Jason shrugged. "He might, but I don't think he would dishonor his father. He hasn't been gone long enough to be permanently swayed by the Wilsons' wealth."

"So . . . so the dance last night is something the people in Pine Valley would like to stop," she answered with a flash of insight.

He nodded. "It's an affirmation of the old ways. It binds us together."

"Did . . . did Jeremy try to stop these ceremonies?" It was when she'd first met Joseph and John Hart in Jason's office that she'd heard the term "Big Head." She also remembered the look of pure hatred John had given her when they'd spoken of the dance and how they hoped there would be no trouble.

Jason studied her. "This was the first we've had here in many years."

"Because . . . because Jeremy would have stopped it?"

He gave her a curt nod, but said nothing.

She looked at Jason. He looked more Indian now than she'd ever dreamed he could. "You . . . you want everyone to remember how it was, don't you?"

"They must," he answered, his black eyes glistening brightly. "Or we'll disappear forever. Our children and our children's children will never know their own history."

Rachel remembered what Joseph had told her about the dance house. "Do they really believe the dance house will save them if the world comes to an end?"

He studied her, the distaste for her naïveté darkening his features. "Don't you believe that your prayers will save you?"

"Well, yes, but . . ." A flashing memory from her childhood stopped her cold.

. . . *If I should die before I wake, I pray the Lord my soul to take* . . .

Suddenly she saw the dilemma. She saw the Christian culture clashing with the Indian, and the pain the Indian people would go through when they tried to hang on to what they knew.

"Is that all you have to say?" he asked, no longer watching her but gazing off into the distance.

She studied his profile. An ache developed in her chest as her love for him grew. He was like no one she'd ever imagined. He was a man with the struggle of two cultures warring within him and she was a part of the culture that was trying to wipe his people out. Anything she said would be meaningless. Nothing she said would be enough.

"I . . . I had a long talk with Dixie this morning."

He picked up a stick and threw it into the fire. "And?"

She gave him an apologetic smile, one he didn't acknowledge, and shrugged. "I . . . I didn't know you were part Indian."

He looked at her, surprise briefly flaring in his gaze. "Half Karok," he supplied, his voice filled with fierce pride.

She didn't know what else to say. It had been foolish to bring it up at all. It was no longer important.

"My father was from Spain. His hair was even lighter than yours, or so I'm told."

All of this information was important only if he wanted to share it, although she realized she was intensely interested in his history. "She said you have a sister." She gazed at the handsome man before her. "She must be very beautiful."

He snorted, his jaw set defensively. "For an Indian, you mean."

"I didn't say that."

"But you meant it," he answered with a smirk. "By the way," he added, his voice harsh. "We're leaving for Pine Valley in the morning. Be ready after breakfast."

She nodded, frustrated that she couldn't bridge this formidable gap that had sprung up between them. He'd already made up his mind that she found him different now that she'd discovered he was an Indian. It was useless to try to convince him that his heritage suddenly meant less to her than her own. Fighting the urge to cry, she turned and walked away, leaving him standing alone by the fire.

Jason stared after her. So that was why she'd seemed so distant. She hadn't known he was a half-breed until Dixie told her. A sick feeling, a sensation foreign to him, burned inside him. He'd thought she'd known. He'd thought that was the reason she'd nearly fainted when he'd first offered her a job. But it was obvious that she hadn't. Her entire attitude toward him had changed since last night.

Last night. . . . They had almost made love in his cabin. He sensed that they would have if Buck hadn't been there. She'd been ready for him, he knew it. And she would never know how ready he'd been for her. He wanted her like he'd wanted no other woman, not even Regina, and he still didn't understand why. Now he'd never know, and that was best. But he wondered why, then, the ache continued to squeeze his heart.

Rachel turned sideways on the buggy seat and watched the trees enclose the reservation. The sun was warm, the weather positively balmy. She thought about March in the Dakotas and shivered involuntarily. There could still be snow as high as her upstairs bedroom window, as there had been many winters. She didn't really miss it, but she did realize that without a sharp delineation between seasons, she might not remember when things happened. She'd always thought in terms of winter, summer, spring, and fall.

The last of the cabins disappeared behind her, and she felt a sadness in her chest. She'd made some friends, people who had prejudged her because of Jeremy, she suspected. And, she thought humbly, she'd done some prejudging of her own. But not anymore.

The winter sun was wonderful and warm. Closing her eyes, she lifted her face toward it. The awful news that Dixie had disclosed about Jeremy and Harry still weighed heavily on her mind and her heart. She had so many feelings about it. A part of her told her it was all rubbish, too melodramatic to be real. Another part of her chided that where there was a rumor, there was often a thread of truth. Dixie's disclosure had been more than rumor. Especially regarding poor Harry. She made a face. *Poor Harry*. She'd have to stop thinking of him as a victim. She'd have to force Ivy to tell her exactly what had happened.

Suddenly she realized that Jason must have known all of this, yet not told her. Swinging around on the seat, she studied his profile. Her heart bumped against her ribs. He was the most beautiful man she'd ever known. Just looking at him did funny, warm things to her.

"Why didn't you tell me?"

His features didn't change. "Tell you what?"

"About . . . about Jeremy and . . . and Harry." The memory of what she'd learned still made her ill.

He tossed her a quick glance before concentrating once again on the road ahead of them. "What about them?"

He was being evasive, and it irked her. "I . . . I'm sorry, but I think you know very well what I mean."

"You're *sorry?*" he asked with disbelief.

With an impatient shake of her head, she amended, "I . . . I didn't mean it that way. And don't change the subject. Why didn't you tell me what you knew about Jeremy and Harry Ritter?"

He was quiet for a moment, his face pensive. "What did you hear?"

Anguish battered her insides. "Do I have to repeat it? I can't . . . I can't. I don't want to believe it—" She finished the sentence on a sob, then cleared her throat, regaining control.

"If you heard that your husband treated the Indians badly, then you heard right. If you heard that Harry Ritter was a weak little pissant who deflowered virgins and enticed married Indian women into barns, you heard that right, too."

Even with the harshness of his language, Rachel felt he was holding back. If there was more to this than she'd learned, she wasn't sure she wanted to know. She sighed, swinging her gaze to him again. "Why didn't someone tell me sooner? Why didn't you?"

He shook his head. "It wasn't up to me. Would you have believed it? Do you believe it now?"

She felt empty, tired. "I wish Ivy would have told me."

He gave her a derisive snort. "Would it have been more credible coming from a White?"

She whipped around on the seat and stared at him. "No, that . . . that's not what I meant, I—"

"Never mind what you meant," he interrupted. "If Dixie didn't convince you, go ahead and ask Ivy. Ask Earl. Ask any damned White in Pine Valley, and you'll get the same answer. Harry Ritter was a rapist, and your husband was a thief and a cheat."

He meant to hurt her, she knew that. Neither the words nor the sound of his voice held any gentleness or sympathy.

"So," she said softly, "everyone in town is painting me with the same brush. Guilt by association." She smiled wanly. "It hardly seems fair."

He gave her an insulting laugh. "Just as fair as assuming all Indians are murdering savages."

The implication hit home. He was right. Until her visit to the reservation, she'd viewed Indians as all alike. Had she known Jason was an Indian, she'd *never* have gone to work for him. She would have avoided him as she'd tried to avoid every Indian she approached on the street. But she didn't think he'd believe her if she told him that had all changed.

Suddenly the buggy lurched sideways, sending the horses into a wild frenzy. Rachel clutched the seat with both hands but was thrown against Jason anyway.

"Whoa, Bell, whoa, Midnight," Jason soothed as he tried to get the horses back under control.

The horses snorted and whinnied, then stopped, prancing in place like marchers in a band. The buggy leaned dangerously to one side, and Rachel was pressed hard against Jason's body. She tried to move away, but it was useless.

"Hold on." He slipped from the seat onto the ground, bringing her with him.

"What happened?" she asked as she quickly moved out of his embrace.

He hunkered down next to the wheel. "I thought this had been fixed." He fingered the bent wheel rim.

"Is it broken?" She stood behind him, looking over his shoulder at the lopsided wheel.

"No," he barked. "All wheels roll at a forty-five-degree angle, hadn't you noticed?" he added, his voice laced with sarcasm. "Of *course* it's broken." He stood and shrugged out of his jacket. "There are some tools in the back. Get them for me."

"Yes, master," she muttered under her breath. "I hear and I obey." Before turning away, she realized he'd heard her. Feeling herself blush, she knew that even a week earlier she wouldn't have dared say things out loud that she'd been saying to herself. As she rummaged through the bit of clutter on the floor behind the seat, she marveled at how she'd changed. She wasn't sure it was for the better. Some things were better left unsaid.

"Is it a box with a green handle?" she asked, spying it way in the back.

"Is there more than one back there?"

She made a face in his direction, recognizing his ever-present sarcasm. Reaching back, she pulled the heavy box toward her, then lifted it out of the carriage. She gripped it tightly with both hands and hauled it to his side, dumping it unceremoniously beside him. Dust sifted into the air as the box came to a heavy stop . . . dangerously close to his foot. He glanced up quickly, giving her a suspicious look.

"It was heavy," she said in her defense.

He mumbled something she didn't understand, then set to work on the wheel.

"Is there anything else I can do?"

His gaze bounced warily from her to his foot. "I don't think so."

Shrugging, she wandered away, settling herself against a boulder. The sun was warm, sending a feeling of lethargy through her as she watched him work. Beneath his shirt, his back muscles bunched and relaxed. A slight breeze ruffled his hair, causing the sun to find threads of gold among the dark waves.

She wondered what his father had looked like. Remembering pictures of Castilians she'd once seen in a book, she let herself imagine that his father had been one of them. Tall, blond, incredibly handsome. Her imagination went further, to picture his attractive, blond father wooing a beautiful Indian maiden. The best of both races had been brought out in Jason, she decided.

The sun's warmth sent her lethargy into lassitude, and she no longer fought to keep her eyes open. She drifted into sleep, her thoughts focused on the man in front of her.

*   *   *

Jason had stripped off his shirt, finding the heat of the late morning sun a welcome balm on his skin. Glancing over his shoulder at the napping Rachel, he allowed a half-smile to touch his mouth. Her head lolled a little to one side, and her lips, those sweet, soft lips, were parted slightly as she slept.

He thought about how much she'd changed in the week they'd spent at the reservation. Dixie, Matthew, Joseph, and half a dozen others had warmed to her. It hadn't surprised him. Who wouldn't, once they got to know her? She was sweet, gentle, almost innocent in her reactions to life—and love.

Swearing, he went back to work. In that respect, she still puzzled him. Days ago, maybe even earlier than that, he'd given up pretending she was an evil woman merely acting naïve. From the day she'd learned that her bastard of a husband had had a mistress, she'd unknowingly convinced him that she was an innocent pawn in one of Jeremy Weber's cruel games.

He swore again, remembering how he'd shouted at Dixie after learning that she'd divulged so much of the truth to Rachel. Dixie had refused to back down, meeting him toe to toe, scolding him for keeping the truth from her. But they'd parted amicably—as they always did. He'd never understand how the women he knew could have been blessed with so much good sense. Most other women, with the exception of his mother, Summer, Nell, and Ivy, were vacuous and foolish.

His job finished, he turned in time to catch Rachel stretching lazily against the rock.

"You snore," he teased, momentarily forgetting that they were at odds with one another.

She gave him a dimpled grin. "You lie."

A warmth that had nothing to do with the sun invaded his chest. He wanted to take the distance between them in two strides, pull her into his arms and kiss her, hold her, caress her . . . continue where they'd left off the night of the dance.

He suddenly realized she was no longer smiling. She seemed frozen with fear, her gaze fixed on his torso. Frowning, he looked down at the mass of deep, crooked scars that zigzagged across his chest.

The horror of understanding sped through him. The morning of the massacre played out in the theater of his mind, and he saw himself stripping off his shirt to cover the bloodied bodies of the victims. He envisioned a frightened woman staring at him through a small hole next to the fireplace, a woman who'd just witnessed the brutal murders of her husband and his best friend . . .

"You!" She still hadn't moved, but her eyes accused him of everything.

He let her stare, refusing to cover up, wanting her to know that he had nothing to hide.

"*You* were there," she whispered, her eyes still filled with terror.

"Of course I was there. I don't deny it." Her unspoken allegation regarding his guilt didn't surprise him. It angered him.

She continued to stare at him, her chest heaving. "Why . . . why didn't you tell me it was you?"

He scowled, his pride holding firm. "My being there had nothing to do with what happened."

"No," she said, not even listening to him as she backed away. "No, you wouldn't have told me, anyway. It was you all along. You're one of them. You're one of *them*," she repeated, her voice filled with shaky loathing. "It's no wonder they can't find the murderers. You . . . you're probably hiding them—"

"Don't be a fool." He reached for his shirt and shrugged into it. She was almost hysterical. It would be impossible to reason with her.

She closed her eyes and swayed back against the rock. "You . . . I should have known it was you," she answered, her voice quivering.

Her hatred continued to eat at him. He understood her

clearly now. "If you hadn't just learned that I was a half-breed," he began as he buttoned his shirt, "you wouldn't have jumped to such a stupid, ridiculous conclusion."

She still refused to look at him. "If you're so innocent, why didn't you tell me you'd been there that morning? You . . . you've had weeks to do it. *Weeks.*"

His own anger and frustration grew. "What good would that have done? By the time I got to your cabin, they were both dead. Believe me, I checked." His pride severely battered, he added, "Who do you think reported it to Tully? Who do you think arranged for your husband's funeral? You sure as hell didn't have the sense to do it."

He tossed the toolbox into the back of the carriage, suddenly not caring what he told her. "Did you ever wonder why so few people came to the funeral? Did it even dawn on you that it was because everyone hated him?"

He tucked his shirt into his denim jeans. "You're lucky anyone in Pine Valley would give you the time of day, considering how they felt about Weber. If Ivy hadn't picked you up as she does all strays, I'd hate to think what might have happened to you that morning."

He turned and studied her. "I'd hate to think what might have happened to you if *whoever* killed your husband would have found you, too. Did you even think about that?"

She stared at him, all the color draining from her face. Bringing her hand to her mouth, she let out a shuddering breath and slid to the ground.

Swearing to himself, he knew he'd said far more than he'd meant to. For some damned stupid reason, she brought out the worst in him. He knew better than to let his emotions rule his head, but ever since he'd first seen her, she'd drawn from him a response too deep for him to understand. Now, all of the hot, exciting notions he'd nurtured about the two of them suddenly seemed impulsive and ludicrous. His weakness for her had made him a fool.

"Get back in the buggy. We have to make it back before dark."

She pushed herself away from the boulder and, like a

sleepwalker, moved woodenly toward him. Her face was stunned into a mask of horror and disbelief. Recoiling dramatically, she refused his hand when he offered to help her up.

They rode back to town in painful, uncomfortable silence.

❧ Chapter Nine ❧

Rachel threw back her covers, padded to the window seat, and curled up on the cushion. The moon illuminated the shed and the outbuildings behind the cafe, carving a sharp delineation between earth and sky. The clock in the restaurant had just struck two. She'd heard it strike midnight and one as well.

Her mind whirled with her recent discoveries. First, she'd learned that Jeremy'd had a mistress, and everyone knew about it but her. No doubt the whole community had laughed at her behind her back, but she knew that what other people thought wasn't all that important.

But Jeremy's betrayal was something she'd never get over. She still felt his infidelities were her fault, but she couldn't do anything about that now. It just continued to hurt, deep down inside where it was almost impossible to heal.

Then there was her confrontation with Jason yesterday morning. Because of his anger, she'd been forced to see herself as others saw her: a shy, naïve, helpless, pathetic, artless, unsophisticated— Oh, *damn,* but she could go on and on heaping adjective upon pitiful adjective and it wouldn't get any better.

Drawing in a deep sigh, she thought back to the funeral. Just who did she think had made the arrangements? Ivy? The marshal? Yes, probably. She hadn't really given it much thought. Someone had always taken care of those kinds of things, things that required thought and planning. If they hadn't, they just wouldn't have gotten done, and that was that. She had no initiative. No one had ever asked her to do anything truly important, because she hadn't been important enough to carry out the task. This wasn't self-pity, this was fact. At least, it was what she'd been told when she lived with her aunt and uncle.

All of the words Jason had flung at her in anger were true. He'd thought he was hurting her. But she was beyond that. What had bothered her so very much *more* was her reaction to his scars. She'd dredged up a picture of Elbee, the ultimate traitor, and immediately decided Jason was a traitor as well.

She'd always prized her ability to judge people, but obviously she wasn't a good judge at all. All of the natural sense she'd thought she had acquired over the years had been just dumb luck. She couldn't automatically weed out right from wrong. *That* had been painfully clear when she'd learned about Harry—and Jeremy. She'd been quick to come to their defense, even though the facts had been laid out before her. Yet, when she saw Jason's scars, she'd also jumped to the conclusion that he was involved in the murders.

Although she knew she was falling in love with Jason, the memory of Elbee's betrayal all those years ago hadn't faded. She'd trusted Elbee, and he'd killed her parents. She loved and trusted Jason, yet briefly, because she'd discovered he was an Indian, she'd felt betrayed.

Of course, she'd regretted her outburst immediately, but it had been too late to take it back. With every sense she possessed, to the depths of her soul, she'd known Jason wasn't capable of murder. But her memory of that morning was still too fresh; she couldn't just brush it aside. And because she couldn't, the recollection had taken hold of her and pushed her face in it, forcing her to scream out loud and gasp for breath, or she would have suffocated.

But it had been the surprise, the shock of seeing those scars—the same scars that had frightened her that terrible morning. Now, she knew the fear she'd felt had been simply a response to the whole gruesome morning—and her horrible past.

But there were still so many other things about that morning that kept her awake at night. Every so often, she'd get a whiff of some smell, and the musty, woody odor of the crawl space where she'd sat, her knees to her chin, would rush back at her.

Shivering, she reached for her robe, then changed her mind. As she groped for and found her underwear, she thought back to what she'd told the marshal weeks before about the face of Jeremy's killer. She hadn't been able to remember it then, and she couldn't now. But she could still see that man standing there, bare chested, the scars gleaming white against his brown skin. With the kind of clarity that sharpens as time passes, she remembered thinking the man might discover her and hurt her. Yet she also knew, even then, that he wasn't a man she should fear. Fright, trepidation, and innocence had prevented her from being rational. Those feelings had come back to haunt her yesterday.

Sighing, she slipped her arms from the sleeves of her flannel nightgown, using the garment as a cover against the cold as she pulled on her drawers and fastened them at the waist. She also slipped into her camisole, buttoning it up the front. Sucking in a deep breath to prepare herself for the invasion of cold air on her skin, she pulled off her nightgown, shivering and hunching her shoulders as she rummaged around in the darkness for her clothes.

Once she'd dressed, she went back to the window and curled up on the cushion. Craning her neck, she peered through the buildings behind the cafe. She'd discovered weeks ago that if she stretched far enough, she could see the front of the building that housed Jason's office. Not the office itself, but the rooms next to it, where he lived. With a little shock of surprise, she realized that one of the windows showed signs of lamplight. A tiny thrill darted through her.

Closing her eyes, she rested her back against the wall and brought back the image of his wide, bronzed shoulders as he worked on the buggy wheel. She remembered wondering

how it would feel to trace his muscles with her fingers, dipping into the grooves, swooping over the bulges. Even
though she'd worked as a nurse, she didn't have that much
experience with the human anatomy.

She opened her eyes and shook her head at her foolish
musings. Considering how they'd parted, she knew that he
probably wasn't thinking about *her* at all.

The clock bonged three times. She glanced at the window
again, making a decision. Bounding off the seat, she hurried
to the coat rack. With her cape over her arm, she quietly
opened the door and stepped into the hallway. After listening for sounds of movement from Ivy's rooms and hearing
none, she fastened her cloak around her shoulders and left
the cafe.

Jason grunted in disgust and put the leather-bound edition
of *Hamlet* facedown on the table beside his bed. He was in a
brooding mood and felt Shakespeare could appease it. But
tonight it didn't work. Tonight, instead of seeing a faceless
Ophelia moving through the script, he saw Rachel. And,
although it really didn't apply, he found himself in the role
of Hamlet, telling the lovely, beguiling Ophelia-with-Ra-
chel's-face to "get thee to a nunnery." A wry smile cracked
the edges of his mouth. . . . *And quickly, too.*

Perhaps he should have read "The Wife of Bath's Tale"
instead. Chaucer was raunchy and humorous, and he needed
his spirits lifted tonight, not weighed down with the morose
musings of a Danish prince.

Thoughts of Rachel drove desire deep into the region below his waist, warming and filling him. He spit out an expletive. Sleep would elude him again.

He slid out of bed and crossed to the stove to feed the fire.
As he shoved in a piece of wood, he looked up and thought
he saw someone pass in front of his window. It could be
nothing; the moon was out, creating changing shadows everywhere even though there wasn't much wind.

He waited, listening for the code. Everyone knew the
code. If they needed him and it was after midnight, they

were to knock on his window four times—two quick, two slow. He heard no one at the window . . . . but someone did enter the office.

Quietly, stealthily, he went to his dresser, slid open the drawer, and pulled out his gun. He moved soundlessly to the door that led to his office, pressing himself against the wall in order to get the advantage over his intruder. The barely audible footsteps came toward him slowly, with the slightest swish of movement.

Now!

He reached around the side of the door and grabbed an arm, pulling the intruder swiftly into the room. A gasp, then a shriek followed.

He pressed the barrel of his gun at the intruder's head— against a mass of familiar brandy-hued hair.

"Rachel?" He moved the gun away, dropping his arm to his side.

She slowly turned and looked at him, her eyes round with fear.

He crossed to the dresser, dumping the gun where it belonged. "What in the hell are you doing, sneaking around in the middle of the night?" Surprise made him angry.

She stood where he'd stopped her, apparently unable to move.

"Well?" he repeated, pulling his shirt off the bedpost and shrugging into it. "What are you doing here?"

Glancing nervously around the room, then at the floor, she answered, "I'm . . . I'm not sure. I just couldn't sleep."

He frowned. "Is something wrong?"

She continued to look at the floor, refusing to meet his gaze.

He looked her over. She stood before him in her voluminous cape, her head bowed and her hands clasped together looking like a Christian martyr, awaiting the cross. "I suppose you know what time it is."

She nodded. "But I can see your room from my window. I . . . I saw the light."

He raised a sardonic eyebrow. Sometimes she was so to-

tally open and without guile. Most women would have acted
coy, batting their eyelashes at him and tittering like rabid
squirrels. Not Rachel. Suddenly everything he'd said to her
yesterday soaked through him like pig swill. He should apologize to her, but he didn't think he could. It wasn't in his
nature.

"And why couldn't you sleep, Rachel?"

She took a deep breath and glanced around the room. Her
gaze slid to his bed—then quickly away. "I didn't really
mean that . . . that I thought you'd killed Jeremy. I know
you're not a murderer. I . . . I guess," she added, "I guess
I've come to apologize." Her nervous fingers fiddled with the
edge of her cape.

His own self-loathing grew. How easily she apologized for
everything. How impossible it was for him to do the same.
His pride wouldn't allow him to go to her in the middle of
the night the way she'd come to him.

He walked over and stood in front of her. She still kept
her eyes fastened on her shoe tops. "Apology accepted." She
smelled of flowers and fresh air. He remembered picturing
daisies, then roses between her thighs, and desire surged
forth. *Damn Hamlet!* Damn his hormones, damn the seduc-
tive differences between men and women, and most of all,
damn *her*.

She coughed, a nervous sound that seemed to strain past
her throat. "Well . . . I guess I should be going . . ."

He felt the pang of her earlier rejection, when she'd
learned he was a breed. Forcing himself to feed on it, to free
himself from wanting her, he snarled, "Nervous being in the
same room with a savage?"

She looked at him, and, finding his gaze on her, she
glanced away. "Of . . . of course not. I've been in a room
alone with you before."

He lifted his black eyebrow again. "At night? When everyone else is fast asleep—in their warm, snug beds?" Her
discomfort spurred him on. "It's bad for your reputation, you
know. After all," he added, stepping so close that their
clothes touched and her sweet scent assaulted him, "you're

an upstanding widow, and I'm the dangerous, dastardly half-breed."

Her lips quivered. They looked soft, sweet, and delicious. She opened her mouth as though to answer him, but nothing came out. Panic flashed in her eyes.

"That's it, isn't it?" He forced himself to feed on what to him was her shallow rejection. It relieved him of guilt. He could say what he wished. He could say what he felt. He could hurt her again.

"How relieved you must be that Buck interrupted us that night. Just think," he hissed, "you almost let a *savage* touch you. I wanted to, you know." He saw the pink flush darken her cheeks before she looked away again.

"You can't imagine the number of times I've dreamed of your breasts, naked and full, in my hands."

"I've got to go," she whispered, turning away. "I—"

"Oh, no. Not yet, sweet witch." He grabbed her arms and held her in front of him.

"Do you want to know something even more ridiculous? This ought to really make you laugh. I'd sit and think about undressing you. Peeling away your clothes, layer by layer," he said, drawing the words out so she'd get a vivid picture, "until your luscious pink nipples were exposed, just for me. For *me*. Isn't that a laugh? Then I'd go crazy, imagining myself feasting on a sweet strawberry lollipop, licking it, washing it with my tongue, watching it bead up into a tight, hard bud . . ."

A tiny sob escaped her mouth, blending with a moan. "Don't," she gasped. "Please don't—"

He gripped her harder. "Why aren't you laughing? Isn't this funny? Isn't this the funniest damned thing you've ever heard?"

She shook her head, tears streaming down her cheeks.

Jason couldn't stop. He ached for her even now, when he was purposely hurting her. God, she drove him crazy! He wanted to wound her, humiliate her. He pulled her even closer against him, pressing his groin against her.

"And the funniest thing of all is that ever since that day you put a sprig of those damned daisies in a vase on my desk, I've wondered if they grew from that virginal place between your thighs."

She shook against him, suddenly gasping out a ragged sob. "Stop it! Stop, please. Why are you doing this?" She finally looked up at him, her eyes filled with pain and her face so wet with tears they were dripping off her chin.

A knife, sharp and long, seemed to twist into his heart. Squeezing his eyes shut, he pulled her into his arms and hugged her tight.

Just as quickly, he released her. She stumbled backward, her eyes wide and her hand over her mouth.

He felt an odd, uncomfortable pressure building behind his eyes. He hated himself for what he'd just done to her. He also hated her for bringing these emotions out in him. "Maybe you should go."

She clung to the chair by the door as if it could shield her from further abuse. "Yes," she whispered.

"I didn't really mean to hurt you, Rachel." Then why, *why* had he done it? God, but he hated himself. Life was so much easier to bear when he didn't allow himself to feel.

She slipped onto the arm of the chair, her head lowered. "Some of what you said to me yesterday was true."

Her voice was so low, he had to strain to hear her. "No," he argued, hating himself more because she didn't seem to. "No one has the right to hurt someone else." No one knew better than he the truth in that statement. Sweet Jesus, what had happened to him?

She gave him a watery smile. "But it didn't hurt. It was true." She shrugged. "I've never been given much responsibility. Not until . . ." She looked at him, her face soft and filled with an odd yearning. "Not until you gave me a job."

He didn't want her vulnerability to touch him. He didn't want to see those emotions that she clearly couldn't hide. "I thought you worked for your uncle."

Nodding, she replied, "But he didn't trust me to do the right thing. He didn't trust me to say the right thing. He

. . . he just didn't trust me . . ." She stood and turned to leave.

In spite of his stiff resolve, his heart ached for her. "Rachel." When she stopped, he whispered, "Don't go."

She turned, wiping her face on her sleeve. "Why should I stay?"

"Because if you go, you'll never come back."

She dug into her pocket and fished out a handkerchief. Uttering a shaky sigh, she wiped her face, pressing the cloth against her eyes.

"I should go. I should . . ."

He went to her, untied her cape and slid it off her shoulders. Glancing down at the front of her blouse, he repressed a weary grin. The buttons were askew, as if a child of four had dressed her. "Did you dress in the dark?"

She followed his gaze. "Yes," she answered, giving him an apologetic smile.

"Let me help you," he said, as he unbuttoned the buttons at her neck. The pulse at the base of her throat moved rapidly beneath her skin, matching the sound in his ears.

"You drive me crazy, you know," he said, pressing his finger against the pulsing movement.

"I do?" Her voice was barely audible. "Why?"

He let out a long, ragged sigh, then continued undoing her buttons. "Damned if I know."

Her hand came up to stop him. "That's . . . that's probably enough."

He looked at her mouth and knew that what they were doing now would never be enough.

"No," he answered, continuing his downward path with her hand on his. Soon her hand slid away, and he felt her shiver.

"Come over here," he ordered softly, pulling her toward the stove.

She followed, her head down and her cheeks pinkened with a virgin's bloom. "I . . . I don't care, you know."

He paused. "About what?"

She looked up at him, then lowered her gaze to his chin. "That . . . that you're part . . . part Indian."

His heart did a funny dance in his chest. He didn't know what to say. He just nodded, then slid her blouse off her shoulders, pulling her arms free. Her camisole was cut modestly across the tops of her breasts, but the plump mounds were still visible. God, but he wanted to bury his face there. He balled his hands into fists, clenching them tightly to keep them from shaking.

"Jason," she whispered, her voice filled with anguish. "Please, I . . . I can't stand up . . ."

Scooping her into his arms, he carried her to the bed and set her down on the edge. She sat there, her hands clasped in her lap, her knees pressed together, her face hidden by the long, glimmering fall of her hair.

He sat down beside her, moving her hair away from her face. She was still flushed.

"I don't . . . I don't know—" Shaking her head, she clamped her lips together.

Gently, with great restraint, he ducked his head and kissed her. She softened beneath him, but her mouth still quivered.

He lifted her hair and kissed her ear, her neck, the pounding pulse at the base of her throat, all the while listening to her breath quicken at his touch. His lips touched the sweet, creamy flesh above the lacy edges of her camisole and he reined in his hunger.

Slowly, keeping his need at bay, he moved back and looked at her. She was shivering, yet the stove kept his room warm. He reached up and slid the top button of her camisole out of the buttonhole, watching her as he did so. Her light eyes held his. She was breathing erratically. He persisted, sliding each button out until he reached the waist of her skirt.

Without pulling her gaze from his, she waited for his next move.

Taking the open edges of the camisole in his fingers, he

pulled them apart. Hunger, urgent and deep, lanced through his groin. She was perfect. Her breasts were firm, high, and round. They quivered, moving to the rhythm of her rapid heartbeat. Her nipples were small pink buds of beauty that had already eagerly hardened.

Swallowing, he licked his dry lips, unaware that he'd been staring at her with his mouth open like a callow youth. He touched her, briefly closing his eyes at the boundless pleasure that surged through him. Circling her nipple with his thumb, he listened as tiny gasps escaped her throat.

Slowly, he bent to touch her nipple with his tongue. She gasped and pushed at his shoulders.

He looked at her, a question in his eyes.

"I . . . I didn't . . ." She swallowed, shaking her head.

"Do you want me to stop?" He didn't want to. Hell, he didn't know if he could.

She shook her head. "No, I'm sorry . . . I just . . ."

Relief flooded him when she shrugged out of her camisole. He slid to his knees in front of her, cupping her breasts, teasing the nipples, gently, seductively kneading the soft flesh.

Her knees relaxed, allowing him to move between them. He snaked his fingers up under her skirt and massaged her bare calf, inching his way up until he met the edge of her drawers. She moaned against him, draping her arms over his shoulders.

As his hand moved higher, her breathing became more labored. When his fingers grazed the heated delta of her thighs, he found the fabric hot and damp. She moved, trying to close him off, but it only made his own loins swell with need.

She pushed at his shoulders again. "Oh God," she whispered, her breath ragged.

He didn't understand her. But he wanted her, and he was sure she wanted him. "Do you want me to stop, Rachel?" he asked again. He looked up at her, and her eyes were heavy with desire and her tongue flicked out to wet her lips. He almost lost it.

"Oh no . . . Just hurry," she pleaded, running her hand over his cheek, down his neck and over his shoulders.

Springing to his feet, he pulled her off the bed and into his arms. They kissed, hard. His hands roamed her bare back, then came around to her breasts, down her sides to her hips. He pulled her against him, letting her feel his arousal. She dug her fingers into his shoulders and pushed back.

Groping behind her, he found the opening to her skirt. It fell to the floor, leaving her in her drawers. He drew back and looked at her. Heat, wet and deep, spread through him.

"Take them off," he said, his voice husky with need.

She fumbled with the tie, but soon let the fabric fall. Her eyes never left his face.

His gaze filtered over her. She was perfectly made. High, swelling breasts tapered into her waist, small and delicate. Her hips were seductively curved to drive him wild, and at the base of her thighs, there was a generous thatch of rust-red hair. He'd dreamed of it; he'd imagined it. Yet nothing could compare with the reality of it.

He touched her stomach, dipping his fingers down to gently fluff her pubic hair. She gasped, but didn't pull away. "Get into bed," he ordered, his voice husky with need.

She slid under the covers, bringing the blanket to her chin.

Quickly shedding his clothes, he joined her, dragging her against him. She arched toward him, asking the unspoken question, giving the unspoken answer.

Without further thought, he pressed over her. Her legs moved apart, and he entered her. He drove, intending to go deep, when suddenly she gasped, and her face was pinched with pain.

A horrifying realization imprisoned him, draining him of

his desire. He stared down at her, watching as she tried not to cry.

"Why in the hell didn't you tell me?" Anger, sympathy, and surprise beat a path across his heart.

❦ *Chapter Ten* ❦

*H*e moved off her, rejecting her as she'd known he would once he found out. Turning away from him, she rolled into a ball.

"How in the hell can you be a virgin, dammit?"

He sounded furious. She had thought she'd be able to pull it off. She didn't *want* to be a virgin. She hadn't wanted it for the past two years, hoping her surprise trip to California to be with Jeremy would remedy the hated condition. But what could she tell him? She could feel him staring at her, silently berating her.

"Tell me, Rachel."

"What's there to tell?" The pillow muffled her voice.

He swore. "Rachel—" He heaved a sigh, which ended in an incredulous, humorless laugh. "You've been married for two years."

"I know that," she answered. "Don't you think I know that?" Feeling his hand on her bare shoulder, she waited for more recriminations.

"He never touched you?" he asked, sounding puzzled as he continued to stroke her arm.

She shook her head, his gentleness surprising her.

Pressing her shoulder toward him, he said, "Look at me, Rachel."

Reluctantly she turned. His sultry, magical eyes explored her face as he pushed her hair back behind her ear. He pulled the covers away and gazed again at her breasts. Her nipples puckered automatically. Reaching out, he touched one with the tips of his fingers, then cupped the breast in his palm. She swallowed a shudder.

"How could he not touch you?" He still sounded bewildered.

It would have been easy to tell him—if she'd understood it herself. "He . . . he didn't even try," she finally answered, remembering her confusion on her wedding night when Jeremy had left her to go drinking with his friends.

He pulled the covers down further, until she was completely exposed to his gaze once again. His hand touched her skin, moving over her gently, encircling her navel, and she closed her eyes, praying he would never stop.

"He must have been mad not to find you irresistible." He bent and planted a kiss on her stomach. She nearly flew apart as tears of wonder trickled out of the corners of her eyes. No one had ever touched her or made her feel this way.

Finally, he pulled the covers over both of them and turned her toward him. "Come here," he ordered softly. "Let me hold you."

She went shyly, anxiously, into his arms, biting her lip to keep from crying out the longing that swelled in her heart. It was a feeling she'd never have imagined. He was hard and smooth and warm . . . so warm. And he smelled clean, but his body had a scent special only to him. If she lived to be a hundred, she'd never forget it. Never, never.

Tears welled in her eyes. No one had ever cared before. No one had held her, comforted her . . . loved her. Not since she was a girl. She slid her arms around him and squeezed.

His hands gently threaded through her hair, fingered her back, her buttocks. There was a quickening low in her belly, a warm bursting of pleasure. She pushed her hips toward him, seeking more.

"My poor baby." His voice was hushed and raw as he pressed his hips against hers, answering her quest. He brought her leg up and draped it over his thigh. There was a wet, heavy sensation between her legs, causing her to shudder with anticipation. Every nerve in her body seemed to come alive there.

His hand moved between them, his fingers touching her. The feeling was such a shock and so arousing, she could barely draw a breath. He caressed her, finding secret exciting places on her body she never knew existed. Gripping his shoulders, she squeezed, certain that if she didn't hang on, she'd lose control and fall not only off the bed, but off the edge of the world.

She was lost in a torrent of sensual response. Something was going to erupt inside her, and she swam toward it, pushing herself against his hand. Suddenly she was on the brink. The thought of losing such total control frightened her, and she tried to pull back.

"No," he whispered, pressing his mouth over her breast. He rubbed her nipple with his tongue, flicking it back and forth and around the nub. Splintering desire burned a path from her nipple to that place between her legs.

"Let it go, Rachel. Don't fight it. Come on, sweet baby, don't fight it . . ." He cupped her with his hand, pressing the base of his thumb against a spot that seemed alive with longing.

The eruption came, sending her out of control, tightening her muscles as spasm after wonderful spasm wracked her. Finally, a warm glow, like the feeling of hot candle wax, exploded through her.

She slumped against him, burrowing her face against his shoulder. She felt him lift her hair off her neck. The cool air against her skin made her realize she'd been sweating.

Daring to peek at him, she found him watching her, his expression incredibly gentle.

"You're crying." He wiped her tears with his thumb.

"I . . . I had no idea," she whispered, her voice still shaky. She felt him hard and hot against her stomach. Her gaze shot to his face again. "Oh, dear," she murmured, suddenly realizing that he'd pleasured her, but had gotten no pleasure himself.

"I'm going to remedy that," he answered, a sultry smile lifting the corners of his mouth. "If you don't mind."

Sliding her arms around his back, she snuggled close, pushing her hips against his feverish root. This time when he entered her, there was little pain, only some residual discomfort. But she welcomed it.

Wrapping her legs around his back, she welcomed his thrusts, rising to meet them.

He stiffened over her, his grunts of pleasure sending her blood singing through her veins. They lay quietly, pressed together. Finally he rolled onto his back, his eyes still closed.

She raised herself on her elbow and looked down at his chest. His scars were deep, white, and had healed poorly. Tracing them with her fingers, she felt tears press the back of her eyes. "Who would do such a thing to you?"

He was quiet for a long while. Finally he answered, "There are some who believe I deserved them."

She shook her head. "What did you do?"

A grim smile cut into his face. "I tried to help a friend, and forgot my 'place.' "

"Your place?" She lifted her gaze to his high, hard cheekbones.

"I forgot that as a half-blood I was supposed to be neither seen nor heard."

"Who did this to you?" She ached to bend and kiss him there, but she wasn't sure he'd let her.

He took a deep breath, enhancing the muscular expanse of his chest. "Soldiers."

"I'm sorry," she whispered, lying back on the bed.

He chuckled beside her, but the sound seemed forced. "Leave it to you to apologize for something you couldn't possibly be responsible for."

But she felt responsible, in a detached sort of way. Both her husband and her father-in-law were military men. And she knew how they both felt about Indians.

Rachel awakened slowly, feeling both warm and uncomfortable. She hadn't shared a bed in years, and she'd never shared one with a man. She didn't have to open her eyes to know that Jason's arm was around her, holding her tightly against his body.

Opening her eyes, she looked at the window. It was still dark. Her gaze found the wall clock, and she saw that it was almost five. A tiny prick of panic stirred her complacency. She had to leave before anyone saw her. She tried to move away.

"Not yet," came the muffled response.

"But Jason," she argued, "someone might see me."

"Talk to me, Rachel. Tell me about your mother and father."

The poignant memory hadn't faded. "Someone told you."

"Earl said they'd been murdered by Indians." He paused a moment. "Tell me about it."

She uttered a shaky sigh and began her story. She told him of her happy life before she'd turned eight, of the love and affection given her by her parents. She talked of Elbee, and how much her family had loved and trusted him. She spoke of the farm, her aunt, her cousin, George. Finally, she told him of the night Elbee betrayed them—the night he had their home burned and her family massacred.

"Why do you suppose this happened?"

"I'm not sure," she answered. "Thinking back, I'd say it was probably because so many farmers had come in to take the best land for planting. You know, taking it without thought for the Indians who'd lived on it for hundreds of years."

"Do you think he meant to kill you, too?" Jason stroked her breast casually.

"I don't know. Probably," she added, the pain of Elbee's betrayal still making her sad.

"How did you manage to get away?"

He continued to stroke her, and she began to feel the newly familiar lassitude. "He was carrying me through the corn and lost his grip when I hit him in the face and pulled his hair."

"And he didn't search for you?"

"No, I don't think so. I've thought about that, and if he'd wanted to, I'm sure he could have found me. Surely he was far more clever than I was."

"Maybe he didn't want you to die."

The statement shocked her. "But . . . but why did he betray us, then?"

He drew in a deep breath, blowing it out against her hair. "Maybe he had to go along with the others, make it look good."

"But he killed my mother and father, Jason. I saw him. He shot them right in front of me."

"Yes, I don't doubt you. Maybe it was a less painful death than if others from his tribe had done it."

She heard her mother's screams and her father's curses. "I suppose, but . . . but it's hard for me to believe he killed them because he had to, or let me live because he loved me."

"Were you an only child?"

She shook her head. "I had a baby brother, Lucas. He wasn't even old enough to walk. They killed him, too."

"You saw his body?"

"No, of course not. He was buried with Mama and Papa, though. That's what I was told."

"Who found you?"

"Neighbors. I guess I was crying . . . out of control. I don't even remember that part. It wasn't until late the next day, though. I was really cold. I do remember that. Then . . . then I was sent to live with my uncle Gabe and his family. I stayed with them until I married Jeremy."

Jason was quiet behind her, but continued to caress her. "I want to make love to you again before you go."

She sucked in her breath as his fingers found that place between her legs. It came alive instantly. Though the emotion was new, she sensed she was already prepared for him. Feeling him harden behind her, she pressed against him with her buttocks.

He pulled her tighter, one hand caressing her breasts while the other touched her *there*. She moaned, arching her back and pressing her bottom harder against him. He positioned himself, and entered her from behind.

She gasped as he filled her, still fondling her with his fingers. He pressed deep, thrusting and moving, while his fingers worked their magic as they'd done before. But somehow, there was something else. An eruption stronger than the one she'd had earlier began somewhere deep in her pelvis, and as she felt it come, she bucked out of control, Jason's arms around her the only things keeping her centered in the universe.

He watched Weber's widow slip cautiously around the side of the building and race down the street toward the cafe. His upper lip curled in distaste. The alliance he suspected was one forged in hell. Everyone knew that.

Letting the ragged curtain fall back into place, he turned and crossed to the fireplace, his movements catlike. Lighting a lamp, he rested it on the floor and turned his attention to the loose brick in front of him.

As he worked the brick away from the wall, he thought about the brilliance of hiding Weber's money there. No one would look; no one would suspect. He let his mind go back to that fateful morning of Weber's murder and he couldn't suppress a vicious grin. His plan had been brilliant. But then, *he* was brilliant, brilliant in ways other people didn't understand. And he'd had the perfect alibi. He hadn't been within miles of the cottage all night long, and he had witnesses who could back him up.

He pulled out the leather pouch, replaced the brick, and with the lamp in his other hand, moved into the deepest, darkest corner of the room. Once there, he put the lamp on the floor and settled down to count his money.

Rachel stood before the mirror in her room. Did she look any different? She frowned. Her eyes—they . . . they were shiny. Sucking in a shaky breath, she decided she'd have to keep busy all day. That way, no one would take a good look at her. How could anyone not know what had happened to her? She felt so *different*. She felt beautiful for the first time in her life.

The thought of working beside Jason all day sent shivers down to her toes. This new need was so wonderful. She didn't understand how people in love could hide their feelings from those around them. Why, she knew the minute she saw Jason, her feelings would show in her eyes, on her face, and in places where, thankfully, no one else could see. The sensations he'd awakened in her were glorious. Oh, what she'd been missing all these years . . . but then, would she have felt the same way with Jeremy? Somehow she didn't think so. Maybe she should have, but she surely didn't think so.

She unconsciously twisted her wedding ring around on her finger. The thin gold band had become a part of her. But after last night, she didn't feel right wearing it. She didn't want to wear it anymore, but she didn't know if it was right to take it off. Screwing up her courage, she pulled the ring off and dropped it into her small jewelry box.

Giving herself one last scrutinizing glance, she squared her shoulders, opened her door, and stepped into the cafe.

"Lord have mercy, Nancy, didn't you see that mess up in that corner?" Ivy, her arms akimbo, stared at the juncture of the ceiling and the wall. "There's enough spider makins' up there to knit a good-sized sweater."

Nancy shook her head and ambled to the corner, a rag tied to the end of a broom. "You know I don't see as well as Jessie. Why don't you have her do the cleaning?"

Ivy clucked her tongue. "We go through this every week, girl. Jessie don't see anything when it comes to cleaning corners."

"Well," retorted Nancy, "apparently I don't, either."

Rachel crept behind the counter and poured herself a cup of coffee. Ivy caught a glimpse of her out of the corner of her eye.

"Well, there you are." She peered at Rachel. "You feeling all right?"

"Yes," Rachel answered, avoiding Ivy's eyes as she gripped her cup in her hands.

Ivy frowned. "You look a mite feverish." She crossed to where Rachel stood and touched her face. "You sure you're all right?"

Rachel gently pushed her hand away. "I'm fine, really. I scrubbed my face extra hard this morning, that's all."

Shaking her head, Ivy didn't look convinced. She went back to nagging poor Nancy.

Rachel took a seat at a table in the back and watched the activity. Bram Justice, the saloon owner, came through the door promptly at seven o'clock. Ivy had always said she could set her clock by him.

He smiled at Rachel. "Morning, Miz Weber."

She nodded. Guilt coated her stomach. She hadn't paid him anything yet, and she couldn't let it pass without saying something.

"I really will have some money for you soon, Mr. Justice. As soon as . . . as soon as I get paid."

He sat down at the table next to her. "Ah, yes. I hear you're working for the doctor."

"Yes, and I . . . I expect Jeremy's pay voucher any day now," she answered, hoping it was true.

"You're an honorable woman, Miz Weber. I have no doubts that you'll pay me when you can."

Jessie sauntered out from the kitchen to take his order and Rachel glanced at the door, flushing as Jason walked into the restaurant. Every feeling he'd awakened in her the night before, and earlier in the morning, flooded her. Their glances met briefly before he looked away. His eyes were warm, but his expression guarded. He took a seat at the counter facing Rachel. Her heart raced madly.

"Morning, Jason," Jessie called as she came around the counter with Mr. Justice's coffee. "The usual?"

Jason grinned at her. "Nope. I'm hungry as a bear this morning. Bring me the usual plus an order of biscuits and gravy on the side. And," he added, "cook up a mess of those delicious fried potatoes."

Jessie looked at him as though he'd lost his mind. "In all the years I've known you, you've never had more than one egg, a dry biscuit, and coffee in the morning."

"Oh, that reminds me. Bring me *two* eggs this morning." He gave her an innocent smile as she clunked the mug of coffee down in front of Bram Justice.

Rachel bit the insides of her cheeks to keep from smiling. Because of *her*, he was hungrier than usual. She'd felt just the opposite, too excited to eat. A fluttering of warmth burst forth in the pit of her stomach. The warmth turned to ice water when she looked over and saw Abner Bailey, the banker, walking briskly past the window.

Crossing her fingers, she hoped he wasn't coming into the cafe. He was more formidable than Mr. Justice. At least when the saloon owner saw her, he tipped his hat and smiled. The banker would give her a cool, appraising look, as if telling her that if she didn't pay up, she'd find herself in jail. Oh, she knew she was being dramatic, but her conscience bothered her. She hadn't been able to give either man anything yet. As unpleasant as it was to think about, she'd have to ask Jason when he was going to pay her.

As Rachel hurried to work, the bitter March wind pressed against her face. She pulled her hood in close around her and scurried to the office, stepping inside. A fire glowed behind the glass door of the stove, sending its warmth over Rachel's skin.

"Oh." She closed her eyes briefly and sighed. "This feels wonderful."

"And to think I haven't even touched you yet." Jason's voice was edged with humor.

She smiled and blushed. "I . . . I meant that it's nice and warm in here."

He stood by the glass cabinet, obviously searching for something. Turning, he gave her a hot gaze. "Not as warm as it could be."

Oh, how was she going to endure such wicked, wonderful

punishment? Flustered, she took off her cape and hung it on the coat tree.

"Are we scheduled to see anyone this morning?" She walked purposefully to his desk and looked at the charts.

"Not unless someone comes in, unannounced."

The fact that his practice wasn't exactly booming didn't seem to bother him. Yet, she couldn't very well ask him for money if he didn't have any. Most of his patients had no money at all. How was he going to pay her?

She cleared her throat. "Jason," she began, hating what she had to ask, "I know . . . I know I shouldn't ask, but . . . but when will I get—" She couldn't say it. She felt like a fool.

"Paid?" he offered.

She nodded, feeling the blush steal into her cheeks.

He was at her side immediately. "Don't be embarrassed. It's my fault. I should have paid you after the first month, which was three days ago."

She couldn't believe it had been only a month since she'd started working for him. She'd learned so much in that month. She'd learned not to fear every Indian who walked the streets of Pine Valley; she'd learned to stand up for herself a little bit; and, most exciting of all, she'd learned that what she'd felt for Jeremy had been nothing compared to what she already felt for Jason. She'd fallen in love.

"I . . . I don't mean to harp on it—"

"Nonsense. I'll have the money for you by tomorrow morning."

She looked around at the empty office. "I feel awful asking for it, but I . . . I do need it . . ."

His gaze followed hers. "You're worried that I don't have it. Is that it?"

Giving him a small nod, she turned away.

He stood closer. "Didn't I tell you that besides being a physician, I'm a farmer?"

She shook her head. "Don't tease me."

"I've never been more serious."

She looked at him and saw that he was telling the truth. "Farmer?"

"Well," he hedged, "not really a farmer, but a wine-maker."

"You grow grapes?"

"My family is in the grape-growing business, yes."

"And . . . and how does that affect you?"

He shrugged. "Every year at harvest, I put in my share of time." He studied her carefully. "It gives me quite a comfortable income."

She was so relieved, she turned to him and grinned. "That makes me feel so much better."

Giving her a half-smile, he said, "You thought I couldn't afford to pay you."

"Well . . . I was . . . I was a little concerned."

He studied her. "Ivy's not charging you rent, is she?"

"Oh, no," she gasped. "It's not that at all . . . It's just that . . . that Jeremy had . . . had a few small debts that I . . . I want to pay off." She didn't want him to know just how deeply in debt she was—because of Jeremy's frivolous activities.

He turned away, but not before she saw a dismal look cross his face.

"Is something wrong?"

"No," he said. "Not a thing. If you have a chance this morning, which," he added, looking around the empty room, "it looks as though you might, would you straighten the supply closet?"

She arched her eyebrows. "*You* want *me* to straighten a room?"

He gave her another half-grin. "A closet isn't a room."

"Nevertheless," she answered. "It's a surprising request, coming from a man who apparently enjoys his clutter."

His grin widened. "Are you making fun of me?"

A thrill shot through her. "Why, yes," she said, answering his smile. "I believe I am."

He gave her a mock threatening glare. "You'd better get a

move on, or I'll punish you for that." His look was far hotter than his threat.

"Is that a promise?" She stood, stock-still, after the words had left her mouth. Had she really said them as well?

Their gazes locked. Rachel swallowed the lump in her throat and broke eye contact. "I . . . I'm sorry."

"Rachel."

"No," she answered, scurrying toward the other room where he kept his supplies. "I'd better . . . get that closet cleaned."

Thankfully, he didn't follow her. She stepped into the small space, keeping the door ajar so she'd have some light.

She worked industriously until she heard the clock strike ten. She'd been at it over an hour. Suddenly the room went black as the door closed behind her.

"Wha—" She turned, stumbling into his hard, firm chest. A melting sensation heated her insides as she breathed in his scent. That, and his nearness, brought on a heaviness in her pelvis. "What are you doing?" Her voice was barely audible. She could feel his breath on her face.

"I'm punishing you." He pulled her against him, moving suggestively. He was ready for her.

Putting her arms around him, she leaned into him, loving the contact. "I . . . I believe I'm ready to be punished." The darkness made her brave, brazen. Standing on tiptoe, she clung to him, pressing her hips against him.

Raising her head, she found his mouth. They kissed, long, hot, deep kisses that both weakened and energized her. He pulled up her skirt and she helped him, wanting only to feel his hands on her.

With his other hand, she felt him fumble with the buttons of his fly. Suddenly his hot root sprang free. He pulled her skirt up and hoisted her legs around his hips. She clung to him, pushing against him as he entered her through the opening in her drawers. He turned, pressing her against the door as he drove into her. Heat became fire and their ragged breaths intermingled, driving them on.

He came, the force so strong she swore she could feel it

touch her heart. But he didn't let her go, and he didn't pull out. Instead, he held her tightly while he turned, slid to the floor and rested his back against the wall. With her legs still curled around him, she felt him continue to move slightly inside her. The position allowed her freedom to move against him, to find that sensitive nub she'd only discovered yesterday. She became languid, her breathing deepened and she rested her forehead against his. Suddenly that now-familiar feeling welled up inside her and she stiffened, aching for the release she knew he could bring her.

Pushing hard against his groin, she shuddered as she came, spasm after spasm quaking through her.

Bracketing her face with his hands, he gently kissed her. When he released her, she rested her head on his shoulder, her nose pressed into his neck.

"I haven't finished straightening up," she whispered, finding it very difficult to form words.

"It doesn't matter. Whatever you've done is good enough."

With effort she lifted her head. "You didn't send me in here just to take advantage of me, did you?" When he didn't answer, she persisted. "Did you?"

He chuckled in the darkness as he lifted her off him. "Not entirely."

She had to admit that it had been very arousing to be taken by surprise in a dark little room. A tiny part of her loudly questioned what his intentions were. She hadn't been accustomed even to thinking about anyone but Jeremy. She hadn't thought her virginal condition would be changed by anyone *but* her husband. A tiny niggle of shame wormed into her thoughts and she struggled to her feet.

"I have an errand to run this evening. Would you come with me?"

There was nothing she wanted more than to be with him. "Where are you going?"

"I have to deliver some supplies to the ranch."

"Your family's place?" Nervous excitement pounded

through her. She wanted desperately to meet his family, yet the thought of it frightened her just the same.

He opened the door and scanned the room. The light made them both squint. "Yes, my family's home."

Frowning, she wondered whether or not to accept. "And . . . and your parents? Will they be there?"

He nodded. "They've just returned from Washington, D.C."

"Oh," Rachel demurred. "I don't want to intrude—"

"Don't be foolish," he interrupted. "I want you to be there with me."

A thrill shot through her. She looked away quickly so he wouldn't see the raw need on her face. "I . . . I guess I could come with you—in case you need some help," she finished feebly.

He gave her a lopsided grin and turned away. "Where my mother is concerned, I can always use some help."

🌿 *Chapter Eleven* 🌿

Rachel was nervous about meeting Jason's family. The feeling was compounded when she spied the large, two-story home looming ominously in front of her. It gleamed white against the shadowy, tenebrous daylight, lights glimmering from the lower-story windows, sending messages of warmth and welcome. The windows above were dark, foreboding, mirroring the atmosphere outside . . . and the feeling inside her.

She shivered. By now, everyone knew who she was. Her concern was for how his family would receive her—on the basis of what they knew.

Huddled beside Jason, the warm fur blanket tucked in around them, she briefly wished they could stay this way forever. All too quickly, they stopped in front of the imposing adobe house.

A young boy, bundled up in a sheepskin jacket, must have been watching for them, for they hadn't even come to a full stop before he threw open the front door and bounded down the steps.

"Jason! Concetta's fixing your favorite tonight!"

Giving the boy a wide grin, Jason hopped down from the carriage. "I thought Concetta had retired. What's she doing slaving away in the kitchen?"

The boy returned the grin. "Aw, you know she only retires when she's got the *rheumatiz.*" He turned his gaze on Rachel and stared. "Who's she?"

Jason walked around the carriage and helped her out. He

gave her a sly wink. "Where are your manners, Josh? Mother would stand you in a corner if she heard you."

Josh hooted. "Ma? Stand me in a corner? Heck, maybe Concetta would, but not Ma."

Rachel felt Jason's hand on her arm. He gave her a reassuring squeeze. "Sounds to me like maybe she should. Anyway, Joshua Gaspard, I'd like you to meet Rachel Weber, my nurse."

Rachel forced a smile. "It's nice to meet you, Joshua."

The boy peered up at her. "Thanks. I've heard about you."

Rachel's stomach dropped. No hope of being anonymous.

"Josh, take care of the horses, please. Are you eating with us tonight?"

"Nope. I'm eatin' with Dusty at his grandma's." The boy went to do Jason's bidding.

"You'll have to excuse Joshua. He was, you might say, an afterthought. Although Summer and I were adopted, we do have three other siblings besides Joshua. They're all away in boarding school or college." He gave her a smug grin. "Joshua wasn't planned. That's why he gets away with murder."

"Well, he's just a boy. What is he, seven, eight?"

Jason nodded. "He's eight. The same age I was when I first met Anna, my mother."

Rachel remembered Dixie's story about Jason and his sister. "Did your father really kidnap your mother?"

"He did." His answer was light.

She stared at him, finding it hard to distinguish his features in the waning light. "I'd like to hear more about that sometime."

He took her arm. "We'll see."

Remembering Joshua's remark, she asked, "What has your little brother heard about me?"

He turned her toward him, holding her firmly by the shoulders. "Don't start freezing up. There's no one in my family who is so small-minded that they'd have an opinion about you before they even meet you." He gave her a wry half-smile. "Except me, of course."

In spite of his reassurance, Rachel's stomach dipped again. "Well, let's get this over with."

He chuckled. "Yes, we'd better get inside. They knew the moment Josh left the house that we'd arrived. They'll begin to wonder what we're doing out here in the dark."

She tried to smile, but her jaw was clenched so tightly, she knew she'd failed. Before they reached the door, it opened wide again.

"Come in! Come in out of the cold, you two!"

"Mother, my love," Jason said, sweeping the woman into his arms. "You're looking as beautiful as ever. Washington must have agreed with you."

The woman gently pushed herself out of her son's embrace and lovingly touched his face. "No, actually being *home* agrees with me. And," she added, "you're in an unusually fine humor, my moody, cerebral son."

He pulled Rachel forward. "I thought I should be on my best behavior. Mother, this is Rachel. Rachel, my mother, Anna Gaspard."

Rachel murmured a proper greeting. Mrs. Gaspard stood back and looked at her, a gentle smile on her lips. "Yes, I imagined as much. Welcome to our home."

Warming to her immediately, Rachel thought, with an unusual sense of humor, that "captivity" had agreed with her. "Thank you," she answered, allowing Jason to take her cape. Looking around her, she made a quick assessment of the foyer. Tapered candles set in a delicate brass chandelier softened the entry with muted light. The staircase was directly in front of her, the graceful scrolled banister a dramatic accent to the carpet of green and gold flowers that covered the stairs. The deep brown hardwood floors against the pale walls gave an even greater illusion of light and space in the anteroom.

"You have a very lovely home," she said.

"Oh, thank you. We've done quite a lot of remodeling over the years. My husband's father built this house almost fifty years ago." Mrs. Gaspard looked around the room, her eyes warm and her face pensive. "But I'm not sure he'd recognize it if he were still alive today."

"If I remember right," Jason added, hanging Rachel's cape on the coatrack, "Father had to nearly twist your arm to make the first changes."

Her smile changed, and there was a hint of whimsy in her eyes. "We didn't make any changes for years. It was beautifully furnished when we moved in. I saw no reason to buy anything new."

"Yes, well, after being forced to live in a bucolic cabin for so many months, this probably looked pretty good to you."

"Oh, Jason, let's not drag up all of that. Rachel isn't interested in that old history."

But Rachel was. Suddenly she wanted to know everything about them. The little bits of family history were mere teasers.

"Your father will be down shortly. Come," his mother ordered genially, "let's go into the parlor."

Rachel was ushered into the warm, cozy room and took a seat by the fire. Here, again, the walls were painted the color of cream, as was the mantelpiece around the fireplace. Hanging over the mantel, attached to it by an extension of the fireplace molding, was a rectangular mirror. A charming old chime clock sat regally on the mantel. Scroll-shaped brass sconces with graceful tulip shades bracketed the mirror.

"Pour Rachel a glass of sherry, Jason."

"One for you, Mother?"

She shook her head. "I'll wait for your father."

Rachel studied the woman. She was petite and quite beautiful. Her hair, the color of melted caramel, had barely a hint of gray.

"I hear you helped out quite a lot after the fire, Rachel."

"I . . . I did what I could," she answered, grateful that she actually *had*, despite her earlier trepidations.

Mrs. Gaspard sighed and shook her head. "I was *so* sorry to hear about that. And your *father*," she added, rolling her eyes at Jason. "You can imagine what *he* had to say about it."

"I said," came a deep, resonant voice from the doorway,

" 'you can always tell when a fire's been set by angry Indians. They leave clues as big as horse droppings.' "

Rachel watched Anna Gaspard's face when her husband came into the room. She smiled, her eyes filling with love as she lifted her hand to grip his. "We have a guest, darling." Her voice was soft and gentle, although it was obvious she was trying to scold him. "Don't be crude."

He bent to kiss her. "I didn't think I was being crude, my sweet. Remember, initially I didn't say 'droppings.' "

Rachel turned away, feeling like an intruder. Her eyes met Jason's, and she felt her face flush. He was watching her intently.

Her gaze returned to Jason's father. The man continued to stand beside his wife, her hand still gripped in his. Rachel couldn't help but stare at him. He wasn't as tall as Jason, but he was noble looking. His Indian features were obvious, his face stark and severe and his coal-black hair shot with gray. There was a dark scar over his left cheekbone. To Rachel's eyes, he wasn't particularly handsome, but he certainly exuded power. The look of love and warmth he exchanged with his wife was one Rachel yearned for from a man of her own. It was also a look that Rachel felt he didn't share easily.

"Nicolas," Mrs. Gaspard said, "this is Jason's new nurse, Rachel Weber."

Rachel's heart thudded madly. He'd been imposing enough when he'd entered the room, but now that his gaze was on her, she felt the blush steal into her cheeks and all the old insecurities storm to the surface.

If any man on earth could get away with kidnapping, this man could. But, just by the looks of him, she would bet her last dollar that it hadn't been a smooth courtship. She was relieved that she'd put her glass of sherry down on the table beside her, or she'd probably have snapped the stem in her grip.

A brief, secret look, so quick most people wouldn't have noticed, passed over his face. Rachel knew, then, that these people were completely and totally aware of what Jeremy had done.

"You enjoy nursing, Mrs. Weber?"

"Yes. I . . . I worked for my uncle, who was a doctor before I—" Hesitant even to mention Jeremy's name, she stumbled over her words. "Before I came out here," she finally added.

"Jason tells me you're quite competent."

She merely nodded, guessing he was only making conversation, which, she sensed, was something he rarely felt obliged to do. He, unlike his wife, made no attempt to make her feel entirely welcome. Maybe she was just especially sensitive because of Jeremy, but she felt sure that was part of it. She could sense his distance.

An elderly Mexican woman loudly announced dinner. Certain she couldn't swallow a bite of food, Rachel reluctantly took Jason's arm and followed him into the dining room.

The round table, covered with a delicate lace tablecloth, was set with impeccable taste. The china and crystal were simple, yet somehow Rachel knew they were expensive. Jason held her chair for her. She noticed that his father still held his mother's chair.

A young Mexican girl ladled a delicious-smelling cream soup into the bowls on their plates. She wasn't particularly skilled at it, but from her concentrated expression, it was obvious she was determined to do a good job.

"So," Mr. Gaspard began, smiling at the girl as she left the room. "Has Earl come to any conclusions about the fire at the school?"

Jason took a spoonful of soup. "We're sure it was set on purpose. I don't think he's gone beyond that."

"What do you think?"

Rachel brought a spoonful of soup to her mouth, enjoying the creamy texture with the chunks of mushroom in it.

"Well," Jason answered, passing Rachel a basket of dark rye bread. "I've been wondering if maybe Ty Holliday isn't somehow mixed up in this."

His father lifted his eyebrows. "What about Buck?"

They all gave Rachel a brief glance. She quickly concentrated on buttering her bread.

Jason sighed. "I don't want to think so, Dad."

"I'm sure you don't want to think he was in any way responsible."

The young girl came back and hovered nearby until they'd all finished their soup, then quickly removed the bowls from the table. She artlessly piled them on top of each other and hugged them to her chest as she hurried from the room.

Mrs. Gaspard followed the girl with her eyes, then smiled at Rachel. "We don't have many servants, Rachel. But from time to time, when we have guests, we appreciate the help. Olivia," she said, nodding toward the door, "is our housekeeper's granddaughter."

Rachel nodded and glanced at the door as the housekeeper came through with a tray of food.

"Want me to serve?" she asked in thickly accented English.

Mrs. Gaspard shook her head. "We'll manage, Concetta. Thank you."

Jason stood and hugged the heavy old woman, catching her off guard. "Shoo!" she scolded, trying hard not to laugh.

"*Brau krub!* Ah, Concetta, you'll spoil me," Jason said, giving the woman a noisy kiss on the cheek.

Concetta wrinkled her nose. "I already have, you crazy boy. I no understand why you like that Swede food." She clucked her tongue noisily as she left the room. "Tortillas and beans much better."

The dish Jason was so fond of, the one Rachel couldn't pronounce, was served in an ornate square serving dish.

"Do you like dumplings, Rachel?" Mrs. Gaspard reached for Rachel's plate.

Rachel thought the dish smelled wonderful. The soup had whetted her appetite. "Oh, yes," she answered, allowing Mrs. Gaspard to put a spoonful on her plate. "Very much." She discovered that the dumplinglike consistency had chunks of pork throughout. Though the dumplings were an odd shade of gray, the dish was rich and tasty.

Anna Gaspard heaped a large helping on her husband's and her son's plates before dropping a spoonful on her own.

"So," Nicolas Gaspard said between mouthfuls. "You think Ty is involved. Why not Buck?"

Jason took a drink of water. "Buck's mad enough to have done it, I know that. But, no matter what anyone else thinks, I know him. I know what he's capable of. He wouldn't burn down the school."

Chuckling dryly, Mr. Gaspard said, "Maybe because you love him like a brother you're a poor judge of his character."

Jason sighed deeply and shrugged. "I don't think so, Dad."

The family continued to talk of crops, siblings, and the recent trip to Washington, D.C., until Concetta and little Olivia came in to clear the table.

"So," Concetta said as the last of the plates were cleared away. "Now, you eat something good, not something I have to make with blood from a cow."

Rachel's stomach became queasy as she watched Concetta waddle out of the room. *Blood from a cow?* She looked from Jason to his mother, an obvious question in her eyes.

Jason gave her an innocent look. "Didn't you enjoy the dumplings?"

She cleared her throat. "Well . . . of course. But . . . just what were they?"

Jason grinned, his dark, slumberous eyes twinkling. "Blood dumplings. One of my mother's favorite Swedish recipes."

She swallowed and tried to smile. For some reason, the delicious-looking flan that Concetta served them for dessert suddenly held little appeal.

After dinner, when Jason and his father excused themselves to go over some books, Rachel asked where she could freshen up.

She followed the housekeeper up the stairs to the bathroom. After lighting the lamps on either side of the mirror, the woman left Rachel alone. The room, now bathed in light, made Rachel gasp. Never had she known anyone with such a palatial bathroom. Even a flush toilet! She stared at the brass and porcelain pull-flush fixtures and the unique embossed pedestal. Her astonished gaze moved to the roomy, high-sided sink with the brass faucets and she glanced up, finding her image in the mirror.

She looked as she felt—a poor little waif coming in out of the cold, to find warmth in a mansion. She'd only read of places like this. It was, in her mind, the highest form of luxury a person could have. And the *tub*. Room enough for two, certainly. Realizing where her thoughts were going, she blushed, but allowed herself the brief fantasy, anyway.

Sitting in the huge claw-footed porcelain tub with the mahogany rim, water lapping at her breasts, she would look up and find Jason watching her. Her blood would thicken with desire.

Come, join me.

The look he would give her would reheat the water. Without saying a word, he would undress in front of her, dropping his clothes to the floor. Her heart would ache anew when he revealed his massively scarred torso, and she would urge him to get in so she could touch it, wash it, kiss it.

Your look tells me you're anxious, he would say as he slowly, seductively unbuttoned his fly.

I'm very anxious—for you. She would watch, breathless as he slid his trousers down over his hard, lean hips. And there it would be . . . that part of him that she had seen so very briefly their first night together. But she remembered. Long and stiff against his stomach, nestled in that thick thatch of dark hair, it looked as if it might split her in two. But she knew better . . .

A noise from downstairs awakened her from her ill-advised daydreams. She blushed again, glancing at the flowered wallpaper, then at the burgundy and white checkerboard tiled floor. How could she think of these things in his *parents'* home!

After freshening up, she turned down the lamps and left the bathroom with a sigh of regret. As she started back down the hall, she thought she heard singing coming from a room at the far end of the stairs. The door was open. She crept to it and looked in.

A woman, clearly older than Rachel, sat in a rocking chair, singing to a baby. At least, that's what Rachel thought it was until she stepped closer. Her heart pinched with pity when she realized the woman was singing to a doll. She could see her face in the mirror, haunting shadows thrown across it from the dimly lit globe parlor lamp that sat on the dresser. The woman's incredible, exotic beauty caused Rachel to unconsciously let out a ragged sigh.

The woman looked up, catching Rachel's image in the mirror. The large black eyes were warm, yet somehow distant. "Anna?"

Rachel hesitated before stepping closer. "No, I'm . . . I'm Rachel."

The woman continued to rock back and forth, the doll held snugly against her chest. "I'm hurtin' again, Anna."

Rachel stepped to her side and sat down on the needle-point footstool. "I'm sorry you're hurting." She gazed at the woman, noting for the first time the ragged scar that cut into the left side of her face.

The woman shook her head. "I can go for a long time without thinkin' about it, you know?"

Listening to the woman's speech, Rachel would have thought she was merely a girl, not a grown woman. "I . . . I think I understand." She stared at the woman's beauty, wondering what could have hurt her so much that she fled into this private, painful world.

"I get to thinkin' about Molly, you know?"

Rachel felt as though she were snooping into something that didn't concern her or that *shouldn't* concern her. But she couldn't just walk away. "Molly? What about Molly?"

The woman's smile transformed her looks beyond beauty. "She's my baby." She looked down at the doll, then glanced at Rachel. "I know this ain't Molly. But sometimes . . ." She sighed, dropping the doll into her lap. "Sometimes I can't quite forget about the pain . . . the hurt . . ." Her gaze went off to some distant place.

Rachel caught the doll before it fell to the floor. As she was putting it down on the bed, she saw Jason towering in the doorway. Her heart leaped with her newfound feelings of love.

"I was worried about you."

She felt herself flush again. "I'm sorry . . . I heard her singing, and I was curious . . ."

He stepped into the room and looked down at the woman who now appeared to be in some sort of trance. Lovingly touching her hair, he said, "June?"

When she heard his voice, she shook herself and smiled up at him. "Jason. Have you seen Molly?"

"She's away at school. She left three months ago."

June frowned, as if trying to remember. "School? Where?"

"In San Francisco. With Jillian and Martha, remember?"

A beatific smile spread across her face. "Oh, I remember." She grabbed Jason's hand and pressed it to her cheek. "I love you, Jason."

"I love you, too." He continued to touch her hair.

Tears stung Rachel's eyes at this obvious loving exchange.

"I see you've met Rachel," he said softly.

She turned and looked up at him, then at Rachel. She gave him a girlish little laugh. "At first I thought she was Anna. Then, I knew she wasn't." Her smile faded. "I wish things would stay the same . . ."

Jason bent to kiss her cheek. "So do I, June. Is there anything I can get you before I leave?"

She gave him a wan smile. "No. But thank you anyway."

Rachel's heart ached for both of them. There was a bond of pain between them. She didn't have to be intuitive to notice that.

"Who is she?" she asked as they descended the stairs.

He uttered a deep sigh. "It's a long, long story."

"Will you tell me sometime?"

He took her cape off the coatrack and slipped it across her shoulders. "Maybe."

Frustration welled up in her. "Is she a relative?"

"No, but we grew up together."

"In the mountains?" The meager amount of information he was willing to share baffled her.

"Yes, you inquisitive woman, in the mountains."

"I'd really like to hear about it sometime."

He shook his head and smiled at her. "You don't give up easily, do you?"

"I guess not." She answered his smile.

June appeared at the top of the stairs just then and told Jason she needed him.

He gave the older woman a patient look. "I'll be right back," he said, gently squeezing Rachel's arm.

Rachel took a deep breath and gazed around the foyer again. Spying a vase of winter wildflowers on a table against the wall, she wandered to them and pulled their clean smell deep into her lungs.

Suddenly she heard Mrs. Gaspard's voice from behind the door of the study. "You really shouldn't blame the girl for that, Nicolas."

Rachel's stomach dipped. She stepped away, not wanting to eavesdrop.

"But, darling," Mrs. Gaspard said in response to something Rachel didn't hear. "You of all people should know she had nothing to do with *that.*"

Rachel instinctively knew they were discussing her. Letting out a whoosh of air, she stepped quickly back toward the stairs, grateful that Jason was on his way down.

"Anything serious?" she asked.

Shaking his head, he steered her toward the study just as his mother was coming out.

"You're leaving? Already?" Mrs. Gaspard looked genuinely sorry to see them go.

"I have an early day tomorrow, Mother. And Rachel has to be at the office in case we get any business."

Worry lines immediately etched themselves into Anna Gaspard's pretty face. "Oh, darling. Things haven't picked up? Don't those foolish people in Pine Valley know an excellent physician when they see one?"

Jason gave his mother a wry smile. "I get their business slowly, Mother. I'm a patient man."

She broke down and smiled. "You're a *what?*"

He threw up his hands in defense. "I'm *learning* to be a patient man."

She crossed the space between them and gave her son a warm hug. "Take care of yourself. Don't forget the goodies Concetta made for you."

Stepping away, she gave Rachel a tender smile. "It was so nice to meet you. You'll come again, won't you?"

"I . . . yes, I'd like that, very much. Thank you so much for a lovely evening."

With that, Jason picked up his food basket and they left. Once in the buggy, the fur blanket tucked back in around them, Rachel realized she hadn't seen Jason's father since dinner.

"I hope I didn't scare your father away."

He turned, giving her a hard look. "Why would you think that?"

Rachel sighed. "Jason, I could sense the distance he put between us. He certainly knows about Jeremy, and he doesn't like me much because of it."

"You're wrong, you know."

She shook her head and smiled in the darkness. "I'm not wrong. What other reason could he have for disliking me?"

Jason didn't answer her. But when she finally turned and looked at him, the moon bathing his face in light, she was certain she saw pain, deep and permanent, carved into his features.

Rachel stepped into the office the next morning and glanced at the envelope that was lying on the desk. It had her name on it. She crossed the room, picked it up and peeked inside. Smiling, she saw the money and the little note from Jason.

As she counted it, she tried to decide how to divvy it up. Three ways was probably best. Thirds for Mr. Justice, Mr.

Bailey, and somehow she'd have to force Ivy to take a third. She felt guilty living off the woman's good graces.

Slipping the envelope into her purse, she decided now was as good a time as any to start repaying her loans. She left the office and strolled down the street, pausing briefly in front of the dress shop to look at the black silk full-length cape that hung on the mannequin in the window. It was so beautiful. The hood was edged with velvet, and the lining of the cape was velvet, too.

With a heavy sigh, she continued to walk toward the saloon. She didn't need a new cape. Hers was wool, warm and sturdy. Very practical. She made a little face. Everything she owned was practical—except her wedding dress, and what good was that? Every time she looked at it, she was filled with sad, bitter memories, but she was too sensible to get rid of it.

She stepped into the saloon and her stomach dropped further. Harvey, the muscle-bound bartender, gave her a lusty look from behind the bar.

"You here to see me, honey?"

Blushing, she realized she didn't even know how to respond to such banter. "Ah, no. I . . . I wanted to . . . to see Mr. Justice."

"Ah, hell. He's just an old man." Harvey gave her a suggestive grin. "I, on the other hand, ain't old at all."

Rachel was ready to turn around and leave, when Tess ran down the stairs, stopping on the landing. "Harv! Get your ass up here!"

He gave Rachel a lecherous smile. "Another time, sweetheart." He tossed his towel on the counter and followed Tess upstairs.

Rachel shuddered. As she approached the office door, she heard loud voices. She didn't want to interrupt a confrontation. She could pay Mr. Justice another time. Turning to leave, she heard one of the voices say Jeremy's name. Praying she'd be forgiven for eavesdropping, she quietly stepped closer and listened.

"I didn't raise you to be a tramp. Your mama would turn over in her grave if she knew what's happened to you."

Rachel listened to the self-righteous sound of Bram Justice's Southern drawl.

"Oh, Papa, how *could* you? I can't forgive you for that. And I *won't* let you take this away from me. I'm not ashamed. I'm proud to be carrying his child. *Proud.* And if I thought for a minute that you—"

"He was a married man, girl!" he interrupted. "Have you no sense of pride?"

"But he loved me. He truly did. He didn't love her. Papa, he told me he never even *slept* with her."

Rachel became nauseous. Sinking into a chair near the wall, she put her hand over her mouth, not even wanting to hear any more. But she couldn't leave. Where Jeremy was concerned, she seemed to be a glutton for punishment.

"And you believed that? Don't be a stupid fool. No man marries a woman then doesn't sleep with her. Love has nothing to do with sex, girl. Haven't you learned that? Hell and damnation, he came to this establishment to sleep with *whores.* How can you profess to love a man like that?"

"But that's just it, Papa. He *didn't* sleep with a whore. He slept with me. I knew the minute I saw him that he was the man for me. And I *was* a virgin, Papa. He never slept with anyone else after he slept with me."

Justice swore. "I suppose he told you that?"

It was quiet behind the closed doors for a long, agonizing minute. Rachel stood, preparing to leave in spite of the weakness that had taken hold of her.

"Jeremy didn't have to tell me, Papa. I loved him. I knew him."

As Rachel hurried toward the exit, the door behind her opened.

"Miz Weber?"

She stopped, trying frantically to compose herself. Finally, she turned around. "I'm . . . I'm sorry, Mr. Justice. I didn't . . . I didn't realize it was so early. I don't want to disturb you."

His gaze was guarded. "You didn't, ma'am. What can I do for you?"

Smiling nervously, she fished into her purse with shaky fingers. "I have some money for you."

"I don't want to put you out."

Rachel looked up and saw Karleen step into the room behind her father. There was no doubt in her mind that Jeremy had found the girl beautiful, for she certainly was. Her hair, long and golden, hung in unruly curls over her shoulders. She gave Rachel a cautious look.

Rachel glanced away, concentrating again on her payment. "It's no trouble, really. I . . . I've already planned for it." She handed him the money. "I'm sorry it's not more, but I will pay you, every cent." She forced another smile, although she felt as if she were going to throw up. "It will just take a little time."

Justice took the money. "Would you like a receipt?"

Rachel shook her head. All she wanted was to get away. "Perhaps another time. Thank you, Mr. Justice." After giving Karleen a quick glance, she hurried from the saloon.

Bram Justice watched her leave, then turned on his daughter. "Well, do you feel better now, knowing she heard what we said?"

Karleen squirmed. "You don't know that."

"I *do* know that. What I don't know," he added, his gaze returning to the front door, "is how *much* she heard."

Rachel dropped off her payment at the bank, then returned to the office. She was numb. She'd thought she'd put all feelings for Jeremy behind her, but she'd never get used to hearing about his infidelity. It was so very much against everything she'd ever been taught. And it all just went to prove what a gullible, naïve woman she'd been. That she hadn't been laughed out of town was a surprise. There was no doubt about it. When Karleen's pregnancy began to show, Rachel would have to leave. *That* was something she didn't think she could abide. Karleen wouldn't hide the identity of the father. In fact, Rachel felt sure that Karleen would advertise it.

She dropped into a chair by the stove and curled her feet under her. With her chin resting on her fist, she stared into the fire. She heard the front door open, but didn't have the strength or inclination to get up.

Jason walked into the room. "Rachel? Is something wrong?"

It wouldn't be easy to leave him, Rachel thought, but she would if it came to that.

"Karleen's pregnant."

Cursing, he crossed to where she sat. "I'm sorry. Who told you?"

She expelled a tired sigh. "I overheard her telling her father." She stole a glance at Jason. "When she came in here with the fever, I thought she was a saloon girl. I didn't know she was Mr. Justice's daughter. You didn't tell me."

He swore again. "I thought everyone knew. Come here," he added, pulling her out of the chair and holding her.

She stood in his embrace, limp and lifeless. "I could have dealt with his infidelities—eventually. But he *told* her he'd never slept with me. Can you imagine? Good Lord, Jason, what if she tells the world?"

He put her away from him so he could look at her. "Do you really care?"

Rachel shrugged out of his embrace and walked to the window. "I don't know. I . . . I just don't know how to feel. He *was* my husband, 'for better or for worse.'" She shook her head. "How am I *supposed* to feel?"

She sensed him behind her. His body heat was welcome, but she couldn't look to him for answers or support. She had to work this out for herself. His hands came around and tenderly gripped her waist.

"No," she said softly, pulling his hands away. Turning to face him, she saw the cloaked look of pain on his face. Oh, God, she didn't want to hurt him, but she had to do this by herself. "I'm sorry. I . . . I just have to be alone for a while. If . . . if you don't need me, I think I'll go back to Ivy's."

Pulling himself up straight, he nodded briskly. "Of course. Take all the time you need. As you can see," he added, giving the office a scornful look, "I don't really need you here."

Knowing she'd hurt him, yet unable to make it right, she slipped into her cape and hurried down the street to the cafe, and her room—and isolation.

❦ Chapter Twelve ❦

*J*ason dropped off some papers at the bank, continuing to brood about Rachel's earlier behavior. He tried to understand what she was going through, but knowing what Weber had done to her, Jason was hard-pressed to understand why she was grieving. To him, Karleen's pregnancy had nothing to do with Rachel. After all, Weber had never even slept with her. In Jason's book, that made Weber the biggest fool on the face of the earth. How he could have wanted Karleen when he had Rachel made no sense.

Jason had known Karleen for many years, ever since she moved to Pine Valley from New Orleans with her father. She was pretty, but there'd always been something about her that bothered him. She'd been a selfish little brat, for one thing. For another—she had a bland, unpleasant personality.

So Jeremy Weber's preference made no sense to Jason. And considering all of this, he felt Rachel was wasting unnecessary energy and emotion on her late husband *and* his mistress.

As he made his way back to his office, he stopped to observe the train pulling into the station. Ever since the iron horse had made its way west, he'd been fascinated by every aspect of it. As a boy, he'd been especially excited by the wailing of the whistle, the sound dropping in tone as it sped into the distance. And the power in the driving wheels had always intrigued him. Now, the engine chugged and hissed as it rested, occasionally sending great plumes of smoke billowing into the air.

He watched the passengers disembark. There weren't many. Pine Valley wasn't a very populous town. A woman and a child were met by a man Jason recognized as a rancher from the south of town. The owner of the mercantile debarked carrying a heavy satchel. Several other people followed.

As he turned to continue his walk back to his office, he glanced at the man stepping from the observation car. He did a double take. The man was a soldier—an officer—in the U.S. Cavalry. Jason's gaze moved slowly to his face.

His stomach dropped and nausea filled his chest. All of the devices he'd used over the past fifteen years to protect himself suddenly fell away, leaving him vulnerable. His heart pumped, filling his arteries with venom-tinged blood and his chest stung as if the wounds he'd lived with over the years had just been inflicted.

Staggering back into the dim light of a doorway, he closed his eyes and brought his hand to his face. Suddenly everything was fresh, clear and vividly real. He was fifteen years old again . . .

"Take the buckboard, Two Leaf," his mother had said, a worried frown on her face. "I asked June to pick the wild berries near Sky's place, but I have an awful feeling she's down by the river."

Two Leaf turned away before she saw his look of distaste. The buckboard! That was a rig for farmers and women. He hurried to the stable and leaped onto the back of his bay, Cassius. Leaning over the animal's neck, he gave it a fierce hug. A gift from his father, Cassius was probably the closest thing he had to a friend and confidant.

"Why would I take that dumb buckboard when I have you?" he crooned into the animal's mane. In return, the horse whickered and flung his beautiful head high as if to preen for his master.

They left the stable by the back entrance, just in case his mother was watching. If June was swimming, Two Leaf thought, racing onto the path that led to the river, she could just as easily ride home behind him on his horse as beside him on the stupid buckboard.

As he approached the swimming hole, he heard a scream. Frightened, he reined in Cassius, moving his gaze thoroughly from side to side, alerting himself to danger like his father had taught him.

"June?" His voice cracked with fear, and he sounded like Cub. Clearing his throat, he tried again. "June?" That was better. He was a man. He wasn't a whining little boy.

No answer. Topping the rise, he looked into the river. June wasn't there. Suddenly he heard the scream again.

"No! Stop it! Ouch, you're hurting me. You have to stop it!"

The hair on Two Leaf's neck crested with fear. "June?" His voice was high again, exhibiting the panic he felt. Now he didn't care. Leaping from his horse, he tossed the reins into the bushes. Racing over the rise, he skidded down the embankment toward the river, tumbling the last few yards. He quickly righted himself, and what he saw brought him up cold. Fear, panic, and fury rushed over him like a runaway train.

"Hey!" he shouted at the soldiers. "You get away from her!" He ran toward them, leaping onto the back of the big blond one who held June down.

"Son of a bitch," the soldier snarled. "Get him off me."

The other soldier, who had been holding June's arms, left and tried to pull Two Leaf off his companion's back.

"Come on, you little savage." He laughed as he flung Two Leaf onto his back. "Go scalp someone else. Leave us to our fun."

The harsh contact with the ground knocked the wind out of him. Gasping for breath, he watched as the soldier, his blue trousers down around his knees, forced himself into June.

"J-June," he gasped, trying desperately to breathe.

"Two Leaf!" She was crying. "Get him away! Ouch! It hurts."

He heard a loud crack, then a whimper from June. Driving to his feet, he lunged at the rapist's back. The other soldier swore again and tore him off, sending him flying backward once again.

"Goddammit!" roared the rapist. "I can't do anything if that little bastard's gonna pester me. Knock him out or something. Kill him—just *keep him away from me!*"

Two Leaf staggered to his feet, wishing he'd brought his knife. Hate, strong and vile, filled his chest. He'd kill them. They were hurting June. He had to stop them.

He picked up a stick and plunged back into the foray, smacking the makeshift whip wildly against the attacker's back. He was pulled off again. This time he was whacked across the face so hard he saw stars.

"What in the hell is going on here?"

The voice came from behind him. Still nursing his jaw, Two Leaf looked around and saw a big, imposing soldier with flame-red hair sitting on a grand chestnut Morgan. The soldier had Cassius in tow.

"What're you doin' with my horse?"

The man with hair of fire looked at him as though he were less than human. "This animal doesn't belong to you, savage."

Fresh anger surged through Two Leaf. "He does! He's mine!"

One of the other soldiers laughed. "He probably stole it."

Two Leaf whipped around and stared at him. "I didn't. He's mine. My father gave him to me—"

"Shut up, boy," ordered the red-haired officer.

Two Leaf scooted away from the prancing hooves, keeping a close eye on the soldier. He was older than the others. No doubt he was in charge.

"I repeat, gentlemen, what's going on here?"

"Just havin' a little fun, sir."

The soldier who had hit him strolled over and examined Two Leaf's horse. "Nice animal, sir. We gonna keep him?"

Two Leaf lunged at him but was quickly shoved to the

ground. Tasting fear and hatred in his mouth, he glanced at June, who looked as though she'd fainted.

"Who's this?" The officer on horseback nodded toward Two Leaf.

"Some little half-breed." The rapist giggled. "Tried to save the digger squaw."

Two Leaf swallowed the bile that pushed into his throat. Again, he looked at the man in charge. "She's my—"

"Shut up, you dirty little savage." The officer's face reflected the distaste in his voice.

As he scooted farther back toward the water, Two Leaf knew he was in trouble, but he refused to give in. "They hurt her—"

"You done with her?" the officer interrupted.

The attackers looked down at June, revulsion replacing the lust Two Leaf had seen there earlier. "Yeah, we're done."

"Grab the breed," the officer ordered.

The attackers cackled with glee. "Yessir!"

Two Leaf tried to get away, but the men gripped his arms and dragged him toward the officer's horse. One of them whipped out a rope and bound his ankles, leaving him defenseless.

"Take off his shirt and hold his arms."

He was held, crucifixion-style, while his shirt was ripped from his body. He looked up at the officer and knew he'd never forget him. Not if he lived forever.

He was a big man, wide through the shoulders and chest. His hair was so red, Two Leaf wouldn't have been surprised if it had caught fire. And he had that funny beard that grew from his sideburns, down to his jaw, then across his chin. His facial hair was redder than the hair on his head. No, Two Leaf wouldn't forget him.

Unable to curb his emotions, Two Leaf flung a mouthful of spit at the man. It missed his face, landing instead on his highly polished black boot.

"You dirty little savage," the officer growled. He pulled

out his bullwhip and, without warning, launched into a rabid attack of violent flicks across Two Leaf's chest.

Refusing to cry out, Two Leaf clamped his jaws together and gritted his teeth.

"Hit him till he squeals, Lieutenant!"

"No one," the red-haired lieutenant bit out between lashes, "especially a filthy little half-breed, spits at me and gets away with it."

Two Leaf's strength waned. His knees gave way, and he sagged between the two men who held him. His chest stung, the pain sinking deep into his flesh and beyond, into his soul.

The lieutenant stepped closer and grabbed his hair, pulling his head back so hard, his neck nearly snapped.

"You take a good look at me, savage."

Two Leaf returned the hateful, heated gaze. He stared mutinously into the officer's face, memorizing it. He didn't ever want to forget it.

"Have you taken a good look, half-breed?"

Two Leaf didn't respond. He only stared.

"Don't you ever forget what I look like, boy. I will always be your superior. In every way. Do you understand?"

Two Leaf didn't move. He didn't even blink.

"I said," he roared, his nostrils flaring and his eyes bulging with anger, "*do you understand?*"

Two Leaf's stubborn, fierce pride kept him from being sensible. Gathering spit in his mouth again, he flung it at the officer's face. He must have bitten his tongue, because the saliva that hung from the officer's chin hairs was streaked with blood.

Hate, so strong it had an odor, emanated from the officer's body. "Hold him up. I'm not through with him."

Pain, absolute and uncompromised, tore Two Leaf from consciousness. The next thing he remembered, he was home, the doctor and his mother hovering over him . . .

Two sharp blasts from the train whistle sliced through his memory and his pain. Glancing at the observation car, he realized the officer, no longer a lieutenant, but a captain now, had gone. *So. You've come at last, you arrogant bastard.*

A grimace tugged at the corners of Jason's mouth. The man had aged well. Still tall and wide through the shoulders, he exuded power—and evil. His hair had faded with age. But that was all that had faded. Jason's memory was as keen and sharp as ever. The incident could just as well have happened yesterday.

Shoving himself away from the door, he made his way to his office. His thoughts were scabs, covering a hazardous gash. Now, the crusty sores cracked a little and the wound underneath started to bleed.

As he staggered inside, Buck greeted him. "Jesus. You look as though you've seen a ghost."

Jason sucked in his breath, just now realizing how much the memory had taken out of him. "More like the devil, Buck. More like the face of the devil."

Rachel scraped the remains of the roast beef lunch from the plates into a small bucket for Nancy's dog. Since Jessie had come down the flue, Rachel had tried to make Nancy's job a little easier. Although she seemed pleased with the help, she said little to Rachel.

"We were awfully busy, weren't we?" she asked genially.

Nancy shrugged. "No busier'n usual."

"I . . . I guess I'm just not used to it."

Nancy didn't answer. Rachel looked up and saw Nancy's gaze, black and hard, focused on something behind her.

"Nancy, what's—"

"Rachel?"

Rachel's heart plunged to the floor. Her hands shook so hard she almost dropped the dish she was holding. Swallowing repeatedly, she put the dish into the dishpan. She knew that voice. She'd hoped she'd never have to hear it again.

"Have you stooped to scullery work?"

She swallowed again and took a deep breath before turning to face her father-in-law. "Captain," she said, forcing a smile as she smoothed her hair from her face. "You're . . . you're finally here." Standing over the stove had caused her to perspire, and she knew her hair was in tight, messy ringlets near her face. "I thought you'd come sooner."

His arrogant gaze roamed over her. "Have you no embrace for a bereft father?"

Guilt wiggled over her skin. "Of course," she answered, wiping her hands on her apron as she met him on the other side of the counter.

Instead of hugging her, August Weber held her away from him. "Let me look at you."

At some point in her life, she'd have been embarrassed for looking unkempt in front of him. Even though she'd felt inferior from the day she'd married Jeremy, she'd always tried to keep herself neat and clean. Now, with her hair undoubtedly looking like a rat's nest and her apron soiled with the remnants of a beef and gravy lunch, she knew she looked like something the cat had dragged in. She didn't care, and that sent a tiny bit of elation scampering over her apprehension.

"You've changed, somehow."

Shock burst inside her, sending a shower of fear through her. Yes, she had changed, but surely he couldn't see her feelings.

"I . . . I don't see how—"

He gripped her to him, the embrace such a surprise she couldn't speak.

"I've lost my son, but I still have you."

Rachel frowned into his chest. This wasn't the man she'd known. The man she'd known hadn't spoken a civil word to her the entire two years she and Jeremy were married.

Pushing herself away, she asked, "What are you planning to do?"

He sighed, dropped into a chair, and ran his fingers through his faded red hair. For a fleeting moment he almost looked beaten. Glancing around the cafe, he appeared to take note of the few occupied tables toward the back. "Come here," he ordered softly.

Slowly, Rachel sat down across from him.

"Someone murdered my son . . . *your husband*, Rachel. And the law in this town is so damned incompetent, they haven't come up with a clue." He glanced furtively around the room. "I'm here to find the bastards who did this to us," he whispered fiercely. Sitting back in his chair, he studied her. "You've lived here a few months now. It pleases me to know you didn't run like a scared rabbit."

He leaned toward her as if they shared a common secret. "You've come to know these people. I can trust your judgment. We will catch the savages who killed our Jeremy."

Us . . . We . . . Our. She felt as if she were being sucked into a vortex, unable to pull herself free. Forcing down her panic, she said, "The sheriff here is quite competent. You must ask for his help."

August Weber bit out an angry expletive. "That sorry excuse for a lawman? Don't let him fool you, Rachel. I've already seen him." He waved his arm, a grandiose gesture. "He's an Indian lover. He'll be of no use to us."

Us, again. Dread made Rachel's skin crawl. He assumed she was his ally. And why wouldn't he? Thank the Lord he didn't know what turns her life had taken since Jeremy's death.

"But . . . but what did he tell you? Did you see his report?"

Weber snorted. "It looks plain to me. Indians did it; Indians will be punished."

She couldn't argue with him. She'd seen the Indians herself. She'd also seen Jason . . .

A fresh jolt of fear rocked her. She had to hide her feelings from this man. He couldn't know what she and Jason shared. He couldn't know the burning love she'd experienced with him—the kind that had never been ignited by her own husband. She hoped the captain hadn't already heard where she'd been working. Not because she was ashamed of it, but because she didn't want him to get too close to Jason. She knew that her father-in-law was the ultimate Indian hater, and to learn that she was working for one would undoubtedly send him into a rage.

"What of your own work in Washington? How long can you be away from it?"

He waved away her concern. "I've come to find my son's killer. I don't think it will take long, but I'm staying as long as it takes."

Rachel's heart dropped further. "Where . . . where are you staying?"

He gave her a calculated look. "I'd thought to stay with you, in the cottage where you and Jeremy lived."

Rachel's face reflected her dismay. "I . . . I'm not living there."

"So I understand. Why did you leave, Rachel?"

She gave him a shocked look. "How could I stay? I was there when it happened. I saw everything. I—"

"You *saw* everything?" He sat forward, obviously eager to hear more.

"No," she answered, suddenly flustered. "I didn't actually see it. I mean, I was there, but . . . but Jeremy had . . . had pushed me into a crawl space next to the fireplace. I . . . I couldn't see anything," she lied.

"We're going back out there, Rachel."

She bit back a sob. "I . . . I don't want to."

"You'll remember something, I'm sure of it."

Shaking her head, she panicked. "No, please . . . it won't do any good. I've been there. The sheriff questioned me there. He has it all in his report. There's nothing more to say . . ."

He grabbed her hands, squeezing them so tightly she almost cried out.

"If I didn't know better, my sweet daughter-in-law," he began, his voice low and menacing, "I'd think you weren't on my side."

Rachel gasped. Oh, God, she had to do the right thing for once in her life. *Get hold of yourself.* "All right," she acquiesced. "Of course, you're right. I'm . . . I'm sorry," she said, inwardly cringing at the words she'd promised Jason she'd never use again. She had to act her part. She couldn't let him know what was going on in her head or in her heart.

Weber smiled, but his eyes were still cold. "That's better. Now," he said as he stood, "let's visit Jeremy's grave, then take a trip to the cabin."

With a quick glance at Nancy, who appeared to be busy cleaning tables, Rachel took off her soiled apron and allowed her father-in-law to slip her cape over her shoulders. As they left the cafe, Captain Weber put his arm possessively around her waist.

Jason stood at the window and watched Rachel leave the cafe with her father-in-law. She appeared comfortable leaning against him, his arm around her, holding her close. Hate for Weber compounded his frustration and his sense of helplessness. Years ago he'd taught himself that hate weakened a man. That's why he'd put the entire incident with Weber in the back of his mind, where it wouldn't cripple him. Now, his insides were in turmoil again. The nausea that had coated his stomach earlier hadn't left.

Buck came up and stood beside him. "So, there they go," he said, his voice filled with disdain. "Father and widow of the deceased united at last."

Jason ignored the sarcasm, continuing to watch them as they crossed to the waiting buggy. "She came to the ranch with me the other night."

"Your folks were there?"

"Of course."

Buck swore. "Why would you parade her around under your father's nose?"

Jason continued to stare outside, even though the buggy that held Rachel and Captain Weber had clattered out of sight. "She's not responsible for what happened to me." He meant the words, but knowing how they'd parted, and discovering Weber's father on the scene, he wondered where her loyalty would ultimately lie. He hoped he knew; he couldn't be sure.

"Father was aloof."

Buck looked at him. "You're sure as hell not surprised, are you?"

Jason shook his head. "No, but," he repeated, "she's not responsible for June's condition or the scars on my chest. I didn't expect him to take his feelings out on her."

"It would have been *my* choice."

Jason ignored the comment, refusing to encourage Buck's hatred.

"Well," he urged, "what did he do?"

"It wasn't what he did. It was what he *didn't* do. He was barely civil, and he stayed cloistered in the library, refusing to come out when we left."

Buck stepped away, as if needing to put space between them. "You sound like you think she's innocent."

Jason glanced at the street, then looked back at Buck. "I don't know what she is. But I won't crucify her just because she married into the Weber family."

Buck snorted. "Your father would."

Jason gave Buck a look that could melt rock. "I know that's his emotional reaction. But, unlike you, dear friend, he doesn't go off to fight his enemy with his dick exposed." Because Weber had nearly whipped Jason to death fifteen years ago, no one even remotely related to August Weber would ever escape his father's hatred. But Jason knew he'd worked through it just as Jason had.

Buck put up his hands in self-defense. "Truce, all right?"

Jason sighed and raked his fingers through his hair. "Truce."

"I haven't seen June lately. She and Ma usually weave baskets together. Has she been sick?"

Jason stepped away from the window. "She wasn't too good the other night. She still drifts back to that day, forgetting that Molly has become a young woman." He remembered the faraway look in June's eyes when he'd discovered Rachel in her room. "I'm not sure it was a good idea to let Molly go so far away. When she was home, June was fine. Almost happy again."

Buck let out a rush of air. "Women have a hard time separating themselves from their young. June would have given her life to save her kid, even though it was forced on her by those damned soldiers."

Jason gave Buck a look of surprise. Now and then he saw snatches of a real human being beneath his arrogant, swaggering exterior.

"I think on some level she's thanked them for it, and forgiven them."

"For all your smug talk, I don't think *you've* forgiven them," Buck remarked.

"I thought I had," he answered, his voice filled with self-derision. "Until today."

He turned, pinning Buck with a hard look. "He's here to find the killer, you know."

Buck shrugged, returning Jason's harsh gaze. "That has nothing to do with me."

So you've said, over and over again. He studied his young friend. "None of us will escape his lash. Knowing Weber, innocent men will die—"

"And I should throw myself at his feet and admit to something I didn't do, just to save someone else?"

Frustration pummeled Jason's senses. Dammit, he wished he knew the truth.

Buck shrugged again, suddenly appearing extraordinarily unconcerned. "Maybe he's mellowed."

Jason laughed, a humorless, hollow sound. "You're dreaming." And so was he. He'd begun to care for Rachel, certain she felt something for him, as well. It was bad enough trying to fight the memory of a dead husband, and Karleen's pregnancy had served to bring all of Rachel's insecurities back to the surface. Now, with her dead husband's father stirring up trouble, he wondered how soon it would be before she reverted to the frightened, helpless woman she'd been when they first met.

Rachel stifled a yawn as she sat across from her father-in-law in the opulent dining room of the Corinthian Hotel. He'd summoned her to meet him for breakfast, and she tried hard to pretend she was interested in what he was saying. Of course, a man like August Weber always assumed a person was interested in his point of view, so he didn't pay too much attention to her distracted state. She'd never been in this room before; its elegance impressed her.

Pine Valley sported one of the finest hotels north of Sacramento. Chandeliers, dripping with crystal prisms, hung from carved ceiling medallions throughout the room. Tall, gilt-edged mirrors covered the inside wall, the reflection of light simulating another room, giving diners the feeling of illumination and space. The varnished, dark wood molding enhanced the brightly painted walls, contributing to the illusion of height. Rachel felt out of place.

"You're going to move from that squalid room and join me in a suite here, Rachel."

She pulled her gaze from her surroundings. "I . . . I couldn't, Captain, really. I'm . . . I'm perfectly comfortable at Ivy's."

He signaled the waiter. "I insist."

Rachel allowed him to order for her. She felt a panic so strong she couldn't have spoken without shaking, anyway. And she knew what was happening. He was an overwhelming man, hard to argue with. He needed to be in control. If she wasn't careful, she'd end up doing everything he asked before she even knew what had hit her.

"Please, Captain. I . . . I'd prefer to stay where I am. What difference does it make?" She swallowed a shudder as he reached across the table and took her hand.

"We're family, Rachel. We must stick together."

Pretending she needed to cough, she pulled her hand away and brought it delicately to her mouth. "I'd rather stay where I am, if you don't mind."

He gave her an arrogant grin. "But I *do* mind. Before I left, Sada told me to take good care of you."

She lowered her gaze to hide her eyes. Sada, Jeremy's mother, would hardly care what became of her. In fact, when the woman had been told of Jeremy's death, she'd probably raged for days that Rachel should have been killed instead of her son. *Sada the sadist.*

"Well, then we won't tell Sada, will we?" she said with forced levity.

His faded red mustache twitched. "You surprise me, Rachel."

Taking a sip of her water, she looked at him over the top of the glass. She swallowed, the icy water sliding down her throat. "I do?"

He sat back and examined her. "You seem different."

Not as easy to browbeat, you mean. She put her glass down and studied her hands. "I've had to learn to live on my own." She glanced up, giving him a somber look. "I never had, you know."

Resting his elbows on the table, he steepled his fingers before him and continued to study her. "I'm not sure I like you this way."

Anger, fresh and hot, erupted in the pit of her stomach. Of course he wouldn't like her this way. She hadn't prostrated herself before him.

She'd learned that her husband had fallen in love with another woman and had given that woman his seed. She'd learned that he'd been cruel to the Indians, refusing to replace their broken tools and who knows what else. She'd learned that his best friend was a nasty little rapist. And she'd learned that not all Indians were murdering savages.

He might not like it, but she wasn't going to wash his feet with her hair just to prove she hadn't changed.

"Life's been hard, Captain. A woman alone must find her strengths or she won't survive."

He quirked a bushy eyebrow at her. "*Are* you a woman alone, Rachel?"

Caution numbed her. As far as she knew, no one knew about her and Jason. Not even Ivy. Reigning in her fears, she answered, "I don't know what you mean. Of course I'm alone."

He gave her a hooded look. "Indeed."

The waiter brought their breakfast of biscuits, gravy and

scrambled eggs. The food, not nearly as good as Ivy's, gave Rachel a breather from her father-in-law's scrutiny. She forced herself to eat, somehow knowing that she was going to need her strength to keep her distance from this man. He was accustomed to getting his own way. He was forceful, vengeful, and, on a primitive level, almost hypnotic. He would stoop to any means to get what he wanted. And right now, Rachel knew he wanted her undying allegiance.

❧ *Chapter Thirteen* ❧

*F*inally able to get away from Weber, Rachel hurried back to the cafe, bracing herself against the cold, wet wind. As she passed Jason's office, she remembered Ivy's broom, the one with the long handle that she'd borrowed to sweep down the cobwebs from the corners. She stepped inside and listened to the sound of the clock. The quiet, empty room saddened her, although she realized that if Jason wasn't around, her father-in-law couldn't harass him. But if he wasn't around, it also meant he wasn't expecting any patients.

Echoing his mother's lament, Rachel wondered for the hundredth time why the citizens of Pine Valley were such fools. Jason was a wonderful doctor. She'd known that even before she'd fallen in love with him. She smiled grimly. That was one of the reasons she *had* fallen in love.

She grabbed the broom and went back outside. A commotion in front of the saloon stopped her progress toward the cafe. The sheepherders were in town, no doubt still drunk from the night before. Cautiously moving toward the fracas, she listened as the herdsmen taunted someone she couldn't see. The wretched drunks were obviously getting a good deal of pleasure at the other person's expense.

There were few people on the street besides the small mob, and those who did have to pass the disturbance gave it wide berth. Rachel intended to do the same. She'd heard the terrible stories about the herdsmen, and how, after a night of imbibing in "sheepherder's delight," they often disgraced the community by exposing themselves to anyone who passed by. But as she approached the noisy gang, she caught a glimpse of a brightly colored skirt.

Slowing her steps, she listened to the vulgarities being spewed at their reluctant captive, and heard the woman whimper. Briefly the circle around the woman opened and Rachel saw the person being jostled. She gasped, bringing her free hand over her mouth. It was the woman she'd met at the Gaspard home. June. Yes, it was June.

She looked around frantically, hoping to find some help. Everyone on the street had somehow disappeared. She thought about running to the sheriff but didn't think there was time.

Remembering the broom she clutched in her fist, she brought it up and gripped it with both hands. Sucking in a deep breath, she boldly stepped up to one of the drunken, swaying men and smacked the handle of the broom across his back and shoulders.

"Stop that!" Her heart lunged into her throat as the drunk turned and gave her a bleary stare.

"Say, fellas," he slurred, staring down at her. "We got another one here."

In their present state of intoxication, they were happy. They hadn't yet turned mean. It made her brave. "You leave that woman alone, do you hear me?"

They all laughed, the sound boisterous and raucous as they continued to fondle June.

Rachel lunged at them again, smacking them wildly with the broom. "Leave her alone, you . . . you noisy, obnoxious sots!" Her adrenaline flowed; she felt strong. And they continued to laugh at her as though what she was doing had absolutely no effect! Furious, she continued to pummel them. Their strength appeared to have been sucked from them by their lack of sleep and their level of intoxication.

Finally able to reach June, she gave the offenders one last blow, and heard the crack of the broomstick as it broke in two. She took June's arm and pulled her away from the staggering men, their guffaws echoing loudly behind her.

"It's all right," Rachel said quietly. "They're too drunk to hurt you."

Leaning on Rachel's arm, June shuddered and closed her eyes. She shook visibly, undoubtedly from fear as much as from the cold.

Rachel took June's face between her palms. "June? Do you remember me?"

Nodding, June gave her a relieved, wobbly smile. "I want to tell you something. I came to talk to you."

"To me?" Rachel sighed, remembering that June often wasn't completely coherent. She played along. "All right, but first let's get you inside where it's warm." She glanced around. June's cape lay crumpled in a puddle of mud. Briskly removing her own, Rachel spread it across June's shoulders.

"Can you walk?" June nodded, and they made their way slowly toward the cafe. "Did you come to town alone?"

"Joshua brought me in. I wanted to see you. Jason and Nicolas can't know." Her teeth chattered from the cold as she talked.

Rachel closed her eyes and wondered who June thought she was talking to. "Joshua brought you in? Does . . . did his mother know you were coming?"

"Oh, no." June shook her head emphatically. "Anna doesn't let me come to town without her or Sky or Shy Fawn."

Oh, Lord, then why was she here? "Where's Joshua?"

A tiny whimper slipped from June's mouth. "He and Dusty—oh, dear. I'm not supposed to tell."

Rachel rolled her eyes. What a mess. "Come," she ordered softly. "The cafe is right around the corner. At least we can get you in out of the cold."

Warmth from the stove laved over them as they stepped inside.

"Well, Lord have mercy," Ivy sputtered as she hurried toward them, wiping her hands on her apron. "What happened?"

Rachel led June to the stove and gently pushed her into a chair. "She was being harassed by some of those horrid, drunken sheepherders," she answered, resting the broken broom against the stove.

Ivy picked up the short length of broom. "What happened to this?"

Rachel felt herself blush. "I . . . I'm afraid I used it on the . . . ah . . . those men."

Ivy gazed down at the jagged edges of the handle and chuckled. "I'll bet they were a mite surprised." Still smiling, she put the broom handle back against the stove. Her good humor faded when she glanced back at June.

Taking the woman's hands and squeezing them between her own, she asked, "June, honey? What're you doin' in town?"

June's entire body shook as she stared at the stove.

"Joshua brought her in. She said she wanted to see *me*. Obviously she thinks I'm someone else. And," Rachel added, "from the sound of things, the trip wasn't okayed by Mrs. Gaspard."

Ivy clucked. "Well, of course it wasn't. June doesn't come to town without one of the adults. That little Josh," she said, shaking her head. "He's a pistol, that one."

Rachel hurried into the kitchen and fixed a cup of tea, stirring a spoonful of honey into it. She brought it back and knelt beside June again.

"Here," she said, taking June's hands and wrapping them around the warm cup. "Drink this, June."

June clasped the cup, brought it to her lips and took jerky sips. She blinked and sighed, still staring at the fire that flickered behind the glass.

"Have you known June long, Ivy?" Rachel ventured.

Ivy smoothed June's hair away from her forehead. "She was already a young lady when I moved here, weren't you, dear?"

A tiny smile flitted about June's mouth. "Ivy's my friend," she said, glancing at Rachel.

Rachel fixed her gaze on June's pretty, youthful face. The woman didn't look any older than twenty. Except for the scar on her cheek, her face was unlined, smooth as silk. Her coloring was far different from any Rachel had ever seen before. While Jessie's and Nancy's complexions were a ruddy brown, June's was almost pale and had a hint of orchid beneath it. She was exquisite.

Jason hadn't been willing to tell her what June had been through. She decided to test Ivy. "Ivy," she began, "what happened to her?"

A gust of air hit the trio as they huddled around the stove. Rachel glanced at the door and found her gaze pierced by a scowling Nicolas Gaspard and an equally angry Jason.

They strode to the stove. "What in the hell happened here?" Jason's father rumbled.

Rachel shuddered. No preamble, no niceties.

"Oh," Ivy said, fussing with June's hair, "them danged drunken sheepherders was pesterin' June."

Giving them a lopsided smile, she grabbed the broken broom and held it toward the men. "Rachel broke my broom on 'em."

Rachel hadn't found her voice, but she felt herself flush deeper when both men turned and gaped at her.

Jason looked incredulous. "You hit the men with a broom?"

She shrugged, giving him a beseeching look. "I . . . I couldn't just let them maul her."

Nicolas Gaspard's gaze moved over her, softening slightly at her comment. Then, with a gentleness that didn't seem to fit him, he hunkered down in front of June. "Why did you come to town, June?"

She looked up and smiled at him. "I wanted to talk to her."

He glanced up at Rachel, then away. "Joshua shouldn't have brought you," he answered.

"But I wanted to tell her that—"

"It's all right, June," he interrupted, helping her to her feet. "We'll talk about it later. I have an errand to run, but Jason will take you home."

June allowed him to steer her toward the door. Once

there, she stopped and turned. "It's not your fault, you know."

Rachel's insides fluttered. She glanced at Jason, whose features were unreadable. She had no idea what the woman was talking about. The message, although apparently meant to put her at ease, only alarmed her further.

She watched them leave, wistfully eyeing Jason's strong, wide shoulders. She glanced at Ivy's closed expression.

"What did she mean? What's not my fault?"

Ivy shook her head and went behind the counter. "Prob'ly thought you were someone else, dear."

Rachel frowned. "Yes," she answered slowly. "That's what I thought, too." But she wasn't convinced. Even though the message had made no sense, Rachel wasn't convinced June had mistaken her for someone else.

She looked at the clock. It was almost ten. With Jessie still out sick, Rachel had promised to help with the lunch crowd, but she had time to hurry over to Jason's office and see that things were dusted and picked up.

"I'll be back before eleven, Ivy." She went to pull on her cape, then remembered she'd loaned it to June. Glancing at the gray light that filtered in through the window, she knew it was still cold and wet outside. "I'm borrowing your cape," she called as she pulled it off the coatrack and hurried outside.

Rachel added another piece of wood to the stove, then warmed her hands over the heat. It hadn't taken long to straighten things up, she thought, looking around the empty room. Obviously there hadn't been much business. Her heart dipped, aching for Jason. Smiling ruefully, she realized that Jason didn't mourn for his practice at all. He seemed to know that in time he'd be accepted for who he was and what he knew.

As she turned to put away some fresh linen, she heard the bell tinkle over the office door. Silently hoping it was Jason, she smoothed down the front of her skirt and hurried into the other room. Her stomach dropped.

"Captain," she said, swallowing her disappointment. "What are you doing here?"

August Weber shut the door behind him, his presence filling the room. Looking around with disdain, he answered, "I could ask you the same question."

Rachel swallowed hard. "I . . . I came in to straighten up, that's all."

"You're a scullery maid for the half-breed, as well?"

She swallowed again, hating the fear this man instilled in her, and hating herself for weakening when he was around. "I . . . I don't know what you mean."

He tossed his cap on the desk, uttering a deep sigh. "I'm disappointed in you, Rachel." He slapped his gloves against his palm, studying her carefully. "I know why you're here."

Fresh fear careened through her. "You . . . you do?"

He nodded, his expression full of distaste. "You've been working for the breed."

Rachel's first instinct was to deny it. It must have shown on her face.

"Don't cross me, girl. I did some checking when I got into town. It's inconceivable to me that you, of all people, would lower yourself to such depths. Have you forgotten everything from your past? Have you forgotten just what savages like this half-breed did to your family?"

Rachel looked away. No, she hadn't forgotten. But if she had, he would have happily reminded her of it—as he was doing now. Her uncle had done the same thing—reminded her how much she hated Indians, constantly reinforcing her hatred and her fear.

"I demand that you quit. It's disgusting," her father-in-law added, his face a mask of disdain. "You will stop this nonsense right now."

She was suddenly grateful he had such an overbearing personality. His audacity was infuriating. She had no intentions of quitting just because he wanted her to. "No." It came out strong, and she was proud of herself.

"You will quit *now*."

Rachel clenched her fists. "No. I needed . . . I need the money." Oh, *God*, she hoped she could stay strong.

"For what?" he roared.

His arrogance continued to get to her. She felt strength from inside flow through her limbs. "To pay Jeremy's debts."

His face didn't change, but his eyes darkened imperceptibly. "What kind of debts?"

She sucked in a deep breath and busied herself by straightening Jason's desk. "I don't think you want to know."

His expression was hooded. "I'll be the judge of that."

She felt her knees weaken, so she leaned against the desk. "Jeremy left gambling debts. He—"

"What?" he roared again.

His anger fed hers. "He left enormous debts all over town. He even took out a loan against his army pay, and gambled it all away at the saloon."

He swore. "What rubbish. Jeremy wouldn't squander his money that way."

Rachel felt her anger grow. "Well, he did. And try as I might, I couldn't get a job anywhere else in this town. The . . . the doctor is the only one who even offered me one. And I took it. I didn't care where I worked," she added, not bothering to tell him she hadn't known Jason was an Indian when she'd taken the job, "as long as I got paid."

Weber's narrow gaze was filled with scorn. "You voluntarily went to work for the same kind of person who *murdered* all of your loved ones?"

She forced her gaze to his. She wouldn't be cowed, not anymore. "Indians are different. They aren't lumped into a group. They're different, just like we are."

Weber spat into the spittoon. "You can't believe that."

"But I do," she argued, suddenly feeling calm.

He gave her a look of pure disgust. "What's happened to you?"

I've grown. I've come to my senses. I've come to realize just how much I want you and the rest of Jeremy's family out of my life. "I've . . . I've grown," is all she said.

He appeared to take stock of the room, but Rachel was sure he was calculating what to say next. She was right.

"Where are these supposed debts, and how much are they?"

She walked away, needing to keep a good distance between them. Once he heard, she wasn't sure she'd be safe from his wrath. "He . . . I . . . the owner of the saloon, Mr. Justice, gave me Jeremy's IOU." She paused, wishing she didn't have to continue. "It was for three thousand dollars."

"What? Impossible!"

She clutched her fingers into her skirt, ignoring the fact that she was wrinkling the fabric. "I saw his signature."

Weber crossed to the window and stared outside. "And the other?"

"The banker. He owed him a thousand dollars." She didn't add that Jeremy had stolen her brooch, but she wanted to.

"There has to be some mistake. Jeremy wouldn't have gambled away his money."

"There is no mistake. I've . . . I've come to learn many things—"

"*You've* come to learn," he snarled. "You are nothing but a thankless, heartless little nobody. What you've learned means less to me than cow dung."

Rachel stepped backward, almost feeling his hatred. She didn't answer him; she wasn't sure she could.

He turned, giving her the full effect of his derision. "Have you any idea why Jeremy married you?"

Her stomach caved in a little, but she refused to show her feelings. Again, she didn't answer him. She'd learned too much about her late husband to be surprised at anything her father-in-law told her.

"Do you?" he ground out.

Finally, she shook her head.

"He was blackmailed into it."

Her stomach caved in a little more. Her feelings must have been evident, for her father-in-law's face broke into a sinister, snarling grin.

"You surely didn't think it was because he *loved* you, did you? You? A washed-out thing with the spirit of a limp dishrag?"

The sick feeling in her stomach spread, leaving her hurting and nauseous. Blackmailed? She'd never dreamed—

"What . . . what do you mean, blackmailed?" She could barely hear her own voice and was surprised she could speak at all.

Weber's eyes glowed triumphantly. "Your precious uncle was so anxious to get rid of you," he began, "he told Sada and me that if Jeremy didn't marry you and take you off his hands, he'd tell the entire countryside that Jeremy had been responsible for Lulu Morrisey's death."

A tiny laugh escaped Rachel's mouth before she could stop it. "How could he possibly threaten you with something like that?"

Weber didn't answer, but continued to glare at her from beneath his tufty, faded eyebrows.

Rachel stared, too. "Unless," she said, continuing softly, "unless it was the truth." He didn't respond. That, in itself, was more of an answer than she'd have wished for.

She thought back to Lulu's death. Lulu, the beautiful daughter of a local merchant, had died in her family's home shortly before Christmas one year, the victim of a mysterious accident. At least that's what Rachel had been told. Her uncle had taken the body to his office. She'd had a closed casket. Everyone at the funeral had mourned poor, sweet Lulu.

"What . . . what happened?"

"How in the hell do I know what happened?" he roared.

"But . . . but if it was a lie, why did you let my uncle get away with it?"

"That's hardly important now, is it?"

She suddenly knew with utter clarity that somehow Jeremy had been involved in Lulu's death. Staring off into space, she saw again the stilted, sullen face of her husband on their wedding day. She vividly remembered her puzzlement and shame when he didn't come to the marriage bed, and every day after that she'd tried to pretend they were living together like any normal married couple . . . Even after he'd left for California, she followed the lead of other army wives, meeting to commiserate over their temporary "widowhood" and pretending her problems were the same as theirs.

She couldn't have dreamed up a situation like this one. It was too melodramatic, too contrived—too hurt-filled.

"He must have been there when she died," she finally said, unaware that she'd spoken aloud.

"*That* isn't the issue. I wanted in the worst way to punish your uncle for what he did to my family. Then the old goat died before I had a chance to do anything at all. But," he added with a wistful sigh, "I knew he'd found something that implicated Jeremy. Unlike his mother, I knew he wasn't perfect." His voice was raspy with remembrance. "But we'd had such plans for him." His voice turned bitter, resentful. "And they sure as hell didn't involve *you*."

Rachel felt his hatred. She'd never had a real marriage, but his words hurt anyway, as he'd meant them to. No woman wanted to hear that her husband was forced into marriage, that she could never have hoped he would learn to love her.

What a foolish, starry-eyed girl she'd been! She'd been used and abused by her aunt and uncle, by Jeremy's parents, and by Jeremy himself, and she hadn't had the sense to fight back.

She nervously straightened Jason's desk. "If you're through with me, then let me finish my work."

Weber removed his cap from the desk, then caught her by surprise by grabbing her arm. She gasped, but hid her fear.

"Don't think this ends things between us, girl." He stared at her, attempting to frighten her with his expression. Rachel stared back, no longer intimidated. But she sensed that it would not be wise to infuriate him further.

"I don't want to fight with you, Captain. I just want to get on with my life."

His grip didn't loosen. "If you don't help me find my son's murderer, you're as guilty as the murderer himself."

Swallowing her fear, she looked him in the eye. "If I could remember anything else, I'd tell you."

He studied her. "I wish I could believe that."

"But why can't you?"

He continued to scrutinize her. "There's something in your behavior that makes me think you're not telling me the entire truth, Rachel."

She shrugged out of his grip. "I want to find Jeremy's killer as much as you do. Oh, *God!* I've wracked my brain trying to remember something that might trigger a memory. What happened that morning haunts me almost every night, and I wake up, wondering when it will stop. Trust me, Captain," she added, her voice shaky with feeling, "I want an end to this as much as you do."

Heaving a great sigh, he pulled on his gloves and walked to the door. "I'm convinced," he said, "at least for now. My investigation goes into full swing tomorrow. Don't try to hide from me, Rachel. I may need your assistance."

After he'd left, Rachel sagged against the desk. She wished she could find some way to help him. It would send him on his way that much faster. There was no reason for her to be afraid of his digging into the crime. Jason had nothing to hide; she knew that. And if Jason wasn't involved, an investigation shouldn't bother her.

The thing that worried her was that she knew how August Weber felt about Indians. If he ever found the one responsible for murdering his precious son, he wouldn't just kill him. He'd make him suffer, long and hard, before he allowed the savage the blissful luxury of death.

She went back to straightening the linen in the closet and had almost finished when the bell above the office door tinkled again. Her spirits sinking, she walked slowly back into the other room, fully expecting to see her father-in-law.

Her pulse fluttered and warmth burst through her when she saw Jason leaning over his desk, going through the stack of files. He looked tired as he massaged his neck.

Although she'd just seen him, they hadn't talked since before her father-in-law had come to town. She'd left him, needing to be alone with her discovery of Karleen's pregnancy. But it hadn't taken long for her to realize that Karleen's baby had nothing to do with her or the life she had now.

Abruptly, as though just realizing she was there, he raised his head and looked at her. His expression was guarded before he turned his gaze back to the papers on his desk.

"What are you doing here?"

She swallowed her disappointment. His greeting had not mirrored her own feelings. She guessed she couldn't blame him. After all, she knew she'd hurt him when she left, telling him she needed some time alone.

"Is . . . is June all right?"

"June's fine. She's been through a hell of lot more than that." He glanced at her. "What are you doing here?" he repeated.

"I . . . I thought I should at least do a little cleaning—"

"That's not necessary," he interrupted. "Nothing has been disturbed because I haven't had any patients."

A fresh ache settled around her heart. Maybe if she told him about her father-in-law's arrival, he'd realize that was why she'd been preoccupied. The fact that Karleen was carrying Jeremy's baby no longer bothered her. It was history, and she wasn't going to let it affect the rest of her life.

"My . . . my father-in-law is in town."

Although there was no way he couldn't have heard her, he didn't react at all.

She cleared her throat. "I . . . I've been expecting him. He's taking over the investigation from the marshal. He—" She bit her lip nervously. "He's staying until he finds out who killed Jeremy." She watched Jason and frowned. He appeared utterly disinterested. "I . . . I mean, once he's uncovered the killers, he'll leave and . . . and things will be back to normal."

He looked up at her from his desk, quirked an eyebrow at her but said nothing.

"I mean, the . . . the marshal hasn't found any new clues. Captain Weber just wants to help. You can't blame him for that." Now, it sounded as if she didn't believe the marshal could do the job by himself. Of course, she had to admit nothing had been unearthed . . .

"Why wouldn't Marshal Tully want him to help, Jason? Oh," she added, carrying on this ridiculous one-sided conversation, "I know Captain Weber isn't a very personable man. I should know that better than anyone. He never liked me, not from the very first day. It's even worse now. But . . . but I still feel as though I should help him. I mean, why not? If I do, maybe he'll leave sooner."

Jason slammed the chart on the desk and leaned back in his chair. "Are you finished?"

She blinked. "What?"

"Are you finished defending your father-in-law, *and* your reasons for not being at your job?"

"Well, I—"

"Because if you are, then leave. One of my motives for hiring you was because I felt sorry for you. I got along for years without any help, and I can surely struggle through without yours now."

She forced down the nausea that swirled in her stomach. If he was just trying to hurt her, he was succeeding. "I don't believe you," she said softly.

He looked at her, his heavy-lidded gaze moving arrogantly over her. "It's true." Looking away, he added, "Actually, the main reason I hired you was to keep an eye on you. Your husband did some despicable things to my people, Mrs. Weber. I had to make sure you didn't come to continue the reign of terror."

The blood drained from her face, and she groped behind her for a chair. Finding one, she sank into it. "How could you possibly believe that I would hurt anyone?"

He snorted. "A marriage isn't made between a fox and a hare, Rachel."

She glanced away, hating the look of hostility she saw in his eyes. "I'd do anything to make up for what Jeremy did to your people, Jason. Leaving them with broken and unusable equipment was an unprincipled—"

He laughed, a harsh, nasty sound. "That's all you think he did to them?"

Dread coated her stomach further. "I . . . I don't know what else he did. No one—"

"No one told you? Well," he snarled, "let me fill you in." He leaned back in his chair, the muscles in his jaw working furiously. "Each time he received supplies for the reservation, he took most of them and sold them to the squatters."

She swallowed, her stomach now in knots. "Squatters?"

"Yes, squatters. Trashy Whites who *illegally* build shacks on the edges of reservation land, hunt and kill reservation livestock, beg, borrow, steal, and, if they must, buy anything that's been earmarked for the reservation Indians."

Rachel knew he was telling her the truth. What hurt was that he seemed to enjoy punishing her. She focused her gaze on her hands, which were clasped tightly in her lap.

"Besides you, your father-in-law, and Karleen Justice, the only other people in this entire valley who will miss Jeremy Weber are the squatters." His voice was soft, but tinged with disgust.

She didn't defend herself. She would sound shallow and foolish to exclaim that she wouldn't miss her husband, even though she realized it was true. Any feelings she might have had for Jeremy vanished when she discovered his deceit.

"That may all be true," she began, hoping her emotions didn't show. "And I wish more than anything that I could make it up to all those who've suffered because of him. I want you to believe that, Jason."

She tried to look at him, but seeing his hatred made tears press against the backs of her eyes. She blinked and looked away. "But Captain Weber is here. There's nothing I can do about it. And he wants me to help him find Jeremy's killer. He may be no better than his son. Maybe he's worse. I don't know. But if I help him, it's possible that together we can get to the bottom of this. Isn't that what we all want? To solve the murders and get on with our lives?"

He laughed, a derisive sound that spattered over her skin like hot fat.

"You do that, Rachel." He came out from behind the desk like a cat and suddenly was in front of her, his hands on the arms of her chair, his face close to hers. "You and that . . . that arrogant father-in-law of yours solve the crime." He continued to stare at her, studying her. "But just remember," he added, cupping her chin in his hand and squeezing lightly, "just remember that when you find the truth, make sure it's really the truth, and not just what August Weber wants it to be."

Rachel's heart hadn't stopped pounding. Confused by Jason's behavior, she merely stared at him. "There's only one truth, Jason."

He moved away from her, snorting a sarcastic laugh. "Oh, that's what you think. Years ago," he said, facing her again, "my father told me that the white man's truth is many shades of gray. It's never the same, time after time. It's what he wants it to be, and he'll change it to suit him."

She clutched the arms of the chair. "Why would Captain Weber lie about the truth?"

He gave her a derisive half-grin. "The apple doesn't fall far from the tree, Rachel."

Everything she'd just learned about Jeremy, plus all that she already knew, was vivid in her mind. Of course Jason was right. She knew what her father-in-law was. He was arrogant, self-serving, pompous, and felt he was superior to almost anyone else on the face of the earth. And he'd coldly told her to her face that Jeremy had been forced to marry her. But he was also a father who'd lost his only son. If she had any sympathy for him at all, it was because of that.

"I can assure you, Dr. Gaspard," she said, "that I will not be swayed by my father-in-law's blatant prejudices."

He gave her a grim look. "But you can't turn your back on him, can you?"

Sucking in air, she whispered, "No. I can't turn my back on him."

He strode to the coat tree and gave Ivy's cape a violent

tug. "Here," he grumbled, tossing the cape into her lap. "I don't need you anymore."

Pressing her fist against her mouth, she stood, the cape gripped in her numb fingers. She didn't know what she could do. It was almost as if he were making her choose between him and the captain. For some inexplicable reason, Jason seemed to have more hatred for her father-in-law than he did for her late husband.

As she stepped out onto the wooden sidewalk, she barely felt the cold wind whistling through her clothing. Jason's attitude didn't make any sense to her. She knew he wasn't guilty. Trudging toward the cafe, she began to wonder if maybe he knew something about the morning of Jeremy's murder that he wasn't willing to share with her. She couldn't imagine any other reason why he'd be so very angry with her.

❦ *Chapter Fourteen* ❦

*T*he next morning, a cold, icy rain pelted the windows and rooftops. Rachel dressed under her covers, straightened up her room, then hurried into the cafe kitchen and started a fire in the stove. She tied Ivy's apron around her middle and made coffee. Shivering, she glanced at the window where silvery rods of rain hit the pane.

She looked at the clock. It was early; Ivy's room was still quiet. Well, she thought, stifling a yawn, at least someone could sleep. Her night had been punctuated with vivid dreams of Jeremy's murder—again. Then, when she'd finally awakened and been unable to get back to sleep, she'd thought about her confrontation with Jason. His words still stung. She had thought that he, of all people, would understand her need to help her father-in-law. Certainly there was no argument that it was best for everyone if Jeremy's killer was found and punished. It was the only way they could all get on with their lives.

An ache formed around her heart. She'd hoped and dreamed that "the rest of her life" would involve Jason. After yesterday, her fantasies and illusions were shattered. That would teach her to dream, wouldn't it?

The cafe door opened, setting off the bell that hung over the molding. Startled, Rachel crept to the pass-through window and looked out into the large room. A young boy, no more than seven or eight, stood near the stove, warming his hands.

"Yes?" She wondered what on earth a young child was

doing out in such inclement weather so early in the morning. Stepping into the cafe, she asked, "Is there something I can do for you?"

He swung around, his eyes wide and his face pale. Silently, he handed her a piece of paper then made tracks for the door.

Puzzled, she watched him leave then slowly turned back to the stove. Her name was printed on the front of the paper in bold, square letters.

As she opened it, before she'd even read it, a queer sensation made her stomach dip. The note, printed with the same standard lettering, read: "If you want to find out who killed your husband, follow the boy. Come now, and come alone."

A stirring of fear and excitement coursed through her. If she could solve the mystery, her father-in-law would be on a train back to Washington—and out of her life.

Oh, she thought, fresh fear niggling her spine, who was she kidding? As wonderful as that sounded, the thought of actually secretly meeting someone she didn't know scared her to death. She had to face it. She wasn't that brave. The author of the note could be anyone. It could even be Jeremy's murderer. No, she thought, shuddering violently, she wasn't that brave, at all.

Crumpling the note in her fist, she shoved it into Ivy's apron pocket and went back into the kitchen. Her gaze went to the window again. The rain hadn't abated. She wondered if the boy had been told to wait for her until she came. If so, maybe she should go. After all, the thought of a small boy catching pneumonia because of her made her feel awful.

Rolling her eyes, she scolded herself for even thinking about going. She tried to take her mind off the note by doing some of the breakfast preparation, but she couldn't concentrate.

Glancing at the clock again, she realized that if she didn't make up her mind one way or the other very soon, Ivy would be up and the girls would be here to start breakfast. Then, if she really wanted to go, it would be too late.

She stepped to the window and, cupping out the dim light

from inside, peered into the wet darkness. Her heart jumped into her throat. There was a buggy out there! And that poor little child was standing in the rain, as if she'd told him she'd be along in a minute.

It was ridiculous—no, *foolish*—to get into a strange buggy to meet someone she didn't even know. Even though she'd become more spirited these past few months, she wasn't *that* brave or foolhardy.

To even think about going was crazy. She couldn't do anything by herself anyway. And no doubt someone was out there, watching to see that she didn't try to contact anyone, if she *did* decide to go. She'd never go off into the unknown by herself. But the note had said to come alone. Come alone . . . Or what? Or she'd be sorry? Did they want her to come alone because . . . because they didn't want any witnesses?

She tried to swallow the lump in her throat. *Now, don't get melodramatic, Rachel Kathleen. It's not your nature.* Right. She was usually so practical. Peering out the window again, she noticed the buggy was still there—as was the poor, wet, cold boy.

She'd go. Every nerve in her body tingled with fear and her limbs shook at her decision, but she closed her eyes and forced her body to respond. Slowly, she felt herself go calm. The decision made, she pulled off Ivy's apron and draped it over the back of a chair. Hurrying into the cafe, she grabbed Ivy's cloak off the coat tree and rushed outside. The wet, icy wind assaulted her, but she hardly felt it. Her mind was too busy trying to get her body to act like a single entity instead of flying into a thousand unidentifiable pieces—as it wanted to.

The poor child who had handed her the note still stood beside the buggy. Hunching against the cold rain, he opened the door and motioned her inside.

With trepidation filling her chest, she stepped into the buggy and wrapped herself in the warm blanket provided for her.

All during the ride, she told herself what a fool she was for playing this little game with someone she didn't know.

There was no reason to believe she could trust this person— a person who didn't have the decency to sign his name to a note demanding that she meet him.

The buggy stopped. Suddenly she cursed herself for being so absorbed in her thoughts that she hadn't watched where they were going. Rachel looked outside. They were in front of a tiny cabin that stood alone in the night. But there was smoke chugging from the chimney, and a warm light flickered at the window.

Filling her lungs with cold air, she threw off the warm blanket and opened the door. She lifted the hood of Ivy's cape over her hair and stepped to the ground. Her legs were so numb they felt like tree stumps.

The buggy pulled away immediately, deserting her in the driving rain. Calling out to the driver, she noticed it was the child who'd delivered the note.

"Little boy, who am I supposed to meet?"

He continued to drive on; he didn't even look back.

Pulling her cape tightly around her, she stepped to the cabin door and knocked. Nothing. Her heart pumping in her ears, she knocked again. Still no answer.

With more nerve than sense, she lifted the latch and discovered the door wasn't fastened from the inside. Pushing it open slowly, she felt the dry warmth of the room envelop her. She quickly shut the door behind her so no more warm air would escape, then glanced around the room. It was empty.

Puzzled, she walked slowly toward the fireplace, momentarily hypnotized by the hot orange and yellow flames. There was an overstuffed chair by the fire. Next to it stood a table on which she found a small carafe and a cup and saucer. A piece of paper was tented next to the carafe. She picked it up and read:

"Please be comfortable. The coffee is strong, but do not be concerned. It isn't tainted."

She frowned at the last remark. *It isn't tainted? Well*, she thought a bit sarcastically, *thank you so much for putting my mind at ease*. Trusting fool that she was, *that* thought hadn't entered her head.

She lifted off her cape, draping it over the back of the chair to let it dry, then sat down. Huddling in the chair, she glanced around the room again. This was odd. Someone had told her to meet them here, threatened her to come alone, then, like the host of a fine house, offered her coffee. Only yesterday she'd thought her life had taken a melodramatic turn. Today, she was *certain* of it.

Although the fire made the room seem warm and cozy, she noticed that there was only one window in the cabin. It was very small, and crisscrossed with metal stiles. Even during the brightest daylight, the room would be dim and gray.

She looked around, hoping to find a clock. There was nothing on the walls or on the fireplace mantel. And the only furniture in the room was the chair she sat in and the table next to it.

The rain had slackened, no longer beating against the pane. She fidgeted in the chair, finally getting up and going to the window. She wasn't even sure where she was. Daylight met the gloomy darkness of the eastern sky, and she could just make out the railroad tracks. She craned her neck, looking both ways out the window. No one was coming. She wasn't sure if she was distressed or relieved.

As she turned, she noticed a funnel of smoke drifting into the room from the fireplace. Alarmed, she moved toward the smoke, and by the time she'd made it back to the chair, the room was already filled with gray haze. It stung her eyes and attacked her nostrils, causing her to cough. Anxious to get out, she scrambled to the door, lifted the latch, and tried to pull the door open. It wouldn't budge. It was stuck. *Or locked from the outside*.

Frantically, she pulled on the door, coughing as the smoke infiltrated her lungs. It was useless. It wouldn't open. Falling to her knees, she covered her face with the sleeve of her blouse, trying to filter out the smoke. The room was hazy with it, obliterating everything.

She knew she had to keep calm. No one at the cafe even knew where she was. It had been a mistake to come, she knew that now. It didn't matter if this had been accidental or intentional. It was too late.

Crouching on the floor, she crawled to the chair to retrieve her cape. Maybe if she hid beneath it, she could continue to breathe a while longer. The smoke scorched her throat and her lungs, and she took small, short breaths, attempting to use her skirt as a sieve to cleanse the air.

Feeling her way across the floor, she decided against recovering her cloak. Smoke was now pouring into the room from the fireplace, and she would be a fool to move toward it rather than away from it. She dropped to her stomach and began pulling herself along the rough wooden planking. Shards of wood pierced her hands, but she ignored the sting and continued to move away from the intensity of the smoke.

Each breath became more painful, more labored. She was crying—she could tell. Tears . . . tears hit her hands. But it was all right to cry now, for it wasn't fair. Dying wasn't fair. She coughed again, gasping for air that wasn't there. *Too stubborn to roll up and die, aren't you?* Yes, she thought. Too stubborn.

Willing herself to move into the far corner of the cabin, she pressed on, feeling her way along the hard wooden floor.

Jason strode into the cafe, blowing on his hands and rubbing them together to warm them. He walked directly to the stove. Ivy was sitting at a table with Bram Justice, her face pinched with worry.

"Morning, Ivy, Bram. Something wrong?"

"Oh, Jason, I'm glad you're here," Ivy answered, getting up to meet him. "You seen Rachel lately?"

Memory of their volatile meeting the day before stirred him, but he kept his feelings hidden. "I saw her yesterday. Why?"

Clucking her tongue nervously, Ivy paced in front of him. "Well, she ain't in her room, and it looks to me like she ain't been there all night."

"I suggested that perhaps she'd stayed at the Corinthian with Captain Weber," Justice offered.

"Reasonable," Jason answered, "but I stopped there on my way over here to check on one of the waiters. Weber was in the dining room, but he was alone."

"Oh, merciful heaven," Ivy murmured. "Where could that girl be?"

Jason frowned. "That's odd. Are you sure she didn't leave you a note or something?" For some unknown reason, fear germinated in his chest.

Ivy shook her head. "I've checked everywhere." Shoving her hands into her apron pockets, she pulled out a crumpled piece of paper. She absently smoothed it out and glanced at it, moving it away from her face so she could read it. She shook her head.

"Jason," she asked, "what does this say? I don't have my spectacles on me."

Jason plucked it from her fingers and read it aloud. " 'If you want to know who killed your husband, follow the boy.' " He glanced at Ivy, their eyes meeting over the top of the paper. She looked puzzled.

"That's it? That's all it says?"

Jason shook his head and glared down at the strong, boxy print. The germ of fear erupted in his chest. "It also says, 'Come now, and—' "

"And? And what?" she almost shrieked.

" '—and come alone.' "

"What? What?" Ivy paled and grabbed back the note, held it at arm's length and tried to read it herself.

Jason raked his fingers through his hair. "She wouldn't go off with someone she doesn't even know, would she?"

Ivy shook her head violently. "No. No. She wouldn't. She wouldn't—would she?"

Jason thought back to their heated conversation the day before. She'd been so damned determined to discover who killed her blasted husband. Normally, he didn't think she'd go off half-cocked, but after yesterday, after everything she'd said to him, he was no longer so sure. She just might jump at the chance to prove she meant what she'd said. His own words to her lashed his memory again, and the bitter, destructive taste of revenge filled him.

Taking the note back from Ivy, he reread it. "What boy is this?"

"I don't know," she said, her voice on the verge of hysteria. "I don't know at all." She gasped, looking toward the door. "Earl has to know. Maybe he can think. Oh, dadgumit, I just can't *think.*"

Bram Justice shrugged into his coat. "Maybe I can help. I'll check down at the stable. Isn't there an orphan lad down there who can't speak?"

Jason turned, surprised at the saloon keeper's offer. "Yes, Willy. Thanks, Bram. That's good of you. It would have been easy for someone to have him deliver such a note. Willy can't talk and he doesn't read or write. The perfect delivery boy."

Nancy and Jessie came in, puzzled at the commotion until Ivy herded them into the kitchen, her voice worried as she tried to explain what had happened.

Jason paced in front of the stove. Dammit, he felt so *useless.* He stared outside, knowing he couldn't just pace. If something had happened to her, he'd never forgive himself. He'd thrown so many angry words at her yesterday, heaping his hurt on her because she felt the need to stand by her father-in-law. He'd wanted to tell her why he hated the man. But he wanted her to discover it herself. He didn't want her pity, and he didn't want her disbelief. But he *had* wanted to hurt her for her loyalty to the bastard.

Tully rushed into the cafe, his cheeks rosy above his oversized mustache. "Mornin', Doc."

He nodded absently and buttoned up his sheepskin jacket. "Rachel's disappeared."

Tully's expression suddenly changed. "What? What do ya mean, she's disappeared?"

Jason handed him the note. He watched Tully's face change again.

"Jee-hoshaphat," he muttered. "If you weren't busy, I was gonna have you come with me to that empty shack out near the junction. It's smokin'. Thought we'd take a look-see." Shaking his head, his eyes still focused on the note, he gave a stunned whistle through his teeth.

"Bram Justice went over to the stable to find Willy. Hopefully he's the one who delivered the note."

Tully studied Jason. "You think Buck's behind this?"

Jason went cold. That hadn't occurred to him. "Does that sound like Buck to you?"

Tully uttered a huge sigh. "Nope, not really." He took off his hat and scratched his head. "Dammit, sometimes I think I'm too old for this job."

"I can't coddle you now, Earl. We've got to find Rachel," he answered sharply as he strode to the door.

"Hell, I know it. If that father-in-law of hers gets wind of this, my ass is in a sling."

Jason stopped. God, he hadn't thought about Weber. He glanced outside as Bram Justice, his coat collar pulled up to cover his ears, hurried toward him.

"Anything?" Jason asked.

Justice shook his head. "The boy isn't there. No one's seen him since yesterday."

Studying the new muddy ruts in the street because of the rain, Jason swore. He couldn't concentrate; he couldn't focus on where to begin. He sure as hell didn't want to confront Weber. Somehow he had to get Rachel back before Weber even knew she'd been gone.

He watched a wagon clatter slowly down the wet brown street, turn and continue past the bank, out of sight. An idea, farfetched and desperate, began to form in his brain.

Justice cleared his throat. "Excuse me, Marshal, I might have an idea where the boy can be found."

Earl straightened. "Well, get on it, man."

Jason watched Bram Justice cross to the boarding house. He was surprised, but pleased that the saloon keeper was anxious to help. It was comforting to know that people always pulled together in a crisis. "Earl?"

Tully glanced over at him. "Yeah?"

"Let's take a look at that shack."

"What about Rachel?"

"If my hunch is right," he answered, "we might find something. But we damned well better hurry."

They crossed to the stable and saddled their own mounts, both noting that the boy who generally helped them wasn't anywhere to be seen.

Striking out from the stable, they headed out of town on the old Stimmler road. They stopped briefly at the junction of Stimmler and Grant.

Jason squinted into the wind and saw the smoke in the distance. Guiding his mount over the seldom-used road that led to the old supply shack, he stared at the pattern in the mud. His heart lifted.

"Earl, look at the road."

Tully peered ahead of him. "Sure looks like buggy tracks."

"And they're fresh." Jason refused to allow his hopes to soar. Nudging his mount's ribs, they sped over the road, mud flying in their wake.

The shack was still smoking. It oozed out from around the window and the door.

Jason slid from his horse and went to the door. Quickly pulling back the latch, he flung the door open and stepped aside, allowing the smoke to billow out into the cold morning air. Both he and Tully squinted and coughed, fanning the steaming air in front of them.

"I'll check around the back by the fireplace," Tully announced, leaving Jason to enter the cabin alone.

Using his high sheepskin collar as a mask against the smoke, Jason stepped into the cabin. The room began to clear as the cloudy haze escaped through the open door. Next to the fireplace sat a once brightly covered easy chair. He strode to it, noting the dark blanket that hung over the back.

The second he touched the black fabric, he knew what it

was. His insides grew cold again as he pulled Ivy's cape off the chair and looked around the smoky, empty room. His frantic gaze fell on the table with the carafe and the cup and saucer. Sucking in a ragged breath, he reached for the carafe, brought it to his nose and sniffed.

The peppery odor was familiar, but he couldn't remember where he had smelled it before. *Damn*, if he could only think . . .

"Rachel!" He tossed the carafe aside, listening to it clatter against the stone fireplace. "Rachel!"

He scanned the bare floor. His heart leaped with hope when he saw the round black ring lying flat against the wood. In a single stride he was standing over it. He tugged on the ring, pulling open the square wooden piece that covered the root cellar.

A blast of wet, musty air hit him in the face. "Rachel?" He slid into the cellar, his heart pounding so hard he could hear nothing else. And the cellar was black as pitch. He stood a moment, trying to adjust himself to the darkness.

"Rachel?" His voice was quieter, saner.

A ragged cough came from the corner.

His heart vaulted upward. He felt his way, stumbling over lumpy sacks. "Rachel? Rachel, it's Jason."

The ragged cough changed to a deep, bronchial sob.

He got to his knees. A foot. A small, delicate ankle. The hem of her skirt. "Rachel? Honey, it's me."

Her hands flew at him, touching him wildly until they came to his face. He pulled her into his lap and hugged her against him. She shivered uncontrollably and her skin was cold. "Ah, sweet thing," he murmured into her smoke-filled hair. He rocked her back and forth against him. Her body shook with quiet, relieved sobs.

They sat in the darkness, not speaking. Jason continued to caress her back, her hair, her shoulders. The sting of tears pressed against his eyes and he felt the wetness on his cheeks.

"I . . . I couldn't—" She coughed, a deep, bronchial

sound that warned Jason she'd inhaled a dangerous amount of smoke.

"Shhh," he answered. "Don't talk. Later. You can tell me later, sweetheart."

Tully's head poked into the cellar. "Jason? The chimney was stopped up with rags."

Swearing under his breath, he lifted Rachel into his arms and carried her to the opening. He would have handed her up to Tully, but she wouldn't let go. Her arms were soldered around his neck.

Tully reached for her but Jason shook his head. "I'll make it," he said, finding the narrow steps that led up to the cabin floor.

He ordered Tully to get Ivy's cape. Tully wrapped it around a shivering Rachel and they left the cabin, stepping gratefully into the clean, cold morning air.

Because Ivy insisted, Jason had allowed her to undress Rachel, clean her up a little, and put her to bed. Of course, she'd balked at putting Rachel in *his* bed, but he'd refused to leave her at the cafe. He wanted her close so he could watch her. Now, as he sat beside the bed and looked at her, he knew there was a deep, secret part of him that cared for her more than he wanted to admit. If he'd lost her, he would never have gotten over it.

"Jason?"

He turned at Tully's whisper.

"She still sleepin'?"

He nodded, got up from the bed and followed Earl into the other room.

"What in the friggin' hell is happening?"

Earl was clearly befuddled. Maybe he *was* getting too old for this job. "Someone must think Rachel knows something."

"About Weber's murder?"

Jason shrugged. "It has to be that." He knew the coffee was important, and he should tell Earl about it, but until he could remember where he'd smelled or tasted it before, he didn't want to say anything. Even so, he wouldn't let Rachel out of his sight.

The more he thought about it, the more he realized Earl was slowing down. And as much as he detested Weber, he understood the bastard's fury at the current status of his son's murder. The investigation was at a standstill.

"Why don't you go over to Ivy's and have yourself a hot meal, Earl?"

A wave of relief washed over Tully's features. "Well, I guess there ain't much we can do right now, anyways." Heaving a sigh, he stood up. "I deputized Ed Gruenwald this mornin' after we found Rachel. He's out at the shack gatherin' up the clues."

Jason thought about the coffee in the carafe—which was now undoubtedly absorbed into the porous wood floor. That clue would no longer be available—thanks to him. "Good. Let me know when he's brought them in. I'd like to take a look."

Tully nodded and shrugged into his jacket. "Hell, Jason. I just ain't the tough piece of gristle I used to be. I'm so tired, I'm thinkin' about hanging up my badge." Shaking his head, he left, still limping slightly from the bullet wound he'd received over two months before.

Jason frowned. That was another thing. Who in the hell had shot him? Now, with Rachel nearly dying in that cabin, he had to wonder if maybe the shot hadn't been meant for her.

On his way to check on Rachel again, he heard the office door open behind him. Thinking Earl had forgotten something, he turned, ready to cajole him. The words froze on his lips.

"Where is she?"

Captain August Weber slammed the door and strode past Jason, barely acknowledging his existence.

Jason hid a smirk. "She's asleep," he answered, feigning a nonchalance he didn't feel.

Weber finally looked at him. Recognition, not surprise,

was evident in his eyes. "I want her out of here and taken to the hotel immediately."

Jason casually strolled to the window and glanced outside. "I can't do that."

"It's an order."

Taking a deep breath and counting to ten, Jason turned and looked at him. "I'm a doctor and she's my patient. She stays here."

Frustration welled up in Weber's eyes. His face and neck turned red. "Still the impudent half-breed. Haven't learned anything the past fifteen years, have you?"

Jason's right eyebrow shot up. How interesting that he could remember so clearly the number of years that had passed. How interesting that he hadn't struck the incident from his memory as easily as one strikes a match. Jason was grateful he'd already exorcised the pain of his own memories.

"I'll let you know when she's well enough for visitors."

Weber's eyes narrowed. "Where do you get off, posing as a civilized human being?"

Revulsion and pity battled for space inside Jason. Revulsion won. "Where do you?"

They stood, toe to toe, glaring at one another. The tension in Weber's body was palpable. He was strung tighter than a fiddle bow, and Jason sensed he would soon lose control. Jason didn't move. He hardly breathed.

Abruptly, Weber stepped back, turned and marched to the door. "Better watch your back, half-breed. If I need a savage to pin this murder on, you're as likely a candidate as anyone."

Jason, remarkably calm, watched him leave. Threats. Childish responses invented by bullies. And Captain August Weber was a bully of the first order.

❧ *Chapter Fifteen* ❧

Rachel coughed, wincing at the soreness in her chest. She tried to open her eyes. They watered and stung, causing her to gasp softly.

"What is it?"

At the sound of Jason's voice, she smiled and squinted up at him, her eyes continuing to water. "It's nothing," she whispered, noting the concern on his face. "My eyes—" She motioned with her hand, shook her head and swallowed. "They sting, that's all." She swallowed again. "And, and my throat. It . . . it hurts."

He took her hand. "Don't talk. You've inhaled a lot of smoke. The less you say, the sooner you'll start feeling better." Reaching over to the table, he lifted off a heavy mug and whisked it past her nose. "Tea," he said. "With honey. I want you to drink as much as you can."

She pulled herself up on her elbow and took a few sips, trying very hard not to make a face as the liquid slid down her throat.

The familiarity of the room comforted her as she settled back against the pillow. This was the room where she'd learned to make love. The bed where she'd finally lost her virginity. Warmth continued to spread through her. She felt safe here.

Looking back at Jason, she gave him a warm smile. But he wasn't smiling. His face was stern, serious. "What's wrong?"

He caressed her arm, shaking his head at her. "I can't believe you went off like that. Ivy was sick with worry."

She wanted to smooth the furrows from his forehead. *And you? Were you sick with worry?* "But, I—"

He put his finger to his lips. "No talking. *I'll* do the talking for a while.

"I'm going to ask you some questions that you can answer with a nod or a shake of your head. Okay?"

She nodded. Instinctively she knew that everything he'd said to her yesterday had been said in anger. He cared for her; she felt it.

"Do you have any idea who you were supposed to meet?"

Frowning, she shook her head.

"And you didn't see anyone once you got to the cabin?"

She shook her head again, remembering the panic she'd felt when she couldn't get away from the smoke. The sting of tears continued to press behind her eyes, from both the discomfort and the memory.

"I couldn't get the door open. I thought I was going to die, and I'd never see any of you again."

"Shh," he soothed as he took her in his arms. "Don't talk. There's plenty of time for that."

She closed her eyes and clung to him when he tried to pull away.

"Rachel," he whispered, gently pushing her back on the bed. "You need to rest."

She looked up at him. "Was someone trying to kill me?" Her voice was hoarse and it hurt to talk, but she had to ask. "I want the truth, Jason, please."

He stroked her hair, pushing it away from her face. Heaving a deep sigh, he finally answered, "It's possible."

She sucked in a wet, ragged breath. "But I don't *know* anything."

"Apparently someone thinks you do."

She pinched her eyes shut. "What am I going to do?"

"You're going to stay here with me. I won't let you out of my sight."

"But . . . but you have work to do. You have to make trips to the reservation." She shook her head. "I can't keep you from all that."

"Then I'll bring someone in to stay with you." He straightened his arms on either side of her and lowered his face to hers. "I'm not going to let anything happen to you."

Flecks of gold floated in his dark, dreamy eyes. She'd never noticed that before. Her body tingled at his nearness. "Are you going to kiss me?"

A smile pulled up one side of his mouth.

"Please?" Warmth burst in the pit of her stomach.

His lips touched hers. Soft. Gentle. Sweet. Reawakening all the memories and feelings she'd thought never to have again. She opened her mouth. Their tongues touched, stroked, cradled. She felt warm, no—hot. Bringing her hands to his face, she pulled him closer.

Suddenly her chest hurt. Reluctantly she pulled away, turned her head to the side and coughed.

"You're not ready for this." He sat back and smiled at her.

She yanked her handkerchief off the bedside table and crumpled it in her fist. "If I'm a real good girl, will you make love to me again? Sometime?" She wondered if she was being too brazen. The look on his face told her she wasn't.

His eyes darkened, his nostrils flared, and he gave her a smile that made her toes curl. "I guess I could think about it."

Returning his smile, she caressed his smooth cheek, then ran her fingers over his lips. "I'm sorry I caused everyone so much concern."

He pulled one of her fingers into his mouth, biting down gently, licking. "For once, you should be sorry." He caught her fingers in his and kissed her sore palm.

Her heart nearly burst with love. "Jason?"

Stroking the top of her hand, he looked at her, a question in his eyes.

"Thank you for coming to look for me."

"You're welcome." He gave her hand a gentle squeeze.

The moment was sweet and poignant. She'd never been so happy to be alive. "I love you."

He dropped her hand, stood, and cleared his throat. "Get some rest, Rachel. Get some rest."

A small part of her was sorry he hadn't said he loved her, too. But it didn't matter that much. He'd come looking for her, he'd found her and he'd saved her. That all meant he cared a little, whether he wanted to admit it or not.

After he'd gone, she turned toward the window and frowned. Why was someone trying to kill her now? Why hadn't they tried months ago, when it had made some sense? Shivering, she curled into a ball beneath the covers and continued to contemplate her skirmish with death.

It had been a week. One week since he'd found Rachel cold and shivering, huddled in the corner of that root cellar. And he'd kept his promise; he hadn't left her alone. Yesterday, when he'd had the emergency at the reservation, Dixie had come by and insisted that she stay with Rachel while he was gone.

Stepping to the window, Jason peered out into the night. There was a cold wind sifting in around the frame. Black, leaf-dappled trees swayed in the moonlight, gently hypnotizing him as he thought about the coffee he'd found at the shack. The aroma continued to tease the edges of his memory.

He winced, rubbed the crick in his neck, and blew out the kerosene lamp on his desk. Glancing at the door of his apartment, he realized he felt a niggle of guilt about not sending Rachel back to her room at the cafe. Physically she was ready to go. Emotionally she was far stronger than he'd ever given her credit for. He just wasn't ready to *let* her go. And that's why he felt the guilt.

He should never have made love to her that first time. She was becoming dependent on him, and it wasn't a realistic relationship. One thing had led to another to make her believe there could be more between them. He'd given her a job when she needed one. Discovering her virginity, he'd taken it, giving her the first taste of full-blown passion she'd ever known. By some stroke of dumb luck, he'd found her in the cabin, and saved her life. In her eyes, he was some sort of hero. She was undoubtedly infatuated with him. In time, the feeling would probably dissipate.

Love was so . . . elusive. He cared for her, he desired her, but . . . love? He didn't know . . . couldn't be sure. The thought of loving someone scared him. He'd loved once —at least, he'd thought it was love. But this time, with Rachel, there was all that emotional Weber baggage between them . . .

He rubbed his neck, unwilling to take that thought further. He hadn't weakened over the past week, having slept on the cot in his back room. Tonight he needed to be farther away from her than that, because she'd been unconsciously —he thought—arousing him all day.

Earlier, she'd stood by his desk and reached to the top of his cabinet, a movement that had stretched the front of her dress across her bosom.

Then, when she'd come to him with a patient's chart, she'd pressed her breasts against his arm as she asked her question. He'd glanced at her, but there wasn't any calculated look in her eyes. She'd touched him and talked to him as one would someone with whom she was intimate, and he couldn't deny that it pleased him.

But enough was enough. Tomorrow she could go back to Ivy's. He or Tully would assign someone to keep an eye on her. She needed a bodyguard until he could discover who was trying to kill her and why. He didn't know who he'd trust with the job, but he'd find someone. Ben sprang to mind, but Jason couldn't ask him to do it over the long term. It was enough that Ben had offered to watch her while he went to Sacramento to pick up supplies for the new reservation school.

Now, he thought, as he crossed to his private quarters, he just hoped he could manage to get through one more night of celibacy.

The lamp was lit at the bedside. She was undressing by the stove, her back to him. He knew he should leave. He told himself to turn around and get the hell out of there, but he couldn't move. He watched as she pulled off her petticoat, tossing it over the chair. With quick, smooth movements, she unbuttoned her dress and slipped her arms from the sleeves.

The smooth white skin of her shoulders and arms drew his gaze and she must have heard his harsh intake of breath, because she turned toward him, studying him, her eyes wide and her mouth slightly open. She didn't smile, nor did she pull her dress back up to cover herself.

He stared at her bosom, watching as her nipples hardened beneath her camisole. Color stole across the pale expanse of skin above her undergarment, then up her neck into her cheeks, staining them a luscious pink.

Dammit, there was still time to leave, but his self-discipline was shot. One week of having her near and not touching her had taken its toll on him. He ached for her. He remembered the sweet, artless sounds she made when she was on the brink of release. Desire, a thick, rich anguish that sank deep into his loins, pressed his need.

"Jason," she whispered, pulling her dress down over her hips and stepping out of it. Then she began to unbutton her camisole, her eyes still holding his. Slowly, hesitantly, she pulled the garment apart, exposing to him her plump, pink-nippled breasts.

Commanding his control, he balled his hands into fists and tried to will away his desire. Again, he ordered himself to leave, and again, he found he couldn't. His root swelled, the delicious, hungry itch sending his pulse pounding.

Her fingers hesitated on the buttons of her drawers, but she pulled the buttons through their holes and let her drawers slip low on her hips.

Swallowing convulsively and swearing at his weakness, he took the space between them in two strides. He reached out and gently tugged the fabric, allowing it to slip down to her thighs, then to the floor. Her brandy-hued triangle drew his gaze. Groaning, he dropped to his knees and pulled her toward him.

Slowly he pressed his nose against her and breathed in her scent. The skin low on her belly was like satin, her fur soft and tightly curled. He kissed her there, aching to make love to her with his mouth, but afraid to do so. She was still innocent.

"Jason," she whispered, her voice shaking above him. "I can't stand up." Her knees buckled, and he caught her to him, lifting her high into his arms.

Her breathing was erratic; her motions restless. She clung to him with one arm and, with the other, impatiently pulled his shirt from his denim jeans. Tugging at the buttons, she eagerly pulled them loose and jerked the sleeve down his arm. He shrugged out of the other arm and let the shirt fall to the floor. Her hand stroked his chest and her fingers moved over his scars like a blind man's over braille.

They kissed, hot, deep, wet kisses that he'd taught her, and the fire in his loins flared. Her hand dipped to his waist, then down over his crotch and he quickened at her touch. She was aggressive—something she hadn't been before. His lusty itch for her grew.

He strode to the bed and dumped her onto it. She was breathing deeply and her face was pink. She watched as his hand went to the buttons of his jeans. His movements slowed. He shouldn't be doing this at all, but suddenly he wanted to tease her, tantalize her, drive her as crazy as she drove him.

Slowly he slipped the top button out of the rugged buttonhole. Her gaze didn't leave his hand. He bit back a hard, lust-filled grin. "Are you impatient, Rachel?"

She opened her mouth but didn't speak. Her fingers gripped the sheet and she scissored her long, shapely legs together, shuddering up at him.

He almost lost control, but held himself back. Slowly, he unbuttoned his fly until his penis poked through the opening and finally sprang free.

She gaped, wide-eyed, innocent, naïve. He slid his jeans down and stepped out of them, delighted that she was so eager to see him. All of his good intentions were gone. He wanted her. He wanted to thrust deep inside her and empty himself into her. He watched as she moved to her knees, continuing to stare.

Still, he held himself back. "Do you want to touch me?" Restraint didn't enter his head. His need to see her desire for him blocked out every rational thought.

She gave him a quivering smile, bit her lower lip and moved closer, her gaze never leaving his erection. Tentatively she reached out and touched him.

Scorching heat filled him, delivering such a surge of blood to his penis that it swelled further and throbbed with a need he'd never felt before.

Gasping, she pulled her hand back. "It's . . . it's hard and smooth . . . and hot," she whispered, giving him a look that sent more blood boiling to his groin. He swallowed a groan.

This time she used both hands, one to gently grip him, the other to touch his sac. He bit back another groan but kept himself under control, breathing with shaky determination.

"Your hair is wiry," she said, touching his bush with gentle fingers.

"Don't be too gentle, Rachel." To him, his voice sounded as lust-filled as his root. If she had any sense, she'd back away, for when he came, he knew he'd come with a vengeance.

She gave him a wobbly smile. "I . . . I don't know what to do."

"Do you want to learn?" Could he last much longer?

Nodding eagerly, she made room for him on the bed.

He joined her and brought her fingers to him. "Like this," he rasped, shards of desire splintering through him as her fingers moved over him. He was hungry, but closed his eyes, allowing her to learn how to please him. Time and again he felt the volatile urge, but capped his release.

Opening his eyes, he gazed at her. Damn, but she took his breath away. Her hair hung in disarray over her shoulders, curling wildly around her breasts. Her eyes were heavy-lidded and her face still stained with the rosy glow of arousal.

Their gazes met. She gave him a dazzling, dimpled smile followed by a lusty shudder, and he clenched his jaw to maintain control.

"Enough," he finally said, his voice husky with desire.

She frowned. "Aren't I doing it right?"

He let out a whoosh of air. *"Too* right."

She snuggled against him. "I . . . I've never felt like this."

"How do you feel?" Her smell was like an aphrodisiac.

"Ooooh," she moaned. "Like I'm going to fly apart if you don't—" She clamped her lips together.

Turning on his side, he ran his fingers over her stiff nipples, exalting in her sharp intake of breath. "If I don't what?"

She rubbed her leg against his, closed her eyes and shook her head.

He concentrated on her breasts, kissing them, tugging gently on her nipples, reveling in her arousal.

Her pelvis moved seductively, and she threw her leg further over him, bringing her womanhood in contact with his skin. She was wet.

He moved his fingers to her, and she pushed against them, gyrating. Quickly he lifted her to straddle him. Her eyes flew open, but when he settled her over him she closed them again and let her head loll back, then forward as they moved together. He brought her slightly toward him, where he knew her pleasure would be enhanced, then let her ride him until she collapsed over him, sweating, breathless, and spent.

Swiftly, he brought her beneath him and drove hard, pressing deep, lunging into her with a fierce possession. He let himself go, savoring the lusty bite of desire as it grew, until he finally exploded inside her.

They lay together, her head tucked between his chin and

his shoulder. She ran her hand down over his chest, then down into the thick black hair around his limp organ. He felt it twitch, responding to her touch and he marveled at how easily she aroused him.

"Jason?"

"Hmmm?" He allowed her to play with him. He pushed away any other thoughts but her touch.

"Dixie told me something."

"Dixie's been a fountain of information, hasn't she?"

"She told me that ever since Jeremy took over as Indian agent, you've used your salary as reservation physician to replace the supplies Jeremy sold to the squatters."

He made a face. "Dixie talks too much."

"But is it true?"

He sighed. "Yes, it's true."

Suddenly she was up on her elbow, looking down at him with those big, light eyes. "What a wonderful thing for you to do."

Tracing her breast with his finger, he gave her a lopsided grin when her nipple drew into a tight nub. "It's nothing, really. I don't need the money. They do."

She continued to look at him, moving her gaze from his face to his torso. Her hand roamed over his chest, over the keloid surfaces of his scars. "Do they hurt?"

"Not anymore."

She lowered her head and kissed each one, her hair caressing his skin. His hand moved over her back, finding the soft underside of her arm, then around to her breast. The nipple hardened for him, and he continued to fondle it as she kissed him.

Finally, she raised her head and looked at him, love and pain shining in her eyes. "I can't understand why anyone would want to hurt you. How did it happen, again?"

Sighing, he looked away. He'd tell her—part of it. "Mother had sent me to find June. She was supposed to be picking berries near the overseer's cabin, but Mother feared she was at the river." He frowned, remembering. "June loved to swim. No matter how many times we'd told her it wasn't safe to swim alone because of the soldiers, she'd forget. I heard her screaming from the river. When I found her, she was with two soldiers. One was raping her. The other was holding her down."

Rachel gasped, putting her hand over her mouth, her eyes still filled with June's pain.

"I tried to stop them, but I was only a kid, and there were two of them. Well," he added, "suddenly their superior showed up—with my horse, Cassius, in tow." He laughed, knowing the sound was humorless. "For months afterward, the thing I hated them for most was that they stole my horse."

"Who beat you?"

He sucked in a deep breath, seeing Weber's red mustache twitching before him. "Their lieutenant. The others bound my feet and held me while he beat the shit out of me."

She flung herself over him, hugging him tightly. "Oh, my darling."

He felt her tears on his skin. Lifting her head, he gazed into her wet face. "Don't cry for me, Rachel."

Fresh tears dribbled down her cheeks. "I can't help it. Oh, Jason. How can people like that live with themselves?"

He embraced her, caressing her back and her sweet, round buttocks. Her hand moved low on his belly, her fingers tangled in his hair. She touched him as though to heal him, and heal him she did. His firm resolve long forgotten, he felt desire sink into his loins again.

He flipped her onto her back. "My turn."

She looked at him through heavy lids. Her lustrous hair fanned out over the pillow. Her arms were flung wide, away from her, and one leg was bent to the side, exposing her to him. Tiny drops of moisture glistened on her rusty-red triangle and she shuddered deeply when he touched her there.

He nuzzled her bud with his finger, loving the feel of her lubricant as she became more aroused. She closed her eyes and opened her mouth, presenting him with those wonderful little sounds as her pelvis moved on the bed. Her head rolled from side to side and her breathing came in shallow puffs.

He loved watching her come. When ecstasy peaked within her, she clamped her thighs together, trapping his hand between them.

Slowly she opened her eyes and smiled at him. "I'm afraid you've made me very sleepy."

He pulled the covers over them. "Then sleep," he ordered, dragging her against him spoon fashion. He didn't intend to stay with her—only until she was asleep. Then he'd go to the cot where he'd slept all week. Now that he was sated, his common sense had returned.

"What about you?"

"We'll worry about me in the morning—after you've gotten some rest."

"All right." She snuggled against him, pressing her bottom against his genitals. He ordered his root to stand at ease, but it didn't listen. Thankfully, Rachel was already asleep when it came to attention and twitched against her backside.

He moved silently through the night, staying in the shadows. With a furtive glance in both directions, he slunk around to the back of the building, pulled out his key and let himself into the dark, vacant room. He could trace the black outline of the boxes against the wall.

Stepping carefully, he maneuvered behind them, to the cold, unused fireplace. Grateful for the practiced sensitivity of his fingers, he moved them along the brickwork until he came to the spot he wanted. He loosened the brick, plunged his hand inside, and smiled. The pouch was still there. After replacing the brick, he went to the window and studied the night, his mind going back to his latest unsuccessful ploy to rid himself of the burdensome woman.

What rotten luck that she'd found the entrance to the root cellar. Had she not, it would have been finished. No one left to tie him to the murders. Except those he'd paid to do it, and they were on borrowed time as well.

Absently, he watched the trees create macabre shadows in the moonlight. Now he'd have to devise another plan to kill Rachel Weber.

Rachel hummed a little song as she flicked the feather duster over the windowsill. She'd been humming all morning—couldn't help it. Way back when she lived in that other life she'd happily left behind, the army wives used to sit around, making fun of their husbands' urges. *They pinch your breast and tickle your bottom, and they're ready to perform.* Or—*I, for one, get good and tired of sex. Why should I work so hard at something I don't enjoy?* Or—*I get so pooped I drag myself around all day.*

Rachel was bursting with energy. Even after this morning, when Jason had nudged her awake with his . . . his thing. She blushed, remembering that he'd told her to call it what it was. Just thinking about their conversation excited her all over again.

The bell over the door tinkled, prompting her to shelve her newly discovered daydreams. She turned, feather duster in hand, and looked down at Dusty, the little boy she knew to be Dixie's nephew. Directly behind him was a tall, lean man she realized must be the boy's father.

This was the man whose wife had died because of Harry Ritter. Swallowing hard, she rephrased the thought in her head. *Harry Ritter raped this man's wife, causing her death.*

She tried to smile at Dusty while shoving the rest of the thoughts to the back of her mind.

"You're Dusty, aren't you?" She avoided the father's gaze. "Did you find homes for all of your kittens?"

Recollection flared in the boy's dark eyes, and he nodded. "Where's Jason?"

The father's voice was raspy, deep and resonant. It also frightened her. "He . . . he's at the reverend's. His wife is—"

"When do you expect him back?" he interrupted, pacing to the window and peering out like a caged animal.

She glanced at the chime clock on the wall. It was almost

noon. Now, more than ever, she was anxious for Jason to come back to the office. Dixie's brother-in-law made her very uncomfortable. "He . . . he'll be back soon, I'm sure. Can I do something for you?"

"No," he answered sharply. "I'll wait."

Dusty rubbed his eyes. He turned and clung to his father's leg, tugging on his jeans. The father hunkered down beside him and listened as the boy whispered something into his ear. He gave Rachel a piercing look. "Can the boy sit on the bed?"

"Oh," Rachel murmured, nodding her head. "Certainly. Is he sick? Doesn't he feel well?" She hurried over and plumped the pillow before Dusty tumbled onto the bed, still rubbing his eyes.

"He'll be all right." The father sat beside him, smoothing his hair away from his face. "You're tough stuff, aren't you?" He gave his son a private grin, one the boy answered with a very weak imitation.

Rachel thought the boy looked feverish. If he was, she could at least start bringing it down—if the father would let her touch his son. As she moved closer, a strong whiff of whiskey rose to her nostrils. She glanced at the man with the angry eyes, noting that his hair, although darker than Jason's, was also lightly waved. But, she thought, wrinkling her nose, Jason smelled so much better.

She touched the boy's forehead, jerking her hand away when she realized he was burning up with fever. Her eyes met those of the boy's father. "He has a terrible fever," she scolded.

He gave her a hard look. His black eyes seemed dead, yet there was an intensity in them that frightened her—and gnawed at her memory.

"I'm aware of that. Jason will take care of it. We don't need your help."

He almost hissed at her. Suddenly she realized that he knew who she was. It shouldn't have surprised her; she'd been around long enough for everyone to know. She straightened and went to dampen a cloth with cool water. Returning to the bed, she thrust the wet fabric toward him. Hesitating only briefly, he took it and laid it across his son's forehead.

He grinned down at the boy, speaking to him in a language Rachel didn't understand. The boy threw her an occasional glance, as if what his father was saying somehow related to her.

Suddenly the boy coughed, deep and croupy, and gripped the front of his father's shirt. It gaped open, not only exposing a wide expanse of his chest, but also revealing a deep, ragged scar in the soft flesh of the area of his upper right shoulder.

Rachel's heart stopped, then began pounding painfully. She broke out into a cold sweat, and her face went slack as she stared, memorizing the wound that she'd seen endlessly in her nightmares. That was why his eyes had frightened her. They were the same eyes she'd seen on the face of the savage who'd murdered Jeremy! And the wound Jeremy had inflicted would have formed a scar similar to this . . .

Swiftly turning away from him, she stumbled to the desk and sank into the chair, fumbling with the files while she collected her thoughts. She had to think. *Think!* She didn't know what to do. She was too frightened to confront him. After all, if he'd killed once, he'd have no compunction about killing again. She sucked in a deep breath, letting it out slowly. When she thought her legs would hold her, she stood and moved woodenly to the window, hoping, *praying*, she'd see Jason.

Relief flooded her when she saw him striding toward the office. Needing to gather her thoughts, she left the window and hurried into the other room, leaving Dusty and his father alone in the office when Jason entered.

She sank heavily onto the sofa and waited, silently preparing her speech for Jason. Pressing her fists over her mouth, she thought about what his reaction would be when she told him. How hard it would be for him to believe his

best friend had killed Jeremy and Harry! But she was certain
he had. Every bone in her body ached with the realization.
Every nerve vibrated. In spite of her fear, she had to tell
him. She had to . . .

❧ *Chapter Sixteen* ❧

*J*ason was writing something in Dusty's chart when Rachel went back into the office. He looked up, gave her a heart-stopping smile, then went back to his task.

She let his smile linger in her memory, holding it tight, fervently wishing she didn't have to tell him what she knew. Taking a deep breath, she let it out slowly and waited until he'd finished.

"Jason?" Her voice sounded weak, anemic.

He flipped the cover on the chart and looked at her with concern, obviously catching the panic in her voice. "What is it? Aren't you feeling well?"

Closing her eyes briefly, she steeled herself against what was to come. "No, I mean, yes. I'm fine." She wanted his arms around her, but he made no move toward her. This would hurt him so much, so very much . . .

"Is Dusty all right?" She nervously picked up Dusty's chart off the desk.

"Just a low-grade fever. He'll be fine. Why did you leave them?"

"He . . . Dusty's father didn't want me to help. He knows who I am." The angry eyes haunted her.

"Buck's still pretty angry with the world, Rachel."

She gazed up at him. "I could tell. But . . . but I guess any man in his place would be. I mean, to lose your wife like that . . ." She shuddered. Although she knew in her heart that Buck was guilty, she didn't hate him for what he'd done. Under the circumstances, she could almost understand it, except that the motive wasn't clear in her mind. Oh, it was for killing Harry, but not Jeremy . . .

"Buck will make it. I can see changes in him already." Jason touched her chin and looked into her eyes. "Something's wrong. What is it?"

Reluctantly, she pulled away. "I have to tell you something."

"I'm listening."

She left him and stood by the window. Buck was riding by on his mount with Dusty in front of him. The boy was nestled snugly against his father's chest. Rachel glanced away, not wanting to see the tenderness.

"Well?" he urged.

"I think your friend Buck is the Indian who killed Jeremy." She'd blurted it out quickly, then closed her eyes and held her breath.

"What?" His voice was deadly.

Expelling the air, she sagged against the window. "Oh, darling, I know this has to be a shock to you, but—"

"What in the *hell* makes you think he did it?"

Finally she turned. Jason's black look made her recoil, but she brought her hand to her shoulder, flapping it nervously. "I . . . um . . . the scar." She saw the disbelief on his face. "I'm so sorry, Jason. I know it's hard for you to believe. Oh, love," she soothed, reaching out to touch him. "I know he's your friend. I'd give anything if—"

"Stop it." With a look of disgust, Jason shrugged off her touch. "There isn't an Indian alive who doesn't carry the white man's scars. Look at *me*. Look at my father, at June. Pick an Indian at random off the street."

Swearing, he raked his fingers through his hair. "I could show you fifteen men who have scars exactly like Buck's. *Fifteen*. Just because Buck's scar is on the same side as the one you saw your husband inflict doesn't mean a thing. Hell, I've seen his scar. I've *treated* the damned scar."

His admission shocked her, sending her stomach plummeting. "Wh-What?"

"Buck got the wound in a barroom fight," he snarled.

She frowned and looked away, fighting the urge to run from his anger and disbelief. "But . . . but he must have lied to you."

"No, dammit, he wouldn't *lie* to me." He scowled, his expression menacing and fierce.

She closed her eyes briefly. He was blind to Buck's faults, that's what it was. She couldn't back down; she was too certain she was right. "It was him. I saw it in his eyes today. I'll never forget those eyes, Jason. Never."

"You were hysterical that morning. Or don't you even remember that? I saw you, Rachel. You were incoherent, and ever since then, you've claimed you couldn't remember the face of the man who killed Jeremy. Now, suddenly, everything's clear to you." The sarcasm in his voice was heavy.

"Now I know what I saw, Jason."

"Ah, hell, you think the thought of Buck's guilt hasn't crossed my mind?" He swore again, then walked away from her, to the opposite side of the room.

"He's the first person I went to see that morning. I had my suspicions, only because I knew Ritter was responsible for Honey's death. I've known Buck too long. He may be a lot of things, and he may have had a motive, but he didn't do it. *He's not a killer.*"

She pressed her fingers to her temples. "I . . . you're too close. Don't you see? Why, even your father said you were too close to Buck to be a good judge. I know what you're feeling." She turned, giving him a pleading look.

"Jason, I couldn't believe Jeremy did those horrible things to your people. Not at first. So, believe me, I know what you're going through." She took a step toward him. "And I was *married* to Jeremy. A person can't get much closer to another than that."

"Don't talk to me about your marriage." He stepped away from her, giving her a cold, hard look. "You didn't even have a marriage. You didn't know him much better than a stranger you'd meet on a train. Hell, *I* knew the bastard better than you did. Everyone in Pine Valley knew him better than you did."

She didn't know what to say. She hated it when someone else always had a better answer for something than she did. And his answer was far better—and made painful sense.

"Jason, I understand your pain. I really do. But . . . isn't it possible he's lying to you? That he was there in spite of what he told you?"

"No." He crossed his arms and presented her with his back.

She stared painfully at his stubborn stance. It didn't do any good to argue with him. He'd made up his mind, but he was wrong. So very wrong. She felt it deep inside. Despite the awful mistakes she'd made in the past, she wasn't making one now.

"I'm sorry you can't see him for what he is, Jason. He's a murderer. Maybe he was driven to do what he did, but he still did it, and somehow he's going to have to pay for it."

He wheeled around and pinned her with a heated scowl. "You'd turn him in?"

Frustration pummeled her. She didn't know what to tell him. Oh, God, she didn't know what to do. "I . . . I don't know."

"Human beings are innocent until proven guilty, Rachel. Just remember that around here, Indians aren't considered human."

Suddenly cold, she pulled her shawl off the back of a chair and wrapped it around her shoulders. It hurt that he didn't believe her, that he would automatically think she'd been hysterical and unable to make a rational decision. But she was beginning to see things clearly now, and what she saw made her hurt even more. Jason had known about Buck from the beginning but hadn't come forward with the incriminating evidence. It made perfect sense; he was protecting his friend. And why wouldn't he? He might look and act like a White, but first and foremost, he was an Indian. He'd stop at nothing to protect his people.

"I'll think about what you've said, but in my heart I know you're fooling yourself. Your friend Buck is the one I saw." Knowing there was nothing more to say, she turned to leave.

"Rachel."

She stopped at the deadly sound of his voice.

"I want you to think long and hard before you make your decision."

She tucked the ominous statement away, and moved toward the door.

"Before you decide, consider this. Inside all of us is a person we'd rather not expose to the world, for whatever reason."

"What's that supposed to mean?"

"Sometimes the most savage exterior hides a tender, sensitive soul. And sometimes the most pious, upstanding facade hides a savage, waiting to spring free."

She frowned. "You're talking in riddles, Jason."

"I'll make it simple. You'd better be damned sure of your facts. You think you know your father-in-law pretty well, don't you?"

"I . . . I know he isn't perfect, if that's what you mean."

"The man—the one who beat me senseless?"

Nodding, she felt a chill chase over her.

"It was August Weber."

The following morning tule fog, thick, damp, and cold, clung to everything. It resembled the feeling in Jason's chest. He hadn't meant to unmask Weber as the man who'd beat him, at least not until he could tell Rachel about it without making it sound as if it were her fault. But her stubborn reluctance to admit she might be wrong about Buck had forced him into it.

Now, he waited. Waited and wondered if she'd follow through and expose Buck to her father-in-law as Jeremy's killer. He hoped she wouldn't. Not because she didn't still believe Buck was guilty, but because he didn't want her to. He'd wanted her to take his word for it.

Before all of this happened, she'd admitted her love for him. Maybe now she'd come to her senses and realize that it had merely been an infatuation. Something deep inside him rebelled at the thought, even though it made incredible sense.

He swore softly. She was a moral person, but she was also compassionate. He hoped that if she thought about it as he'd asked her to, she'd realize that turning Buck in meant certain death.

Unable to convince himself further, he busied himself with his backlog of paperwork and went over the list of reservation supplies he had to pick up at the Port of Sacramento. They would be there by now. He'd leave for Sacramento tomorrow.

Shortly before eight, the office door opened and Dusty tumbled in, his face streaked with tears.

Jason felt a burst of anger. Buck had been ordered to keep Dusty quiet for a few days. "Dusty? What is it?"

The boy rubbed his face with his fist, spreading his tears and the mucus from his runny nose over his cheeks. "I . . . it's my daddy," he whimpered.

Jason went cold inside. "What about your daddy?"

"Th-they came and took him away."

He rushed around the desk, hunkered in front of the boy, and wiped his face with his handkerchief. "Who took him away?"

Dusty threw himself at Jason, clinging to him for all he was worth. "The bad man."

Frowning, Jason rubbed Dusty's back, attempting to soothe him. "What bad man, Dusty? Can you describe him to me?"

"I . . . I don't know," he whined.

Jason took a deep breath. "What was he wearing? Do you remember? Did he dress like the marshal?"

Dusty shook his head. "Not . . . not like the marshal."

"Did he wear a uniform? Like—"

"Yeah," Dusty said with a hiccoughing nod. "A . . . army man."

With a sharp intake of breath, Jason squeezed Dusty hard against his chest. Dammit, she'd done it after all. After everything he'd said to her yesterday . . . Now, guilty or innocent, Buck was as good as dead.

Shivering against the cold, damp air, Rachel tugged the corners of her shawl together and walked carefully through the fog. Her eyes felt heavy and sandy. Another sleepless night. She'd sat in the window seat, staring outside for hours, hearing Jason's voice tell her that August Weber had been the man who had beaten him.

The words had hit her like the lash of a whip. Her sweet, darling Jason. He should hate her. She, who had so foolishly and naïvely taken her father-in-law's side in her arguments with Jason. Why she'd felt the need to defend the man, she'd never know. Maybe it was because she'd so desperately wanted him to find Jeremy's killer and be gone from her life.

No wonder Jason had been so harsh with her when they'd first met. Through the thick curtain of her anguish, she vaguely remembered the terse way he'd treated her that morning. Perhaps what he'd said in anger about hiring her to keep an eye on her was the truth. In light of everything she now knew about her husband and his father, she no longer doubted it.

She bit her lower lip hard enough to make it hurt. Everything was clear to her now. Her husband had stolen from Jason's people and her father-in-law had nearly killed him. It was a miracle Jason could stand to look at her. And how could she look August Weber in the face without revealing what she'd learned about him—and what she now felt?

She'd tossed and turned all night, unable to decide what to do about Buck. Telling Tully or her father-in-law about her suspicions would surely mark Buck as a dead man; Jason was right about that. And if Buck were killed, his poor little boy would be an orphan—as she'd been. That kind of life wasn't fair for any child. She didn't want to be responsible for any more killing. There'd been enough to last a lifetime.

"Rachel? That you?" The marshal's voice, somewhere behind her, penetrated the fog.

She turned, squinting into the wet air. "Good morning, Marshal. I've never seen anything quite this thick."

"Yep, yep, wetter'n rain." He fell into step beside her, shortening his considerably to match hers. "Glad I run into you. Your father-in-law has himself a prisoner at my jail. I don't mind tellin' you the man ain't one of my favorite people, but as a Cavalry man, he's entitled to use my facilities."

Rachel's stomach did a flip-flop. "He has a prisoner? Who is it?"

"Buck Randall."

Her stomach plunged. "Jason's friend?"

"That's the one. Cap'n Weber sent me to find you and bring you to the jail." He snorted. "Actually, it was an order."

His sarcasm was evident. No doubt the captain had barged in and thrown his weight around—as usual, she thought derisively. Nervously, she cleared her throat.

"I wonder what he needs with me." Oh, she didn't wonder at all. She knew what he wanted. Now, after all of her soul-searching, she wasn't sure what she was going to do about it.

"Dunno. Just said to find you and bring you on over."

Rachel's steps automatically slowed. Did he think she could identify him? Is that what he wanted? She'd already told him she couldn't, and although recent events had given her cause to change her mind, there was no reason for him to believe that, for she hadn't seen him in days.

Suddenly they were in front of the jail, and Rachel felt the old, familiar nausea coat her stomach. As she stepped inside, she noticed the fire burning in the stove in the center of the room, the embers glowing from behind the heavy glass door. Captain Weber sat at the marshal's old, wooden desk, writing something in a ledger.

Tossing her a triumphant, arrogant smile, he blotted the page and slammed the ledger shut. "Good news, Rachel. I've caught the bastard."

Her stomach lurched. "You . . . you have?"

"I have." He pushed the marshal's chair back and stood. "Come," he ordered. "Follow me."

Feeling as if a weight had been tied to her ankles, she followed him back into the alcove where the prisoners were kept. As she stepped into the room, the first person she saw was Jason. He stood beside the cell and glared at her, his expression betraying his feelings. It was obvious that he thought Rachel had turned Buck in. She went cold inside.

Shaking her head, she gave him a pleading look, but he turned away, refusing to acknowledge her. She moved toward him, needing him to understand that she'd done nothing to bring about this capture. "Jason, please, I—"

"Rachel," Captain Weber said, coming up behind her. "There's only one thing I want from you."

She turned and stared at her father-in-law, hoping her expression was passive. She knew only too well what he wanted her to do. "What . . . what's that?"

Weber stepped to the cell. "Well, savage. Anything to say for yourself?"

Buck scowled and turned away, moving toward the back of the cage.

"Come closer, Rachel."

Rachel swallowed and stepped closer to the cell. She stared at Buck's back. All she had to do was tell her father-in-law what she'd told Jason yesterday, and this whole nightmare would be over. *Over.* Her glance drifted to Jason. His fists were shoved deep into his pockets and a muscle worked in his jaw. His scowl was revealing. He blamed her. And why shouldn't he? Yesterday she'd left him with the impression that Buck had to pay for his crimes.

"Well, Rachel? Tell me," Captain Weber said smoothly. "Is this the savage you saw that morning? The one who murdered my son . . . *your husband* . . . and mutilated him?"

She winced, remembering the picture of Jeremy's body lying before her, the stumps where his hands had been, still oozing blood.

Once again, she looked at Buck. He had turned and met

her gaze. Hatred made his eyes burn like black fire. He bore his malice for her like a badge of honor. But there was something else, too. A vulnerability. A powerless sense of despair. It made her ache; it made her want to cry.

Her gaze rested on his face. Suddenly, like a bolt of lightning, the picture of Jeremy's killer loomed before her. It pressed forward in her memory as if it had been sketched in harsh, black ink. The sharp nose, the high cheekbones, the black, angry eyes—and the deep white scar slashed across his cheek. Realization was like a slap across the face. Blinking her eyes, she drew them to Buck's cheek. Nothing. Both were smooth except for the faint shadow of black whiskers.

It's not him. Her strength left her, and she leaned against the pillar in front of the cell for support.

"Well, Rachel?"

She blinked nervously, startled by her father-in-law's accusatory voice. "Wh-What?"

"Is this the savage who killed Jeremy?"

"He deserved to die," Buck snarled, stepping so close to the bars that she could smell the faint odor of stale whiskey.

Stunned by Buck's admission, Rachel faltered and stepped backward. Her hand automatically went to her throat and she clasped the edges of the shawl in her fist.

"They both did," Buck spat. "Whoever killed them should be rewarded, not punished."

"*You* did it, you dirty savage," Weber barked. "Don't try to pawn the guilt off on someone else."

Buck's sneer spoke volumes. "Don't I wish. I'd gladly pay for this crime if I'd had the pleasure of committing it."

"No one said you could talk, savage." Weber threatened him with his fist.

Buck's face filled with loathing. "You arrogant, pig-faced son of a whore."

Weber's face turned dangerously red and his eyes bulged, but somehow he restrained himself.

"No one in this goddamn room is innocent," Buck went on. "*No one.* There are only two innocent people in this whole frigging mess. My *dead* wife . . . and my son. And as far as I can see, they're the only ones who've paid."

He gripped the bars and sneered at them. "Do what you want with me. I don't give a goddamn. My life isn't worth shit anymore!"

His hot, angry gaze stopped on Rachel. "And *you*," he said, his voice filled with hatred. "I hope that bastard you married and that fornicating schoolmaster are burning in your sanctimonious Christian *hell*." He flung a mouthful of spit at her.

The glob hit Rachel's hand, slid across her skin, and dropped onto her skirt. She froze, the nausea building inside her. She tried to wipe the spittle away, but she couldn't move her hand. Always uncomfortable with someone's anger, her feelings were compounded when it was aimed at her. She felt sick, hurt. All she knew for sure was that Buck didn't act like a guilty man, only like one who no longer wanted to live.

"Son of a bitch!" Weber yelled, his arms lunging through the bars, his fingers around Buck's throat. "You're dead, you murdering savage!"

Rachel stumbled backward, trying to get out of the way. Jason attacked Weber, grabbing his hands, trying to pry them loose. Buck's face was pushed against the bars and his hands went to the captain's hair, pulling, grabbing, tugging . . .

She watched the fight with a sense of detachment. Even though she'd discovered Buck wasn't the one who'd actually killed Jeremy, she could still implicate him in Jeremy's death. His hatred told her he was probably guilty of something. All she had to do was point her finger. Or nod her head. Or say simply, "Yes, he's the one I saw." But this had to end. The violence and the killing and the hatred—it all had to stop somewhere.

"No," she murmured. The foray continued, Jason and Captain Weber pushing and snarling at one another like angry dogs. "No!"

Everyone stopped. They turned and stared at her.

"Rachel?" Weber's voice.

"He's . . . he's not the one I saw." She sank into a chair and shook her head. "It isn't him. The one I saw had a long white scar over his right cheek." She closed her eyes and put her face in her hands.

"Dammit, Rachel," Weber swore. "This is insane. You said the savage was guilty; I heard you with my own ears."

Unable to believe what he'd just done, she raised her head and stared at him. "No," she replied, quaking with fresh fear. "I didn't tell you that." Her gaze flew to Jason, whose look pierced her soul. "I . . . I didn't tell him that. I *didn't*."

"Rachel, Rachel," her father-in-law said around an evil smile. "It's too late, my dear. The deed is done. You can't go around changing your mind whenever it suits you."

She tried to swallow the lump in her throat. It pressed upward, accelerating her nausea, for he was purposely trying to implicate her. "No," she whispered. "I . . . I won't let you do this. You . . . you can't make me admit to something I didn't say."

Weber's hateful chuckle scraped her skin. "But you *did* say it, Rachel."

"But, I—" She looked at Jason, hoping to find strength or sympathy or support, but she found only hate and disappointment. Turning back to her father-in-law, she said, "If I don't identify him, you can't charge him. You can't."

Weber shrugged expansively. "I'll wait. I have nothing but time, Rachel. Sooner or later, the savage will be dealt with." He gave her a malevolent grin. "I'd rather it be sooner, but," he said with a sigh, "I'll wait. I always get what I want. You should know that."

Marshal Tully ambled into the room. "Sounds like a lot of ruckus back here."

"Oh, Marshal," Rachel said, rushing to him. "If I don't identify Buck, he can't take him away, can he?"

Tully scratched his head. "I expect he can do whatever he wants to, Rachel. He's the army law, and Jeremy Weber was an army officer. Sorry," he said, shaking his head sadly. "Could be Buck didn't actually kill Weber, but he ain't got proof he wasn't there." He gave her a helpless shrug. " 'Fraid it's out of my hands."

"What . . . what about being innocent until proven guilty? What about that?"

"The Injuns don't have that privilege, Rachel."

Jason's words came back to haunt her. . . . *Indians aren't considered human* . . . Turning to her father-in-law, she threatened, "You'd better be fair. You'd better—"

He scowled. "Fair? *Fair?* Was it fair for the savage to mutilate my boy's body? Was it?"

There was nothing she could do. She knew August Weber very, very well, and now that he'd found his man, she had a feeling that nothing would stand in his way.

She thought back to her argument with Jason. No one had heard them. No one was there. Unless—a sick feeling spread through her—unless her father-in-law had been, for some odd reason, listening at the window.

Giving Buck and Jason one last pleading look, she walked slowly from the room, Tully and her father-in-law right behind her. Once in the office, Weber picked up his hat and his gloves. "Don't do anything foolish, Tully."

Tully sighed and stretched his back. "I ain't plannin' to."

"He's still my prisoner. I'll deal with him in my own way."

Tully nodded impatiently. "Yeah, yeah. Just get him outa my jail as soon as possible. Right now, I got more problems than I know what to do with. I got me three dead renegades. They was found less than a mile from the reservation. With my luck, the rest of the band will come in and start shootin' up the town."

Rachel's heart jumped. "Marshal! Don't let him—"

Captain Weber interrupted. "I have some business in Sacramento, Tully. When I return, I'll shackle Randall and take him to Fort Riley. Until then, he's in your hands, and I'd damned well better not find out that you've let him go."

Tully nodded wearily and returned to the alcove with Jason's medical bag, leaving Rachel alone with her father-in-law. He made her sick to her stomach.

"You overheard my conversation with Jason." Her tone was low, accusatory.

Captain Weber smirked. "Lucky for me, wasn't it?"

"How *could* you? How could you turn everything I said around to make it sound as if I confided in you?"

"It all worked out quite well, didn't it?" Weber crossed to the door. "How fortunate that I happened along when I did. I saw the two of you through the window. I crept around to the side and heard everything you said. It's too late, Rachel," he continued, still giving her that arrogant smirk. "I don't think your precious doctor will believe anything more you have to say."

"Thanks to you," she seethed.

"Yes," he replied with a smug smile. "Thanks to me."

After he'd gone, Rachel tossed a wistful glance toward the alcove. She wanted to face Jason now, but she couldn't. He certainly didn't want to hear anything more from her. Somehow she'd have to convince him that she hadn't run directly to Captain Weber and spilled the whole story, then changed her mind after Buck had been arrested. It wouldn't be easy, but she'd have to try.

Marshal Tully came back into the room, gave Rachel a weak smile, but said nothing.

She was stunned to see how easily her father-in-law pushed him around. "How can you let him do that to you?"

Tully gave her a long sigh. "Now, don't go muddying up the waters, Rachel."

"What do you mean, 'muddying up the waters'?"

"I mean, don't go gettin' any fancy ideas about tryin' to get Buck outa here."

"But, Marshal, you don't understand. Guilty or innocent, Buck won't live to see Fort Riley. Captain Weber will see to that."

"Well, now, I ain't so sure he's innocent anyways." Tully sat back in his chair and put his feet on the desk.

Rachel stared at him. "I just told everyone that Buck isn't the one I saw that morning. I'm not lying, Marshal. It really wasn't him. The face I've been trying to remember suddenly became clear in my head." She saw the lack of interest on Tully's face. "What's happened to you?"

"I'm tired, Rachel. I'm damned tired. I don't want no trouble, especially from the army. Leave it be, honey. Your pa-in-law will handle it proper."

She wanted to scream at him; shake him. Somehow he'd changed since she'd first met him—or had he always been this weak and indecisive?

A noise drew her gaze to the alcove, and she remembered that Jason was still back there with Buck. She didn't want to face Jason now. She needed some time. Undoubtedly he did, too.

❧ Chapter Seventeen ❧

*J*ason brooded in front of Buck's cell. The picture of Rachel's face, so filled with pleading, wouldn't leave his mind. Although confused at what she'd done, he was still angry. Yesterday she'd seemed certain Buck was guilty, yet Jason had hoped she'd think about the consequences of accusing him. He knew full well that once the accusation was made, nothing would stop Weber from bringing Buck to justice—his brand of justice, anyway.

Today, Rachel had inexplicably changed her mind, but it was too late. The life of an Indian wasn't important. Whether he was guilty or innocent wasn't an issue; she hadn't understood that. She didn't realize that the slightest hint that Buck could be guilty would send the law down on him so fast, the truth would never be told. Now, Weber had his murderer, and unless Jason could think of a way to save him, Buck was a dead man.

Buck's behavior was another problem. "Are you so anxious to die? Because if you are, you've done the right thing, you stupid bastard."

Buck swung around and faced him. "I won't beg for my life. Not in front of *any* White." He was quiet for a moment, then added, "You said she was certain I was guilty. Why did she suddenly change her mind?"

Jason raked his fingers through his hair, then massaged his neck. "Damned if I know. Maybe she really did remember the face of the real killer." It's what he desperately wanted to believe.

"A lot of good it'll do now," Buck replied with a derisive snort. "She still has that look of fear in her eyes. Believe me, I know that look well. She thought I was guilty as hell and hightailed it to that bastard Weber to tell him so. Never mind that she's changed her tune now. It's too damned late."

"Well, you certainly made it easy for her to hate you. Jesus, Buck. Spitting at her?"

Buck shrugged, as though he couldn't care less. "You'd have thought that would have made her want me dead all the more. And I'm not so sure her retraction wasn't just an act to save her own skin." He tossed Jason a knowing look. "After all, how can she still have you if she accuses me?"

That thought had gone through Jason's head, too. But only fleetingly. Rachel was a lot of things, but she wasn't duplicitous.

"And don't give me any of that shit about how she's changed," Buck snapped. "Once a White, always a White. And why not? They're no different than we are. That's the only thing I can say in their defense. Right or wrong, they believe in their own—at least they stand by them, whether they believe them or not."

Jason scowled. Dammit, Buck made perfect sense, and it irritated the living hell out of him. He hadn't wanted to believe Rachel would turn Buck in, but when it came down to the wire, she would side with her own—just as he would with his. There was no honor in turning against your own people.

"You were pretty hard on her, Buck."

"I'm not sorry for a damned thing I said. I meant every word of it. I'm glad they're dead. Who knows, I might have killed them myself if someone hadn't beat me to it."

"Jesus, Buck. Why didn't you just confess, then? Considering what you said, you might as well have."

Buck's arm came through the bars and he grabbed Jason's shoulder. Jason glared at the hate-filled agony he saw in his face.

"Tell me, good doctor, how I'm supposed to live the rest of

my life with the sound of Honey's laughter waking me from a dead sleep. Shit, I only drink to kill the pain. The only peace I have is when I've drunk myself into a stupor. Unfortunately, goddammit, the minute I wake up, I hear it again."

"Everyone deserves a period of mourning, you lunatic. *You*, on the other hand, have a death wish." Jason pried Buck's fingers loose and moved away from the bars. "What good are you going to be to Dusty if you're hanging from the end of a rope?"

"I've told you, Dusty's better off with Sky and Ma."

Shaking his head, Jason walked away. Damn, they'd had this conversation before—many times before.

He glanced around the room, noting the high, barred windows and the solid brick walls. "We've got to think of some way to get you out of here."

"You think she really remembered who killed her husband?"

Shoving his hands into his pockets, Jason turned, once again taking a good look at his childhood friend. He saw a gaunt, surly half-breed on the brink of alcoholism. On the surface, that's what he was; that's what others saw. But deep in Buck's charcoal eyes, Jason saw the anguished, self-destructive force that would probably kill him. Jason didn't want to lose him. There had to be a way to save him from Weber . . . and from himself.

"I think she probably did. But, more than one person has told me I'm too close to see the real you, Buck." He waited a heartbeat. "Am I?"

Buck groaned and threw himself on the cot. "I'm no smooth talker, Jason. Hell, I went through school kicking and screaming, and the fewer words I have to use to say something, the better. The sack of shit you see," he said, folding his arms under his head, "is the sack of shit you get. You know that."

Jason stared at him for a long time. His normally arrogant sneer was gone. The anguish had won. He looked whipped, broken. Like he'd given up.

"Any idea who might have killed them?"

Buck gave him a sarcastic, lopsided grin. "You should have asked me that months ago."

Jason came to attention. "Why in the hell didn't you tell me before?"

Buck shrugged. "I wasn't sure. It all started with a feeling —along with a few little clues that everyone else had missed. By the way," he added. "Ty Holliday has a scar on his cheek."

Tossing a quick glance toward the door, Jason sidled closer to the bars. "Could he have planned the whole thing and carried it out with so much secrecy?"

Buck smirked. "Not unless he was using someone else's brain."

Jason felt a twinge of excitement. "All right, old friend. It's time to tell me what you know."

Tully strolled into the room. "Oh, by the way," he said with a sigh. "Ty Holliday and two of his pals were found near the ravine this mornin'. They each took a bullet to the head, and they was all practically swimmin' in whiskey."

"Injun lover!"

Rachel winced as the words hit her. The boy wasn't more than eleven or twelve, yet when he shouted at her, his face had been filled with hatred. She knew it was only the beginning. Her refusal to accuse Buck of her own husband's murder would undoubtedly be fodder for dinner conversation at every White home in Pine Valley for days, even weeks, to come.

She stopped at the abandoned building and unlocked the door to the quiet, dusty room that stored the reservation supplies. She stepped inside. Four days ago, Jason had left for Sacramento to pick up provisions. He'd left without speaking to her. In fact, they hadn't spoken directly since the day before Buck was arrested. Intellectually, she couldn't blame him. Emotionally, it was like being stabbed in the heart. What else could he do but think she'd told her father-in-law about Buck? It's what she'd as much as told him she was going to do.

She gave the room a cursory glance. Getting it ready for the supplies gave her something to do. And she'd heard Jason tell Earl that the children at the reservation needed the carton with the shoes. She'd keep an eye out for it while she reorganized the boxes.

The room was damp and cold. Shivering, she pulled her shawl tightly around her shoulders, then crossed to the boxes in front of the fireplace. She couldn't start a fire without moving them. She read the contents of several: brass nails, mending leather, feather dusters—she made a face. *Feather dusters?* Shaking her head, she looked at the bottom box and discovered *shoes* written in bold, black letters.

Slowly she moved all the boxes that blocked the fireplace, leaving to one side the box with the shoes in it. She found a small pile of wood stacked against the wall and took two pieces to the grate, along with some kindling, and started a fire. Rubbing her hands near the blaze to warm them, she glanced casually at the fireplace brickwork. It was old, but obviously hadn't had much use. The mortar between the bricks was still well cemented, and the bricks themselves were red and even.

She frowned. Except that one down there. Curious, she got to her knees and touched it. It was loose. How odd, she thought. She wiggled it, and to her surprise, she was able to pull it out halfway.

A wistful memory washed over her. As a child, she and George had hidden their "treasures" under a board near her bed.

She pulled the brick out. To her surprise, it came away from the rest quite easily.

Squinting into the dim light, she tentatively put her hand into the dark hole, shuddering at the thought of maybe touching something furry . . . and alive.

Instead, she felt something soft. Briefly, she pulled her hand away, then slowly moved it around inside the hole, touching the object again. It felt like a bag of marbles. Grabbing it, she pulled it out and held it, feeling the odd, heavy weight in her palm.

With the bag clutched in her fist, she got up and moved closer to the fire so she could look more carefully at the leather bag. There had once been an initial on it, but most of it was worn away. Squinting closely, she saw the faint outline of the large, gold W. Her stomach fluttered nervously, and her throat went dry.

She pulled at the leather thongs, opened the bag, and shoved her hand inside. *Money.* Swallowing convulsively, she dropped the coins and paper, jerking her hand quickly from the bag.

Tossing a frightened glance around her, she tugged at the thongs, pulling the bag closed. She'd seen it before. Not recently, not even since she'd been in California. But she remembered it clearly, for Jeremy had paid the preacher with money from that bag the day they were married.

She sagged to the floor and leaned against the boxes of supplies. It was what the marshal had asked her about that day at the cottage when she'd picked up her clothes. It was something he'd known Jeremy had . . . It was something that could identify Jeremy's murderer.

Swallowing nervously again, she pressed her fist to her mouth. Jeremy's killer had hidden the money in the fireplace. But, who? Who was it?

She took a deep breath and stared at the bag in her lap. The coward in her wanted her to put it back where she'd found it. After all, whoever had put it there would come back for it. And what if the killer was watching this place, or watching her? Remembering her brush with death in the smoky cabin made her break out into a cold sweat. Jason had as much as admitted that someone wanted her dead. She was beginning to understand why.

She was half tempted to put the money back. Maybe she could watch to see who came for it. But it wasn't possible to spend every waking minute staring at an empty building. And she might miss the thief, and then never know who'd killed Jeremy and stolen the money. Then, again, the killer might discover *her*.

With a shuddering sigh, she stood, making her decision.

She'd take the money. In spite of her fears, she refused to leave it behind. After all, it was rightfully hers—and she needed it desperately. But she also realized that she couldn't tell anyone she'd found it. She couldn't even tell the marshal. She no longer believed he could do anything about it, anyway.

She wondered if there was any way to discover whether or not Buck knew of the money and the fireplace. Oh, the last thing she wanted to do was face the man again, and no doubt he'd refuse to talk to her anyway. But . . . he *was* behind bars, and couldn't hurt her, and someone would have to bring him his lunch from the cafe. Nancy usually did it, but . . .

Shuddering again, she turned to leave. Then, remembering the box of shoes, she shoved the bag of money into the deep pocket of her apron and hoisted the box into her arms.

She'd go back to her room, count the money, then decide whether or not to confront Buck. Lord, she didn't think she was that brave . . . she hoped she wasn't that foolish. Maybe he wouldn't even talk to her. Maybe he'd tell the marshal to get her out of his sight.

Her mouth lifted in a half-grin. Or maybe she'd forget the whole stupid idea. At any rate, since the money was rightfully hers, she'd think about dropping a payment off at the bank. At least she could get her mother's cameo out of hock. Then, after that, she'd take the shoes to the reservation. It would keep her mind off everything else.

Struggling around the box to open the door, she looked outside, scanning the street and sidewalk to make sure she wasn't being watched. Then, as casually as possible, she hurried back to the cafe.

Stunned, Rachel sat on her bed and stared down at the money. *Fifteen hundred dollars.* She sucked in a mouthful of air, expelling it slowly. The bills had all been rolled into a wad with a binder wrapped around them. They were a little damp. The coins had been loose at the bottom.

She counted out what she still owed the bank, slipped it

into her purse, then stashed the rest of it in an old cloth bag of her own. She hid the bag inside one of her shoes, and shoved the shoe to the back of the wardrobe, laying towels over it to cover it.

After folding the empty leather bag as best she could, she put it in her purse, then stepped into the cafe. Nancy was putting a cloth over Buck's lunch tray.

"Nancy?"

The woman looked up as Rachel came toward her.

"Is . . . is that the prisoner's lunch?" Rachel's heart was in her throat.

"I'm taking it over there now," Nancy answered.

The cafe was filling up. "Listen," Rachel said, "why not let me take it?"

Nancy gave her a strange look. "Why would you do that?"

Rachel laughed nervously. "Oh, it's not . . . not like I'm going to give it to him personally. I . . . I just have to go to the bank, and the jail is on my way."

Nancy glanced around the noisy cafe, then shrugged. "Fine with me. I have plenty of work here."

Rachel didn't know if she was scared or sorry that Nancy had given in so easily. Anyway, it was up to her, now. As she picked up the tray, she decided that she could simply leave it with the marshal if she wanted to. But, if she had the nerve, she'd follow through with her little plan.

Marshal Tully was busy arguing with a couple of ranchers when Rachel stepped into the jail. He turned and stared at her, obviously surprised that she was delivering Buck's lunch.

"Wanna put it down over there, Rachel? I'll get it back to him when I have a minute."

Rachel's grip on the tray was so intense, her knuckles were white. Nodding, she stepped to the table on the other side of the room while he went back to his heated, noisy debate.

The ranchers, obviously cattle owners, were complaining about the sheep ranchers who used the land near theirs. If

Rachel had learned one thing, it was that cattlemen and sheepmen had no time for each other.

She glanced at the door to the cells, then down at the tray, which she still had gripped in her fingers. Tossing Marshal Tully a quick look, she put the tray down on the table and took the empty leather pouch from her purse. With her back toward the men, she spread the pouch, faded gold W facing up, beneath the plate that held Buck's lunch, then smoothed the big napkin over the tray again.

Taking a deep breath, she walked into the alcove and found Buck lying languidly on his cot, reading a book. That, in itself, surprised her. She stood, unmoving, and watched him.

Suddenly, he raised his head and looked at her. With a look of disdain, he turned back to his book, shutting her out.

Rachel swallowed hard. She put the tray on the floor, and hurried away without a backward glance. However, once outside the alcove, she stepped to the narrow slot in the wall that the marshal used to observe his prisoners and waited for Buck to eat his lunch—and discover the evidence.

It didn't take long. Once Buck was sure she'd gone, he tossed his book on the cot, reached through the bars, and whipped off the large napkin. Through an opening between the floor and the bars, he pulled his plate off the tray and into the cell.

Rachel put her hand over her mouth and held her breath as Buck paused, staring down at the tray. She watched his face. He put his plate on the floor and reached through the bars to pick up the bag.

He frowned, then looked quickly at the door, as if expecting her to step through with an explanation. After a few seconds, he shifted his attention back to the bag. He turned it over and over and held it toward the light, appearing to try to make out the faded letter.

With a puzzled little laugh, he tossed the bag back onto the tray and devoured his food, obviously untroubled and only mildly puzzled by the presence of an empty leather money bag on his lunch tray.

Rachel let out a long, quiet breath, and continued to watch him. When he was finished, she scurried back into the alcove and picked up the tray. The plate covered the bag, and Rachel didn't even glance at Buck before she tossed the napkin over the tray, picked it up and left the room. Before leaving the jail, she stuffed the empty money bag back into her purse, and left the rest of the tray on the table. She hurried out of the jail unnoticed, the marshal still in a heated discussion with the ranchers.

At the bank, Rachel stepped up to the window and asked for Mr. Bailey. The elderly teller told her to take a chair and wait. Someone would be with her shortly.

She sat, trying to digest what she'd just learned about Buck. Guilt ate at her. His actions proved he was an innocent man.

The door to Mr. Bailey's office opened, and he stuck his head out. "Mrs. Weber? Come in, please."

Rachel marched confidently into the room. "I've come to pay off my . . . Jeremy's loan, Mr. Bailey."

Abner Bailey had taken his seat behind the desk. "I see. You've been paid, Mrs. Weber?"

"I . . . well, of course," she murmured guiltily. "Here," she said, fishing into her purse and pulling out the round wad of bills. "It should be exactly enough."

He stared at the money, then quickly glanced at Rachel. "Your debt has been paid, Mrs. Weber."

Stunned, Rachel gaped at him. "It has? But . . . but who could have . . . I mean, who paid it?"

Bailey took a deep breath, letting it out slowly. "I'm afraid I'm not at liberty to say."

"You're not at liberty to say? But . . . but that's ridiculous."

"Ridiculous or not, I can't divulge that information, Mrs. Weber."

Rachel was surprised, yet wary. Who on earth would pay her bills for her? No one, except the marshal and Ivy, knew she had debts. And neither of them had the money.

She smiled at the frosty Mr. Bailey. "I . . . I guess it's good news, then. At least I can get my cameo out of jail," she said, trying to sound glib.

The banker frowned and pursed his lips. Rachel didn't like the look at all. "I . . . I *can* get my cameo back, can't I?"

He stood and came around to the front of his desk. "I do regret this, Mrs. Weber."

"Regret what?" Somehow she knew she was going to hate what he had to say.

"Whoever pays the debt gets the collateral."

Rachel's stomach lurched. "You mean . . . you mean you gave my brooch to . . . to someone else?"

He shrugged. "It was all quite legal, I assure you."

Rachel dropped into a chair and stared at her lap. "Mr. Bailey," she pleaded. "Can't you please tell me who paid Jeremy's loan? How . . . how can I possibly get my pin back if you won't tell me where it is?"

"I'm sorry. I made a promise; I must keep my word."

Rachel rose quickly and turned away, fighting the tears that stung her eyes. "I . . . I see. Well, th-thank you anyway, Mr. Bailey."

Feeling helpless and puzzled, Rachel left the bank. As she trudged down the sidewalk, she realized there was another person who knew of her debts: August Weber. She'd told him herself. But she had no reason to believe *he* would bail her out. It wouldn't benefit him at all. Unless . . .

Her stomachache returned. Unless he thought that by paying her bills, he could force her into accusing Buck as Jeremy's killer. And he would. He'd dangle the *paid in full* receipt and her precious brooch in front of her like a carrot on a string.

She found herself at the door to the saloon. With a shaky sigh, she realized it didn't matter which debt she paid, just as long as she paid. But if she found that Jeremy's debt to Mr. Justice had been paid as well, she didn't know what she'd do.

The saloon was relatively quiet. Harvey, the muscle-bound pest, was behind the bar, cleaning glasses. He tossed

Rachel a lascivious grin, which she ignored. Tess was laughing and flirting with a local rancher—a man who Rachel knew had a wife and children. Ignoring them, she stepped quickly to the office door and knocked.

Bram Justice's cultured drawl bade her enter. She went into the office, closing the door behind her.

Justice straightened a stack of papers and gave her a courteous smile. "Miz Weber. What a pleasant surprise. What can I do for you today?"

Rachel dug into her purse and pulled out the wad of damp bills, still rolled as she'd discovered them in the pouch. "I want to pay you something, Mr. Justice."

"Ah," he answered, sounding enlightened. "I see you've been paid again."

Rachel cleared her throat. "Er . . . yes. I . . . I have," was all she could utter as she handed him the bills. Guilt assaulted her again.

He took the money, slowly unrolled the bundle, then looked at her. "Drop them in a puddle?"

Panic froze her. "I . . . I'm sorry?"

His fingers moved over the bills. "They're damp."

"Oh," she answered, swallowing nervously. "I . . . I don't know why they would be wet."

He gave her a strange smile. "I see. I'll get you a receipt this time. Do you mind waiting a moment?"

She was tempted to tell him not to bother, then bolt from the saloon. "No," she answered, shaking her head. "Not at all."

He slipped into another room off his office and closed the door. Rachel paced nervously in front of the desk, tossing furtive glances at the closed door. She felt guilty as sin. She'd read something into everything Bram Justice had said or done. She was afraid that if she didn't leave soon, she'd break down and admit to anyone and everyone how she'd come by the money.

Scolding herself, she tried to calm down. But when Mr. Justice came back into the room, she jumped guiltily. He handed her the receipt.

"There you are, Miz Weber. You must be careful when you carry so much cash around," he reminded her. "It isn't safe, you know."

She tried to smile. "I . . . I suppose not, but I was anxious to pay you, so I didn't dillydally."

He gave her a hooded look. "Of course you didn't."

He was making her nervous. She knew it was her own guilt that worked against her, nevertheless, she was anxious to get outside.

"Well," she said lamely, "thank you, Mr. Justice."

He nodded. "Miz Weber."

She pulled open the office door, her feelings of guilt compounded when she saw Harvey loitering nearby. Had he been listening? Burdened with shame, she hurried from the saloon, eager to get away. She knew it was probably her overactive imagination and her guilt, but she thought Bram Justice had acted quite strangely toward her. Of course, no stranger than Mr. Bailey had.

She almost laughed. What a terrible criminal she'd make! *Guilty* could just as well have been stamped across her forehead. And this wasn't even a crime, for heaven's sake. She'd found money that had been stolen from her husband, and had spent some of it on *his* debts.

But the rest of it, what was safely tucked away in the back of her wardrobe, she wouldn't touch. Not until—well, not yet, anyway. There wasn't enough to pay off Jeremy's gambling debt. She'd been thinking about his final pay voucher, too. With a now familiar surge of anger, she realized that he probably owed the army money, rather than the army owing him. And since she was pretty sure that Jason would fire her when he returned from Sacramento, the stolen money was all that she had left in the world.

❧ Chapter Eighteen ❧

The mountains rose up around the valley, tall, pine-studded peaks laden with snow so white it blinded him.

He stopped his mount behind the manzanita brush and settled down to wait. How tempting it would have been to grab the Weber widow by the throat and demand to know where she'd gotten the money! Unfortunately, it hadn't been necessary. He'd recognized the curled bills immediately. He'd counted them often enough. Pushing good sense aside, he'd made his way to the empty building, dreading what he would find. His instincts had been correct. The money was gone.

He cursed himself for not moving it sooner. It had been foolish to think it was safer there than within his own strongbox. But it had given him perverse pleasure to skulk into the building unseen, and count and recount the ill-gotten money.

However, since the Weber woman had found his cache, she could inadvertently stumble on other clues. He'd been certain she knew what was going on, anyway. After all, not only was she the last survivor of his little massacre, but she'd discovered the stolen money. It seemed a shame to kill such a sweet, naïve woman, but he couldn't risk the possibility that she'd heard something that morning. Of course, the savages he'd hired professed to have kept their mouths shut, but with savages, one never knew whether they told the truth or just what one wanted to hear.

He'd decided months ago that the Weber widow was like a cat with nine lives. Twice he'd tried to get rid of her, and twice he'd failed. The first time he'd hit Tully—a rather unfortunate accident, but the old coot hadn't been hurt too badly. The second time she'd been clever enough to find the opening to the root cellar. That was a damned shame. And having the building refuse to catch fire was another thing he hadn't counted on. He'd been a fool to leave any clues at all, but so far, no one had traced back to him the one clue he had left. Fortunately, Tully was getting old and tired.

He squinted in the direction of the reservation. She should be coming along any minute, now. The third time was supposed to be the charm. Too bad Mrs. Rachel Weber wasn't as easy to kill as that drunken renegade, Holliday, and his ragged cronies.

A sly smile split his mouth. Damned fool Indians, thinking he would actually pay them for doing his dirty work. Not that they hadn't done a good job. Mutilation had been an ingenious idea, and so appropriate. Of course, had it been his idea, he'd have—

He stopped musing and listened. Yes, someone was coming. Excitement pumped through him. It was hard to always appear cool and collected when so often his blood ran hot with the thrill of the hunt. He sometimes wondered if perhaps he had purposely failed to kill the little widow the first time because he enjoyed stalking her so much.

Hiding behind the thick manzanita greenery, he rested his rifle on his shoulder and took aim.

Rachel struggled with the reins. It was hard enough for her to handle a team under normal circumstances, but today it was almost impossible. Since June still hadn't returned her cape, she'd been forced to wear one of Ivy's big, fleece-lined jackets. Although it was warm, it was bulky and difficult to maneuver in, for the sleeves kept slipping down over her hands. And the team was easy enough to control on the flat road, but here, on the stretch between the reservation foothills and the valley, the horses seemed spooked by the imprisoning mountains.

She smiled sadly as she rattled along. If the horses were spooked, she'd probably passed her own fears on to them. It wasn't fair to curse the poor animals with her own apprehensions.

The mountains seemed to pull in around her, causing her to fight for breath. She really thought she'd come to terms with them. She'd begun to love their beauty, slowly learning the variety of pines and firs, and even able to recognize certain birds by their song.

Everyone in California took the mountains for granted; to most, they were merely part of the landscape. But the first time she'd seen them, she'd felt they blocked her view. Always accustomed to seeing far onto the distant horizon, she felt the mountains were like great walls of granite that offered neither door nor window to what lay beyond. And she was accustomed to knowing what lay beyond. She'd much preferred the flat, treeless expanse of the Dakota plains. Even in the valley she felt safer, seeing the mountains at a distance.

Maybe her yearning for the flatlands was enough to help her make the decision to leave. But she still wanted to stay. A sad longing for what she and Jason might have had washed over her.

Suddenly, a rifle shot split the cold, quiet air. It crackled, echoing off the granite that surrounded her. Panic rose in her throat as the horses bolted, running headlong down the partially frozen, rutted path. She grabbed the reins with both hands and pulled back, bracing her feet on the board in front of her.

"Whoa!" she screeched. "Whoa, girls!"

She didn't have enough strength to stop them. The reins slipped slowly from her grasp and she steeled herself against the imminent crash. Forcing her gaze straight ahead, she held on and prayed. Her eyes stung from the blustery onslaught and she could hardly breathe. The cold, wet wind whistled around her ears and tunneled up the gaping sleeves of Ivy's jacket, sending a chill clear through to her bones.

The horses raced toward the sharp curve in the road, the wagon rattling and bouncing over the hard, deep ruts. Suddenly she heard a loud snap, and the horses galloped away, their gear flapping and dragging along behind them.

Rachel held on and slid to the floor of the buckboard, pressing herself under the seat and cushioning her face with the pillow she'd used to sit on. The wagon lurched sideways, into the thick, prickly brush that grew on the slope beside the road. She felt herself turning, moving, jolting hard against the underside of the seat. Abruptly, the wagon slid to a stop on top of her. She didn't move. She hardly dared breathe. She waited, just thankful she was alive.

Someone had scared the horses. It was unlikely that it had been just a random shot by a hunter, although it was possible. But she had a terrible feeling in the pit of her stomach that it hadn't been something as innocent as a hunter—unless, she thought, fresh fear chilling her, she was the hunted.

Stay calm. Don't move. She almost laughed. As if she *could* move. Pressing her mouth against the thick sleeve of her jacket, she tried to calm her ragged breathing and her racing heart.

She held her breath and listened. Her heart jumped into her throat once more when she heard dry brush snap and a horse snort very near the wagon. Instinct cautioned her to stay quiet. Minutes passed, and seemed like hours. Her ankle began to throb, and she realized that she'd somehow twisted it, probably when the wagon rolled over on top of her.

Suddenly she heard another shot, and the horse and rider near her bolted and galloped off, into the brush. She waited again, hardly daring to breathe.

"Mrs. Weber?"

Her insides quivered, then relaxed. It was Ben's voice. He'd just helped her unload the wagon at the reservation. She felt a twinge of relief.

"Mrs. Weber, are you all right?"

"Ben? Is . . . is that you?" Her voice sounded muffled even to her.

He lifted the wagon until he could see her. "Can you move at all?" he asked.

"I . . . I think so," she answered, pulling herself out from under it. When she'd crawled free, he let the wagon fall backward, down the hill.

He hunkered down in front of her. "Are you hurt?"

"I think I hurt my ankle."

"Can you move it?"

She gingerly rotated her ankle. "I can move it," she said around a gasp as pain shot up her leg.

Ben put his fists on his hips and shook his head. "Something spook the horses?"

"Yes. A shot." She sat up slowly and looked around. "I heard a shot."

Ben nodded, but said nothing. "I guess you'll have to ride into town with me. Think you can get up?"

"Yes, I'm fine. I'll be fine." She clenched her teeth and tried to get up without his help. She couldn't do it. Suddenly she wondered just how wise it was to trust Ben. After all, she hardly knew him at all.

He gripped her under the arms and helped her to her feet, then onto the back of his horse. He must have caught the apprehension in her eyes, because he said, "I didn't spook your horses, Mrs. Weber."

Feeling foolish and remorseful, she replied with a small smile, "I didn't really think you did."

He nodded. "It could have been a hunter."

"Yes," she answered a little too quickly. "I'm certain that's what it was." She wasn't convinced, and she didn't think he was, either. But she didn't want to dwell further on the possibilities.

"No doubt the horses are already in town," he remarked. "Everyone will wonder what's happened to you."

"Yes, I imagine they will." Anxious to get her mind off her present troubles and her painful ankle, Rachel changed the subject. "How is your son? Is he still with the Wilsons?"

Ben gently nudged his mount forward. "He's home with me now, but I still want him to learn to read and write English. Mrs. Gaspard, Jason's mother, has a school at the ranch. She's been kind enough to take my boy in with the other children."

"That . . . that's good, Ben." The pain in Rachel's ankle prevented her from blocking out her fears. Tossing anxious glances at the shadowy trees and shrubs alongside the road, she wondered if whoever wanted to kill her would try again. Finding the money had made her a prime target. If the idea hadn't frightened her so, she'd have thought it might be a good way to flush the killer out into the open.

She and Ben rode together in silence, down through the sloping hills, past the cold river and onto the lush green valley floor.

When Ben pulled up in front of Ivy's, he dismounted and helped Rachel hobble into the cafe.

"Rachel, honey!" Ivy hurried up to her, grabbed her shoulders and gave her a stern look. "What's happened? What is it?"

Rachel allowed herself to slump into Ivy's waiting arms. "Oh, Ivy, please, I can't stand up," she said shakily.

Ben and Ivy helped her sit down, and Ben carefully propped her leg up onto the chair across from her. Her ankle throbbed mercilessly.

"Something spooked the horses," Rachel said, reluctant to blurt out the words that someone was trying to kill her. "If Ben hadn't come along, I don't think I'd be here to tell you about it."

"Them horses roared into town just a few minutes ago. Jason took them over to the livery. Lan' sakes, he'll be just sick when—"

"Now, don't go exaggerating, Ivy. I'm fine. It's all very innocent, I'm sure. Something spooked the horses, and the wagon tipped over, but I'm fine. Honest, Ivy, *please* don't make a big issue of this." Her pulse fluttered. So, Jason was back.

Out of the corner of her eye, she saw him sprint into the

cafe, then slow down when he saw her sitting there. She'd never gone so many days without seeing him. All sorts of magical things happened inside her. She flushed, her pulse raced, her breathing became ragged . . . She loved him so fiercely.

He crossed to where she sat, his long, fluid stride filled with purpose and his lean hips unconsciously sending her erotic messages.

"Are you all right?" The question had all the warmth of a winter rain. The familiar hollowness in her stomach returned.

Their eyes met briefly, but he pulled his away. With the same professional detachment, he concentrated on her leg.

She didn't want to cry, but she felt tears anyway. They didn't come from her painful ankle, but from her pain-filled heart. "I . . . it's my ankle," she said carefully, unwilling to let him see her feelings. "It's nothing, really. I'll be fine."

"Dang it, she won't be fine, Jason. Lord a'mighty, she could have been killed out there." Ivy hovered over her like a lioness.

Jason took off her shoe. His hands moved over her foot and ankle, sending fluttering messages into Rachel's stomach in spite of the pain. She gazed down at the top of his head, aching to run her fingers through his thick, coarse hair, desperately wanting to pull him close and lose herself in his embrace.

"It isn't broken," he said without feeling.

"I know that," she snapped, angry at herself for allowing her dreams to interfere with reality. She wanted him so much, but knew she was a fool. All she could hope for was that he'd just go away, for having him near was more painful than any sprained ankle.

"Ivy? Get some cold compresses, would you, please? Does anything else hurt?" he grilled her, his voice terse.

Yes, you fool, my heart. With a weary shake of her head, she shrugged out of Ivy's enormous jacket and held it in her lap. She had no strength to put on an act. Had she not gotten hurt, she might have been able to convince even herself that she'd become strong and self-sufficient. It had been important that she appear independent. She didn't need him feeling sorry for her. And she'd wanted him to know that she could be stubborn and mule-headed, too . . . but it just wasn't her nature. She was too forgiving. She'd always been that way. That was a part of her she couldn't change.

As she'd watched him work on her ankle, she realized that he didn't appear worried about *what* she was feeling. She knew she looked horrible. Her skirt was filthy and had a long tear in it, her stockings were snagged, the eyelet hem of her petticoat was ripped clean off, and her hair had pulled free from its pins and was now a snagged, tangled mass that fell in disarray over her shoulders. It wasn't quite the way she'd hoped Jason would find her on his return from Sacramento.

She thought back to the other times Jason had tended to her cuts and bruises. It seemed he always saw her at her absolute worst.

"Nancy," Ivy called. "You bring Rachel some tea, and Jessie, get some towels and make a compress." She gripped Rachel's hands and looked at her sternly. "Were you coming from the reservation?"

Rachel nodded, then smiled up at Nancy as she set a cup of tea down in front of her. "I took the shoes out there. The children needed the shoes."

"Shame on you!" Ivy scolded. "Jason? Did you hear that? She went to the reservation by herself. Me and Earl warned her about that." She gave Rachel a stern look. "What were you thinking of, girl?"

Rachel wasn't in any mood to be scolded. Ignoring Ivy's little tirade, she glanced longingly at Jason's broad back. He'd ordered compresses for her ankle, then left her. He treated his horse with more care than he'd just given her. In spite of that, she ached for him.

He was still angry; she deserved his anger. If she'd been wise and had kept her feelings about Buck to herself that day, Buck wouldn't have been arrested. Whether she'd meant it or not, it was all her fault. And this time she wasn't just taking the blame because it was her nature. She took the blame because it was hers to take.

Everything Jason had ever said to her about his people, all of those things about how they weren't considered human and weren't allowed the same rights as Whites, had once seemed an exaggeration. She'd listened with polite, even sympathetic interest, but she hadn't entirely believed him. After all, he was seeing things from the other side of the fence. It had taken so much tragedy for her to realize that he'd been right all along.

But she had so much to tell Jason. She wanted to go back a few weeks and start over again. She needed to tell someone about the money, and she wanted it to be Jason. Because whether he believed it or not, he was the only person she truly trusted. She wanted to tell him about Buck's response to the leather money pouch that had been stolen from Jeremy's safe. And about the disappearance of her mother's cameo brooch . . . She wanted his confidence again. She wanted his trust. And, she realized, pressing her lips together to keep them from quivering, she most desperately wanted his love. But that, she realized, was something he hadn't even given her before.

Now, there he stood, completely and utterly shutting her out, his eyes focused on something outside, on the street. If he'd turn and take just one step in her direction, she'd do the rest. She'd run headlong into his arms, hobbling all the way, begging him to forgive all of her foolishness. She ached with longing. Her anguish deepened when he hurled himself away from the window and stormed out the door, leaving her without so much as a backward glance.

Jason deliberately slowed his pace as he crossed the street, trying to get a handle on his feelings. His heart had rammed into his rib cage when he'd seen Rachel, her face drawn and white and her sweet mouth trembling with fear. But at least she was alive. He'd feared the worst when the horses had sped into town without her or the wagon. She was bedrag-

gled and hurt and he'd treated her with the same indiffer-
ence as he had the first time he'd ever laid eyes on her. He
hadn't known her then, but now there was no excuse. She'd
nearly been killed, yet he couldn't meet her halfway. Damn
his stubborn pride! Thank God he'd asked Ben to keep an
eye on her while he was gone in case she ventured out of
town. He couldn't have lived with himself if something had
happened to her.

She didn't seem like a very strong woman, but when he
thought about what she'd already been through in her short
time in Pine Valley, he realized she had an inner strength
that matched the strongest he'd ever seen.

How he'd wanted to pull her into his arms. Just touching
her foot had sent crazy waves of longing crashing through
him. Longing for what they'd once had . . . he wondered if
they'd ever have it again. If there was a chance, everything
that was standing in their way would have to be cleared up.
And it was up to him. He knew he could hold a grudge
forever. He didn't think she was capable of it.

Now, he had a damned good idea who was behind all the
little mysteries concerning Weber and Ritter. And, if he was
right, he also knew who'd been trying to kill Rachel. He
didn't know why, and he knew he couldn't prove anything,
but he had a gut feeling.

Stepping into the saloon, he pulled the pungent coffee
smell deep into his lungs. An alarm went off inside his head.
Yes, this was where he'd smelled that special brand before.
So, now he knew *who* had been behind the attempts on
Rachel's life, but he sure as hell didn't know *why*. Not yet.

Harvey glanced up at him from behind the bar. "Well,
Doc. Haven't seen you in here for months. Can I get you
something?"

Jason's gaze went to the office door, then drifted slowly
back to the bartender. "Your boss in?"

Harvey looked away, busying himself with a row of bottles. "Yeah. He's . . . he's been in there all morning."

Jason's eyes narrowed. *You're a liar, Harvey.* He strode to the office door just as Bram Justice opened it. The saloon keeper stepped back, surprised.

"Jason," he said with a quick smile. "Is something wrong?"

Jason nodded. "I'd like to talk to you."

Justice, fully composed, ushered him into his office. "Can I offer you a cup of coffee?"

Jason swallowed a smile. "Yes. Thank you."

Bram poured the coffee, then set the china cup and saucer down on the desk in front of Jason. He inhaled the aroma again. This was it. His heartbeat sped up, adrenaline pressed through him. This was the coffee he'd smelled that morning he'd found Rachel huddled and shivering in the black corner of a root cellar.

Schooling in his thoughts, he casually sipped the coffee. "Unusual-tasting stuff. Sort of the 'sour mash' of coffees, wouldn't you agree?"

Justice ignored him.

"Do you get it around here?"

Bram was at his files, his back to Jason. "It's not so unusual, really. The mercantile has it."

"But they ship it in for you, don't they? From where, New Orleans?"

Bram turned around slowly. "And if they do? Does that make it a crime?"

Jason gave him an expansive, innocent smile. "Certainly not. I just said it had an unusual taste."

Bram gave him a careful look. "Of course."

He sat back, trying to enjoy the exquisite taste of the coffee. "How's Karleen?"

Bram stiffened. "What do you mean?"

"I'm a doctor, Bram. Even if I hadn't heard she was pregnant, I would have guessed it, back when she was running that high fever."

"She's fine." His answer was sharp, contained.

"Is she going to keep it?"

Bram turned, his black eyes glowing with hatred. "Not if I have anything to say about it."

Jason sighed and put his cup on the desk. "That's a dangerous choice, Bram. Have it done wrong, and she could die."

Suddenly, Bram attacked. "This is *my* business. I don't want or need your opinion. No half-breed is going to make the decision for me."

Jason raised his hands in a gesture of defeat. "Just remember what I said. Abortion could kill her *and* the child." Keeping in mind what he'd come into the saloon for, he asked, "Have you been here all morning?"

Bram's expression was carefully closed. "Why?"

Jason shrugged. "Harvey said you've been working in here all morning. But," he added, shifting in his chair, "I thought I saw you race into town just a short while ago."

Bram turned away, busying himself at his files again. "Harvey was mistaken. I . . . I did go out for a few minutes."

"Where?"

"I don't think that's any of your business. Or are you doing Tully's dirty work? God knows he's not capable of doing his own anymore."

So, he wasn't the only person who'd noticed Earl's lack of energy and interest. It probably gave Bram a false sense of security, knowing the marshal wasn't as quick as he used to be. "No, I'm not doing Earl's job. Just curious, I guess."

He rose to leave. "Thanks for the coffee."

Justice merely nodded, but continued to watch him until he was gone.

Once outside, Jason crossed to his office. He found Ben waiting for him inside.

"Well? What spooked the horses?"

"Not 'what,' but 'who.' "

"Bram Justice?"

"How'd you know?"

"I saw him ride into town just before you brought Rachel in. Did she say anything to you?"

"No," Ben answered. "She was pretty shook up. The wagon tipped over on top of her, but she somehow had curled up under the seat so she wasn't hurt." He paused.

"She could have been, though. Bram was poking around, probably looking for her body when I scared him away. I think he would have finished her off, Jason."

Jason let out a long sigh, then rubbed his neck. He didn't want to think about a world without Rachel in it. It was people like her who made it bearable for the rest. "Thanks, Ben. I'd hate to think what might have happened if you hadn't been there."

Ben shrugged. "You were right to have someone watch her."

"Yeah, now I have to watch *him*." And he also had to figure out a way to keep a closer eye on Rachel.

Rachel had felt listless ever since her accident. Her sore ankle gave her an excuse to do little, and she'd have happily stayed in her room, but Ivy refused to let her sulk. Of course, Ivy didn't know she was sulking, for she always pretended to be interested in Ivy's prattle.

"I think you should go."

"What?" Rachel asked, pulling herself away from her daydreaming.

"I said, I think you should thumb your nose at this whole danged town and go to the basket social."

Rachel laughed, but only to cover her feelings of emptiness. "Why would I want to put myself through that kind of punishment?"

"Oh, now, everyone doesn't think you're an 'Injun lover,' you know. And anyways, what's wrong with it? I like Indians just fine. Most of us do."

Rachel picked up the feather duster and dutifully went over the rungs on all the chairs at the table where they sat. "But most of them would gladly point the finger at any Indian who supposedly killed a loved one, wouldn't they? That makes me lower than low, Ivy."

"But you said you were sure that Jeremy's killer had a scar on his cheek."

"That's right. He did. But I didn't remember that until I

really came face to face with Buck. Something cleared in my head, like fog rolling away. It was the strangest sensation."

"Well, I don't want you moping around here anymore. Get out," Ivy urged. "Get out and meet some new people. If you're gonna stay on here, you'll have to make some friends."

If I'm going to stay on here, I'm going to need Jason's love.

"Oh, but I—"

"Now, don't back-talk, girl. Take out your prettiest dress, you know, the light blue one you rolled into a ball that day at the cabin."

The thought of wearing her wedding dress no longer made her ache. She'd gladly buried her feelings of hurt regarding her wedding and everything that had gone along with it. "And what am I supposed to do with it?"

Ivy shook her finger in Rachel's face. "I said, don't sass me, girl. That basket social at the church starts in three hours. You go get ready, and I'll put together a basket that'll have every man there droolin' over you *and* your lunch."

"But, Ivy. It's a summer dress. I'll freeze to death in it, especially since I don't have my cape."

Even though Ivy had often offered hers, every time Rachel put it on, she smelled the smoke that still permeated the fabric. She realized she'd rather freeze to death than wear something that reminded her of her close encounter with death.

Ivy wouldn't be dissuaded. "Then you can use mine. Smoke smell or not, it's better than nothing. And if you won't wear it, I'll find something else for you to wear. I ain't lettin' you get by with spending your time in that little room. If Jason don't know what he's got—"

"Jason?" Rachel interrupted, her heart leaping.

"Oh, now don't go thinkin' I haven't been aware of what's goin' on between the two of you. You wear your heart on your sleeve whenever you see him. And he's been slammin' around here for days, ornery as a mule with a boil on its butt.

"Now," she said, refusing to let Rachel argue, "I don't know what happened, and it ain't none of my business. But I *do* know when two people belong together. Now, if he's gonna be so stubborn, give him something to stew about. Get on over to that basket social and find yourself another beau."

Rachel bit back a sad smile. "Just like that?"

Ivy nodded. "Just like that. I'll drag you over there myself if I have to. The reverend was by earlier. His brother-in-law is in town, and I think the reverend was lookin' to fix the two of you up. Now, get—"

"Oh, no you don't." Rachel swung away from her. "I won't go if I'm going to be fixed up, Ivy. Honest, I won't go."

"Well, why in tarnation not? What's the harm?"

Rachel shook her head violently. "If it will get you off my back, I'll go to the social, but *please* don't try to fix me up with the reverend's brother-in-law."

Ivy stood back, her hands on her hips, and considered her. "Seems it would put a bee in Jason's britches if you let me fix you up with a beau."

Rachel drew in an exasperated sigh and rolled her eyes. "If you don't stop worrying about my love life right now, I'll pack my things and leave."

"And where would you go?"

"It doesn't matter. I'll go back East where no one knows me. I'd rather live like a spinster than have some strange man forced on me."

"Now, you really wouldn't leave, would ya?"

Rachel rubbed her temples. "Ivy, I'll go to that silly basket social if you'll please just leave me alone. I don't want any help from you."

Ivy looked away, appearing hurt.

"Oh," Rachel said. "I didn't mean to hurt your feelings, Ivy. I . . . I just don't want or need a man in my life."

Ivy sniffled. "You promise to go to the social?"

Rachel sighed again. "I promise."

"I'll make you the best basket," Ivy said, her enthusiasm quickly restored. "I have some chicken I just fried this morning, and some lemon pie, and I'll whip up some fresh buttermilk biscuits . . ."

She was making Rachel tired. "Fine, fine," she said as she limped to her door. She turned back to say something, and Ivy had already disappeared into the kitchen.

Going through her sparsely furnished wardrobe for something special to wear depressed her further. Besides the dress she'd worn for her wedding, which hadn't even really been a wedding dress but a garden dress, she had few nice things.

Rummaging through her clothes, she came across the light blue-figured batiste hanging on a hanger. She gently ran her fingers over the open oversewn lace inserts at the hem and the waist. At the neck she stopped, imagining the cameo nestled in the folds of the lacy fabric. The sleeves were long, Juliet type made of net, but certainly not warm. Should she wear it anyway?

Why not? Now wasn't the time to brood. And she might as well forget how the cameo would look, because it was gone. She did know that when Captain Weber returned from Sacramento she was going to confront him about it.

A sick feeling burrowed into her stomach as she glanced at the dress. She didn't want to wear it. It was like an open admission that she was out looking for a man. Tossing the dress one last look before washing up, she wondered why she was even bothering to dress up at all.

She was overdressed and she felt foolish. The other women wore serviceable, warm dresses. Hers was neither. It wasn't appropriate for a rural basket social. And the reverend's brother-in-law, a young blond man with an eager, pleasant face, hovered nearby. Once he'd discovered her hobbling into the church hall on a makeshift crutch, he apparently decided to become her slave. He'd told her he'd get her anything she wanted.

She *wanted* to go home. She was cold, miserable, and sick to her stomach. The over-eager suitor caught her eye and smiled. She smiled back, hoping she wasn't as sick looking as she felt. Surely he didn't think this was a date. The reverend had introduced them when she arrived—what was his name, again? Oh, yes. Darwin . . . Durwood? No, Darwin. Darwin something-or-other. Poor man, he was probably very nice. He had kind brown eyes. Sort of puppy-dog eyes. And a puppy-dog personality, always eager to please.

She frowned and looked away. When had she become so cynical?

"Is . . . is something wrong, Mrs.—er . . . Rachel?"

He was at her elbow. She gave him a weak smile and shook her head. She wished the afternoon and the evening would end. So, this is the way it would be for the rest of her life. Meeting perfectly nice men, then comparing them to Jason.

If she hadn't been so miserable, she might have laughed. Comparisons should have put every man ahead of Jason, considering his sarcasm, stubbornness, arrogance, and lack of trust. But for some reason, she couldn't imagine living the rest of her life with a mild-mannered man who seemed to know her every desire—and acted upon it—before she even knew it herself. It made her feel shame, because she didn't think there was a woman alive who wouldn't adore that trait in a husband.

The reverend went to the podium and raised his hands. Everyone fell silent.

"This is a wonderful turnout," he said with quiet enthusiasm. "I've been blessed twofold this week, and I want to share my joy with all of you." He tossed a warm, loving smile at the pale woman sitting across from Rachel.

"My beautiful wife, Birgit, has been given a clean bill of health by our own Dr. Gaspard. Of course, he told me to hire someone to help with the children until she gets stronger, but I have no problem with that."

Rachel glanced at the reverend's wife, who was returning her husband's special, secret look. Rachel's quiet envy ate at her, and she felt ashamed.

"Secondly, her brother, Darwin Thorpe, is staying with us for a while. Please make him feel welcome." He looked at Rachel, who couldn't move away from Darwin without making it look obvious, and added, "Seems he's already made a good friend."

There were snickers from the other single men in the back of the room. Rachel was sure she heard "Injun lover," but perhaps she was just overly sensitive. She wanted desperately to go back to the safety of her room.

"Now," the reverend continued, "the baskets look beautiful and smell delicious. I know all you men are anxious to start the bidding. Why don't we get at it?"

Rachel had to stop herself from running from the room. She'd purposely put her basket in the back, hoping it would go unnoticed. And it might have, she realized forlornly, had it not been for Darwin Thorpe.

The baskets began to disappear, each one bid upon by an anxious suitor or a faithful, complaisant husband. As Rachel's came closer to the front, she felt that familiar, anxious stomachache.

"Now, this sure is a pretty one," Reverend Toland said as he picked up Rachel's basket. "How much am I bid for this?"

"Fifty cents." Darwin Thorpe's voice was a bit high-pitched, but very confident.

The reverend smiled. "I have fifty cents." He bent over the basket, pulled in a deep breath and closed his eyes in ecstasy. "This smells mighty good, fellas. I wouldn't let this go for fifty cents if I were you."

There was some good-natured elbowing by the few remaining single men who hadn't already bought a basket, but there was some snickering, too. Rachel heard it clearly.

The room was deathly quiet. Everyone who had already been paired off stopped what they were doing and watched the tragedy play out before them. A tragedy from Rachel's perspective, anyway. She wanted to crawl into a hole and pull it in after her.

"Come on now, fellas," the reverend cajoled. "This basket is worth three times that. Do I hear a dollar fifty?"

Silence. The single men shuffled their feet and looked at the floor. Darwin Thorpe cleared his throat nervously. Rachel wanted to evaporate.

"Twenty-five dollars."

Rachel's head snapped up and she stared at the door. Warmth flooded her and her heart nearly burst in her chest. Jason stood at the back, his dark gaze blazing a hot path over her skin.

❧ *Chapter Nineteen* ❧

Rachel heard the reverend's voice, but she was no longer listening. She watched, her heart in her throat, as Jason strode purposefully through the crowd to where she sat.

As he reached her, she saw the quiet defiance in his eyes, as if daring her to refuse him—no matter what he asked. She knew there was nothing she wouldn't give him.

"Yes, Reverend," he said, not taking his eyes off Rachel, "twenty-five dollars for that basket."

Quietly, Rachel asked herself what this meant. Her own answer was joyous, but still she held back.

"Rachel?" Jason took the cape he had draped over his arm and held it for her. With disbelief she stared at the cloak, realizing it was the one she'd seen in the merchant's window months ago—black silk, with hood and shawl, all lined in black velvet.

Something winked at her from the shiny dark fabric. Pinned high on the shoulder of the cloak was her mother's pearl-encrusted cameo. Biting her lips to keep them from trembling, she stood, leaning on her crutch, and allowed him to drape the cape over her shoulders.

The reality of what he'd done left her speechless. "Thank you," she whispered, turning and looking at him over her shoulder. Everything about him—his smell, his presence, his voice—rushed over her with wonderful, warm familiarity.

He gave her a private smile. Stepping away from her briefly, he pulled out his money clip and peeled off a couple of bills. "This is for the basket, reverend. And this," he said, taking out a few more, "is for the ceremony."

Rachel's heart flip-flopped in her chest and she stared from Jason to the reverend. She knew her mouth was hanging open.

"Ceremony?" The Reverend Toland was perplexed.

"Please," Jason said, nodding toward the sanctuary. "Could we talk in there?"

Reverend Toland gave him a tentative, warm smile. "Certainly. Of course. Of course."

"And," Jason added, "Birgit? Would you come, too?"

Rachel's face was wet with tears. She hardly dared think about what was happening. "Jason? What are you doing?"

He gave her a stern look. "You'll see." He handed her the basket, lifted her into his arms and followed the reverend into the sanctuary.

Rachel pulled back and looked at him, adoring the haughty slope of his incredible eyes. "Would you like to tell me what's going on?"

He gave her another private grin. "I'm afraid if I do, you won't let me do it."

She hardly dared to breathe. "Do what?"

"Marry you."

A worrisome little question sprouted in her thoughts, asking her why he'd do this, but she shoved it far back into the attic of her mind. It hardly mattered why. She wanted this. "Oh, you know I'll marry you. But . . . but what's the hurry? Ivy should be here, and . . . and Earl—" It didn't dawn on her to argue, much less refuse. She loved him too much.

"They're on their way," he answered, giving her a chaste kiss on the mouth.

"And . . . and you love me? Do you, Jason?"

He gazed at her for a long, poignant minute. The pause would have bothered her if she hadn't been so much in love.

"Would I ask you to marry me if I didn't?"

It wasn't the answer she'd hoped for, but it would do. She looked down at her dress and thought of the irony of it all.

The last time she'd worn it, she'd thought she was happy. Then, she'd been a starry-eyed, naïve girl. This time she wasn't. Well, maybe still a little starry-eyed. Loving Jason did that to her. She suddenly remembered the speed with which she married the first time.

"But . . . but what's the hurry? What about your parents? Won't they—"

He covered her mouth with a deep, impetuous kiss. One she couldn't ignore. The intimacy with which he kissed her was yet another thing she'd missed. The taste of him, the way his mouth and his tongue could send dandelion fluff whirling around in her stomach, then deeper . . . It had been so long . . . so long . . . She had a dozen questions, but they could wait. They could all wait until later.

When he finally pulled away from her, she was as anxious to go through the ceremony as he was. Questioning him about his hasty decision was the furtherest thing from her mind.

Rachel sat on the bed and studied the ring Jason had given her. An emotion stronger than she could hold burst through her, and her eyes filled with tears of joy. The ring had belonged to Anna's grandmother. It wasn't fancy, it had no large stone, but the lacy gold filigree was delicate and lovely. Nothing could have made her happier.

Her gaze shifted to the table and the scattered remnants of their picnic lunch. Jason had insisted they eat it *au naturel*. Now, watching him pour her a glass of champagne, Rachel realized that although she still wasn't comfortable with her own nudity, she'd become very comfortable with his. She'd never tire of seeing his body, or the casual way he displayed it for her.

Staring first at his wide, hard shoulders, then down his back to his tight buttocks, she shuddered as she remembered gripping him there whenever he came into her. He turned, moving toward her, a full glass of champagne in each hand. She still felt physical pain when she saw or touched his chest. Everything he'd gone through so many years ago was transferred to her. She didn't ever want that to change. She always wanted to feel his joy as well as his pain. Though he surely hated August Weber, Rachel had never heard him say the words.

Her gaze trailed lower, to where his root sprang from the heavy bush of black hair. Although they'd just made love, she wanted him again, but she still wasn't accustomed to being the aggressor.

He stood beside the bed and grinned down at her. "What are you looking at?"

She gave him a lazy smile. "I was just thinking that even though you have no hair on your chest, you *do* have it in all the important places."

Arousal flared in his eyes. "You've become quite a brazen hussy, haven't you, Mrs. Gaspard?" He handed her a glass, and they gave each other a silent toast.

"Thanks to you, Dr. Gaspard." She still had the bedcovers hiked up over her breasts.

He grinned down at her. "Are you cold, or just shy?"

A wave of warmth washed over her. "A little of both, I guess." She glanced at the window. "It's still daylight, Jason, and we've . . . we've already . . . done it."

His eyes sparkled with humor. *"Done it?* Don't you know what it's called?"

She blushed, truly feeling shy. "Of course I do."

"Then say it," he answered, sitting beside her on the bed.

Forcing her eyes up to meet his gaze, she said, "We made love."

He gave her a good-natured smirk. "Oh, we did that, all right. But what else?"

She took a long, nervous gulp of champagne. "We . . . we had intercourse."

"Yes," he agreed. "We had that, too. But don't get technical, Rachel love. Tell me," he said, running his fingers across her breasts, then on down to the triangle at the crest of her thighs, "what we call it when we're so damned hot for each other we can't get out of our clothes fast enough?"

The champagne was beginning to loosen her up. The

place between her legs throbbed. "You mean like that time in the closet?" She still remembered the urgency of that coupling, and it aroused her further.

"Exactly," he answered, letting his gaze rest on the hardened points of her nipples beneath the sheet.

She knew what he wanted her to say. It excited her when he whispered those things to her. It made her feel lusty and sensual when her every thought was centered on the feelings between her legs. "Oh, Jason, I know what you want, but . . . but no matter how much I want you, I . . . I just can't say it out loud."

His eyes softened. "Can you whisper it to me?"

"You . . . you don't think it would be awful of me?"

He took her glass and put both of them on the table beside the bed. "It's not an awful thing for a wife to say to her husband, Rachel, believe me. In fact, many men like it."

"And you? Would you like it?" She was so aroused she could hardly breathe. She was afraid she was going to climax without him even touching her.

"Oh," he answered, his stirring gaze answering for him, "I'd like it a hell of a lot."

She was ready to spontaneously combust. "All right," she said around a shy smile, "come here."

He bent close and she whispered the raunchy, erotic words into his ear. His sharp intake of breath and the condition of his manhood told her he was pleased. She, on the other hand, was ready to burst into flames.

He moved away and tugged at the bedding, revealing her nudity. "There's something I've always wanted to do."

Swallowing a delicious shudder, she asked, "What's that?"

"Brace yourself." He retrieved his glass from the table and tipped it just enough so that a small trickle of champagne splashed onto her stomach, pooling in her navel, then tunneling on down into the soft hair that grew low on her belly.

She sucked in a quick breath and let it out shakily as he dipped his head and lapped up the moisture. His tongue slid down into her hair and she stiffened, raising up off the bed.

The sensation wasn't unpleasant at all, but it had taken her completely by surprise.

"I guess you're not quite ready for that," he said, his voice soft and teasing.

"What . . . what were you going to do?" Her heart pounded so hard in her chest, she thought it might break free.

He continued to grin at her. "Think about it for a while, Rachel love. Just think about what I could do down there with my mouth."

Before she could imagine what he had in mind, he bent and kissed her stomach. Heat, deep and powerful, burned inside her. Her need for him intensified when he worked his way up to her breasts, pulling and tugging on first one nipple, then the other, until she wasn't sure she could stand it anymore.

Spreading her legs, she felt him nestle against her. He teased her with his hard tip, touching, rubbing the maddening itch of her burgeoning bud. When she thought she could take no more, when every nerve ending was alive with desire, and she was hanging on to him with all of her strength, he finally slid into her, pressing deep.

She clung to him, pushing against him so tightly, she felt the coarse hairs of his bush entwine with hers. Wrapping her legs around him, she waited impatiently for him to move inside her. Then he began. He didn't pull out and thrust again, but rocked slowly. She felt her climax start deep in her womb, a slow bubbling of intense desire that suddenly shook her as spasm after spasm wracked her, and she heard herself cry out.

Jason continued rocking, harder and faster until she felt him explode inside her. She held on, refusing to let him go. The last thing she remembered before she fell asleep was being rolled to her side and feeling the covers tucked in around them.

When Rachel awakened, it was dark. She sensed that Jason was awake beside her. "Jason?"

"Hmmm?"

She gently touched his chest, running her fingers over each scarred furrow. "I . . . I have to tell you something."

"Yes?"

"Remember . . . remember the money the marshal said had been stolen from Jeremy's safe?"

"I remember," he answered, absently stroking her hip.

She swallowed hard. "I found it."

He sat up. "You *found* it? Where?"

She told him about going into the warehouse to make room for the other supplies, and how she'd found it behind a loose brick in the fireplace.

"What did you do with it?" His voice was strained.

"Well, I . . . I figured the money was mine. And . . . and Jeremy had left so many debts all over town, I thought it . . . it wouldn't hurt to start paying them off."

She didn't mention her surprising trip to the bank or the mysterious disappearance of her mother's cameo.

"So, who did you pay off?"

"Well, first let me tell you what I did to prove to myself that your friend Buck wasn't involved."

He chuckled beside her.

"What's so funny?"

"Is this about the leather pouch?"

She stared at him in the darkness. "How did you know?"

"Buck told me you'd planted it on his lunch tray. He had no idea what it was all about, but that it was a pretty transparent attempt to find out something."

She felt a rush of foolishness. "He probably thinks I'm a real ninny."

"No, he really doesn't, Rachel." His hand returned to her hip and he stroked her tenderly.

"Maybe not, but he still must blame me because he's in jail."

Jason shifted beside her. "It's odd. Jail has given Buck time to think. He's actually become quite philosophical." He paused for a moment. "And he doesn't want to die."

"Jason, I didn't tell Captain Weber what I thought about Buck. He admitted to me that he'd overheard our conver—"

"I know," he interrupted.

"How did you know?"

"Well, I didn't know at first. At first, I was angry. I'd decided that even though you tried to do the right thing once you got to the jail, it was too late. Weber had already made up his mind about Buck. So, I wanted it to be your fault."

"Oh, darling, I—"

"No," he interrupted again. "If you're going to apologize, don't. Buck's innocent. We both know that. Somehow, we'll get him out of there before Weber takes him to Fort Riley."

She cuddled against him. "I feel so safe now that I'm with you."

"Rachel," he said, absently stroking her breast, "where else did Jeremy owe money besides the bank?"

Fresh adoration flushed her skin. "Thank you again for getting back my cameo. I . . . I didn't think anyone knew of Jeremy's debts besides me and the captain. And . . . and of course, Ivy and the marshal."

He pulled her close. "I'd seen you come out of the bank months ago. I had a feeling Weber had money problems."

"Well, thank you, again." She ran her hand down over his warm groin and cradled him in her palm. His root twitched and grew slightly at her touch.

He stilled her hand. "Not so fast. Where else did Jeremy owe money?" he repeated.

"He owed Bram Justice three thousand dollars."

Jason swore, then pulled her into his arms. "Dammit, Rachel, Justice is the man who's trying to kill you."

She went cold. "Oh, dear heaven . . ." She clung to him, her mind whirling. "Do you suppose he's the one who stole the money?"

"I think that whoever he hired to kill Ritter and Weber stole it for him."

Even though she was tucked safely into Jason's arms, she began to shiver. "I'm really in trouble, Jason."

"I know you are, Rachel love." He stroked her back and her buttocks soothingly.

She pulled away slightly. "You don't understand. I paid off part of Bram's loan with the money I found. And if he's checked on his stash, he knows it's gone."

The two little boys had coerced Concetta, the elderly Gaspard housekeeper, into packing them each a hearty lunch. They were off, they had told her, to track the wild buffalo that hid in the hills beyond the vineyard. They took Bruno, Dusty's grandpa's hound, with them.

The early April sun was warm. It was like a summer day. Joshua and Dusty tramped through the brush, content to explore every crevice and tree hole. Bruno loped on ahead, breaking the trail, sniffing out clues to the whereabouts of the elusive buffalo.

Joshua took his walking stick and pushed over a rotting log, sending the denizens beneath it squirming and wriggling against the bright daylight.

Both boys squatted and watched, fascinated by the flurry of activity.

"Them's maggots," Dusty said, his face intense.

"Naw, they're just boxer bugs."

Dusty nodded, obviously impressed with his older friend's knowledge. "Let's pee on 'em."

"Yeah."

Both boys opened their flies and drowned the bugs with urine, delighted to see that some of them floated, belly-up, to the top of the puddle.

Dusty eyed Joshua's penis. "Mine's browner than yours."

Joshua pulled on his. "Mine's bigger."

"Yeah, but you're older. Mine'll get bigger, too. One day it'll be *real* big."

"Yeah, mine, too."

Confident the bugs were dead, they shook off their little peckers, poked them back in their shorts, and rolled the log back where they'd found it.

They trudged on, their lunches safely hidden away in the makeshift backpacks strapped to their backs, and their pockets filled with treasures, both dead and alive.

"I'm hungry," Dusty whined.

"Me, too. Let's eat over there by that tree. Bruno!" Joshua shouted. "Stop your barkin'."

The boys pulled off their backpacks and flopped to the ground, resting their backs against the big trunk while Bruno continued to bark.

"What's he barkin' at?" Dusty took a bite out of his sandwich and peered at the dog.

Joshua shook his head. "Prob'ly a coon or something."

They ate hungrily. Joshua looked at his last bite of sandwich. "Here, Bruno," he called, holding out the morsel. The dog ignored him. "C'mon," he said to Dusty. "Let's see what he's barkin' at."

The boys slowed down when they saw the dog, his nose poked into the hole of a small cave hidden on the side of a rocky hill.

Dusty swallowed hard. "Maybe it's a bear."

Joshua tried to quell the fear in his belly. "Naw, a bear would've growled at him or somethin'." He crept up behind the hound, trying to look inside the cave without getting too close. He caught a flash of something light.

Grabbing hold of Bruno's collar, he tugged the dog sideways. "Dusty, hold Bruno back while I look inside."

Dusty took a few tentative steps, just close enough so he could grab Bruno's collar when Josh let go.

Arming himself with his walking stick, Joshua got down on his hands and knees and peered into the cave. "Well, shit my britches," he whispered, unable to believe what he saw.

"What? What is it?" Dusty craned his neck but couldn't see beyond Josh's rump.

"A boy. Jeee-zuz cripes, Dusty, there's a boy in here!"

❧ Chapter Twenty ❧

*J*oshua and Dusty coaxed the boy out of the cave with food. He was ragged, dirty, and half-starved. Unaware of who he was or where he lived, the boys urged him to come home with them.

As the three of them and Bruno trudged up the path that went to the kitchen, Concetta burst from the house, Joshua's mother on her heels.

Concetta nearly smothered the boy with affection. *"Dios! Dios!* Poor little *niño."*

Anna bent down and looked at the boy, whose face was so dirty it was hard to tell what he looked like. "Where did you find him, Josh?"

"In a cave. Bruno found him first. He don't talk, Ma. He don't say anything."

" 'Doesn't,' Josh, not 'don't,' " she said absently as she continued to look at the child.

"What'll we do with him?" Dusty asked.

"We keep him, that's what," Concetta said hotly, hugging the tiny boy to her ample chest.

"Concetta, he might have a family. We can't just keep him. Someone must be worried sick about him."

The elderly housekeeper peered up at her employer. "Can we at least give him a bath and a meal?"

Anna smiled softly. "Of course. And Josh, he looks to be about your size. Why don't you go up and get him some clean clothes?"

As Josh and Dusty raced toward the house, Anna's gaze

went to the barn. "Jason just rode in. He's in the barn with his father. After you've given him a bath, we'll have Jason look him over to make sure he's all right. Then," she added on a sigh, "somehow we'll have to find out who he is."

Rachel was relieved when Jason told her Willy had been found and was currently staying at the ranch.

"Why do you think he ran away?"

Jason removed his jacket and tossed it on the bed. "Probably because he was threatened by whoever had given him that note."

Rachel took Jason's jacket off the bed and hung it up. "Poor little thing. What happens to him now?"

Jason chuckled. "Concetta won't let the poor kid out of her sight. Dad said she's acting the same way toward Willy that she acted toward him when he stumbled onto the ranch almost forty years ago, looking for his father."

"Will he stay there?"

"I don't see why not. He's safer there, at least for now." He laughed softly again. "Poor kid doesn't know what he's in for. Mute or not, Mother will see that he attends the vineyard school, and Concetta will make him take a bath once a week, whether he needs it or not. And," he added, shaking his head at the thought, "she'll keep him so full of tortillas and beans, he'll gratefully sneak away with Josh and Dusty to eat dandelion greens in the woods."

Rachel was filled with warmth. "Is that what you did?"

"Many times," he said, answering her smile.

A horrible thought struck her. "What will happen if Bram discovers where the boy is? Would he try to harm him?"

"No one has to know where he is until Bram's been dealt with, Rachel. And that's another thing. You're not to go anywhere alone. *Anywhere*. Is that clear?"

"Do you really think Bram Justice would harm a defenseless little child?"

Jason raked his fingers through his thick mane of hair. "I wouldn't put it past him, honey. He's tried to kill you, hasn't he?"

He was right; Rachel knew it. When he began rubbing his neck, she gently shoved him into a chair and massaged it for him. "I can always tell when you're tight as a rope, darling. As a doctor, you should know that all that tension isn't good for you."

He gave her a pleasure-filled groan and flopped his head forward onto his chest.

Rachel pressed her thumbs into the tight cords on either side of his spine and worked her way up into his neck and down his back. "What are we going to do?"

"We aren't going to do anything. Is that understood?"

She stopped massaging his back just long enough to give him a fierce hug from behind. Nuzzling the back of his ear with her nose, she whispered, "Understood." As long as Jason loved her, she wouldn't jeopardize her own safety. She had too much to live for now.

"I have to go out to the reservation this afternoon. I want you to stay here. Don't go anywhere. Not even to Ivy's. Is that clear?"

She hugged him again. "I'm not a child, Jason. I understood you the first time."

"Hmmm," he grunted. "Seems to me I know someone who nearly got herself killed because she went off to a vacant cabin without telling anyone."

"That was then. This is now. I won't go anywhere alone." Kissing the back of his neck, she added, "I have enough paperwork to keep me busy, anyway."

He gently squeezed her arms. "As long as we understand each other."

"Why can't I go with you?" She ran her nails up and down his back, loving his contented sigh.

"Because Birgit Toland is supposed to stop by with a sputum sample, and I want to make sure someone is here to take it."

"Is she really better?"

"Yes," he answered, getting up from the chair and moving away from her. "She'd be better off in a warmer climate, but her husband takes good care of her. He's hired June to help with the children."

She smiled. "Oh, that's wonderful. June is such a sweet person."

"And she needs the distraction right now. With Molly gone, she just doesn't have enough to keep her mind off the past." He gathered some things into his black bag.

"Oh, darling," Rachel said quickly, "I have to pick up something from Ivy's. Can you stay until I get back?"

He gave her a stern look. "All right, but if you have to visit, tell her to come over here. I want to leave by noon."

Rachel crossed to the door, then stopped, turning to look at him. "Aren't you going to kiss me goodbye?"

He gave her a heart-stopping look of hunger. "It won't distract you from your mission?"

"I would hope so," she said with feeling, reaching out for him as he came to her. She went into his arms and raised her face to his. "You have the most beautiful, incredibly sensual eyes of any man on earth," she whispered. "It's the first thing I noticed about you."

He grinned and pushed his pelvis against hers. "What was the second thing?"

She reached down, squeezing him gently through his jeans. "I didn't notice *that* until much, much later."

They kissed, a deep, wet tonguing that left them both intoxicated.

"I'll finish that tonight, when I get back," he warned, his eyes black with arousal.

"I can't wait." She tamped down her excitement as she left the office.

Less than forty-five minutes later, she was on her way back from the cafe, so ecstatic her feet barely touched the ground. She felt a little guilty stretching the truth about picking up something at Ivy's, but she wanted some "girl talk," and she wanted it *now*.

She'd missed her monthly cycle. It had been two weeks, and until now, she'd never been late by more than a day or two. Even at the most stressful times in her life, she'd still gotten her menses on time. She prayed she was pregnant. It was too early to tell, Ivy had told her. Oh, but she wanted Jason's baby. Not just one, but many, many babies.

It would be hard to keep it a secret for very long, especially from a husband who was a doctor. But she wanted to be sure. She wanted to miss two periods before she said anything to him at all. She also hoped he wouldn't curb his lusty lovemaking after he found out.

Giving her flat stomach a happy hug, she went into their apartment through the side door.

She heard voices in the office. She crossed the room, intending to enter the office until she heard her name. Sucking in a startled breath, she stopped and listened.

"I can't believe you did that."

It was Jason's father's voice. He sounded angry and disgusted.

"I did what I had to do." Jason's voice was cold.

"But did you have to *marry* the girl? Wasn't that just a little extreme?" Nicolas Gaspard swore. "Most men would have hired a bodyguard or a nursemaid to protect her. Why in the name of hell did you have to *marry* her?"

Rachel felt sick. Pressing her hand over her mouth, she slumped against the wall, briefly closing her eyes. She should have known. It had all been too good to be true. Quietly, she hurried back outside. Her joy and happiness had evaporated like steam on the wind. She cursed herself for eavesdropping. She'd only learned awful things that way, things that hurt her deeply. One would have thought she'd learned her lesson the first time.

So, she didn't have the perfect marriage after all. But, she thought with a little hope, it was still a marriage, and she loved Jason fiercely. That he didn't love her also hurt, but she would make him love her. It surely wasn't the first time she'd had to work for something she wanted. She thought back to her wedding day, to his answer to her question about loving her.

Would I marry you if I didn't?

Yes, of course he would; he had. She thought of their

nights together, and she knew he desired her. And she thought of the child she might be carrying. She still hoped she was pregnant, but all of the excitement and anticipation had gone out of her dreams. Living with Jason would hurt, but she'd put up a good front. She'd make him happy, and hope he would never be sorry he'd married her. But he could never know that she'd overheard him talking with his father. It would only make things worse—for both of them.

She'd make the best of this; she'd been making the best of bad situations since the death of her parents. Her first marriage had been a sham. This one wouldn't be. She wouldn't let it be.

Biting back tears, she realized that as long as he didn't love her, letting him be intimate was going to be the hardest thing she'd have to endure. It would be hard to get lost in the glory of passion now that she knew he only married her to keep an eye on her.

Composing herself, she walked purposefully to the office door and stepped inside. Feigning surprise, she met her reluctant father-in-law, who was on his way out.

His smile was somewhat warmer than she'd expected. "Welcome to the family, Rachel."

"Why, thank you, sir," she said with forced enthusiasm.

He pulled back, surprised. "*Sir?* Now, we can't have such formality. Please call me Nicolas."

She smiled gaily, and bravely returned his wave. Inside, she felt empty and nauseated. Turning toward the office, she found Jason in front of her, studying her.

"Is something wrong?"

Laughing quickly, she brushed off his concern. "Of course not. What could possibly be wrong?"

He frowned. "I don't know. I thought maybe someone had said something to you. I know people are still snickering about your marriage to a half-breed."

She melted at his concern. "Oh, don't be silly. What other people say doesn't bother me." She gave him a sad little laugh. "I've developed a pretty thick skin since I moved here."

"Well," he said, shuffling nervously, "if everything's all right, I'd better leave for the reservation."

She had to force herself to kiss him. Not because she didn't love him, but because, in spite of everything, she loved him too much.

"Is that all I get?" He touched her shoulders. "You weren't even gone an hour, and you got much more than that. I'll be gone all afternoon. Come here," he ordered softly.

Rachel moved easily into his arms. His kiss was as passionate as always. The moment their lips touched, she was lost—and confused. She was glad when he left, for she immediately burst into tears.

The chime clock had just struck two when the office door opened.

Looking up from Jason's desk, Rachel was surprised to see Nell. "Nell? Is something wrong?"

Nell's gaze flitted nervously around the room. "I've just come from the reservation. Jason wants to see you, right away."

Alarm spread through Rachel. "He . . . he does? What does he want?"

She cleared her throat. "I have no idea. He just told me to tell you to come."

Rachel rose slowly. Nell's animosity toward her hadn't changed. "Now, that's odd. He told me not to leave the office alone under any circumstances." But, she thought, already thinking ahead, Birgit Toland *had* dropped off the sputum sample, so there was nothing to keep Rachel there.

"Well," Nell said after a pause, "I'm to take you there so you don't have to go alone."

"Oh, that makes sense, I guess." Rachel went to get her cape, then glanced at Nell's mannish pants. "How are we getting there?"

"I'm afraid I just have my horse. Do you ride?"

Rachel grimaced. "Not very well, but I can hang on. If you can wait just a minute, I'll change into something else."

She went into their apartment, changing into an old

linen shirtwaist and a pair of twill trousers she'd found in one of Jason's drawers. Going back into the office, she shrugged into the fleece-lined jacket she'd borrowed from Ivy, and strode to the door.

Nell's gaze fluttered over her before she turned away. "Oh, one other thing. The money you found?"

Rachel faltered and her insides went cold. "The . . . the money?"

Nell quickly attempted to calm her. "Don't worry, Rachel. Jason told me all about how you found the stolen money."

Rachel felt a twinge of annoyance that Jason would confide in Nell so quickly and easily. "Oh, he did, did he?"

"We've been friends for a long time. There's hardly anything we don't tell each other."

Rachel narrowed her gaze at the Indian woman. She wondered if perhaps Jason had also confided the real reason he'd married her. No doubt he had. A slow burn simmered inside her.

"What about the money?" Rachel refused to just take her word for it.

"He wants you to bring it."

Nell's gaze was straightforward and honest. Rachel could think of no reason why she'd lie to her. "Did he tell you why he wanted it?" She tried to curb the anger in her voice.

Nell shrugged. "Something about using it as evidence against someone."

Rachel hid her feelings as she crossed to the safe and took out the money, which she'd replaced in the original leather pouch. She wasn't a bit comfortable about this. "I suppose he told you who?"

"Of course he did."

Rachel shoved the pouch into her jacket pocket and met Nell at the door. She stood, staring at Nell for a long, tense minute, trying to decide whether or not to trust her. "Who is it?"

Nell gave her the faintest flicker of a smile. "Bram Justice."

The wind went out of Rachel's sails and she felt limp as a

dishrag. She began to wonder if Jason told this woman *every-thing* that went on between them. "Let's get going, then."

Rachel hung on for dear life. Completely unfamiliar with the correct way to straddle a horse, she found her buttocks smacking the horse's rump with every step. She gritted her teeth, knowing with certainty that she was going to be very sore in the morning.

Once they were into the foothills on the road to the reservation, Nell nudged her mount off onto a narrow side road.

Alarm shot through Rachel. "Why are you taking this road?"

"It's a shortcut," Nell answered, tossing the words over her shoulder.

The foliage was dense and dark and tree branches hung over the path, like the tentacles of some stark, ghostly monster. A strange sensation prickled the hairs on the back of Rachel's neck. "I'd rather stick to the main road, Nell."

"This one will get us there much quicker. Quit worrying. God," she said with a disgusted sigh. "You're such a worrywort."

Yes, Rachel thought, she probably was. Still, she had the most uncomfortable feeling . . .

They rode to a small opening where a tiny ramshackle old miner's cabin squatted beneath the trees. There was a horse tied up at the post on the porch.

"Nell, what are we doing here? Whose place is this?"

Her question was answered when the door opened and Bram Justice stepped outside. Everything she'd learned about him registered clearly, coldly. A feeling, hollow and chill, spread through her stomach and her chest.

"Well, Mrs. Weber. How nice of you to come," he drawled.

He sounded as though he'd been expecting her for tea. Rachel wasn't sure if he was just extremely well composed, or completely crazy. She was afraid he was the latter.

Nell dismounted and tied the reins to the hitching post, her eyes purposely avoiding Rachel.

Rachel covertly took in the thick woods around her, wondering what her chances would be if she ran. As she slid off the horse's rump, she glanced at Bram and noticed the pistol he had tucked into the waistband of his pants. Considering that he'd already tried to kill her at least twice, she knew he wouldn't hesitate to use it now.

"Please," he said politely. "Come in. Come in."

Knowing what he was capable of, and believing he'd ordered the deaths of Jeremy and Harry, Rachel decided her wisest move would be acquiescence—at least for now. Although her knees felt as if they wouldn't hold her, she walked sedately into the cabin.

The interior, so similar to the cabin where she'd almost died, filled her with panic. She took several deep breaths to calm herself.

"I'll take my money now." Nell stood at the door, her arms crossed over her chest.

Bram gave her a condescending smile. "Oh, I don't think so."

A variety of emotions played over Nell's face. "What do you mean? I did what you asked; I delivered her to your door. You promised me the money, and I need it."

Bram pulled out his pistol and waved her inside. "I never give savages money. They don't know its value."

Nell scowled, but kept her mouth shut. Inching past him, she gave the dark, dank cabin interior a frantic look.

Bram closed the door, picked up a length of rope off the table, and turned to Rachel. "Tie up the squaw," he ordered, handing her the rope. "Squaw, sit down. There," he said, pointing to one of two chairs in the room.

Rachel's hands were cold and sweaty and she still felt sick to her stomach. "Why do you need both of us? Why not just let Nell go?"

"Tie her up!"

Swallowing hard, Rachel gave Nell an apologetic glance before she pulled the woman's hands behind her back and tied them together.

"What are you going to do with us?"

Rachel could tell Nell was frightened, but she put on a brave front.

Bram smiled. "Why don't you tell her, Mrs. Weber?"

Rachel decided not to correct him regarding her current wedded status. She didn't want to bring Jason's name into this. She tied Nell's hands as tightly as she dared, then tied her ankles together. "What makes you think I know?"

He moved quickly toward her and plucked out the money pouch from her pocket. "This is why I think you know."

Rachel's stomach plummeted and she broke out into a cold sweat. "The money is mine, Mr. Justice."

"Now it's mine," he said silkily, shoving the pouch into his pocket. "You can't imagine how startled I was to see you with that money, Mrs. Weber. Oh, I recognized the damp, curled bills immediately. Please," he added, "tell the squaw why I can't let either of you go."

Rachel swallowed again. "Because . . . because he's responsible for killing my husband and the schoolmaster, Nell."

"What!"

Justice motioned Rachel to the other chair. Her legs already stiff and sore from her ride, she crossed to the chair next to Nell and sat down. She winced several times as Bram pulled the rope tightly around her wrists and ankles.

"You're quite clever, Mrs. Weber." He stood and studied both of them.

Rachel stared back. "What I don't understand, is . . . why?"

"It's too bad you won't live long enough to have a child of your own, Mrs. Weber. Then, you'd understand."

"This has something to do with Karleen?"

His face came close to hers, and his eyes were black with hate. "She was *perfection*. She was completely unspoiled, exactly like her mother had been. I had every intention of keeping her that way until a man of *my* choice came along."

Rachel threw caution to the wind. "But . . . but if she and my husband were in love—"

"*Love?*" He swore, a hard, violent epithet that wasn't

softened by his Southern drawl. "That bastard slept with every woman in Tess's stable."

Rachel remembered the conversation she'd overheard. "But I thought . . . Karleen said—"

"She was thinking with her crotch," he spewed. "And he came here diseased. He gave her *crabs*, for Christ's sake."

"Crabs?" Rachel asked innocently.

"Lice, you foolish woman. He had *lice* thriving off his filthy pubic hair!"

The contents of Rachel's stomach rose to meet her throat, and she swallowed violently. Her nausea wouldn't be appeased and she continued to shudder.

"But that doesn't explain why that little fornicator, Harry Ritter, was killed and so beautifully maimed," Nell said, breaking her silence.

Justice suddenly smiled. "Mr. Holliday and his cronies were ingenious enough to do the maiming without being asked." He expelled a deep sigh and stared at Rachel. "I rather wish they'd castrated your husband, too. But," he added, spreading his hands before him, "dead is dead. And I didn't even have to leave my poker game to get it done."

Rachel glanced at Nell, who gave her a sorrowful look and mouthed, "I'm sorry." She gave her a wan smile.

He paced in front of them. "None of this would be necessary if I hadn't missed the first time, Mrs. Weber."

Rachel's heart fluttered nervously. "The first time?"

"Yes," he answered, nudging his chin with the muzzle of his gun. "Poor old Tully got the worst of that one."

"That was you?" Rachel couldn't hide her shock.

"I'm afraid I'm not a very good shot when it's dark. But," he added, shrugging expansively, "no harm done."

Rachel lowered her gaze so he wouldn't see her revulsion. "I hear they found little Willy."

Rachel's head shot up, and she met his smug gaze.

"Yes," he said with a malevolent grin. "I thought so. I'd heard a rumor that he'd been found."

"You wouldn't harm a child, would you?" she asked, hoping to penetrate his insane fog.

"Ah, Willy." He made a grim face. "I'm not a monster, you know, but . . ." He gave her a dramatic sigh. "Loose ends will not be tolerated."

Rachel closed her eyes. She knew that the most dangerous animal in the jungle was the one you couldn't see and didn't expect to attack until it was too late to protect yourself. Bram Justice was clearly that animal.

"But, why? He can't talk. He can't even read or write."

"You know, you may be right," he said, tapping his gun muzzle against his lips. "But I just can't take the chance. Of course," he added, "I fully expected you to die in the cabin fire, Mrs. Weber. I'd been planning that for so long, I hadn't taken into consideration the dampness of the weather. With you burned up in the cabin and the boy dead, there would be no witnesses. Then," he said, expelling a little laugh, "the boy ran away before I could get my hands on him."

Frustration continued to eat at Rachel. "But I don't understand why you wanted me dead. I didn't see or hear anything that morning. I was too frightened. All I knew was that Indians had killed my husband. If they spoke, I didn't listen. And if I'd listened, I wouldn't have understood them, anyway."

Justice nodded and frowned. "Yes, I see your point. But," he said with a shrug, "what difference do two more deaths make when you're already responsible for . . . so many others?"

An uncontrollable chill shook Rachel. She wondered how many others, besides those she knew about, there were. And he was right—what difference did two more make if you've already killed once? Staring at the door, she willed Jason to come and save her life again.

Chapter Twenty-one

Ben had seen Rachel leaving town with Nell and had followed them to the miner's shack. He hadn't gone far beyond that when he met Jason on the road and told him what was happening. Frustrated and angry, Jason wondered why in the hell Rachel had refused to stay put after she'd given her word that she would.

Now, he was within shouting distance of the miner's shack, although the heavy brush hid him from view. Two of the renegades from Ty Holliday's band stopped at the edge of the road near him. The one called Leo had completely shaved his head, save for a hank of hair flowing down his back. The other one, Cam, had blackened his face, making him appear fierce and menacing—which he was.

"The saloon keeper killed Ty," Leo told Jason. "All Ty did was ask for his money, and the White killed him. We didn't help kill the two soldiers, Two Leaf, but we know that Ty and the other two did. Now, the saloon keeper must pay for Ty's death, and the deaths of the others."

Jason didn't answer right away. There had to be a way to do this without causing any more bloodshed. "The law will take care of the saloon keeper."

Leo nudged his mount forward. "No," he replied firmly. "White man's justice is no good. They won't punish him for killing Indians."

"But they *will* punish him for killing the soldiers. After all, he hired Ty to do it. And he attempted to kill the soldier's woman many times. All of these things will keep him in jail, maybe even worse." Jason watched their faces, hoping they would agree with him.

"They might kill him?"

Jason nodded tentatively. "They might."

"Then why not let us do it? I dream of it every night," the menacing one said, thirsty for Justice's blood.

"Because if you do it, the white man's marshal will come after you." Logic. Would they see it?

"The white man's marshal is weak; he won't bother to chase us."

Everyone saw Tully's weaknesses. Even Tully. He'd told Jason just the day before that he'd requested a replacement. "But Marshal Tully is going to retire. And surely whoever replaces him will be young and strong. And anxious to do a good job."

The two rebels looked at each other. Finally, Leo asked, "How can we be sure the saloon keeper will get what he deserves? Whites are never punished for doing bad things to our people."

"I promise you I'll see to it, even if I have to take him to Sacramento myself," Jason vowed.

"I'm not happy with this," the menacing one groused, nosing his mount toward the cabin.

"Wait," Jason called softly. "Help me do it my way first."

"Why should we?"

"Because Nell is in the cabin with the soldier's woman. If the saloon keeper knows we're coming, he might kill both of them."

The renegades paused. Besides being one of their own, Nell was a valuable herb doctor. "All right," Leo answered. "We will try it your way first. But remember, Two Leaf, if your law does not punish him, we will find a way to do it ourselves."

Jason breathed a sigh of relief, but he knew it was only transitory. "We can't waste any more time. This is what we'll do," he said, huddled with the bloodthirsty renegades.

Suddenly the menacing one jabbed his heels into the ribs

of his mount and took off toward the cabin, his earsplitting war whoop cutting through the air.

One moment the cabin was quiet, the next, there was an explosion of sounds, the most frightening of which were the high-pitched shrieks of the black-faced Indian who kicked open the door.

Rachel's heart stopped and her breath caught in her throat. The savage swung a lassolike tether at Bram, intending to rope him like a calf, but Bram was quick. He turned and fired, hitting the intruding Indian in the chest. As the Indian staggered backward, Bram dove behind Rachel's chair, pressing his forearm against her throat.

"Easy, now, Mrs. Weber. No quick moves."

Briefly closing her eyes, Rachel strained back against the chair. The slightest indication of a struggle, and she knew he'd cut off her breathing. She'd had him pegged for a dandy; his athletic prowess surprised her.

She stared at the open door. The fallen Indian lay lifeless across the threshold. Glancing carefully sideways, she saw Nell look furtively at the window beside her. Rachel followed her gaze and saw the top of a bald head pass beneath it. She quickly looked away, unsure if she should feel relief at the possibility of being rescued, or more frightened than she already was.

Bram's focus was on the door. "Ladies," he said quietly, "I have no bad feelings for either of you. But I'll kill you both before I let another savage come through that door."

There was a slight sound behind them. Suddenly Bram grunted, releasing his hold on Rachel.

The Indian they'd seen at the window dragged Bram out from behind them, a lasso firmly in place around his torso and his hands already tied behind his back. Bram began cursing violently, threatening to kill them all.

Rachel had no idea how the bald Indian had gotten into the cabin. It was as though he'd miraculously materialized inside until she glanced behind her and saw the wooden covering to the root cellar flipped over on its back. Some root cellars had outside entrances; this one must, too.

Glancing back at the open door, Rachel went limp with relief as Jason appeared on the threshold. He bent to check the pulse of the fallen Indian, then immediately crossed to where Rachel sat, still tied to the chair.

Without speaking to her, he untied her chafed wrists.

Rachel was so happy to see him she nearly wept. "Thank God, thank God, thank God . . ." she murmured over and over again.

He said nothing until he'd untied Nell. "I don't think I want to know what went on here, Nell, but can I assume that you're responsible for this?"

Nell, usually so proud and defiant, bowed her head and nodded. "I . . . I thought he just wanted to kidnap her for the money. Honest, Jason, I didn't know he meant to kill her."

"He'd have killed both of you." Jason's voice was calm, but Rachel could see the tension building in his body.

"Two Leaf." The bald savage held a knife to Bram's throat and nodded toward his fallen friend. "He killed Cam. I must kill him."

With her eyes on Jason, Rachel absently rubbed her irritated wrists. She could almost see the wheels churning wildly in his head.

"I thought we'd struck a bargain," Jason replied carefully.

"That's right." Bram's eyes were wild. "Don't let him kill me. I swear to God I wasn't going to kill the woman. I was just going to frighten her. I'd *always* meant to just frighten her."

The bald Indian took out a rag and stuffed it into Bram's mouth, then tied a handkerchief around it to keep it in place. "White man's words come out of his mouth like puke."

"He'll be properly punished, Leo. Don't kill him. I'm not saying he doesn't deserve it," Jason said, "but I don't want anything to happen to you. If you kill him, you know you'll have to pay."

Indecision flashed over the Indian's face. "White justice doesn't have anything to do with us."

"And it never will if we keep acting like savages," Jason reasoned. "Sooner or later, like it or not, we all have to change and make a few concessions."

The Indian released Bram and shoved the knife back into his belt. "All right, Two Leaf, we'll do it your way. But if this pile of donkey dung is not punished, you have my promise that I will do it myself."

Rachel hadn't realized that she'd been holding her breath. She let it out in a rush and hurried to help Nell move the dead Indian outside onto the ground.

"I'm sorry, Rachel." Nell wouldn't look at her, but her words seemed sincere.

"Let's just forget it." There was a mingling of sadness and relief in Rachel's heart. She was anxious to get home, in spite of the chastisement she'd receive. But it wouldn't be the same now that she knew Jason's reasons for marrying her.

Bram Justice was taken to the Pine Valley jail and locked in a cell. Rachel gave her statement, and Marshal Tully whistled, astonished at what Rachel had to say. She left out nothing, implicating Bram in the deaths of the soldiers, Ty Holliday and his men, the theft of her money, and the numerous attempts on her life. Because he'd planned on killing her too, he'd told her everything—including the fact that he'd hit Tully by mistake outside the church those few months before.

Still, Tully said he couldn't release Buck without authorization from August Weber. That worried both Rachel and Jason, although it seemed to weigh far more heavily on Jason's mind.

They'd eaten a quiet dinner in the Corinthian Hotel dining room. Back in their apartment next to the office, Jason finally spoke to her.

"I told you not to leave." His voice was stern and angry, but contained as he stormed around the room.

Rachel swallowed and stared at the floor. "I know."

"Then, explain it to me, Rachel. Dammit, I can't watch you every minute. I've got to be able to believe what you tell me."

"Nell said you needed me," she said defensively. He made her feel like a wayward child, and she didn't like it.

He threw his vest over a chair, then turned and studied her. "But I told you not to leave."

Disbelief made her outspoken. "And what if you really *had* needed me? What if I'd ignored her request, and something had happened to you?" She swung away from him angrily. "How could I possibly have known Nell hated me enough to have me kidnapped? I'm sorry, Jason, but my mind doesn't work that way. I'm not a vindictive person, so my first thought isn't always that someone is out to get me."

"Well, maybe, after all that's happened to you out here, it *should* be." His level of anger surpassed hers.

They stood and stared at each other.

"Maybe it should," she answered quietly. "Maybe I should take lessons from Nell." It was a nasty little dig, and beneath her, but she couldn't let it pass. After all, Nell, the "perfect woman," was Jason's closest confidante, and that fact had been eating at Rachel all day and long into the evening.

He grunted a sigh and walked away from her. "I'm not so sure that's very clever, either. Hell, she almost got herself killed today, too."

"Well, please forgive me for not being *clever* enough to suit you," she sniped, angry with herself for her jealousy.

"What in the hell is wrong with you tonight?"

"*Me?* What's wrong with *me?*"

"Yes, you. You're petulant and peevish. You're not acting like yourself at all."

She sniffed dramatically. "If I sound out of sorts, it's because I was nearly killed *again*. That sort of thing doesn't have to happen to me too many times before I begin to feel just a little bit uncomfortable," she grumbled, her voice edged with sarcasm.

He raked his fingers through his hair and stared at her. "I

guess you do have a reason to be irritable. But," he added, approaching her with a small smile, "you're safe now."

She automatically froze, and she knew he saw it in her face.

"What is it?"

Stepping away nervously, she answered, "I'm just tired, Jason. Really tired." And she was, but until today, she'd never have admitted that to him. She'd have gone into his arms eagerly. Willingly. She'd have found comfort and strength there. But not tonight, and probably not ever again.

She could feel his eyes on her, and his scrutiny scared her. Not wanting to give him any reason to delve into how she was really feeling, she forced herself to smile at him. "I *am* tired, Jason. I'm sorry I sniped at you."

Escaping behind the privacy screen, she got into her nightclothes and crept into bed, pulling the covers up to her neck. She lay there, still as a corpse, barely breathing as she waited for him to join her. As he moved about the room, removing his clothes, she found she had to turn away. He was so beautiful to watch, all brown muscle and sinew. But his gaze was different now. It no longer made her melt; it made her want to cry. It had turned her cold, and it hurt.

She felt him watching her. Bravely she turned over and looked at him. She loved him so much she thought she might burst. Blinking back tears, she waited for him to join her. She almost hoped he didn't. If he got into bed, it would be so tempting to curl up next to him.

He stood there, staring down at her.

"Are . . . are you coming to bed?"

He gave her a disgusted sigh and turned away. "I've got some work to do." He slipped back into his shirt and was gone, leaving Rachel alone, as empty inside as she was in the bed.

The morning sun awakened Rachel, punishing her with its brightness. She automatically groped for Jason. When she discovered he wasn't there, she remembered what had happened the night before, and the hollowness returned to her stomach. Glancing at his pillow, she realized that he hadn't been to bed at all.

She curled into a ball and closed her eyes. Yesterday, when she'd overheard the awful news that Jason only married her to keep an eye on her, she'd thought she could continue on as if nothing had changed between them. Now she wasn't sure. The more she thought about it, the more she knew it would only cause her more pain. And she *did* have some pride, although it had taken her a few months to realize it.

Staying with him in spite of everything had seemed a brave thing for her to do yesterday, but after lying awake half the night, she realized that it was no way to run a marriage. She wasn't such a fool that she'd lower herself to ruining her life or Jason's by pretending everything was wonderful. Yes, she loved him, and yes, she wanted to be his wife. But, she realized she wanted him to love her, too. Not just pity her because someone was trying to kill her.

And what would happen now that Bram Justice was in custody, and there was no longer a threat on her life? Jason's whole reason for marrying her no longer existed. Surely he was anxious to get on with the rest of his life.

Giving her head a weary shake, she flung the covers aside and rose from the bed. She grabbed a towel, went behind the privacy curtain and gave herself a quick, cold bath, adding lavish amounts of jasmine essence to her rinse water. With her towel wrapped snugly around her, she came out from behind the screen. Her pulse raced and every nerve in her body began to quiver, for Jason leaned against the door jam, staring at her.

"Jason." Her voice was breathy, surprised. "I . . . I didn't hear you come in."

He gave her a hot, secret look. "I know. I love to listen to you when you bathe."

The flush of desire crept into her cheeks in spite of her earlier resolve. She schooled in her hunger. "I'm so happy I amuse you. What is it you enjoy listening to? Do I grunt? Groan? Squeak?"

Obviously unaware of her inner turmoil, he merely grinned and gazed at her towel-covered nipples. "Nothing like that, Rachel love."

Gritting her teeth, she turned away and hoped she could stay strong. She hated it when he called her that—it made her feel breathless and weak-kneed. She marched to the wardrobe and pulled out clean underwear, trying to ignore him.

"Don't you want me to tell you what I imagine?"

Strutting past him on her way to the stove, hoping he couldn't sense her confusion, she asked, "Do I have a choice?"

He still didn't appear to see the change in her. "Ah, sexual banter," he said, moving slowly toward her. "I love sexual banter."

Pretending to discover a flaw in her drawers, she prolonged the need to drop her towel and dress in front of him.

"I imagine," he said, tugging at her towel, "what it would be like to be that little square of cloth that you generously lather. I think about being pressed to that sweet, soft womanhood of yours, being rubbed back and forth, back and forth," he replied, pulling then releasing his grip on the towel. " 'Ah, that lucky washcloth,' I say to myself, imagining how you'd feel, how you'd smell, all clean and sweet, but with that special musty smell that comes after we've made love—or fucked, as you like me to say."

She gasped. "I do *not* like you to say that," she answered, barely able to contain her desire. She closed her eyes and let herself be drawn against him, her back against his chest.

"You're a liar." He held her tight, snaking his hand beneath the towel to cup her at the apex of her thighs.

She almost wept. She had no discipline over her feelings for him. Suddenly she didn't care that he didn't love her. He desired her, and she knew she'd hate herself for weakening afterward, but right now, she wanted him desperately.

The towel fell to the floor, giving him access to all of her. Her head flopped back onto his shoulder and she let him tease her nipples and stroke her between her legs. She was so wet for him, she could feel it trickling down the insides of her thighs. She shuddered, grinding her buttocks against his groin, feeling him harden beneath his jeans.

Unable to stand it any longer, she turned in his arms and feverishly opened the buttons on his fly. Plunging her hand inside his jeans, she felt the hot length of him pulsating against her fingers. She stroked him, cradled him, combed her fingers through his crisp hair.

He picked her up, carried her to the bed, and dropped her. She sat, bracing herself on her palms, her knees bent and her legs spread wantonly as the cool air licked at her groin.

He removed his jeans and joined her on the bed, but didn't come into her. Resting on his knees between her legs, he grasped her calves and pulled them up over his shoulders.

She inhaled sharply as he pulled her toward him, so close she could feel his breath on the center of her desire. Gripping his thighs, she held on, perplexed and debauched as wave after wave of passion raced through her. Nothing prepared her for the sensation of his tongue as it moved over the slick, wet skin between her nether lips. She flailed hungrily and he held her firm. Suddenly an enormous spasm shook her, sending her higher against his mouth, and she cried out her release.

He let her slide to the bed, then, spreading her legs once again, he entered her, driving deep. She clung to him, waiting for him to find his satisfaction. When he did, she cried again. This time, for what might have been.

❦ *Chapter Twenty-two* ❦

Rachel vacillated in making a decision about her marriage. It had been almost a week since her confrontation with Bram Justice, and she hadn't made up her mind what to do with her life. It was partly because she didn't want to decide. At night, when she and Jason were entwined in each other's arms, it was easy to convince herself that he might learn to love her someday. In the morning, when the cold reality of the world set in around her, she knew it wasn't fair to hold him to his wedding vows.

Jason hadn't seemed to detect the change in her. He was too preoccupied with a way to get Buck out of jail to notice any subtle alterations in her personality. She was good at hiding her feelings. She'd been doing it for years. But now, loving Jason as desperately as she did, it was getting harder and harder to cover the way she felt.

As she cleaned and dusted their small apartment, she felt a twinge of dread. Her father-in-law was back from Sacramento. He'd ridden in late yesterday afternoon. Jason was at the jail now, trying to convince him to let Buck go. Rachel had a bad feeling about that. She knew August Weber well enough to know that he never backed down, even if proven wrong. Somehow, he'd always gotten his way. Probably by intimidation and threats, she thought with a wry twist of her mouth.

She went to the window and stared outside. The showy white petals of a flowering ash caught her eye and she momentarily marveled in the glory of spring.

Someone shouted a greeting beyond the window, and reality intruded. Moving back into the room, she picked up
the shirt Jason had worn the day before. She brought it to
her face, pulling the scent of him deep into her lungs. She
loved the way he smelled. So clean. So masculine . . .

She'd never tire of watching him stride into a room and
stop, searching out the space between them until he found
her. It was almost as if there was some special current between them. Almost as if they were meant to be together
. . . Just thinking about him sent her heart racing out of
control.

She took a deep breath and thought again of their problem: Captain August Weber.

Jason wouldn't get any answers from him, and neither
would Marshal Tully. And her father-in-law had a lot of
clout in the army community. In spite of what she'd learned
about him, she knew he was highly revered among his peers.
They didn't know he'd nearly beaten a young Indian boy to
death all those years ago, and God only knew what other
atrocities he'd committed in the name of the white man.

Then again, she decided, her own disillusionment surfac-
ing, maybe they did know. It was certainly possible that
other soldiers had brutalized Indians as badly as he had.
Maybe that was the mark of a "successful" soldier.

Glancing at the grandfather clock, she felt a sinking in
her chest when she realized she only had a few hours before
she was to meet her father-in-law for dinner at the Corinthian. She hadn't told Jason about it, but he'd casually informed her that he had to be at the reservation later in the
afternoon and probably wouldn't get back until after dark.
She knew that in spite of the fact that he didn't love her, he
wouldn't want her to undergo the verbal abuse that her father-in-law would undoubtedly heap upon her. Especially
since by now he knew she had remarried. A half-breed.

She shuddered violently when she thought of his reaction.
But she knew that he might tell her things he wouldn't tell
anyone else, and maybe she could find out what he planned
to do with Buck.

* * *

Once again, Rachel sat across from Captain Weber in the opulent Corinthian dining room. She'd dressed carefully in a gold and brown velvet brocade-on-satin dress with drop bustle and three-quarter sleeves that Jason had bought her. The chenille fringe that edged the hem had whistled against the fabric as she'd walked to the hotel. She'd been reluctant to waste the new gown on a man for whom she had neither liking nor respect. Unfortunately, it was the only decent evening dress she owned.

With covert care, she glanced at her dining partner from beneath her heavy lashes. He was staring at her. She quickly looked away.

He slathered butter onto a roll, and bit into it, sending the crusty crumbs scattering over the tablecloth. He motioned to the untouched plate of food in front of her. "You're not eating," he said around a mouthful.

She looked down at the meat and potatoes swimming in gravy and swallowed hard. She'd been queasy all day. Nothing had appealed to her, much less the plate of runny slop in front of her. But she had to at least try to eat something.

"I'm not really very hungry," she answered, picking a roll out of the basket and breaking it in half on her bread plate.

Working his tongue over his teeth, he poured himself another glass of wine. Rachel thought it was at least his third, if not his fourth. The bottle was poised over her half-filled glass, but she shook her head and put her hand over the top of it.

"I've heard some very disturbing news, Rachel." He put the bottle down and casually continued eating. "I can't make myself believe it."

Her stomach jumped. Here it comes, she thought. "What have you heard?"

He belched quietly, but didn't cover his mouth. "That fool of a marshal let it slip that you married the half-breed savage."

"He's not a savage." She bristled.

He arched a bushy eyebrow. "He's a savage, Rachel, believe me."

"He's a *doctor*, for heaven's sake." She took a nervous sip of wine, willing it to stay down.

He grabbed another roll and broke it into pieces, dropping them on his gravy-soaked plate. "They're all savages, Rachel. Remember what they did to your *real* husband? And to your poor mother and father?"

Emotional blackmail. He was a master at it. Strangely, Rachel didn't feel herself weaken. "There are atrocities on both sides," she answered. "The Indian doesn't have the market on cruelty, Captain."

"I don't know what's come over you since Jeremy's death. Something must have snapped in your brain that morning."

Rachel gaped at him. He was serious! "I've never felt better in my life."

He gave her a condescending smile, then shook his head. "Sad. It's sad. Well," he said, taking another slurp of wine, "you'll just have to come home with me. Sada will take care of you."

Oh, Lord, there had to be another option. "How can I leave when I'm married to Dr. Gaspard?"

He snorted. "*Married?* Don't be foolish, Rachel. Think." He jammed his forefinger against his temple. "*Think* about what you've done. Isn't there anything left in that head of yours? Is it empty?"

She knew it was fruitless to argue, but she suddenly realized that this was the way he'd always been. Always accusing someone of being a fool or crazy, until the person begins to believe it himself.

"So," she finally said conversationally, hoping to learn what had gone on with Buck. "Where did you spend the day?"

He poured himself more wine. "At that laughable little building they call a jail."

"Oh? What are you planning to do with . . . with the Indian now that Bram Justice has been brought in?"

He waved away the remark. "The Indian's guilty."

Rachel felt a cold wash of fear. "But he isn't the one I saw that morning. And he isn't the one who had been trying to kill me, Captain."

He steepled his fingers and gave her a pensive, but bleary look. "Mr. Justice has said he's sorry, Rachel. And he didn't kill you, did he?"

"But . . . but he ordered Jeremy's death. He *told* me that he wanted him dead, and why. You must have read the report. It's all there. How he had Jeremy killed because of . . . of his daughter."

Again, Weber waved away the remark. "I don't have to read the report to know what *really* happened, Rachel. Indians did it, Indians will be punished."

Rachel sat back and stared at him, her fear escalating. He wasn't even going to read the report. He didn't want to know the truth. She took a small bite of bread and chewed it slowly. When she swallowed, she had to force it past the lump in her throat. "What are you planning to do with the Indian then?"

He drained his glass of wine. "I'm putting him in chains and hauling his savage ass to Fort Riley."

"When?" she asked casually, although she was taut as twine.

He belched again, then drew his napkin over his faded mustache. "Soon."

Rachel lowered her gaze. *Soon.* She didn't dare question him too much. "Soon" could be tomorrow or . . . or next week. But she guessed he wouldn't wait a week. "Well," she said after a moment, "maybe we could have breakfast together one of these mornings."

His cold eyes warmed, and he gave her a sloppy smile. "Yes, soon."

"Tomorrow?" she asked with forced gaiety.

Frowning, he motioned the waiter to the table. "Tomorrow's not good. No, not tomorrow. I have to take a short trip tomorrow. Won't be back again for nearly a week."

Her heart bumped her rib cage. He was too drunk to realize that he'd tipped his hand. Maybe he was transporting

Buck to Fort Riley. She would find out if she had to get up before dawn to watch him herself.

"When I get back from Fort Riley, we'll get you packed up. Sada will be so happy to have you home again."

A sick feeling coated her stomach, aiding her ever-present nausea. "Packed up?"

"You need medical care, Rachel. Being around these savages has made you crazy."

She briefly closed her eyes and pressed her fingers against her mouth. She couldn't go back with him. She wouldn't! Her marriage might not be perfect, but it was a far better alternative than going back to North Dakota with her father-in-law and being forced to live under Sada's ruling thumb.

Anxious to get away from him, she pretended to be interested in his slurred conversation while she toyed with her dessert. When the painful meal finally came to an end, she realized she wouldn't have made such a clean escape, except that the captain had been too drunk to care.

After carefully hanging up her new gown, Rachel slipped into her nightclothes and waited for Jason. She was *not* going to slink away like an abused dog. She had to face him. Attempting to read, she found that she nearly jumped out of her skin every time she heard a noise. So, she paced. Finally, she recognized Jason's footsteps.

He walked into the room and stopped. Her expression must have warned him something was wrong. "Rachel?"

She took a deep breath. "I have something to say to you, and I don't want you to interrupt me until I'm done."

He raised his eyebrows, but said nothing.

"I . . . I think you'd better sit down," she said, motioning him to the chair by the stove.

He complied, settling back and resting his elbows on the arms of the chair.

She pulled in another breath. "I know what we have isn't perfect. I know why you married me, and—"

"Just why *did* I marry you?" he interrupted.

"Shhh, I told you to be quiet until I was done."

Raising his arms in defeat, he nodded.

"I know why you married me, and I'm grateful. But now that the threat is gone, I'm sure you'd like to get on with your life. I understand that, Jason, I really do." No matter how many times she'd said the words to herself, they hadn't hurt nearly as much as they did now, saying them to his face.

"You understand that." He pursed his lips and looked very grim.

Her stomach dipped, but she forced herself to continue. She'd practiced this speech for hours. "Yes, but . . . but you see, I could be very helpful in your career. You . . . you really do need someone to work with, and although you probably think Nell is better equipped than I am, I mean . . . since you tell her everything anyway, I think you need me. Well, for one thing," she continued, blathering away like an idiot, "I'm a White, and maybe I can bring in more patients for you."

She stared at him, trying to gauge his reaction. She could read nothing from his expression. She began to weaken.

"Oh, who am I trying to fool? Jason, Captain Weber thinks that because . . . because I married you, I've gone stark raving mad. He thinks that seeing Jeremy murdered snapped my mind. He also thinks I'm going to willingly pack up my things and go back to North Dakota with him." She smiled sadly and blinked back tears. "It's his opinion that I need some help."

Jason shifted in the chair and cleared his throat. "And you want to stay here, rather than be shut away in some asylum in the backwoods of North Dakota."

Her stomach sank further. He didn't sound very enthused about it. She hadn't thought much about *his* reaction to all of this. "I'm not crazy, Jason. I lo—" She coughed, catching herself before she blurted out the words, even though she'd said them to him before.

"You—what?"

She gave him a nervous smile. "I . . . I *loathe* the idea of going back with him."

He nodded. "You'd rather stay here."

She rolled her eyes in frustration. "Jason, I eavesdropped on your conversation with your father. I deserve the pain I've been going through for listening, I know I do. I heard you tell your father why you married me." She held her breath.

"You did? What did I say?"

Pushing out a lungful of air, she scolded, "You know perfectly well what you said."

"No," he argued. "I don't remember at all. When was this?"

"The day . . . the day that Nell came and convinced me you needed help. Before that, I'd gone over to Ivy's. When I came back, I went in through the other door and overheard your conversation with your father."

He looked at her cautiously. "What did I say? Refresh my memory."

She suddenly found the satin piping on her dressing gown very interesting. Moving her finger along the pink braid, she answered, "Well, it wasn't so much what you said as your father's response to your having told him you married me."

"And that was what?"

She closed her eyes, not wanting to watch him as she recited, " 'Did you have to marry her? Hell, Jason, most people would have hired a bodyguard or a nursemaid. Wasn't *marrying* her kind of extreme?' Or something like that."

Lowering his gaze, he ran his hand over his mouth. "Hmmm. Yes, it was something like that. But do you remember what I said to him?"

Her stomach caved in a little further. "Yes, you said, 'I did what I had to do.' "

"That's right. I did."

She nodded, suddenly feeling very tired and sick to her stomach. "You married me to keep an eye on me and keep me safe from Bram Justice."

"Partly, yes."

She gave him a wan smile. "It *was* a little extreme, Jason. Your father was right. You could have hired a bodyguard."

He gazed at her carefully. "Would you have preferred that?"

Pressing her hands against her stomach, she crossed to the bed and sat down. How was she going to put this? She didn't want him feeling sorry for her. Pity was something she couldn't handle—not from the man she loved so desperately.

"If . . . if it would have made you happier, then, yes. I wish you'd have hired a bodyguard. I don't want to ruin your life, Jason. If . . ." She took a deep breath. "If you want out of this marriage, then . . . then I won't fight you."

He was quiet for a long time, then swung around to look at her. "Is that what you want?"

No! No! No! "If . . . if it's what you want."

"Did you happen to hear the rest of my conversation with my father?"

Giving him an embarrassed smile, she answered, "Oh, no. I hurried outside and came in through the office, hoping you wouldn't know that I'd been listening."

"So, you didn't hear anything else?"

She shook her head, kicked off her slippers, and slid under the covers. She was so tired. She closed her eyes briefly, and when she opened them again, he was standing by the bed.

"Is something wrong?" His face was etched with concern.

She yawned. "No, I'm just tired."

He grinned at her. "And pregnant."

Her stomach dropped and her hands went down as if to protect it from the fall. "How . . . how did you know?"

He gave her an intense look. "I know everything about your body, Rachel."

She rolled onto her side away from him. "I didn't want you to think you had to stay married to me because of . . . of the baby." She felt his weight on the bed as he sat down beside her.

"Can I stay married to you because I love you?" He stroked her hair.

She rolled back and stared at him, her heart certainly in her eyes. "Don't say it unless you really mean it, Jason."

"After you'd apparently left, you didn't hear me tell my father the reason I'd married you."

"No," she answered shakily. "I didn't."

"I told him I'd done what I had to do. I married you because I'd fallen in love with you."

She went limp. "Oh, you have? You really have?"

"How could I not? You've proved ten ways to Sunday that you love me. In spite of your initial meakness, you found that inner bravery that is only bred into special people. You believed in me, even though you'd known the Webers longer. I don't think that belief ever faltered, no matter how much Weber tried to convince you otherwise." He shook his head and gazed at the floor. "I don't deserve you."

Her heart filled, spilling over with love. "Oh, don't say that, my darling. Please, don't ever say that." She turned on her side and flipped back the covers. "Just tell me you love me again, and come to bed."

"I love you, again and again and again."

She held out her arms to him.

He threw off his clothes and joined her in bed, hauling her against him. "Thank God we've got that settled. Now, what's this nonsense about Nell being my confidante?"

Rachel snuggled against him. "She said you told her everything."

He snorted a laugh. "God knows what made her say that. I think maybe she's a little jealous of you."

"You don't tell her everything?"

He kissed her forehead. "Never have, never will." He ran his hand down over her stomach. "Have you been sick?"

A delightful shiver shook her. "A little queasy today."

"How do you feel about being pregnant?" He settled her against him.

She yawned, smiling lazily against his shoulder. "I *love* it. How do *you* feel about it?"

He hugged her tight. "I think I'm a pretty damned good stud."

She smiled sleepily at his boast and tried to stay awake.

There was something else she was going to tell him, but she was just too tired and too much in love to think. Burrowing her nose against her husband's neck, she drifted toward sleep. Tomorrow. She'd tell him tomorrow.

❧ *Epilogue* ❧

A fierce March wind howled through Pine Valley, rattling the windows in a frantic effort to reach inside. The year had been kind to some, not so kind to others.

Rachel Gaspard felt blessed. Sitting near the stove in their small apartment, she held her infant son, Lucas, named after her own baby brother, to her breast. The stinging pull of the milk as it drove to the surface of her nipple and into her son's mouth thrilled her. She rocked gently back and forth, humming a sweet, poignant lullaby she'd learned from her mother years before.

Looking up, she felt her pulse thrum heavily as her husband stepped into the room, one arm behind his back. Her milk came forth with such a surge, the child sputtered and choked, coughing as the rich liquid dribbled from his mouth and over his chin.

"Such a greedy, demanding little beast you are," Jason chided, once the child began to nurse again.

Rachel gazed up at Jason, loving him so much she thought she might fly into pieces. "Much like his father."

Giving her a hot, private look, he pulled his arm from behind his back and presented her with a small bouquet of daisies.

Every week since the birth of their son, he'd presented her with either daisies or roses. She swore he was some kind of sorcerer, able to manufacture flowers out of thin air. "Oh, they're beautiful. When are you going to tell me where you find them in the middle of winter?"

Turning briskly from her, he answered, "It's my secret. The only one I'll ever keep from you, I promise." He put the flowers in water, returned to her and lifted his son into his arms. After burping the child, he nestled him into the beautiful hand-carved cradle that had been a gift from the happily retired Earl Tully, and his new bride, Ivy.

Rachel's gaze swept Jason's dark, arrogant profile as he put their son to bed. Even now, she thrilled at the sight of him. He turned, his eyes suddenly filled with concern.

"What is it?"

He crossed to her again and took her hands in his. "The new marshal got word today that August Weber has finally been stripped of his captaincy."

She sighed, relieved. She often relived the morning she'd secretly discovered her father-in-law hauling Buck off to Fort Riley in chains. She was still grateful she'd been able to help convince the authorities that Buck was innocent. Bram Justice was serving a life sentence for his crimes. Karleen had gone into labor shortly after her father's sentencing, and because she'd allowed Tess to deliver her child instead of Jason, the baby was born dead—the cord wrapped tightly around its neck. Karleen buried her baby next to its father and left Pine Valley to be near her own.

Gazing at her husband again, Rachel noted his pinched expression. "I thought that news would cheer you up more than this," she said softly, rising to touch him.

He turned and pulled her into his arms. "I'm worried about Buck."

Hugging him fiercely, she asked, "Still nothing?"

He shook his head. "He's been gone for months. There's been no word to me or his family. He hasn't even contacted poor little Dusty." He let out a ragged sigh. "That's what concerns me the most."

Rachel unbuttoned her husband's shirt, kissed the old scars, then rested her cheek against his chest. "He told you not to worry about him, Jason."

"I know, I know. But how can I help it? He'd just begun to come back from self-destruction, then he took off."

"In his heart, he's a renegade, darling. A rebel; a maverick. Don't cry for him; he wouldn't approve."

"I think of Buck out there somewhere, cold, drunk, maybe even d—"

She pressed her fingers against his lips. "No. Don't say it. If nothing else, Buck's a survivor. In your heart you know that, too."

He squeezed her hard. "I want so much for him. He's closer to me than my own brother. I want him to have what we have. Is that so much to ask?"

Rachel stared out into the night, seeing beyond the trappings of man and nature. Somehow, in all that had happened between them, she and Buck had developed a unique, if tenuous, bond. Though she wasn't gifted with any special powers, the peace in her heart told her he was out there somewhere, fighting to survive.

"No, my darling, it's not so much to ask." She turned her face toward her husband's and they kissed. "If he can find even a fraction of the happiness we have, he'll be blessed."

HERE IS AN EXCERPT FROM *FORBIDDEN MOON*, JANE BONANDER'S NEXT EXCITING HISTORICAL ROMANCE:

The sounds of Nicolette attacking a Bach invention on the piano faded as Molly strode purposefully into the barn. The interior was shadowy. Light filtered in from a window high at the point of the roof, the beacon a shaft of dancing particles of dust. An odor of hay and manure reached her nostrils, but it was faint enough to be merely earthy, not pungent. The darkness and the quiet were provocative, titillating.

She paused when she saw Buck and rested her shoulder against the rough wooden doorway. He was shirtless, the muscles in his back moving, bunching, releasing as he curried the brown stallion. He still murmured words of confidence with each stroke of the brush. The animal's ears twitched, as if focusing on the sound of Buck's voice. She wondered what it was about him that had changed. Of course, he was seven years older, but that wasn't it. He seemed more contained now, less apt to fly into a rage. He'd always been so angry. At her, at the Whites, at the world. And, more often than not, working hard at getting good and falling down drunk.

She raised her eyebrows. That was it. So far, she hadn't seen him drunk.

"What are you doing here, brat?"

She jumped, his voice startling her. He still hadn't turned. "How did you know it was me?"

He chuckled, and the raspy, tobacco-rough sound made her breath catch in her throat. "I can tell."

"Impossible," she answered, meandering slowly toward him. "You must have glanced over your shoulder."

"Didn't have to. I've always been able to tell when you're around. I could seven years ago, and I can today."

She snorted lightly. "Have you got an extra-sensitive nose or something?"

He still hadn't turned around. "When it comes to your scent, I have."

He could smell her? Well, that was an attractive notion, she thought dryly. Even so, an odd heaviness gathered in her pelvis. "That's ridiculous. I've never worn perfume, and I'm not wearing any now."

He stopped brushing, turned and stared at her. His dark eyes smoldered as his gaze raked over her. "It's not perfume I smell, brat."

She wanted desperately to give him a blazing retort, but found it hard to breathe, much less talk. All of her energy was centered elsewhere—in dark, warm places that swelled with unwanted desire. Finally, "That . . . that's ridiculous," she whispered. "And . . . and don't call me 'brat'."

He merely shrugged and put the currycomb on the ledge near the door. He was closer now, and she could smell him as well. The sweat of man and animal, leather, tobacco, hay, and the dark, secretive odor of the back room in the barn. The erotic overlay of all the scents mingling in the electric air between them made her heart thump and her knees weak.

"What are you doing here?" he asked again.

Finally coming to her senses, she pulled herself up straight. "Are you flirting with Nicolette?"

A humorless sound erupted from his throat. "Why in the hell would I flirt with a sixteen-year-old girl?"

Molly swallowed, watching the corded muscle flex in his arm as he braced it against the wall beside her. She followed the hard, vein-threaded lines of his limb until her gaze met the thatch of black hair under his arm. She tried to control a shiver. "She has a crush on you, you know."

"I know," he answered simply, his gaze never wavering. "I liked your hair better last night."

She wanted to move away but didn't . . . or couldn't, as the memory of his hands opening her robe throbbed behind her eyes. "If Charles . . ." she began weakly, then took a deep breath. "If Charles has any reason to believe you're leading the girl on, he'll kill you."

"I can take care of myself."

Anger erupted inside her. She took a step and grabbed his arm, trying to pull him around. "Don't be a fool. You're the one who warned me about Charles' feelings for breeds. You know it's dangerous to play games with him."

With whiplash speed he turned and gripped her shoulders, his gaze burning into hers. "Listen to yourself. What in the hell do you think he'll do to you when he finds out the game you're playing?"

A stab of fear plunged through her, making her dizzy. "It will be different with me," she heard herself say. "He's in love with me."

He swore, the sound oozing disgust. "There's a name for a woman like you, a woman who marries a man just because he's rich enough to give her everything she thinks she wants."

Looking at Buck, she saw the hatred simmering in his eyes. It was so strong, she could feel it. "What's he done to you? What in the *world* has he done, to make you hate him so much? Is it because he's a rich white man with everything in the world you want, but can't have?"

He turned back, concentrating on the stallion, but his back muscles tensed, as with anger. "That's your desire, brat, not mine. Not all breeds lust after the white man's world like you do. Unlike you, I've never envied the white man for what he has. I've just hated him for what he is."

The disparaging remark didn't sit well, but she ignored it. "Then you will stop encouraging Nicolette?"

He turned again and faced her. "Why in the hell do you care? What I do with my life is my business. I don't encourage the girl, but I'm going to be civil. And you," he snarled, suddenly angry, "can stay the devil away from me and my affairs."

The sparks between them erupted into flame. They stood, nose to nose, like the combative adversaries they'd always been. She could see his pupils dilate, darkening against the circle of gold that rimmed them. She could smell him, feel him, almost taste him . . .

Suddenly his mouth was on hers, clamping hard, punishing, tormenting, berating. It took her by surprise, took her a moment to respond. Then, when she did, she knew it wasn't right. Buck wasn't the one who should be kissing her, Charles was.

She struggled against him, pinching her lips together, pushing, twisting, and shoving to get out of his embrace. He held her tightly, wearing down her resistance as he continued to press himself against her from mouth to knee.

He was hard all over. His bare chest was a solid surface of warm flesh. She reached up, intending to push him away. Yet when she touched his shoulder, she couldn't resist cupping the skin that encapsulated his muscle.

Suddenly, something akin to a juice-filled fruit exploded low in her belly, sending gushes of hot liquid into her pelvis. Her mouth opened beneath his. It was so good. So hot. So tempting. And fires of hell, it felt right . . . She allowed him to probe her tongue with his, the heat in her nether regions intensifying.

He lifted her slightly and pulled her close, grinding his pelvis against hers, pressing her against him with blatant familiarity, punishing her with his need. Wanting desperately to melt into him, she wrapped one leg around his, bringing his stiffened manhood closer to the source of her own desire.

A throaty chuckle escaped his mouth, triggering an alarm inside her. With all of her energy and willpower, she turned her head away and shoved at his chest.

He glanced down at her, his eyelids heavy. Smirking, he released her slowly. "So, you've—"

On solid ground again, she slapped him hard across the face. "No. Whatever you were going to say, the answer is no."

He touched his cheek, the old scar denting it devilishly as he smiled. "I don't believe you."

"I don't care what you believe. I—"

"I think you've missed our little battles. I think you've been wondering for years what it would actually taste like to have my tongue in your mouth. I think I should have given you a taste years ago, when you begged for it."

Anger and desire made her gulp back a powerful shudder.

"As I said before, you can go to hell. I forgot about you the minute I left the vineyard." Taking a deep, shaky breath, she touched the wild tangles of hair that had come loose from her carefully twisted coiffure and marched toward the door. The sound of his husky chuckle followed her as she rushed from the barn . . . .